M3

The Outsiders

Millennium Series

Staci Morrison

A.

For Mark, who inspired me, made me laugh, survived the fire, and like all good heroes got his happy ending.

And for Max, whose passions run deep, my life and work are far richer for having you in them. Thank you.

Table of Contents

Enter the Millennium

Welcome back! The reader will recall that years in the text are indicated with ME, Millennial Era, instead of BC or AD. Thus, 999 ME is 999 years into the Millennium.

Character names use a Hebrew construction, whereby 'ben' means child of, so Josiah ben Eamonn means Josiah son of Eamonn.

So, what is the Millennium, and when will it occur?

It is a prophetic time, the next great age. Our world today will not continue ad infinitum. At some point in the future, the Lord will appear in the Heavens and call His church to Himself. This global cataclysmic event is called the Rapture and sets off a series of events that will usher in the Tribulation, seven years of wars, famine, earthquakes, fire, and pestilence; hell on Earth. But in the end, the evil forces are defeated. The Lord returns to rule, ushering in the Millennium, one thousand years of paradise, a return to what was lost in Eden.

Series Notes

As the series progresses, we move deeper into the tale, often going on the "other side of the door". And while each book could technically be read as a stand alone, I do not suggest it. The breadth and depth of the story is fleshed out in vivid detail by reading the series in order. I am not big on recapping, but I do my best to anchor each part where appropriate. Sometimes I leave those things to the reader, as I think it adds some little tidbits to discover.

Just prior to the launch of M3-The Outsiders I created a "Bonus Section" on alanthia.com that offers readers a timeline of events from the previous novels. If you like that sort of thing check it out.

I am honored and humbled to have you back, so from the bottom of my heart, thank you. Take my hand; I am going to tell you an amazing tale.

He reveals deep and hidden things; he knows what is in the
darkness, and the light dwells with him.

—Daniel 2:22

Part 1 - Prologue

December 13, 990 ME (Five Years into Rebellion)

Midnight Ramen - New City, Alanthia - Himari Nakamura

"I guess the club scene wasn't happening tonight," Ken Yamato said, turning away and leaving Himari Nakamura alone in the drizzle.

The smell of bleach water and broth wafted into the alley. Inside the narrow galley kitchen, the light over the sink cast his complexion in a sallow glow. He was closing for the night, as she knew he would be. "I came to see you," she said, her voice travelling on the mist like a genie loosed from a bottle.

"Why?" he asked flatly, not looking at her.

She deserved that. "Because I miss you."

"You have a hell of a way of showing it, Himari," he growled and turned his back, chucking his dirty apron into the linen bin.

She took a tentative step inside, mindful of her four-inch heels on the freshly mopped floor. "It's not too late," she whispered, hating the note of pleading that rang hollow and pathetic in her ears.

"Nothing has changed, Sunflower. Go home."

February 13, 997 ME (Twelve Years into Rebellion)

Instinct - New City Palace - Mack ben Robert

Standing in Prince Peter ben Korah's empty bedroom, Agent Mack ben Robert hissed, "What the hell do you mean you haven't seen him for over a month?"

"Exactly what I said, Agent. Prince Peter left the night of his birthday on an extended trip." Jarrod ben Adriel, the unflappable valet, drew himself up with dignity, fighting an icy finger of fear that crawled his spine.

Mack swore under his breath and gestured out the door. "If he's gone, then why is his entire contingent of staff still in residence?"

Jarrod stilled, then lowered his voice. "We were notified that you arranged for a special security detail for a sensitive state visit."

"Who told you that?" Mack demanded, vibrating with banked fury.

Jarrod's eyes shifted around the room. "The King."

Mack froze. "Since when does that son of a bitch let Peter do anything other than cut ribbons?"

The color drained from Jarrod's face, both at the disrespectful way the agent referred to King Korah and his dead certainty that these walls had ears. "I surmised that once the Prince reached the age of nineteen, the King saw fit to give him more responsibility?" He ended the statement with a question.

Mack flared his nose in skepticism. "Did you pack? Did you see him leave?"

Jarrod lifted his chin and inhaled deeply before replying, "No, Agent. I did not."

Instinct fired like an electrical storm, raising every hair on Mack ben Robert's body. It was the premonition that told him to frisk helpless old ladies who turned out to be knife wielding jihadists, and for seven years those gut instincts kept Prince Peter ben Korah alive. "He's got him somewhere, if Peter's not dead already. Come with me and be quiet."

Last Call - Redding, California - Lavinia ben Anthony

She did not belong behind a bar, even a nice one. Lavinia ben Anthony's elegant features and lithe figure begged for designer silks and obscenely expensive Italian pumps. Instead, she dressed in gypsy skirts and peasant blouses that teased the olive-skinned perfection of her shoulders and calves. Her signature gold bangles shimmered in the dim light, clinking together as she worked, the sounds blending into the background noises of the band and murmured conversations of late-night drinkers.

With practiced ease, she hefted a rack of glasses on the counter, still hot and dripping. Pulling mugs out one at a time, she dried and put away without conscious thought. On the small, raised stage, a local band wrapped their final set, singing a soft melodic tune for the few remaining patrons. It had been a busy night at the Cipollini Bar and Bistro, and the succulent aroma of chicken picatta and Pacific salmon gave way to the more mundane scents of vinegar-based table sanitizer and dish room soap.

The eyes of every lonely man at the bar followed her movements, but Lavinia did not notice, lost in a world all her own. The silver ring hanging from a chain swung free as she bent down to retrieve a dry towel. She tucked the necklace away, pausing for a moment to remember the only man she ever noticed.

Lavinia glanced at the clock, just after midnight, February 14th. In the Last Age, lovers celebrated this day by exchanging hearts and chocolates, promising to love, to stay, to be there. She sighed.

"Last call, gentlemen."

May 27, 999 ME (Fourteen Years into Rebellion)

Tourist - Bologna Italy - Kayah ben Samuel

He was Mossad; she could tell by the way he moved. She thought it must be their training, it changed the way their bodies functioned, giving them a stealthy, lethal grace. Kayah ben Samuel kept an eye on the agent across the piazza and inhaled the scent of wet limestone, courtesy of the ancient fountain that made this place such a draw for tourists. A warm, southerly breeze bathed her face in fine mist, refreshing in the heat. She fumbled in her large bag, pulling a brochure from its depths. Pretending to study the map, she surreptitiously adjusted the Italia souvenir visor over her eyes.

The Mossad agent was hunting.

Kayah yawned and relaxed onto a bench, making a show of turning to the sun, pretending to enjoy a respite in the beautiful park. Through determined practice, she calmed her thumping heart, ignored the instinct to run, and harnessed the adrenaline. She refused to even glance at the quilted bag at her feet. Instead, she listened.

"I don't think he saw us. Do you?" A whisper floated from behind Kayah's bench. A teenage girl, by the sound of her.

"I hate that Egyptian," came the reply, another young girl.

"I hate the Greek more."

Kayah stretched and turned slightly, her eyes concealed behind a pair of oversized sunglasses. Sitting cross legged under a tree, the speakers appeared to be two boys, and they were the object of Mossad's surveillance. The agent watched them, unnoticed and tucked away behind a florist cart.

Kayah adjusted the strap of her sandal, satisfied she was not the target. She stood, stretched, and disappeared behind the fountain, carrying a middle-aged woman's flowered handbag, which held a million shekels worth of computer technology she had stolen that morning.

December 25, 999 ME (Fourteen Years into Rebellion)

God Help You All - New City, Bunker - Himari Nakamura

Hidden underground, in the predawn hours after the police arrested Astrid, Davianna, and Josiah, Alaina ben Thomas stretched her long legs and dropped her hands from the keyboard. "I've added the extra layers, Peter. There is not a hacker in the world that can trace us back here."

Himari Nakamura's snort conveyed exactly what she thought of that sentiment.

Alaina shot her a look that dared her to try but addressed her comment to the Prince. "Given what we already had in place for Code Black, the redundancy makes us impenetrable."

Prince Peter ben Korah nodded. "Do your thing, Himari. Tell me what we have."

Himari gave him a flippant salute and started. Her task this morning was to review the encrypted emails sent to The Resistance minutes before the arrests. She needed to ensure the messages carried nothing nefarious. Opening the third document, the sender became clear. She knew this code, and her blood ran cold.

Embedded in the text was a language she had not seen in fifteen years. The message read, "I'm sorry, Himari. Tell Kayah I was wrong, tell Lavinia she was right. It was an accident. I set it free. God help you all."

Part 2 - The Alcatraz 5

September 11, 982 ME (Three Years Before Rebellion)

The Original Bunker

They should not have been there. They should have been in class. Instead, they sidled along the outside wall of the gymnasium, getting ready to run. Himari Nakamura rationalized they were only skipping one class, her least favorite, Social Studies. Kayah ben Samuel hated school and her English Literature teacher, Mr. ben Donnelly, spit when he talked, so she needed very little encouragement to join Himari that afternoon.

Free from the ever-watchful eyes of teachers and administrators, they exchanged conspiratorial a nod before making a break for it. They sprinted around the dugout and disappeared into the woods behind the baseball field, following a well-traveled footpath; illicit adventure and a secret underground bunker awaited.

Their friend, Lavinia ben Anthony, was already there, but she had early release and never skipped class. She could have graduated at the end of their sophomore year. Truth be told, she should have forgone high school altogether and entered university when she turned ten, but she hated being the kid genius, and her mother understood that. Chewing on a red licorice stick, Lavinia stared at the algorithm Gus ben Allen thrust at her the second she walked in the door. He hadn't looked up from his work, merely grunted and handed her the paper.

Gus had the look of a man who recently lost a tremendous amount of weight and was in the process of rapidly gaining it back. However, his appearance tended to rank near the bottom of his priorities. Gus possessed an extraordinary mind that wandered into complex mechanical and electrical applications, often in the middle of a conversation. His pale gray eyes would glaze over as he disappeared into the labyrinth of a mechanical wonderland.

Lavinia understood the lure of that place, and by extension, Gus. She took a gulp of her sugary cola and thought again, "There go I except for the grace of God."

An hour later, Lavinia heard footsteps and smiled as her two friends swept through the heavy metal door, looking flushed and windblown.

Kayah walked over to Gus' workstation. Placing a hand on his big shoulder, she asked, "How long have you been here?"

He hunched low in his seat, narrowing his eyes at the copper coil he was twisting.

Not dissuaded by his silence, Kayah said, "No… if you want to be allowed to stay. You have to answer."

Gus grunted, "Today, I got here today."

Kayah leaned forward and sniffed. "You bathed?"

"Just like you told me." He smiled up at her, seeking approval.

"That's good," Kayah said, giving his shoulder a squeeze. "Did you cut your hair with the dog clippers again?"

He pursed his thick lips. "Yeah, but they work just the same. I don't know what the big deal is."

Kayah rubbed the back of his head. "You missed a spot."

He ran his hand over the stubble. "Oh, I'll have momma fix it."

"Fair enough," Kayah said, giving him a reproving look. "Now, tell me what you are working on."

Gus hunched, his low voice monotone. "The transformer."

"Are you almost done?" Kayah pressed because he looked guilty. His notebook was full of fifteen new pages of calculations, but the model remained untouched. "Gus, we can't keep standing still. This was supposed to be ready today."

Gus deflated and pulled the papers in front of him, writing.

Himari stepped between them. "Don't be such a hard ass, Kayah."

"Bull shit, Himari. Somebody has to push him. Somebody has to tell him to bathe. Somebody has to tell him that he has to talk. And somebody has to make him do his fucking work. Otherwise, we will spend another two years down here with Gus still scribbling on that damn pad."

Lavinia chewed a licorice stick, watching the interplay. It had been building for weeks, and she fell firmly on Kayah's side of this particular argument. Since she knew where she stood, she lost interest and returned to her figures, ignoring their raised voices, until her mind registered a new person.

"Quit bickering." The slamming door punctuated Stephen ben McSwilley's command. "I swear every time I walk in this room, you two are at each other's throats."

Himari wrapped her slender arms around Gus' neck. "Tell her to stop picking on Gus."

"Whatever, Himari! Stephen, you talk to him because he hasn't done shit." Kayah threw up her hands and stormed out.

Stephen looked at Lavinia, who lifted a shoulder. "Kayah has a point."

Stephen made a long-suffering sigh and said, "Himari, do your thing. I'll sit with Gus."

Kayah returned to their small workroom, dressed in coveralls, a long silver flashlight and assorted tools slung around her waist. "I'm going down to Quadrant G," she said through pursed lips and slammed the door, leaving silence in her wake.

Kayah was right. Gus was behind.

Quadrant G

Kayah stalked through the underground tunnels, furious. The freaking geniuses drove her crazy. They were on the verge of discovery, and they should be testing. Instead, she was playing archeologist again.

Wary of broken linoleum tiles, she avoided the worst of them by habit, having already lost one pair of shoes to their razor-sharp edges. Her flashlight bobbed with her steps, illuminating the industrial gray walls, still ugly after a millennium. Not quite alone down here, the ancient structure hosted an assortment of subterranean animals and rodents. Their scampering feet ceased making her edgy, though that had not always been the case.

At one point, the facility had been an underground server farm and research lab. Kayah suspected it was a highly secured facility because it withstood the earthquake that buried it at the end of the Last Age. The hermetically sealed chambers fascinated Kayah, representing a world long gone, where people flew and drove, talked across miles, and accessed knowledge at their fingertips, a wonderous age. For two years, she and the geniuses explored the ruins, dreaming of what had been and what could be. It was all here, the greatest treasure trove of Last Age computer technology ever discovered.

Originally, they believed the equipment found inside would circumvent years of work and research. Kayah thought they would have a functioning machine in six months, tops. To that end, she did her part, every time, on time, more than they asked. She fancied herself the salesperson, the visionary, the entrepreneur, who knew the commercial value of what they were building and understood its impact. Visions of wealth and freedom drove her underground, bound her to this motley crew, and pushed her down the dark tunnel.

Quadrant G remained the final unexplored section of the complex. The security door eluded them. It responded neither to force nor guile. They did not dare detonate explosives, lest they bring the whole place down or alert others to their presence. Last month, they managed to awaken the keypad, but their jubilation turned to defeat when they realized without a code, they were no better off than when the blasted thing was dead.

However, two days ago, Kayah discovered a badge.

She did not examine her motivations for keeping it to herself. But trust never came easy, and she harbored a proprietary possessiveness toward this place. She discovered it, though she never disclosed the circumstances. They did not need to know that—nobody did. But the bunker was hers. Let the geniuses sit up there in that windowless room with their equations and their formulas. Kayah was the pioneer, and this was her frontier.

When she rounded the corner, her heart began to thump. On the wall, the battery pack hung from the keypad by yellow and red wires, Gus' handiwork. She softened toward the big lug. He really was extraordinary.

She squeezed the badge, but the edge cut into her fingers so she released it, afraid it would crack. The beam of light illuminated her target and focused her mind. Tucking the flashlight under her armpit, she activated the battery pack. The keypad lit up, casting the hall in an eerie blue hue. With the yellowed plastic quivering in her hand, she slid the card down the side and waited. Nothing. She tried again. Still nothing. Kayah flipped the badge over and stared at the black stripe and tried once more. The keypad blinked, and the lock clicked. She jumped back in surprise.

Standing outside, she looked at the ceiling and gave a quiet chuckle. "One small step for a girl… one giant leap and all that rubbish."

The door opened without a sound. A rush of stale air greeted her, dusty with an odd hint of metal and decay. She coughed and waved it away, then peeked inside. Computer equipment lay smashed and scattered around the room, but unlike the rest of the facility, this was intentional. The sledgehammer propped in the corner confirmed it.

When nothing moved, she inched the door open, noting the wall of cracked screens, six of them. The frenzy and force of their destruction made her nervous, as if the malevolent force that wreaked such havoc might be lying in wait.

"Hello," she called, then felt absurd.

A four-person desk faced the screens, bare of everything save a single sheet of paper, a rectangular device, and a skull. Beside one of the chairs an ancient handgun mingled with a pile of human bones.

Kayah backed against the wall, blood roaring in her ears as sweat broke out under her coveralls. Ready to flee, she imagined a ghost rising from the dust, banishing her.

Quadrant G was a tomb.

However, the only sounds that broke the silence were her quick pants. When no specter materialized, she stepped forward, curious about the blood-spattered note on the desk.

It got to the point.

'*I killed it, leave it dead.*'

Her nerve failed.

Without forethought, she grabbed the rectangular object off the desk and fled. The flashlight created strobing patterns on the walls as she ran, and the rodents, sensing her terror, beat a hasty departure. She dared a glance over her shoulder, hoping the door remained shut.

Halfway back to the workroom, she bent over, gasping, a pool of light at her feet, her right hand clutching the artifact. As her breathing slowed, she straightened and tucked a sweaty blonde curl behind her ear and palmed her treasure, examining it under the flashlight, an old phone, a mobile device. Her fingerprints disturbed the thick film of dust, and she wiped it clean on her pantleg. It looked new, not a scratch on it.

One of these in good condition sold for thousands on the black market. If Gus ever got the electrical supply working, and they could figure out how to activate it, it would be worth millions. Kayah panned her light down the hall, ensuring she was alone. This was hers.

She took a left into Quadrant D, their first excavation point, and hid the artifact.

It Doesn't Work That Way

Security protocol dictated they leave the bunker one by one. The first alarm, at 5:45 pm, belonged to Himari. Her strict parents insisted she be home from her afternoon "study" sessions in time to eat with them. Closing the marked-up manual, she said, "I'll see you all tomorrow. Gus, see you on Friday." Turning to Kayah, she added, "Be nice to him." With a swing of her long black hair, she left.

Nine minutes later, Lavinia's alarm sounded, which she failed to notice. Stephen pushed the snooze button and nudged her shoulder. "Vinia, time to go."

She looked up, distracted. "Give me a minute," she said, scribbling figures with a furrow between her fine eyebrows. Two minutes later, she set her pencil down with a note of triumph. "I've got it. We're ready."

"That's good. See you back here in two days." Stephen

beamed.

Lavinia threw her three empty soda cans in the trash and winked at Kayah. "See you tomorrow." Halfway to the door, she stopped and dug in her bag, pulling out a geometric printed t-shirt. "Here's that shirt I said you could borrow."

Kayah took it with a coo of appreciation. "Thanks, Vinia. This will look amazing with my black jeans."

"And your hair, too. The analogous color scheme does not compliment mine."

Kayah grinned, chewing her gum. "The browns, Lavinia, it's fine to just say the color."

"Right, browns." Lavinia nodded and drained the last of her soda before departing.

Stephen's alarm went off next, but he motioned to Gus. "Gus, go ahead. I need a word with Kayah."

Gus put down his soldering gun. "I'm not done yet."

"It's okay, big guy. It will be here on Friday," Stephen said, using a tone that cut off further argument.

Gus looked between his two friends. "Don't yell at her, Stephen. Kayah's right." He rose like he did everything, slowly, and left the room.

Kayah crossed her arms and shot Stephen a hostile glare, ready for a fight. "What?"

Stephen matched her posture, his dark eyes penetrating. "What did you find, Kai?"

Kayah snorted. "I didn't find shit."

"Don't lie to me," Stephen warned with a jut of his prominent chin, looking determined. "You came back here pale and sweaty, like you'd seen a ghost. What did you find?"

Kayah gathered her belongings. "Nothing, same as the last fifty times we've tried to breach that damn door. I came back because I'm sick of working on it."

Stephen made a disbelieving hiss. "You got in, didn't you?"

Kayah tied her shoe, refusing to look at him. "No."

"Liar." Stephen's thin upper lip curled in derision. "You can't keep secrets, Kai. It doesn't work that way. And you, of all people, know how important this is. Do you really want everything to fall apart because you are hiding things?"

Kayah gave him a narrow-eyed stare and tilted her head, considering. "Fine, I got in. It's a tomb."

Stephen threw his arms up in exasperation. "What the hell, Kai?" He stood up, radiating equal amounts of fury and excitement. "Show me."

Kayah sighed. "Come on."

She showed him the tomb, not her treasure.

October 23, 982 ME

The Alcatraz Five

Five weeks later, they were ready. From the discovery of the bunker to their first test, it had taken twenty-six months. They nicknamed the place Alcatraz, after the ancient prison ruins in the Bay. In many ways, the bunker became a prison, though self-imposed. To avoid suspicion, they worked three days a week: Monday, Wednesday, and Friday. They never discussed their secret outside the bunker's walls, and if the girls saw the boys above ground, they pretended not to know each other. This proved difficult for Gus but crucial for the safety of the group. Their activities could get them thrown in jail for the rest of their natural lives, and they knew it.

Most of the equipment in the bunker was useless, degraded by age and time. They painstakingly excavated and salvaged the best, reassembling the parts in the workroom. The obstacles were astounding, components, power, and expertise, all of it lost. The Millennium was paradise, at least on the outside. For the Alcatraz Five, life was anything but.

The day of the test, Gus ben Allen arrived first. At nineteen, he was the oldest of the group, the fifth of seven children. Moving into the dark room, he set about readying the place, as was his routine. Battery powered lamps, of his making, illuminated the cinderblock walls. They arranged the five workstations much like a classroom, each bearing the equipment, personal effects, and style of its occupant.

Kayah gave up trying to remind him to put down cardboard or craft paper, so his table bore the unmistakable marks of a mechanic, solder burns, grease smudges, and copper shavings. He had a stray piece of straw stuck in his auburn hair, and his hands bore calluses of a manual laborer, earned working on his family farm.

Most people assumed he was simple. In some ways, he was. He did not speak until he was seven, even now he didn't say much. His parents accepted that he was different and did not try to force him to change. Once, he overheard his mother tell a lady at church, "It was just one of those things, a rare difficult birth. The cord wrapped around his neck, poor baby. It deprived his brain of oxygen too long."

If he ever thought about it, which was not often, Gus surmised they were probably right. He was different. However, he suspected the power that should have dispersed over a normal brain concentrated and settled in an area that processed complex equations and electrical engineering concepts. Gus did not blame his family for failing to understand what went on inside his head. He had not told them. Besides, one mean-eyed doctor called him retarded, and everyone believed it, until he turned twelve.

He built a wind-up toy dog, and it changed his life. Mrs. ben Trey, his teacher, noticed. Several days later, she produced a box of gears and components, but best of all, she left him alone. Gus needed to be left alone when he tinkered. Two days later, he finished a mechanized tank, complete with a rotating turret gun that could fire a small projectile.

Within the month, they reassigned him to a new school, Euler Preparatory Academy for the gifted and talented. He did not know anyone there, but he enjoyed the engineering program, and no one gave him a coloring book.

Unfortunately, he flunked out.

"Gus, I am sorry, but you are just not adapting as well as we hoped." The administrator pointed to two projects on his paper-strewn desk. "This is what you were supposed to make, a miniature water pump, but this is what you made." He gestured to a model of an automated feed dispenser. "While we appreciate the clever design and its practical applications, this was not the assignment."

Gus stared at the water pump, pondering the best place to put one on his parent's farm, and stopped listening to the administrator.

"You have failing grades in almost all of your classes, Gus. Your teachers report that even if you do the work, it is late, and never to specifications. I am sorry, but we are transferring you back to general education."

"I wasn't in general education," Gus said, paying attention now. "I like Euler. I don't want to leave."

He was sixteen and never went back to school.

Settling in at his workstation, he waited for the others and thought that was perhaps not such a bad thing.

Stephen ben McSwilley was sweating. His palms felt clammy, his heart thumped, and the burning sensation in the pit of his stomach had become all too familiar. He pushed through the bunker door and found Gus hunched over his notepad. He did not look up, just kept calculating.

"Hi, Gus," Stephen said, not expecting an answer.

They met when Gus joined the engineering program at Euler. Stephen would never forget the horror he experienced seeing his new lab partner the first time.

"He stinks, and I swear he had pig poop on his overalls today," he complained to his mother, Joan, when she came to their rooms on her afternoon break.

"Now, be nice," his mother admonished. "I grew up on a farm, and so did your father."

Stephen gave an impatient gesture around their well-appointed sitting room. "Mom, you were born at Gilead, the Palace of the Princes, not a farm. Stop."

"My father worked on the farm at Gilead, Stephen. Sometimes he smelled like manure."

"Well, you don't, neither does Dad, and we do not live on a farm. We live in the Palace."

Joan waved him away. "Just because we live in the Palace does not mean we are from the Palace. Your father and I are working people, just like your new friend Gus."

Working people… Stephen hated that phrase. To him, it meant servitude, relying on the whims and capricious behavior of the spoiled royals they served. He had no desire to waste his life doing laundry or scrubbing floors. To be fair, neither of his parents did those things, and living in the Palace had its benefits, even if they were in service.

Joan read his dubious expression and said, "Try to work with him, lad. They put him with you for a reason. Make the best of it."

He took her advice and discovered Gus was off the charts brilliant. With a little coaxing, Stephen channeled that brilliance, and to his delight, they got top marks on everything they did, which was fortuitous, because mechanical engineering proved difficult for him, though he would never admit it. Unfortunately, he and Gus only had two classes together, and Gus failed miserably without Stephen to keep him on task.

When Kayah approached him with her idea, the first-person Stephen thought of was Gus. "I know another guy who might be perfect."

"No way, we can't risk it. People talk," Kayah said.

"I'll let you meet him." Stephen smiled. "He doesn't talk."

And thus, began the plan that would launch Stephen ben McSwilley into the stratosphere. He was ambitious, though he hid it behind the veneer of humble, self-deprecation ingrained in him from birth. But he had a talent for recognizing the abilities of others and organizing them in a way that maximized the outcome.

Pacing around their workroom, he said as much to himself as Gus, "Today is the day. Today is finally the day."

The morning of the test, Himari Nakamura left her parents' overly decorated apartment in the Japanese section of the New City and hurried down the sidewalk. The tourists and lunch crowd had yet to arrive, but the shopkeepers and restaurant owners all stepped into the crisp autumn air as if to check. They called greetings to each other as the restauranteurs smoked dark tipped cigarettes and the florists arranged their buckets of flowers just so.

"If you were mine, I would not let you out of the house," Mrs. Yamanaka muttered as Himari walked by.

Himari ignored her. With a determined step, she vowed to remain oblivious to the unanimous disapproval directed at her. It was her attire. She was used to their scorn, but no matter how much they glared and whispered in low Japanese tones, she refused to dress like them. They looked ridiculous.

When she was ten and got accepted into Euler, she decided she was going to school dressed like everyone else. She and her mother argued for weeks. Finally, Himari put her hands on her hips and declared, "You will not catch me dead in a kimono. I will go naked before I wear another one."

Why everyone in her neighborhood insisted on dressing differently than the rest of the New City residence was beyond Himari. She chose to blend into her city, which prevented her from ever truly being a part of the community where she lived.

But no matter how she dressed, her face and stature identified her as Asian. And try as she might, she did not fit in anywhere. She straddled the middle; her mixed blood ensured it. Her biological father had been Alanthian, her mother second generation Japanese. They met in high school and married right after graduation, but their relationship lasted less than two years. Enough time for Himari to be conceived, and for her father to discover he would never fit in among his wife's people; she had no desire to fit in among his. He left when Himari was seven months old. Her stepfather, Kunimoto Nakamura, adopted her when she was two. Himari was fifteen when she discovered he was not her actual father. A neighbor told her.

However, at Euler they accepted Himari, and she fell in with a group of misfits. Descending the steps of their underground hideout, Himari Nakamura recognized she and the misfits were about to make history.

"*Addio*, Mamma," Lavinia ben Anthony called from the front door of their bungalow on Fibonacci Avenue.

"Have a good day, precious, and do not forget, your father will be here when you get home."

Lavinia had forgotten that. She paused at the door, going back to the kitchen where her mother was clearing breakfast dishes. "He is in port?"

Violet beamed. "Yes, the Singapore Bridge docked around midnight. He has four days leave."

Lavinia patted her thigh, pensive. "I already have plans. Kayah and I are going on a double date," she lied. For effect, she smiled and added, "You haven't seen Pappa for six months. You two enjoy your night. I will see him when I get home or in the morning."

Violet flushed, trying to hide the smile pulling at the corners of her mouth. "Who are you going out with?"

Lavinia waved the question away, the gold bangles, a recent gift from her father on her eighteenth birthday, made a pleasant tinkling sound. "I'm just a stand in. The date is Kayah's. I don't know the other boy, but I told her I would go."

Violet suspected the boy felt otherwise. "Is he from school?"

Lavinia paused, then nodded, trying to control the nervous flutter of her fingers tapping her thigh. She hated lying to her mother, but it was becoming easier.

"All right. Be careful."

"I will," Lavinia assured her and leaned in for a goodbye kiss.

Drying her hands on a dish towel, Violet tried to squelch her anxiety about her daughter dating. Lavinia had been the prettiest baby anyone had ever seen; strangers often stopped Violet on the street to ooh and ahh. And she had grown into an elegant young lady.

All parents think their children are the most beautiful and intelligent creatures in the world, but in Violet and Anthony's case, it might be true. Lavinia was special. The doctors claimed they did not have tests that could quantify her IQ. She was literally off the charts, a certified genius. How she came by this, no one knew. She read at eighteen months, did complex math at six, and spoke five languages, including Danish and Japanese, by the time she was twelve. She also lived in a world all her own.

Violet walked to the window and watched her daughter disappear around the corner, hoping the world that Lavinia was oblivious to would not chew her up.

No one questioned Kayah as she ran out the door, simply because Kayah had nobody. She was a throwaway kid, a ward of the state, who lived in a squat brick orphanage and made up names for herself. Her current favorite was Kayah ben Samuel because she liked Samuel in the bible and thought he had been abandoned too, so that was what she went by. However, her legal name marked her for what she was, Kayah ben Alanthia. But it sucked going through life with a label like that, so she changed her name and changed her story.

She earned her spot at Euler, though most of her classmates believed she was part of some non-existent quota program for underprivileged. It was bullshit, and only one preppy boy with his hair parted on the side ever dared say it to her face, and then only when he was surrounded by teachers and his gang of rich douche bags.

The following day, the administrators held a special assembly to warn students about a dangerous vagrant who attacked a student as he walked home. No one ever accused Kayah of being a charity case again.

Despite being a stunning blonde with hazel eyes and porcelain skin, her smart mouth, disregard for authority, and overall bad attitude prevented her from being adopted. She gave up that fantasy when the last family who showed interest in her took her back to the orphanage without bothering to go inside. She was six.

Running fifteen minutes late, her black ankle boots beat a rhythmic pace down the sidewalk. Paired with Lavinia's printed t-shirt and holey jeans, the outfit gave her an urban, edgy look. The cheap leather bag slung over her shoulder held the artifact from Quadrant G sewn between the lining. A few shekels littered the bottom of her purse, all the money she had in the world, but she never kept anything of value at the orphanage.

With her make-up done and her hair curled, she looked older than her eighteen years, and even if the men craning their necks to watch her walk past had realized her age, they would not have cared. The expensive perfume she wore, while stolen, made her feel powerful, better than who she was. And she, more than the rest of the Alcatraz 5, knew October 23, 982 ME would change her life forever. ABC's

At 10:42 am, the Alcatraz 5 huddled around the newly refurbished monitor on Himari's workstation. Since programming was her forte, they agreed she should be the one operating the commands. That they even got the machine to turn on seemed like a miracle. It took a tremendous leap of courage to even power it up. They feared the unit might fizzle and short out, which had happened before. But they learned, adjusted, and this time felt different.

The pointing arrow flew across the screen in jerky movements before reappearing in unexpected places. Stephen kept giving excited directions. Kayah suppressed the urge to lift Himari out of the chair and take over. Gus listened to the computer's fan speed and watched the pulsating light, catching the imperceptible flicker of the three-phase electrical transmission powering the machine. Lavinia calculated the Euler Angle on the calibration of the mouse and decided she needed to adjust it for smoother scrolling.

Himari hovered over the file, looking at each of her companions. They nodded, breathless with anticipation. It was the most logical place to start. The first file, ABC, start there. She squeezed her eyes shut and double clicked.

An hourglass appeared on the screen, flipping over and over. Himari opened her eyes and watched. Even Gus came out of his reverie, fascinated by the little cartoon icon. They held their breaths, waiting.

Then, the notes of a thousand-year-old song filled the room.

Himari shot out of her seat. Stephen hugged Lavinia. Kayah leapt on Gus' back. They jumped and danced, laughed and cried. The Alcatraz 5 had done it.

November 11, 982 ME

The Key to the Future

After the initial jubilation of their discovery, they got to work. They learned exponentially, and the bunker drew them deeper and deeper into the knowledge of the Last Age. The more they probed, the further they got. It mimicked a drug.

The day after they played the audio file, they all snuck into the bunker to discover everyone else had the same idea. Their self-imposed work week was sacrificed on the altar of progress.

The number of hours and days they worked was not the only thing that changed. At school, three weeks after their first successful test, Stephen said hello to Lavinia in the hall, not to Himari or Kayah who were walking with her, just Lavinia.

Kayah muttered a curse under her breath, and she and Himari exchanged knowing glances.

Lavinia looked between them, confused. "What?"

Kayah shook her head. "That's not good."

"What are you talking about? I said good morning to Stephen." Lavinia scrunched up her face at Kayah, who was suspicious of everyone and everything.

"Well, it's against the rules, for one thing," Himari said without moving her lips. She glanced around surreptitiously. "For another, he's been giving you moon eyes for a month."

Lavinia's olive complexion paled. "No, he has not."

Kayah snorted. "Get out of your algorithms and look up every once in a while."

Lavinia groaned. "No, not Stephen. I hate it when that happens. It ruins everything." She looked at Himari in panic. "You tell him, but do it nicely, in a way that lets him stay in the group and keep his pride. Being Japanese, you know how to do that…"

Kayah elbowed Lavinia and grinned. "You don't want me to do it?"

Lavinia shook her head. "Kayah, you pull the wings off flies."

"I do not," Kayah protested, but her chin got just a bit sharper with suppressed amusement.

Himari laughed. "I'll be sure to tell my mother you think I've learned my Japanese charm lessons well. She and my father will get a good laugh." Himari struck a pose and bowed.

"Do it," Kayah encouraged.

"Yeah, do it," Lavinia seconded.

Himari composed her face, though her almond-shaped eyes sparkled. It was a game, one she played with her friends, mocking her culture, especially her subservient mother. "Oh, master Stephen-san, you are so smart and so handsome. But I humbly ask you," she bobbed over her steepled fingers, "to leave Lavinia the fuck alone."

They exploded with laughter.

But after it settled, they still had a problem.

Since they met in eighth grade homeroom, the three girls became inseparable. Over time, four boys had joined their group as friends. But to a one, they fell in love with Lavinia. It was pathetic. Boys never intended to fall for her, they just did. It was impossible not to. Kayah teased that she emitted a pheromone, and once they caught the scent, instinct took over. Lavinia could do nothing to stop it. She never encouraged them, at least intentionally. Truth be told, she spent most of her time lost in some complex mathematical calculation, which gave her beautiful face a wistful glow the boys misinterpreted as ardor, for them. It was maddening for everyone because it ruined their friendships. The boys left, leaving everyone sad and embarrassed.

They hoped Stephen and Gus would be immune. Gus was, but it turned out Stephen wasn't. Damn. They should have known. In the last ten months, Stephen had grown from an awkward, gawky engineer to a slightly handsome, well-spoken, confident young man. But they were busy, and no one noticed it was happening again.

Now the group was in trouble, and Kayah was furious. Sitting in class, she fumed. The rest of them had their futures laid out, neat and tidy. But at eighteen, the only thing keeping a roof over her head was the fact that she was still in high school. In June, she would receive her diploma, a couple thousand shekels, and the best wishes of the Alanthian Social Services Department. Her only hope of not sleeping on a park bench was the successful sale of the contents of the bunker, specifically the device she hid in Quadrant D.

Euler taught business classes, though most of the geniuses did not bother to enroll. Kayah took every one of them. She held her own in the technical courses, excelling in physics and biomechanics, but without a degree, nobody was going to hire her, and she determined sales was her best chance of making a living. She read people, could put on a show, and convince almost anyone to do what she wanted.

To that end, six months ago, she began sneaking off to attend business conventions and symposiums, looking for an employer and a prospective buyer for her treasure. She shopped the thrift stores, picking up second-hand suits, silk blouses, and only slightly scuffed leather pumps. Skillfully applied make-up, a French twist, and a trim black suit transformed her from schoolgirl into junior sales executive. She sat among the conference attendees, crossing her extraordinary legs, taking notes, and hanging on every word. Men always came to sit beside her.

Alanthian business executives were flirting with technology. It ran in the blood of the New City, a heartbeat pumping just below the surface. The Alcatraz 5 were not the only ones conducting secret research, despite Prince Eamonn's governmental crackdowns and impassioned speeches against it.

Kayah despised Prince Eamonn on an elemental level that bordered on hatred. Perhaps because his portrait hung in every "home" she ever lived in, but more likely it was his patronizing manner. He absolutely grated on her. She preferred his brother, Korah, and was drawn to the younger Prince, always had been. Soon after mingling with the city's business executives, she understood why. It was a poorly guarded secret; Korah believed in tech and the future it held.

So, with less than a year before she found herself sleeping on a park bench, Stephen's sudden infatuation with Lavinia was intolerable. Unlike the rest of them, Stephen had access, dangerous as it might be, to Prince Korah. The more she frequented the conventions, the more she heard, the more men told her in hushed tones, she convinced herself that her instincts were correct. Prince Korah held the key to her future, and she knew exactly how to get his attention.

December 6, 982 ME

Test of a Leader

Stephen took the news like a man. He denied it, but Lavinia's love-struck ones always did. But unlike the others, he did not sulk or slither away. Stephen bore up well to Lavinia's rejection, though Kayah still caught the longing in his eyes, it was impossible to disguise. But he did not act on his feelings or make any untoward advances. They pretended it never happened, except for Gus, who had not realized.

Over the next several months, Lavinia and Stephen found themselves at odds, not over his unrequited love, but over the ruins in Quadrant G. The place gave everyone the creeps. Not Stephen, it drew him. They often discovered him sifting amongst the rubble with the macabre skeleton looking on with slack jawed amazement at his audacity. Lavinia took the dead man's message seriously. Stephen argued the note was nothing but the ramblings of a man gone mad at the end of the Last Age. Himari was more circumspect because she knew some secrets needed to stay hidden. Kayah agreed with Himari, for once. But Gus settled the argument.

"Mechanically, there is nothing we need from this room. There is no reason to continue fighting about it. If there is something dead down here, we ought to leave it." He paused before continuing, staring at his big feet. "When I was six, I dug up our pet cat after it died." He walked away, adding quietly, "I shouldn't have done that."

The three girls exchanged looks and turned to Stephen, united in their determination to abandon the tomb and equipment to the ghost who guarded it.

Stephen met their eyes, outnumbered, and out voted. His continued leadership of the group hinged upon his ability to accept that he would not always get his way. He nodded once and motioned for them to depart. Making a final inspection, he looked around, then pulled the heavy door closed with a thunk.

Lavinia surprised them by taking a mallet and smashing the keypad to smithereens, ending their forays into Quadrant G.

January 6, 983 ME

The Birthday Party that Changed the World

In the course of human history, they could say with relative certainty, it was the first time a five-year-old's birthday party changed the world. Then again, it was no ordinary birthday party, and he was no ordinary five-year-old. Anyone who met Prince Peter ben Korah could attest to that. Prince d'Or did not earn his nickname by accident, he earned every golden ray of sunshine.

He charmed the guests, flirted with the little girls, and flattered the waitstaff, even the temporary help brought in to serve. Stephen used his influence to get Kayah hired for the party. Dressed in sober black and white, she found herself the recipient of the little Prince's legendary charm. "They usually do not let pretty girls serve in the Palace." Peter winked at her before accepting the lemonade from her tray.

Someone trained in service would have demurred in a manner befitting their different stations; Kayah was neither trained nor demure. And her mission today had nothing to do with hustling lemonade. She grinned at the young Prince. He was adorable. "Being pretty is only one of my talents, as I am sure you understand."

"I have talents, too." Prince Peter grinned. "I can ride like the wind and am not afraid of the horses, even the stallions."

Kayah went for it. "I can make music come out of a box."

He raised a golden eyebrow. "Are you a magician?"

Kayah raised her brows back at him. "Sort of. I might even show your father. I hear he is interested in things like that. Maybe he will buy it for you as a birthday present."

Peter laughed, a bit too cynical for a child his age. "You would have better luck with my mother," he said, gesturing toward the lovely pale redhead watching them across the lawn. He winked and strutted off to join the rest of the posh children, lining up to take their shot at the pinata.

At the blast of a trumpet, everyone paused. Kayah took her cue and bowed her head, as Prince Eamonn and Prince Josiah made their appearance. The first thing that struck Kayah was that Prince Eamonn was tall, much larger than his portraits conveyed. The second was his son was his mirror image, in looks and carriage, albeit a thirteen-year-old version. The third was that Prince Eamonn had the most penetrating eyes she had ever seen. He caught her glance as he walked three feet from her. She supposed the rest of the servants had their heads bowed, but she wanted to look at him.

She should not have; it was a disaster.

Orphans recognize that look, it said, 'You do not belong here.' She had seen it a thousand times, from mothers on playgrounds who realized their daughter's new friend was not a suitable playmate, to dream killing guidance counselors who smiled and told her to set more realistic goals for her future. She saw it on the faces of clerks in nice stores, who suspected she was there to shoplift, which she was, but how the hell did they know? Standing on the Palace lawn, held by Prince Eamonn's piercing gaze, she wondered if there was a class somewhere that taught it because it was the same across social strata. It cut her to the quick and reminded her that she was the lowest of the low. He did not stop or address her, but he went a step further, narrowing his eyes and silently banishing her. If she thought she hated him before, she was dead certain afterward.

She did not cower or lower her chin; she returned his hateful gaze with one of her own. It screamed, 'Right back at you, asshole'. Then she smiled, insincere and sweet, prepared to be man-handled off the property, which was the usual course of events. Five minutes later, the guards came. If she could count on anything, it was that her betters never appreciated when she fought back.

Stephen sidled up beside her, as she stormed toward the servant's quarters. "What did you do?" His face was ashen, his lips the same hue as his wheat-colored hair.

"Apparently, I was too pretty." Her high blonde ponytail swung with each angry step.

Stephen faltered, turning red. "Oh, I was a little worried about that."

"Never mind, you said you were going to get me into see Prince Korah," Kayah hissed.

He scratched his head and looked chagrined. "He's not here."

Kayah rolled her eyes. "He missed his son's birthday party? That's kind of shitty."

"Prince Korah," he cut himself off, his face flaming. "We don't discuss the personal lives of the family. It's a tenet of being in service."

"Unless he is back in the next fifteen minutes, which is how long I have before they toss me out. You have to do it." Kayah's frustration boiled over. "Don't screw it up, Stephen. This is my only chance."

"What exactly do you want me to do?"

Kayah looked around and pulled him behind a tall hedge just outside the kitchen entrance. "Give him this and tell him there is more where that came from." Kayah took a drawstring bag from her pocket, which contained the Quadrant G device. "This is what I planned to show him. We've got one shot."

His brief glimpse of the contents shook him to his core. "I could go to jail for the rest of my life for having this."

"What do you think we've been doing for the last two-and-a-half years? You think this has been a game, some sort of make-believe adventure, so you could hang out with hot girls and make goo-goo eyes at Lavinia?" Kayah grew fierce. "You want to be the leader? Then fucking lead. Get that in front of Korah. He'll pay."

Stephen looked at his open palm, dumbfounded as she stalked away. He stuffed the bag in his pocket and retreated to the kitchen to get more drinks. The glasses made tinkling noises when he went back to the party. He could not stop shaking.

Ten minutes later, Kayah was thankful Stephen had her treasure. It really did not pay to be a pretty girl at the Palace. Three guards waited for her outside the locker room. A female guard searched her, including the contents of her purse. Summarily escorted from the property they took her to a nearby coach station. The blue-eyed man in charge handed her an envelope full of cash and bowed. "Thank you for your service. Please do not return."

Kayah wished she did not need the money. But she snatched the envelope and stalked away with her head held high, her face scorched with humiliation and anger.

The Best Place to Cool Off is Underground

"How did it go?" Himari asked the moment Kayah walked through the door.

Kayah threw her bag on her desk, still in a fury. "It's all up to Stephen now."

Gus looked up from his circuit board, his deep voice troubled. "What happened, Kai?"

"Apparently, I'm too cute."

Gus' smile grew slowly. "Well, I could have told you that."

Kayah blew him a kiss, then said in a full-blown sulk, "I got thrown out."

"What? Who gets kicked out for being cute?" Himari exclaimed. "I wouldn't be allowed to go anywhere if that was the case."

"I suggest you don't go to the Palace, at least not dressed as a maid. It's the only thing that I can figure. I had a word with Prince d'Or, that was his take on it." Kayah sat down in a huff.

"You spoke to the little Prince?" Himari rolled her eyes. "That's probably it. You aren't supposed to talk to them."

Kayah bowed up, defensive. "He talked to me first. I wasn't going to just ignore him, *that* would have been rude."

Himari put her hand on her hip. "Instead you pulled some other crap, didn't you? I know you, Kayah. I've seen that temper. What happened?"

Kayah threw up her hands in surrender. "I swear, nothing. I exchanged five words with Prince d'Or, then Prince Eamonn came in, he took one look at me, and I was gone."

Gus furrowed his brow. "That's weird."

Kayah smiled at Gus, she could always count on him to take her side. "It was weird." Kayah looked around the room, Lavinia's absence registering. "Where's Vinia?"

Himari ran her tongue over her upper teeth and shook her head. "They had a death in the family. She and her mother left for Redding this morning. Her grandfather passed away."

Kayah felt a momentary pang of envy. "Oh, that's sad. He's the one that runs that vineyard she loves."

"Yeah, her grandparents run a bar and bistro up there, too." Himari pursed her lips. "She said her mom might move up there and take over."

"That would suck." Kayah tightened her ponytail. "Though, Lavinia will live on campus next year, so she'll still be in the New City."

Gus went back to work on his circuit board but said, "My momma made wine one time. It was terrible."

Kayah chuckled. She always enjoyed Gus' strange segues. "Why was it terrible, Gus?"

He shrugged a big shoulder. "It tasted like vomit."

Himari and Kayah exchanged looks and laughed.

"That's what you do after you drink too much wine, not before," Himari teased.

"I don't know what she did. Everyone said it tasted like vomit, not just me."

Kayah turned on the monitor, deciding to work. "I am sure Lavinia's grandfather's wine doesn't taste like vomit."

"He wouldn't be in business very long if it did," Gus intoned.

"Well, let's just hope Stephen can get Prince Korah to take the bait. If he does, we will be in business," Kayah said, staring at the ceiling, looking wistful.

Himari covered her eyes. "If not business, then jail."

"Don't even say that, Himari. Don't even say it."

January 8, 983 ME

A Bad End, Eventually

Kayah half expected it, but when it occurred, it still felt like a bad dream. It sounded like thunder, and at first that's what she thought, which would have been preferable to what it was—boots. Boots that ran down the steps, invading the bunker. Boots surrounded them, holding weapons. Boots whose owners seized and handcuffed them. Boots confiscated more than two years' worth of work, carting it away in front of the four frightened kids who discovered and recreated the wonders of the Last Age.

Boots destroyed everything.

Lavinia was in Redding, attending her grandfather's funeral the day the soldiers came. Himari's parents hired a lawyer who had her out of jail in eight hours. They released Gus into the custody of his parents in seventy-two. Stephen never saw the inside of a cell.

Kayah met her lawyer, for the first time, a week later.

The buttons on his white shirt pulled across his belly, and his sport coat had a mustard stain on the lapel, which hadn't come out in the laundry. The stain had been there awhile. He kept calling her Karen, and Kayah stopped correcting him.

Six weeks after her arrest, he came back. "I'm sorry, Karen, but I am afraid," he glanced at his notes, "Stephen ben McSwilley cut a deal with the state in exchange for his testimony against you."

"Just me?"

The fat lawyer gave her a patronizing smile. "Himari Nakamura is still a minor. I spoke with the federal prosecutor, he offered her a plea, one thousand hours of community service for her promise to never handle technology again."

He turned the page on his notes. "They dropped the charges against Gus ben Allen. Yesterday, a judge agreed with the state's evaluation, deeming him nonverbal and incompetent. Thus, he cannot be held responsible for his actions and will not stand trial. They placed him in the permanent custody of his parents."

Kayah buried her face in her hands. That was ridiculous, but if it kept Gus out of jail, she was okay with it.

"Karen, I am afraid this is going bad for you. The prosecutor plans to portray you as the mastermind behind the whole thing. You found the site, you recruited the others, so you are the one responsible." He pushed a paper across the cracked wooden table. "Here is the indictment."

Kayah blinked. It was two pages long.

"Six of those charges carry mandatory minimum sentences. I've argued that your age, your background, and your circumstances should play a role." He wiped a gleam of sweat from his brow. "But with Stephen's testimony and your fingerprints all over the crime scene." He paused, looking pained. "Taken with the testimony of your house master that you disappear on a regular basis? You have little hope at trial. I'm sorry, Karen, this prosecutor is not budging. The best deal I could get is that you serve your sentences concurrently."

Kayah's breathing became ragged. "How long?"

"Fifteen."

"Years?" she cried, though she knew it wasn't months.

"It's the best chance you've got. If you go to trial, they will incarcerate you for life."

A week later, dressed in an orange jumpsuit from the county jail. A judge rapped his gavel and sealed her fate.

No one uttered a word about Lavinia, including Stephen.

The injustice of the whole thing was galling, but everybody knew Kayah would come to a bad end, eventually.

June 20, 983 ME

She Will Not See Me - Redding, CA

Six months later, Lavinia walked into her grandparents' old bistro in Redding. She found her mother in the kitchen, washing dishes. "Mamma, she would not see me. I went every day for three days, and she would not come down. Why?"

Violet looked over her shoulder and smiled. Her face registered a lifetime of love and understanding. "I lost my job several years ago. Do you remember?"

"At the payroll company?" Lavinia looked up from her intense study of her hands.

"That's right, dear. My friends from work wanted to see me. They wanted to have lunch because they worried about me, since your dad was at sea." Violet dried the big pot they used for tomato sauce and put it on the metal rack. "I kept making excuses. Do you know why?"

Lavinia shook her head, misery written all over her face.

"Because I was embarrassed. I was ashamed to be out of work, and I was sad. It was too hard pretending that I was fine, that what my boss and the company did was okay. I did not want to see my friends because it brought everything back." Violet took Lavinia's hand. "Do you think Kayah might feel the same way?"

"But Mamma, she is my friend. I am worried about her. I want to see her, to tell her I am sorry," Lavinia lamented, her frustration heightening her color.

Violet patted Lavinia's hand. "Vinia, it's not about you."

Lavinia's pained expression telegraphed her difficulty processing the nuances her mother tried to convey. Old instinct kicked in, and she retreated, equations dancing in her head. Since her mind was spinning, she settled on numbers that spun: signal processing. e jwt. e jx = cos(θ) x + J sin(θ)x. e -jx = cos(θ) x + J sin(θ) x. Calculating complex exponential magnitude, she plotted it on a plane and watched it spin, beautifully.

"Come back," Violet cooed.

Lavinia squeezed her eyes shut. "It is so much easier in there."

Violet did not laugh, because she understood. "I know for you it is, but life is not numbers. This is important."

Lavinia groaned and returned; her lips pursed. She was trying.

"People will not always give you what you want. They cannot always give you what you need. Sometimes, you have to sacrifice for the people you love and give them room to do what they have to do, even if it hurts." Violet gathered both her daughter's hands. "That does not mean they don't love you, and it does not mean that deep inside they don't want to give you what you want. Sometimes they just can't."

"So, what you are saying is that Kayah probably wanted to see me. She still loves me, but she just can't do it right now?" Violet nodded, her smile sad. "And I have to love her enough to let her make that decision?" Lavinia rested her head on her mother's hands. "Can I go back another time? Can I try again?"

"That's what love does; it persists." Violet took her daughter into her arms and held on.

July 4, 983 ME

The Price to Pay

Lavinia did not even recognize Himari. "Why are you wearing that?"

"Shh," Himari hissed, "not here."

"Himari, that is a Shinto wedding gown. You are not Shinto, no one has been for a thousand years." The elaborate kimono was stunning, but so out of character for Himari, a pale stranger stood before her.

Himari pulled Lavinia into a supply closet and shut the door. "It's the price, Vinia."

"The price for what?" Lavinia stared, in awe of Himari's elaborate headpiece.

Himari looked at her red slippers and mumbled, "For what we did."

Lavinia covered her mouth. "They are making you do this?"

Himari looked up, her eyes begging for understanding. "It's not so bad. He's not so bad."

"You don't even know him." Anguish washed over Lavinia. "He barely speaks English, and when I spoke to him in Japanese, he ignored me."

"You have not been properly introduced. It's our way." Himari bit her lip.

"Your way, Himari?" Lavinia whispered.

Unshed tears glistened on Himari's short eyelashes. "I have to try, Vinia. You know I have always been an outsider among my people, but I promised to try."

"I understand what it's like to be an outsider, but this is not you," Lavinia pleaded. "Himari, you successfully installed an operating system that had been dead for a thousand years."

"But at what cost? For Kayah…" Himari drew herself up. "This is what it cost me." Bitterness crept into her voice. "It didn't cost you anything."

Lavinia recoiled. "It cost me Kayah. It cost me Stephen. It

cost me Gus." Her voice faltered, becoming lower and huskier than normal. "And I think when you walk down that aisle, it is going to cost me you, too."

They held each other's gazes, two young hearts breaking inside a broom closet, hidden, like always.

Lavinia turned away, with her hand on the doorknob she stopped. Himari stood frozen, framed in the dark closet with a string mop leaning on the wall behind her. It made the ridiculous headdress look like a gray fountain sprang from the top of her head. "Forgive me if I cannot bear to watch it. I love you, my friend. Be well, be happy."

As Lavinia left the chapel, tears coursed down her cheeks, the bitter irony of the date was not lost on her. July 4th, the day ancient Alanthians celebrated their freedom, and the day her friend sold herself into an even more ancient form of slavery.

You Look Well

Gus ben Allen sat in the hard, uncomfortable chair with his large shoulders slumped, his head down. He methodically rubbed his thumbs against his forefingers. The rough calluses made a small sandy noise he concentrated on because the loud banging doors and buzzers kept startling him. He waited for a long time. They said they would call him, but they had not. So, he sat there. People came and went. He took a tentative glance at the clock, 14:00. Visiting hours would be over soon, and he had been here since 11:00.

Finally, a woman in a tight uniform with big hips motioned him forward and led him down a hall to a little room. The door scraped in the upper left-hand corner when she opened it. He saw the hinge was not properly installed. He could fix it if they let him, but he was too afraid to ask. Gus did not like this place. It felt like the hospital they put him in after the soldiers with the boots came to the bunker, except worse, it smelled like pee. The room had two benches bolted to the ground. He waited another half an hour.

When he looked up, Kayah stood in the door, and it was worth the wait.

Kayah strutted in the room, her ponytail swishing, a huge smile on her face. "Gus."

He rose and took a step toward her, but a mean-faced man pointed a finger at him. "No touching."

Gus obediently sat down.

Kayah relaxed onto her bench, one foot stretched in front of her, the other, bent at the knee. She leaned her head against the wall and gave him a half-lidded appraisal. "You combed your hair for me."

He smoothed his thick auburn waves, tamed with copious amounts of hair gel. "Like you told me."

She sniffed delicately. "And put on cologne." Roughly a half a bottle by the smell. The entire space reeked, and her heart broke with affection for him.

He nodded eagerly. "I took a bath, too."

Kayah approved. "That's good, because if you don't take a bath you stink."

"Like I used to, before we met. But I take a bath every day. Even though you are not there to tell me. I want you to know that."

"That's good, Gus." Kayah swallowed a sudden lump in her throat but kept her expression light. "People will like you if you don't smell bad."

Gus shook his head; he knew it did not work that way. "I'm not stupid, not like they said."

Kayah's eyes shifted to the guard. They were listening. "I know you aren't, but it is better that you are home."

"But you're not home, Kayah." His deep voice grew even deeper, and his soulful eyes registered his distress.

"No, but this place isn't so bad." She smiled, false and bright. "Tell me, what new innovations have you made on the farm?"

His shoulders reached his big ears when he shrugged, but he launched into a detailed explanation of a pulley system he was constructing to lift hay bales from the wagons to the upper floors of the barn. She watched his expressions when he spoke, remembering the many hours they spent together, the times she wanted to shake him and tell him to shut up and just do it. Now, she simply wanted to sit and listen to him speak all day long.

It seemed but a minute, though it was thirty. A knock on the door told them they had less than sixty seconds. "I have enjoyed seeing you, Gus. But I have to get back to work now. They keep me very busy here." Gus' eyes widened. "I work in the library, among the books. I study and read all day."

He relaxed. "That's good, Kayah. I was afraid for you."

"Pfft!" she dismissed him. "Don't worry about me, Gus. It's fine in here."

The guard motioned for her to stand. Kayah plastered a big smile and blew him a kiss. Gus' cheeks flamed.

As the guard escorted Kayah out, he noticed her hands had been in handcuffs, the whole time.

Part 3 - Broken Hearts Club

December 12, 990 ME (Five Years into Rebellion)

The Broken Hearts Club

The loud banging on Himari's door could only be one person, only one person in the world knocked like that, her neighbor Filippo ben Vincente. "I am not home," Himari yelled, refusing to leave her nest on the couch.

"I have your favorite… amaretti. Still warm from the oven," Filippo coaxed.

Himari looked at the junk food wrappers scattered on the coffee table and thought about her empty kitchen. Filippo's cookies were divine. "Make me a cappuccino, too?"

"Yes, I make you two cappuccino. Come on."

Himari rolled her eyes. She stopped correcting his English, especially when she found it charming. Shuffling to the door, she pulled it open and gave him a reluctant smile.

He threw up his hands and said, "Mamma Mia, look at you, eh? What is this you are wearing? It's the same clothes since two days ago, and they were disgusting then."

"Shut up and give me cookies." Himari moved past him, seeing his studio door ajar.

"It is not good, what you are doing." He playfully pulled one of her lopsided ponytails, then added in a gentle voice, "But I understand."

Light infused Filippo's apartment. Its high ceilings gave the space a larger feel than the actual footprint, ideal for his work. Paint, easels, and drop cloths rested under three large canvases. Himari froze at the sight of a long-legged blonde perched on the edge of Filippo's low-backed couch, a plate of almond cookies in front of her, untouched. Himari grew instantly irritated. Models were annoying, and she was in no mood to meet anyone.

Filippo sensed it and pushed her through the door before she could bolt. "Himari, I have a new member of our Broken Hearts Club. This is Alaina. We met today when I was taking photos in the park. She has just arrived in the city, she doesn't know nobody, and she's a sad, like us. So, I bring her here, we eat cookies, we drink espresso, and it's her birthday. We take her out and get drunk, dance, and maybe tonight, we no cry."

Himari looked up at him, amused. He did the exact same thing to her when she moved in last month. The hangover lasted for two days. Whether or not she cried that night, she did not remember. It was fun, that much she recalled. Himari smiled and offered her hand to Alaina. "I'm Himari. Nice to meet you."

When she stood up, Alaina towered over her. "Alaina. Nice to meet you, too." Her accent was deep South, but her clothes were well made, and Himari glimpsed quick intelligence flashing behind her aquamarine eyes. The girl was impossibly beautiful.

"Himari, you tell Alaina the rules of the Broken Hearts Club while I make you a cappuccino." Filippo kissed her cheek and moved with quick efficiency to the open kitchen where a commercial grade coffee maker dominated the countertop.

Himari and Alaina settled into the modern and surprisingly comfortable furniture. Himari called over her shoulder, "They are your rules. Why don't you tell her?"

"Because it is good for you to remember them, eh?" He threw his hands up at her in such a typical Italian gesture, both women smiled.

"He is impossible, but I have to admit," Himari confided, "he has a point." She held up her hand, counting the rules. "First, we never speak the name of our former lovers. To do so, brings their ghosts and binds them to us even stronger. If we wish to move on, we don't say their names."

Alaina looked down at her hands self-consciously. A two-carat diamond engagement ring sparkled in the white light of the studio. "I think I can do that."

"Second, we don't tell our stories, not about them. The hurt does not get better with the telling, it just stirs it up." Himari tried to keep her expression neutral. She largely succeeded, but not quite.

A ghost passed over Alaina's face, and she declared, "I know I can do that."

"Third, we work," Filippo said over the spluttering milk froth. "We pour our passion, our love, our pain into the work. It makes it better, beauty from ashes. Get something from it. Himari, she is not there yet, but she promise me she is going to work."

Himari ignored the jab. He was right, but she had not touched a computer in seven years. And though she would never admit it, she was afraid. In no mood to rehash that argument with her stubborn neighbor, she directed her question to Alaina. "You've come to the New City for modeling?"

Alaina chuckled, embarrassed. "No. Filippo just found me at the park. Before I knew it, he was hustling me about taking pictures. But that's not why I'm here."

Himari considered her closely. "It would be a waste if you weren't here to model."

"Exactly what I told her." Filippo presented Himari her double cappuccino, a delicate milk heart swirled on top. With a flourish, he offered a plate of warm almond cookies. Himari smiled and accepted both.

"You should see, oh, the photos I took of her today, bellissima! The one, oh it is the Mona Lisa, exquisite." He settled with lazy grace and crossed a gorgeous Italian loafer across his knee.

Alaina blushed. "I highly doubt that but thank you. It was fun."

Filippo scoffed, "You no doubt me. I am an artist." He gestured around the room. "I have good eyes. I know what I see and what a face you have. So interesting, not round or oval, or square, like a hexa… hexa… how you say?" He turned to Himari. "Like a five sided." He flung himself out of his chair and took Alaina by the chin, staring intently. He tapped her beauty marks and said, "Just right, perfecto."

Alaina covered her eyes, embarrassed. "Well, I don't think the computer monitors are going to care what my face looks like."

"Computers?" Filippo exclaimed. "You two stunning creatures want to hide behind computers. Such a waste."

"Computers?" Himari asked.

Alaina sparked to life, the haunted air about her banished in an instant. "Absolutely. That's why I'm here. I start technical school in January."

"Really? I know a little about computers." Himari munched on a cookie.

Filippo snorted. "Do not let this one lie to you. She is a famous slacker."

"Hacker," Himari laughed. "Though, slacker might describe me better for the last few years."

Alaina leaned forward, her eagerness palpable. "Truly, you are a hacker?"

Himari's own ghost moved across her face. "I used to be, before I got married." Filippo shot her a warning look, which Himari waved away. "I didn't say his name, but I am allowed to say I am married." She turned back to Alaina. "Where are you going to school?"

"New City Technical Institute, I was supposed to start last Fall." Alaina's voice trailed off, and she took a nervous nibble of her almond cookie.

"Eh, more lovers. We are a sad lot. Tonight, we go drinking. Like I said, it is our lovely Alaina's birthday, and we celebrate by getting her drunk, so she forgets. I will be the jealous of all the men in the club, to show up with the two most beautiful women in the New City on my arms." He gestured, the tight muscles of his forearm showing a smudge of green paint, a wealth of black hair, and the remnants of a faded tattoo.

They made quite a trio, international stair steps, from the tiny Japanese Himari, to the trim and suave Italian of medium height and impeccable Continental style, to the statuesque Alanthian beauty.

"It's your birthday. How old are you today, Alaina?" Himari

asked.

"Nineteen." Alaina tucked a tawny strand of hair behind her ear, and murmured, "There won't be any accordion music, I'm sure."

"There he is. You see him in her face, Himari? Definitely, we get her drunk." Filippo rose and walked to his camera laying on the worktable. Reviewing the pictures, he stopped on one and showed it to Himari. "He's in this picture, too. But oh, look at that."

Himari took the camera and stared at the image. Filippo was right, it was stunning. "Well, I suppose it was just serendipity that brought you to that park today, Alaina."

"Oh, that is it! You are amazing, Himari. That is what we call this picture, and you and me?" He indicated toward Alaina. "We gonna make a fortune on this one."

When Doves Cry

Later that night, Filippo threw the door open to his hired hack and called to Himari "Get in, I take you home."

The staccato of Himari's heels echoed off the narrow walls of the alley behind her husband's shop as she raced toward the shelter of the carriage. The rain fell in earnest now, hiding her tears. "He wouldn't even look at me."

Filippo jumped out of the cab and took Himari's elbow, ushering her inside. The dark interior held the mingled scents of wet hairspray and cologne, booze, and the vague tang of dancing bodies. Alaina, who embraced Filippo's admonition to get roaring drunk, was passed out on the opposite seat with Filippo's cape draped over her legs for warmth and modesty. He put his arm around Himari and knocked on the window, signaling the driver. Seeing the devastation on Himari's face, he gathered her to his chest, rocking her with the sway of the carriage.

"I told you to go home. How did you know?" Himari straightened and wiped the tears from her eyes, mascara coming off on her fingers. She was a mess and did not care.

"Eh, he is a pig head, that one, and a fool to let you get away. Not one time does he come to see you." Filippo shrugged. "The world is full of idiots. Look at Alaina. Some nitwit let her get away. And me," he opened his arms, presenting his trim body, all dark artist and sexy, "someone let me get away. Break my heart, it's terrible."

Himari bit her thumbnail and said, "Broken Hearts Club, indeed."

"It is still early. We put the little one to bed, and you and me, we drink many bottles of wine tonight. You bring your music, and we dance," Filippo dictated with confidence.

Himari narrowed her eyes at him. "How do you know about my music?"

Filippo dismissed her with a shrug. "Our bedrooms share a wall, no? I hear you weeping, and I hear your music. I like the dove crying song."

Himari gasped and then covered it with her hand. "Don't say that out loud. I was not supposed to keep any of that stuff. I could go to jail." She shuddered.

"For music? Bah, that is ridiculous." He seemed outraged at the notion.

It was not the music; it was where she found it. Even with the tech ban lifted, there were certain things the government did not want to come out and music from the Last Age topped their list. But after her painful encounter with Ken, Himari felt defiant. She was tired of the rules, sick of being afraid, weary of hiding everything. "Fine, you bring the wine. I've got the music."

Back at the apartment, Filippo did not bother to knock at Himari's door, coming in with two bottles of wine. "I settled her down in bed and put a trash can beside her, *molto trieste*." Himari gave him a look, and he translated. "So sad, the little one."

Moving into the kitchen, he uncorked the cabernet and poured their glasses. "To our newest friend, we look out for her, eh? She's just a *bambina*."

Himari toasted. Alaina reminded her of Kayah, and somebody should have looked out for Kayah. Himari certainly hadn't. None of them had. The wine tasted bitter, like the memory. With a visible shake, she pushed the melancholy away and drained her glass in a single gulp. Filippo looked at her with disapproval but gave her a refill without a word.

"So, we listen to the dove crying music?" Filippo winked. "I like candles better for dancing." He gestured to Himari's battery powered lanterns with disdain. "This light has no soul."

"They also won't burn down the apartment building. But go ahead and light the candles. I know I can't stop you," Himari said and went to her room. Hidden under her bed were a pair of speakers Gus made and music the cops didn't get.

She had to admit he was right. The candlelight flickered and danced, chasing away the darkness. Himari queued up the song. When she turned, her eyes were dark and fathomless, with an oval tilt that revealed her Alanthian blood. "If you want to know what my marriage has been like, listen to this." With a definitive press of the button, a screeching guitar filled the room.

They danced, remembering lovers who did not love them enough.

Four bottles of wine later, he knew most of the words to Purple Rain. He kissed her cheek and said, "Now I go paint, my friend."

Alaina found him the next morning, sprawled in a chair, purple paint staining his fingers. But there was no canvas in evidence, and he would not show her what he created.

December 30, 990 ME

Beauty From Ashes

Three weeks later, Filippo deposited Alaina on the bed in the room she was renting in his apartment. He shook his head and said quietly, "The little one, she is scared, no?"

It amused Himari that 5'9" Filippo called Alaina 'little one'. Himari grunted as she hefted Alaina's legs onto the mattress. "Haunted is a better adjective for what she is. We are going to have to stop getting her drunk."

"Bah." Filippo pulled the pink and rose quilt over Alaina. "She forgets when we dance. The drink? It helps her sleep. She won't do it long, already she wants to work."

Himari rolled her eyes. "Don't I know it; she won't leave me alone."

Filippo gave Himari a playful shove out the door. "It's good for you, too. Teaching. Every day... I see you."

She scrunched up her face at him. He was right and too damn observant for his own good. "She's smart as a whip. You wouldn't think it by looking at her."

"What? Beautiful people cannot be smart? You think the good Lord have a limited amount of material, you either smart or beautiful? You prove that wrong, every time you look in the mirror, and me too, of course." He gave her a half smile and doffed his stylish hat with a gallant flourish.

Himari snorted. "So humble."

He threw up his hands and gestured toward the work area. "I speak the truth." Then he confided, "I sold a painting today."

Himari's face lit up. "You did?"

He nodded in slow satisfaction. "I did. I also have six offers for the Serendipity."

"Six?"

"And three modeling agencies want to talk to the little one. I told them; we are a package deal. Too many wolves out there, they would eat her alive."

"Does she know?" Himari looked toward Alaina's closed door.

"No. Her heart, it is broken; broken hearts make bad business decisions. One offer, a quarter million." He grinned and admitted, "I sent them other pictures."

"She doesn't want to model."

"Quarter million? Don't be foolish. She can do computer work with you at night. In the day, she will model with me. Good for all the Broken Heart Club members. You see, we work. Beauty from ashes, like I say."

"Maybe I will teach her." Himari walked over to the window, her reflection wavering in the glass. The Himari who stared back at her held a challenge.

"Maybe you teach more than her? Maybe you stop hiding, Himari. Come out from behind the ramen counter. It's time."

"Freaking ramen… it ruined my life. I swear he chose it over me." The bitter edge to her voice cut through the air.

"No, it's not his choice now. Himari, this is your choice. Who you going to be?"

She stared at the woman in the glass wearing a sparkling shirt, black mini, and red high heels. She liked this Himari, this new person who drank wine, danced to ancient music, and helped lost kids from Mississippi learn how to hack. It bore no resemblance to the subservient Japanese wife Ken forced her to become. "I think I am going to take on the whole damn world."

She picked up her small purse and walked out the door, Himari 3.0.

January 15, 991 ME

Surprise Patron

The interruption came at the worst possible time. Filippo yelled through the door, "Go away." The light was fading, and he could not stop. The knock came again, more forcefully. "I said, go away." Instead of going away, he heard the door open. He did not turn. "I do not know who you are, but you must wait."

A clipped New England accent spoke behind him, "I will wait, Mr. ben Vincente."

"Then you no talk either." He cast a quick look over his shoulder. The woman was obviously not a thief, so he did not add no stealing, which was on the tip of his tongue. "Make yourself an espresso. The light will be gone in five minutes."

Soft clicking heels moved across the wood planked floor into the kitchen. He heard a bar stool pull out, but no coffee. Filippo finished and turned to face his visitor.

She regarded him dispassionately, rose, and offered her hand.

He looked down at the paint stains with a helpless shrug, wiping his fingers on the towel tucked in his belt. "Let me wash, the azure blue, it stains."

"By all means. I apologize for dropping in unannounced. I'm Sarah Landry, of the Lenox Foundation."

Filippo bobbed his head in greeting and moved to the kitchen, washing his hands. The name, at least the foundation and the money behind it, was well known to him, and figured she was a potential patron come to call. "May I offer you an espresso, perhaps some wine?"

She lifted a corner of her mouth in a smile that did not quite reach her eyes. "An espresso would be nice, thank you."

"Of course." Filippo emptied the still warm grounds.

Sarah Landry accepted the coffee with genuine appreciation.

He tempted her with the almond cookies, but she declined. Turning her intense gaze away from the sweets and back to him, she asked, "May I see your work?"

His arm swept the studio in a theatrical gesture. "With pleasure."

Classically trained, Filippo was an extraordinary artist, combining renaissance pigments and colors, hues, tones, and perspective with a dignity and soul that was all his own. He was no abstract artist daubing odd paints across a canvas. There was realism and depth to his paintings, stronger than real life, more soulful than the naked eye could capture.

The piece he had been working on when Sarah came to the door was of Alaina in profile, her arm propped on the back of the sofa, hand resting gently against her forehead, one leg tucked under. It captured a moment of contemplation and a sadness so profound the viewer wanted to weep. Across the room, the original enlargement of the Serendipity photo was displayed prominently.

"She is an extraordinary girl, isn't she?" Sarah said quietly.

Filippo stilled and turned his head slightly. "You know her?"

Sarah's laugh sounded breathless, her eyes sad. "Yes."

"I see." Filippo deduced this visit was not what he supposed. "So, she is your business here today?"

Sarah lifted her chin. "She's living here with you." It was a statement, not a question.

"It is better than a hotel or a small apartment on her own." Filippo regarded her warily, unwilling to tell this woman anything until he knew who she was and why she was interested in Alaina.

The charged air was imperceptible but obvious. Time to get down to business. "Shall we sit, Mr. ben Vincente?"

"After you, Mrs. Landry." Filippo made a formal bow and gestured to the dining table. He held out her chair then settled across from her.

Her brown eyes assessed him, calculating and shrewd. "Alaina ben Thomas is engaged to my son." She let that hang in the air, gauging his reaction, no doubt trying to see if he was Alaina's new lover.

Understanding dawned. "Her broken heart man."

Sarah covered her mouth, closed her eyes, and nodded. "Yes. He is not well at the moment." She did not elaborate. "Regardless, we consider Alaina a Landry, and as such, she is under our protection." Sarah dared him to contradict her. When he did not, she continued, "That photograph you took of her, it is stunning. What's the latest offer on it?"

A corner of Filippo's mouth lifted. "One point two million."

"I will give you two." She held up her hand. "Under these terms, the first is that you split the money with her. The second is she does not know who bought it, or that I was here. The third, and most important, is that you send all contracts for our review before she signs them." She slid a business card across the table. "These are our lawyers."

Filippo regarded her and asked, "Your son, is he going to be okay?"

Sarah blinked rapidly and took in a sharp breath. "I am sure he will, but we don't know how long it will take. In the meantime, my role is to ensure that she is safe. Don't fuck with her, Mr. ben Vincente, or I will bury you."

Far from being offended, Filippo was reassured. "I look out for the little one, Mrs. Landry. She is in good hands. Now," he rose and brought her the plate of almond cookies, "eat your amoretti. I have a picture to wrap for you."

March 31, 993 ME

Papers

Two and a half years after arriving in the New City, Alaina could afford to buy her own house. They had enough money to leave the apartment off Singlewood Avenue, but moving was a hassle, and neither she nor Filippo spent enough time in the New City to make a difference. Her modeling career, and by extension his photography career, shot into the stratosphere. The irony of their success was that neither chose the work, but it was too lucrative to walk away from. The small apartment was their way of holding on to their true dreams, Filippo his art, Alaina, her computers.

Himari was in the same situation, at least money-wise. When

she was still living with Ken, a letter came. She had thrown it on the counter with the rest of the mail where it sat for a week because she paid bills on Thursdays for the shop and their small apartment. She had not even flipped it over when she slid the letter opener under the tab. If she had, she would have been prepared.

It read in part: "With the full repeal of the laws prohibiting technological research and development, Himari Nakamura is hereby released from the judgment against her. Her record is expunged, and her ban is no longer in effect."

It was signed by King Korah ben Adam.

She hid it from Ken. The only person she told was Lavinia. It felt like an insurance policy, and she tucked it between her mattress and box springs. The day she left Ken; it was the first thing she packed. At Filippo's urging, Himari 3.0 applied for and received a teaching position at the New City Technology Institute.

She distinguished herself as an acid tongued instructor and genius. The Singlewood Avenue apartment was within walking distance of the school, and she created a comfortable home for herself amongst the wreckage of her personal life.

Alanthian divorce took an exceptionally long time. The archaic laws sought to prohibit the practice; thus, they were difficult to obtain. Ken filed the week he learned she had taken the job at the Institute. No longer welcome in the Japanese section of town, her family ostracized her and stood firmly by Ken's side.

On the first day of Tabernacles last September, she made a final appeal, but they refused to even answer the door. Himari may as well have been a ghost.

Alaina was in Los Angeles for Fashion Week, and Filippo was painting. The Institute was on Spring Break, and Himari was hiding. She did that periodically. Sometimes she was deep in a computer puzzle, other times deep in depression.

Filippo knew she was in her apartment because he heard her moving around, but for two days she refused to answer the door. Finally, he used his key.

With the blinds drawn, she surrounded herself with an odd assortment of pillows and blankets. In the dim light, her pale face reminded him of a porcelain doll. Her eyes darted to her bedroom, and he got the distinct impression she would have bolted if she had the strength. Instead, she huddled deeper into her nest and made a keening noise.

"*La mia piccola ragazza triste,*" he crooned, my sad little girl-friend. "What has happened?"

The corners of Himari's lips quivered as she gestured toward the littered coffee table.

He cleared away several used tissues and chocolate wrappers, unearthing a thick sheaf of documents—final divorce papers. Beside them sat a handwritten note in Japanese.

"It's from my mother," she said, her voice small. Her eyes were swollen, but no tears fell, as if the well had run dry. "They disowned me."

Filippo's soft heart broke. Deprived of his own family, he knew what she felt. Dropping to his knees, he pulled her into an embrace. The arms that hugged him back were weak. She smelled musty, and her hair matted to the back of her head. He lifted her off the couch and dragged her by the hand into his apartment.

She looked around, finding his studio a welcome change. The familiar mix of paint, turpentine, and espresso soothed and revived her.

With infinite care, he guided her to a bar stool, avoiding the couch. She had spent enough time on the couch. Wordlessly, he brewed her a double cappuccino, a broken heart crafted in the foam. She drank it in four huge gulps.

"Now, you eat."

At her first bite, she felt like crying. She had subsisted on chocolate and potato chips for three days. The simple salad, bread, and her favorite, fettuccine Alfredo, worked a miracle. When she looked up, she was a semblance of herself, not the haunted waif.

"Go take a shower, Himari. You no smell so good, eh? I go get you some fresh clothes."

She nodded and started for her apartment.

"No, you cannot go back in there, there are ghosts living there right now. It is better for you to wash them off here. You stay a while." He pressed a glass of wine into her hand. "Drink this while you shower, it will make you feel less jagged."

"Thank you, Filippo." Her forehead crinkled, and she looked as if she might burst into tears.

He waved her away. "You don't thank me. I thank you for

taking a shower, eh?"

Himari guzzled the wine and held out her glass for more. He gave her a thoroughly disapproving look, but the corner of his mouth lifted, glad to see the tiny spark of life.

Breaking Rule Number Two

Himari looked at the clothing he laid out on Alaina's bed dubiously. "This is what you brought me?" Water ran down her legs, but she held the towel firmly in place.

He shrugged, and she recognized the stubborn set of his jaw. "It is armor, make you feel powerful."

"There are no panties."

Filippo shot her a lecherous grin. "Like I said, make you feel powerful."

Himari accepted the wisdom of her Italian friend. "Fine. Get out of here."

He winked and left the room with a small chuckle.

She appeared in the doorway several minutes later, her hair still damp but free of the tangled mess. The skin-tight jeans hung low on her small hips, and red high heel sandals peeked out from the tattered hem. A shimmering red halter top showed off her flat stomach, and loose sleeves fluttered around her elbows. Himari put her hands on her hips, feet spread apart, and said, "You were right."

Filippo eyed her with appreciation and snapped a picture. "Now, you come. I will show you how to pour the pain into the paint and leave it there." He beckoned her forward.

Himari caught her breath. Filippo let no one touch his brushes or his canvases. With reverent steps, as if she were approaching a holy altar, she went to him, never breaking eye contact. He had not shaved and was himself a bit rumpled. The wet canvas in the corner told the story. He left his work to check on her.

Filippo turned her to face the blank canvas, draped a clean smock over her neck, and tied it two times around her waist. As if she were made of clay, he moved with her, placing the palette in her hand, squeezing the paint, and selecting the brush. Whispering encouragements, he guided her hand, giving her what she needed.

There was no form or subject; this was not art, it was pain.

"In spite of how we began, I loved him." Blue Cerulean dotted the white surface.

"I was a virgin. He was not." The fan brush created Indian Yellow tracks across the bottom.

With Rose Madder, she whispered, "So he said he would teach me how to love." She spent a long time on the pink, then blended it with Cadmium Red, finally Perylene Black. "He would not let me touch him… ever." Her chin fell.

Filippo lifted it, whispering, "Into the canvas, Himari, not into your heart."

She took the large mop brush and hit the canvas with a slash of Alizarin Crimson. Her chest heaved. Filippo wrapped his arms around her waist and rested his chin on her shoulder, both of them staring at the shimmering paint.

When her breathing slowed, she considered the colors and selected Light Raw Umber and a fine rigger brush. "He was an amazing teacher, an amazing lover. He could bring me to orgasm in less than a minute." She made short little strokes with the brush. "Anywhere, anytime. Once, I was taking an order. He came up behind me, put his hand down my pants, under my apron, we were hidden behind the counter, and he made me cum."

She arched her back at the memory. Filippo stiffened and pulled her close. She stopped painting. "I became his slave and everything I ever hated."

Filippo's voice sounded ragged. "Paint."

The angle brush outlined Indigo as she continued, "I worked from morning until midnight in that damn restaurant. Boiling bones, smiling at customers, serving soup." Vandyke Brown, Venetian Red, Clear Naples Yellow swirled across the canvas like steam from a soup bowl.

Black Japanese characters flew from her brush, beautiful and haunting. "I spoke Japanese, I bowed, and submitted. I did everything he asked me to do," Sap Green melted down the painting in a sad rivulet. "And I died."

He buried his face in her neck, murmuring in Italian, his English gone.

Small capillaries of Copper Red filled the white spaces. "My

Alanthian blood would not be denied. It refused to lie down, it refused to stay hidden forever, it refused to become a slave." She drew the symbol for man. "My father's blood had more power than I could ever fathom."

She pressed her body backward and felt his arousal. Her chest heaved as she squeezed Azure Blue onto the pallet. With the flat of her hand, she pressed the blue into the dripping red heart. "In the end, more than anything, it was the Purple Rain."

Filippo spun Himari in his arms and kissed her.

And Then There Was That

Himari met his kiss with a fire held in check for two and a half long years. The feel of his mouth was intoxicating, strange, exciting. He tasted of wine and coffee, smelled of oil paint and the mint shampoo she used an hour before.

"I let you touch me, Himari. I take away your pain."

She buried her mouth in his neck, biting, thrusting her small hips against his, reveling in his arousal. Shedding smocks and clothes, they stumbled together into his bedroom, never breaking the kiss. Light flooded the room, there were no dark shadows, neither hiding anymore.

She pushed him onto the bed and jumped on top of him, glorying in the power position. There was no preamble, no gentle foreplay. Raw hunger and animal desire overtook her as she straddled him.

Their eyes met. They knew what they were doing. There was no turning back from this moment.

She lifted herself and took him inside with a cry.

Filippo let her find her rhythm, deep and hard. He resisted the urge to touch her, knew she needed to do this on her own. Content to let her take what she needed, to give her what she required, he watched her while she did it.

Her orgasm, when it came, rocked her soul and freed something terrible. Achieved on her own, without coaxing and touching, without demands and orders, it was Himari's alone, and it was beautiful.

He enjoyed it all, felt her dark brown hair tickle his thighs, and heard the lovely little sounds of pleasure as she crested wave after wave. His artist's eyes appreciated her small breasts, their soft brown nipples, puckered and taut. Filippo held himself back, banked his own orgasm. Saved it for her, for later.

She collapsed against him, her forehead to his and thrust her tongue down his throat in a passionate kiss. Himari knew the gift he had given her and was going to enjoy every precious second of it. Her chest still heaving, she slid down his body and stood at the end of the bed, her eyes, fierce and dominant. "Spread your legs," she ordered huskily.

He grinned, laced his fingers behind his head, and complied.

She started at his feet, gently stroking them with her delicate finger, enjoying his twitch when she hit a ticklish spot. Through hooded eyelids she watched his face when she took his big toe in her mouth.

Filippo murmured something lovely in Italian.

When she teased his toes with the tips of her nipples, he smiled. She licked the inside of his thigh, inhaling his warm, male scent, her desire marking him. He arched his hips. He was drawn up tight and fully aroused. She cupped him tenderly, watching in fascination as his body reacted to her touch. The kiss she pressed to the tip of his cock tasted of salt and silk.

He groaned and closed his eyes.

Himari's hair fanned around his hips as she ran her tongue along the length of him.

Filippo swallowed audibly.

"I want to take you into my mouth, lover."

Filippo wet his lips. "Do as you wish; I am yours to play with."

She nuzzled him and murmured, "You might live to regret that."

"I doubt it."

A Change Gonna Come

"No, I insist. I have not been out of the apartment in days. I will go to the store and buy the steaks. You start the risotto, open the wine, make the salad. I'm ravenous." Himari kissed him full on the mouth and said, "This changes everything, you know?"

Filippo gave her an Italian shrug. "For the better, no?"

Himari agreed with a satisfied smile, "For the better, yes."

It was not quite dusk, but their funky neighborhood thrummed with color and commerce. The narrow streets handled a mixture of cars, bikes, and horses, all equally at home in this part of the New City. A talented busker played blues guitar outside their corner market, Himari stopped and listened, a tattooed girl with black and blonde hair sang. Himari was mesmerized, and decided indeed, a change gonna come.

She threw a substantial amount of money in the hat and went inside to buy their steaks.

When she returned to the apartment, she decided to shower again before going to dinner. Everything had changed. She dabbed on mascara, noting a peaceful woman stared back at her. Another incarnation of Himari, the latest version—Himari 4.0.

She paused outside his door, her hand frozen just above the nob. She withdrew it and knocked. When he opened, his expression conveyed something was wrong. He looked pained, his color high.

"Himari," a false smile showed all his teeth, "it is so nice to see you. Please come in, there is someone I would like you to meet."

Himari's eyes grew large, but she followed his lead and fixed a neutral expression.

A scrawny woman with long sandy hair and straight cut bangs stood in the center of the studio, flashing a huge little-girl smile, incongruent with the wrinkles at her eyes. Unfortunately, her high baby-talk voice matched her smile, and Himari instantly hated her. "Hi, I'm Malibu!"

Himari tamped down the urge to heave the woman out on her ass, but Filippo was panicking beside her, so she refrained. "Hello, Malibu. I'm Himari." She shot Filippo a deadly look.

He moved beside Malibu and put his arm around her shoulders. "Malibu, Himari is my neighbor." He closed his eyes, then looked up, a devastated smile on his face. "Himari, this is Malibu, my wife."

Himari froze and squeezed the handle of the grocery sack. "Your wife?" she breathed, doing everything in her power to control the lightning strike of shock and pain electrifying her body. Clearing her throat, she managed to say, "Well, then I guess you two might enjoy these steaks I brought over… for your reunion." She thrust them out with a jerk.

Malibu skipped forward to accept the present. "Oh, thank you. That is so sweet. I am so excited to be home. How did you know?"

Himari's eyes did not leave Filippo's. "I guess it was just serendipity." She swallowed thickly, and before she burst into tears, turned and left the apartment.

April 1, 993 ME

Good Friends and a Bottle of Wine (or Two or Three)

Himari looked over her glass at Lavinia, drunk. "You damn Italians with your wine."

Lavinia shrugged. "It's in the blood." A slight breeze blew strands of brunette hair around her oval face as she rolled the wine over her tongue, detecting a distinctive tannin that settled in the front of the mouth.

Himari gave Lavinia a crooked smile. "It's certainly in my blood right now."

"Mamma would say, 'It is good for what ails the heart but tomorrow it hurts the head.'"

"I don't give a shit about tomorrow or my head. My heart? I don't have one anymore, it's broken into a thousand pieces." Himari leaned her cheek heavily against her palm.

"Historically, today was called April Fool's Day."

"I certainly feel like an April Fool." Himari took a sip of wine. "Wife? What the hell, Vinia? He never said a word."

Lavinia studied the color of the merlot in the fading light, a recent experiment and one she was quite pleased with. "You said you had rules."

"Screw the rules. He at least knew I was married. I thought he just had some lover that jilted him and broke his heart. He never even mentioned her," Himari sulked.

"You've lived beside him, how long, roughly eight hundred and seventy days? Where's she been?" Lavinia topped their glasses.

Himari made a gurgling sound of disgust. "Some little girl's school by the sound of her voice." Himari pitched her voice deep.

"It was nauseating."

"We hate her." Lavinia raised her glass in toast.

"Yeah, we hate her." In a high falsetto, she said, "Malibu." Then added with a sneer, "What kind of stupid name is that? Who names their kid after a beach?"

"Or a doll from the Last Age, with impossible long legs and big tits, Malibu Barbie. We hate her, too."

"Yeah," Himari agreed drunkenly, glancing down at her small boobs, "we hate everybody and everything named Malibu. It all sucks."

Lavinia was catching up to Himari in degrees of intoxication. While she had not specifically tested it, the merlot obviously packed a stout alcohol by volume. "I think men suck."

"Yeah, especially painters… and freaking ramen cooks. Japanese… Italians… I need a good, red-blooded, Alanthian boy," Himari slurred.

Lavinia blew out a deep breath. "I had one of them. Let me tell you, he was hot."

The meeting of the She-Woman Man Haters Club officially came to a close when Himari leaned forward and said, "Tell me about this man, Vinia."

Lavinia fanned herself, from the memory or merlot, she was not sure. "Oh, my goodness, he was so… earthy."

"Earthy, like dirty?" Himari settled back in her cushioned chair, a view of Lavinia's vineyard in the distance.

Lavinia's fine brow lifted. "Sort of, more like edgy, with music, spice and heat. And fantastic muscles all packaged inside a tough godly man." Lavinia rested her hand over her heart. "He was one of those guys you know would fight to defend you against anything and everything. But he wasn't one of those belligerent chest pounding assholes. He was a man who could fix the tractor and afterward show up with a bouquet of wildflowers, take you to a nice dinner, and then lay you down." Lavinia's eyes softened when she sighed. "He was not neat; he's complicated and doesn't fit into a tidy box."

Himari snorted. "Did he get in your box?"

"I let him touch the wrapping paper," Lavinia said coyly.

Himari raised her glass in salute. "Look at you with nuanced repartee. You've come a long way, Vinia. And you let him touch the box."

"Well, you would have too, if you'd have seen him. As far as nuanced repartee, one does not tend bar for a decade and not learn how to banter." She raised an elegant shoulder. "It creates an environment for better tips."

"You are wasted behind that bar." Himari scowled. "You have one of the most brilliant minds on the planet and you sling beer and grow grapes."

Lavinia dismissed her with a wave.

Until that moment, Himari never realized how quintessentially Italian Lavinia was. It sent a spike through her heart.

"I own a bistro and a vineyard, there is a difference," Lavinia countered.

"You don't have to be a genius to do either."

"I don't know. This merlot has hints of genius, and the plum notes are divine. Besides, you served ramen for seven years."

"You calculated the variance in exponential properties of the subatomic light frequency of matter in the black quadrant of Magellan."

Lavinia's mouth hung open in astonishment. "What?"

A great grin split Himari's face. "Whatever, you know what I mean."

Lavinia laughed, the irony was, she had calculated the beginning of the equation as Himari spoke. "Now, about this black quadrant of Magellan?" She bent over, her slender arms hanging at her sides as she dissolved in hilarity.

Himari held up a finger and mimicked Stephen's voice. "I think there are some practical applications to it."

Lavinia straightened, an exasperated look on her face, Kayah to the bone. "If you geniuses would just hurry up and get it done."

Himari examined her glass closely, her shoulders hunched, her voice deep. "Well, I don't know if I can use this glass, it doesn't look too clear."

They howled with laughter and remembrance.

"Oh, that was so much fun." Lavinia smiled.

Himari agreed, a wistful note in her voice. "It was fun, Vinia."

The ghost of Kayah came for a visit. They raised their glasses in silent salute.

April 8, 993 ME

I Should Have Changed the Lock

"What are you doing in here? I don't want to talk to you," Himari said after she recovered from the fright of finding Filippo in her living room.

"Well, you are going to talk to me." He rose from the couch.

"Where's your wife, Filippo?" Himari dropped her suitcase in the foyer with a thud.

He looked around the room, a guilty expression on his face. "She's gone to visit her parents."

"Then how did you know I would be coming home?"

He shot her an aggravated look. "You are a creature of habit, Himari. I know you, eh?"

That infuriated her, and she stalked toward him. "I thought I knew you."

He seemed to deflate. "You do, Bellissima."

Himari stopped short. "Don't call me that, not with your wife across the hall."

"No, you are right." Filippo blinked, agony and resignation on his handsome face. "But please, sit down. I have to explain." She looked like she was going to argue. "My friend, please?"

Himari perched on the edge of her chair, her hands gripping her knees as she arched a brow at him.

He nodded and began. "I was here, new to Alanthia. I knew nobody. In art school, she was a model. I painted her, and after class I asked her for a date." He shrugged, his smile melancholy. "She was so lovely, full of life, and I was young. We ran away and got married. I knew her for one week." He threw his palms up in surrender.

"She's a, how you say?" he rubbed his forehead. He lost his English when he was stressed or tired. "A tortured soul, some days, very happy and lots of energy, and some days… she a so sad. It's on those times, she try to get better. She takes the drugs, eh?"

Himari said nothing.

He shrugged. "The ones the doctors give, they make her like this." He drew his hand steady across the air. "And she's okay. I tell her I don't mind, but she hates it. She say they make her fat." He rubbed his temple and continued, "So, she goes off the drugs, and then she breaks my heart because she goes crazy. Three times, I find her. She tries to kill herself. We send her to hospital, she comes out, everything is okay. Then she do it again."

Filippo tilted his head in irony. "The last hospital, they give her a drug she likes. It makes her feel better, but they will not let her have it for the long time, it is a short time drug. But Malibu… she wants it for the long time." He rose and went to the kitchen, opening a bottle of wine and pouring two glasses.

Himari accepted hers with a brief nod of thanks.

"She pretended to have a cold, and she steal a doctor's prescription pad where they write the drug orders. You cannot do that, it is illegal." Filippo shook his head in resignation.

"They put her in jail." His voice broke, "My little Malibu, in prison? She is like a child, eh? She don't belong in jail, but that is where they put her. I could do nothing to stop it."

"Oh, Filippo, I'm so sorry." Himari wanted to comfort him, but they had crossed a line and that was no longer an option.

"The divorce papers, I drew them up two years ago, but you know how long it takes. Her mamma, she begged me, 'Please do not do it while she is in prison, eh? Wait until she is free.' I tell her it is better to do it when she is inside, so she cannot do the drugs, but her mamma she begs me." Filippo shook his head. "So, I did not.

"I did not know she was coming or even that she was out. I would not have made love to you, if I had known. You have to believe me. I would never want to hurt you." Filippo's nose flared. "But I cannot leave her, Himari. It would be like kicking a kitten."

Himari balled her fist up against her lips, desperately trying to hold everything inside. She took a deep breath and croaked, "I cannot watch it, Filippo." She steepled her fingers and closed her eyes. "If she would have come just a couple hours earlier, you would still be my friend."

"Bellissima…" The heartbroken word held all the joy and wonder they almost had.

April 15, 993 ME

Three is Definitely a Crowd

Alaina stormed into Himari's apartment. "Save me from that woman." She flopped down on Himari's couch with a whoosh. "You cannot leave, Himari. You cannot leave me alone with them. It is unbearable."

Himari snorted. "Nothing is keeping you there, Al. Move."

"It takes time to move, as you have figured out." Alaina snatched up the apartment brochures scattered across the coffee table. "I am going to take you up on your sublease offer, though. I cannot take another day living with that woman."

In spite of herself, Himari asked, "What has she done now?"

Alaina lifted her lip in disgust. "Nothing. That's just it. She does nothing. There is nothing redeemable about her. She's just sort of there, when she's not simpering or talking to herself." Alaina gagged, then added in a high-pitched voice, "Oh, Filippo, here is your espresso. Look at this stupid little flower arrangement I made, isn't it precious?" Alaina shuddered. "She follows behind him and cleans his brushes. Waits on him like a servant. It's awful."

Himari shuddered herself. "In some sort of evil twist of fate, it seems Malibu Barbie should have married Ken."

Alaina gave Himari a confused look, which Himari waved away. "Nothing, just my inner Lavinia coming out." Himari paused in her packing. "Are you serious about the sublease?"

Alaina yawned and stretched, her feet hanging over the end of the sofa. "Yes, but on one condition."

"What condition?" Himari asked, considering whether there was a container that went to the lid she held in her hand, decided against it, and threw the lid in the trash.

"Tell me what happened between you and Filippo while I was at Fashion Week."

The paper Himari was using to wrap the glass seemed abnormally loud. "Nothing happened. Why do you ask?"

"*Dis-moi la vérité*, you tell me true, *chèr*." Alaina's expression became shrewd.

Himari cocked her head, if Alaina went to the bayou, she was dead serious or roaring drunk. "It's nothing. We're friends. That's all."

"You have not stepped foot over that threshold since I've been home, not once. And he has not been over here, either."

"From what you've told me, I'm not missing anything." Himari examined a set of ornate red and gold salt and pepper shakers, a wedding gift. She chucked them in the trash.

"No, you are not missing anything, except a vomitorium, but that is beside the point. What happened?" Alaina moved to the bar.

"My divorce went through. I was having a rough day. He helped me paint, we had a moment, then Malibu came. No big deal." Himari dismissed the subject.

"What sort of moment?" Alaina pressed.

Himari moistened her lips. "Just a moment, Al. No more, no less, between friends." Himari desperately tried to convince herself it was true.

"You know he loves you."

Himari's mouth twisted. "Stop!"

"He has for a long time. I think since you first moved in, but you were so heartbroken over Ken." Alaina pursed her lips. "Don't leave, Himari, if you do, you are going to leave him to her, and he is dying inside."

"He's not the only one," Himari whispered.

"Oh, I know what that feels like." Alaina twisted her ring. "I live with it every day, but I know one day, he will come back."

"But is he married, Al? Does he have an unstable wife that might kill herself if he leaves her?" Himari's voice cracked, "Do you commit adultery just by loving him? Do you dishonor and shame yourself? I don't really give a shit, but I know him. I know what would happen to him if I stayed." She hurled a teacup across the kitchen and turned, her face flaming. "It's one of those commandments. Do not commit adultery. Do you know where it ranks? I looked it up, just after murder!"

Alaina drew back at the thunderous expression on Himari's face.

"Because if I stay, we will do it. And that might end up killing them both."

Angry hot tears rolled down her cheeks and she gasped, "Do you think he is the only one who has been in love since the beginning? How could I not love him?" She threw up her hands in an unconscious imitation of Filippo. "With his crazy hats, and his almond cookies, and too damn much espresso? The way he dances, the way he moves, the way he loves clothes and the way he makes me laugh? How?" she screamed, shaking her fists. "How can I not love the only man who has ever truly seen ME? Not the woman he wished I was, or the hot Japanese chick in the dance club, or the sexy computer professor, but ME?" She pounded her hand on her chest. "The girl who sings off key and gets sad and does not bathe or brush her hair? The one who does not know where she fits in this world except when she is with a temperamental Italian painter who makes cappuccino hearts out of frothed milk!"

Alaina covered her face with her hands and cried. She cried for Himari, she cried for Filippo, but most of all she cried for herself and Beau Landry, who was still lost in the bayou.

Part 4 - Charm School

September 14, 986 ME (Eighteen Months into Rebellion)

New Lawyer

Sir Preston ben Worley, the lawyer waiting in the interview room for Kayah, sported the most prodigious moustache she had ever seen. It reminded her of a bratwurst, complete with twisted ends. And while impressive, the facial hair was overshadowed, if possible, by untamed eyebrows, which sprouted wild hairs that curled in haphazard profusion. She wondered if they ever interfered with his vision but amended the thought when she stared into his piercing gray eyes. Perhaps he let them prosper to prove he could still grow hair because only a smattering of thin gray strands clung stubbornly to his age spotted scalp. His hands, though, told another story, large and big knuckled, with thick blue veins showing through his papery skin. They looked like mallets, which was perhaps a good thing in a lawyer.

"Please remove the restraints," Sir Preston said.

The prison guard cleared his throat. "I advise against that, Sir."

"I do not converse with my clients whilst they are bound. Remove the restraints." His imperious manner left no room for argument.

The guard's dubious look clearly conveyed the folly of this request, but he complied. "Mind your manners, Kayah."

Kayah smiled sweetly. "I always do."

The guard flinched when she rubbed her wrists, her right hand fisted.

"I'll be outside," the guard's beady eyes narrowed at Kayah, then he added, "in case you need me."

"I am certain that will not be necessary," Sir Preston said curtly.

Kayah straightened her top, squared her elegant shoulders, and stood before him like a Princess rather than a convicted felon. She wore her long blonde hair in a ponytail that sat high on her head. Even clean of make-up, her face was arrestingly beautiful, symmetrical, and fine-boned. Her large eyes were an interesting light hazel, rimmed with blue and green. They reminded Sir Preston of a September wheat field set against a morning sky. By far, the most striking feature of her oval face were her lips, full and perfectly shaped, with an enticing bow to the upper and sensuous fullness to the lower. Prison would not have been easy with a face like that.

He rose from his chair and, through sheer force of will, stifled a groan because he never gave into old age, ever. "I am Sir Preston ben Worley, of Worley, Blake, and Standish, Attorneys at Law."

Kayah shook his hand and appeared surprised when he moved around the table and held her chair. "You are a step above my last lawyer."

Sir Preston dug into his bulging leather briefcase, noted the name of her public defender, and scoffed. "A first-year law student would have been a step up from your last lawyer, Miss Kayah."

Her raised golden brows telegraphed her agreement, but she said nothing. If the last four years had taught her anything, it was to let them speak first.

"As you likely know, this week the legislature officially passed Bill Number 16.1-35. The duly signed Act lifts Alanthia's ban on technological exploration. To prepare for its passage, all cases of technology crime have been under review by the Alanthian Attorney General. My firm, Worley, Blake, and Standish, are participants in said review, and your case fell to us." He rested his forearms against the table, observing her reaction.

She crossed her arms and looked at him impassively.

"With the repeal of statutes," he referred to the papers spread before him and recited a series of numbers that sent her to prison, "the conviction of one Kayah ben Alanthia, aka Kayah ben Samuel, becomes a manner for the state to subrogate, at their will."

For the first time, Kayah's glacial facade faltered, giving the merest blink. Her initial fifteen-year sentence had been amended three times—for violence.

"So, you see, Miss Kayah, this puts your case in a special light, does it not?"

She uncrossed her arms, and her countenance became one of an innocent, lost girl. "I was merely defending myself."

The act did not fool Sir Preston for a moment. He knew her history. She spent as much time in solitary confinement as she did among the general population. The last assault added ten years to her sentence because the guard she attacked was on permanent disability. "Be that as it may, it will require considerable legal wrangling to extricate you from the mess you have created."

Kayah studied her nails before cocking her head and pursing her lips. With the little girl gone, the shrewd felon fell back into place. "What do you want?"

She was perceptive. He was not disappointed. "I have been counsel to the highest government and royal officials in the land for the last sixty years." He let that sink in before continuing. "As such, I am in a unique position to see that you walk out of these doors."

Kayah noted that he did not add a free woman. "In exchange?"

He shrugged dismissively. "I have a certain education and reform program you might find intriguing."

"Does it involve me spreading my legs?" Kayah asked, trying to shock him.

Sir Preston did not miss a beat. "In general, no."

Not an outright denial, which a pimp would have given. Somehow, it caused her to trust him a degree more. "What exactly do you have in mind?"

"For now, suffice to say, that a woman of your extraordinary talents may find my program provides a better path than your current trajectory."

Kayah judged him in that instant, cunning and sly, but not perverted. She steepled her fingertips and rested her chin against them, considering. She had little choice, and he knew it, but she was not going to give in that easily. "On one condition," she held up a graceful finger, "I never come back here or any other penitentiary."

The corner of his mouth lifted under that moustache. "That, my dear, will depend entirely on how well you learn your lessons." Buried in the paperwork of his briefcase, he had her psychological and aptitude evaluations. With an IQ of 160, he knew she would learn her lessons well.

She knew it, too. Her smile was pure predator. "You have yourself a student, Sir Preston."

October 31, 986 ME

Time For a Change

Six weeks later, Warden Jackson ben Michael's pen hovered above a set of release papers he knew were ill advised. The girl might not have come into the system a dangerous psychopath, but she was leaving one. Prison did that to some. It was supposed to reform, it rarely did. With a rueful shake of his head, he put pen to paper and signed the forms, thinking, "God protect us, she is free." He looked up, feeling sick. They set her loose with a legal name change, Kayah ben Samuel.

Kayah's smile chilled him to the bone. "Why so pale, Warden?"

Jackson ignored her taunt and handed the sheaf of documents to the elderly lawyer, who took them like they were pedigree papers for a new puppy. The man did not realize he had a jackal. "Sir Preston, I believe all is in order." He stood, ready for them to depart. "Kayah, I am sure we'll be seeing you again."

She winked. "You won't see me coming, Warden." Then she rose with imperious grace, placed a gloved hand in the crook of the elderly gentleman's arm, and walked out of the room, a free woman.

The guard behind his desk exhaled audibly. "I've been in this job for five years, Warden, and I have to admit, that one scares me."

Jackson pinched the bridge of his nose. "She should, Sigmund."

"I think she killed Stubby," the guard asserted. "I can't believe they are letting her out."

Jackson laughed without humor. "Do you know who her lawyer was?"

"The old guy? No, sir."

"That was Prince Eamonn's personal attorney, and before that he was Prince Adam's closest advisor and friend." Jackson shook his head. "With all the unrest brewing… they are going to turn that girl into a weapon."

Sigmund's boots scuffed on the cracked wood floor. "I just hope they don't turn her on us."

Jackson took a long swallow of his anti-acid medicine and seriously considered requesting a transfer.

Outwardly, Kayah appeared as composed as an Ice Princess as her high heels echoed down the drab gray hall. She dressed as a lady in a black and plum suit that clung to her figure in chic perfection. Afforded hair pins for the first time in years, she styled her blonde mane into an elegant twist and positioned the small hat over her left eye. She suspected the ensemble was the first of many costumes.

"You look lovely today, Kayah," Sir Preston complimented in a solicitous tone, as if they were out for a stroll, not leaving a penitentiary.

"It beats the hell out of what I wore in here," Kayah said drolly.

"A more appropriate response would have been, thank you, Sir Preston," he said, not looking at her as he motioned for the guard to unlock the gate.

The clatter of metal, the sound of keys, the deafening slam reverberated inside her brain. As they stepped into the sun, Kayah vowed she would never hear that noise again. Fixing a smile, she mimicked his cultured tone and replied, "Thank you, Sir Preston."

He chortled. "See, that was not too difficult. Your first lesson, how to accept a compliment with grace." He bowed and gestured to the liveried footman waiting by an stylish coach.

Kayah paused on the step and said over her shoulder. "You will find that I am a fast learner."

His gray eyes sparkled. "Which is exactly why you are here."

Kayah settled into the comfortable leather seat. There were other reasons, but she was content to find out what they were in time. She was leaving prison behind, and she was never coming back.

November 9, 986 ME

Grapefruits for Breakfast

Lessons on deportment, table manners, how to walk, talk, dance, play piano, and speak French began the moment she alighted from the coach and entered Sir Preston's luxurious townhouse in the New City. His servants had better manners than she. But it did not take long before that, and everything else about Kayah ben Samuel changed, at least outwardly.

On the morning of November 9, 986 ME, she was mastering a grapefruit spoon. Sir Preston watched with interest, which she found irritating first thing in the morning. Nonetheless, he had been kind, and thus far, no one tried to have sex with her, so she endured.

"Why do we even have grapefruit? This thing is vile." She resisted the urge to spit it out.

"Salt it," Sir Preston said over his cup of tea. A footman moved to the sideboard.

"Salt? That's odd." Kayah accepted the saltshaker from a silver tray.

Sir Preston seemed pleased with himself. "An unexpected ingredient that changes the entire experience."

"Or an ill suggestion that creates a disaster," Kayah countered.

These little exchanges had become commonplace over the last ten days. He was always teaching.

"It is the amount that makes the difference. A few shakes and it is glorious; dump the salt, and it is ruined."

"Thus, subtlety in the unexpected," she shook several grains onto her open palm, "and perhaps a little flair." Kayah raised her hand above her head and sprinkled the salt between her fingers.

"In the appropriate circumstances, absolutely. Your problem is, Kayah, you do not know what those are yet."

She made a show of segmenting the grapefruit with her spoon and raised it in a toast. Chewing, she considered the change. "Marginally better. It's still bitter, though."

"That's the pith, the thin membrane, inside it is sweet."

Kayah studied the grapefruit dispassionately and dug into a segment without the membrane, annihilating the delicate fruit. She held up a soggy mess for his inspection. "Seems the grapefruit enjoys having its bitter pith, holds it together."

Sir Preston stirred his English tea. "Which is why one needs a delicate touch when peeling a grapefruit."

The Old Man Inside

The messenger arrived at ten in the morning. As Sir Preston read the missive, Kayah caught the first glimpse of the old man who lived inside her mentor's body. His hand convulsed, and he made a low keening noise. It scared Kayah. Everything depended on his continued patronage, and he looked like he was about to have a heart attack. "Sir, are you okay?"

His entire body shook.

Kayah crossed to his side as the letter fluttered to the floor. "Sir, what is it?"

His large-knuckled hand covered his eyes, and he hugged himself. "Oh, Alexa, what have I done?"

Sir Preston's personal servant and valet, Jarrod ben Adriel, moved quickly. "Excuse us, Miss Kayah. I believe Sir Preston needs a moment."

Kayah's instinct was to argue, but Sir Preston began to weep. She narrowed her eyes at the paper, reading the words:

"We regret to inform you that last evening Princess Alexa ben Seamus was found murdered."

She felt her face pale and said to Jarrod, "Of course." At the doorway, she paused. "Sir Preston, I am sorry for your loss."

His pallor was the same color as his moustache. "Thank you, Kayah. It is a greater tragedy than you can possibly imagine."

November 12, 986 ME

Escape to New York

The kingdom mourned the death of their beloved Princess, donning black armbands, and hanging yew wreaths on their doors. The staff draped the windows of the Richardson Avenue townhouse in crepe, as everyone went about their duties in silence. They held Princess Alexa's funeral in the Alanthian National Cathedral, and when he returned, Kayah surmised Sir Preston ben Worley had aged ten years.

At 7:00 pm that evening, a servant tapped on Kayah's bedroom door. "Sir Preston has issued instructions for the household. I am to ready you for immediate departure to New York."

"New York?" Kayah rested the open book in her lap. "What's happened?"

The maid bobbed a curtsey. "I don't know, Miss, but it is a dreadful sad day."

Kayah nodded. She caught a brief glimpse of the murdered Princess that fateful day at the Palace. For the first time, she considered the little Prince and the horror he must be going through. "I feel sorry for her son. I think he loved her very much."

"Yes, Miss, I suspect you are right. They visited once. He is a charming little boy."

"Indeed." Kayah closed her book and helped the maid pack.

They escaped the New City a few days before the fighting broke out. Sir Preston drilled her on lessons while they flew cross country. It seemed to take his mind off his grief, and Kayah absorbed the knowledge like a sponge.

January 19, 987 ME

The Wrong Girl

"Who invented French conjugation?" Kayah pushed the book away in frustration. "My friend Lavinia would have been a much better student. I think she speaks twenty languages."

Sir Preston crossed his arms and leaned back in his over-stuffed chair. "I find it intriguing that not a single one of you ever named her."

Kayah stopped being surprised by the old puppet master several weeks hence. It was futile to deny the truth of his words. "She was not there."

"No," he twisted the end of his moustache, "not the day you were arrested."

"There was no reason to bring her into it." Kayah walked to the window. "It would not have made a difference to me; except I might have had a more interesting cellmate."

"She came to see you," he paused, "five times, yet you would not see her."

She raised her lip in derision. "Turquoise was not my color."

"Yet you saw Gus."

Kayah cleared her throat. "That was different."

"How so?" Sir Preston narrowed his gray eyes.

"Leave me alone, Old Man." Kayah turned, exiting his study with a slamming door. No one stopped her as she escaped the townhouse.

Outside, she stalked down the street, angry Sir Preston was poking around in the past. Kayah was fond of Himari, tender toward Gus, but Lavinia was Kayah's one true friend, the only person Kayah loved. That love kept her quiet when they were arrested. Prison was no place for Lavinia, and neither was Sir Preston's lair. She headed straight for the park, fuming.

The brisk winter breeze cooled her anger, and she took a moment to appreciate her surroundings. She liked New York. It had an edge that appealed to her, a light and shadow that drew her in. Unlike the New City, with its undertone of sterile ambition and innovation, New York reminded its occupants of who it was, had been, and would become again. There was a toughness to it, a blue-collar backbone that declared, "I'm still here, deal with it." New York was a male city. Kayah often thought of things in those terms. The New City was decidedly female, albeit a harlot. New York was a bruiser that would punch you in the face, then walk over your body. By contrast, the New City would kidnap you from your bed and torture you in a sterile clean room. Kayah grew up in the New City, she learned New York in prison.

She glanced at a newspaper, abandoned and fluttering on a park bench. 'Fighting Rages on the West Coast!' Underneath the fold, it read, 'Civil War enters third month of bloody battles.'

She shook her head, not terribly interested in the war, except for how it might affect her. The rest of the Kingdom watched with interest, and rebel fighters joined the foray from all regions, especially the south. They blamed Korah for the drought and turned out in droves. Given history, Kayah thought that was both ironic and portentous.

She took no side in her mind or with Sir Preston. For obvious reasons she supported the repeal of the anti-technology laws but was not too keen to support a government that put her in prison. She left the ideological wrangling to the firebrands and the lawyers, let them kill each other over it. The outcome was of no consequence to her.

"Hey, hey! Pretty lady, how about you come over here and give me some company?" called a youth leaning against a tree. His companions grinned. Eight pairs of eyes swept her with leering menace.

Kayah's sidelong glance was full of loathing. "Fuck off."

The group erupted in laughter; except the boy she had cursed.

He stormed up to her. "What'd you say, bitch?"

Kayah slowly turned to face him. If humiliation had not clouded his brain, he might have read the intent in her eyes. He should have stopped; he should have run. "I said, fuck off, maggot."

"I'll teach you!"

He tried to grab her. The hand he pulled back a few seconds later would grab no one again. With ruthless efficiency, she broke six bones in rapid succession. He fell at her feet, screaming in agony. His gang of friends pointed and laughed.

Kayah did not spare him a second look as she strolled away. Prison had not been a complete waste of time. She earned an education behind bars. They transferred her from cell to cell. She orchestrated it and quickly absorbed whatever criminal knowledge her cellmate might have to impart, if any. Then she moved on.

They thought solitary confinement was punishment. Quite the contrary, she spent ten hours a day strengthening her body, the remainder, her mind. She could do a hundred pushups balanced on index fingers and big toes, grab her ankles in a backbend, or kick a man's teeth out with a single strike. A double joint in her thumbs rendered handcuffs useless, though they did not know that. At least Stubby hadn't, until it was too late.

The filthy bastard thought it was funny, the first two months she was in prison, to put her in a straitjacket and fuck her on her cot. It had not ended well—for him.

Something About It

Sir Preston offered his arm after supper. "Come, we will enjoy a brandy before we retire."

"And a cigar?" Kayah deadpanned.

"Impudent chit," he chuckled. "I shall perhaps teach you how to smoke a cigar. It might come in handy."

"Planning a revolution in Cuba, Old Man?" Kayah was only half teasing.

Sir Preston snorted. "I believe one revolution at a time is sufficient, wouldn't you agree?"

"I hear vacation homes become much more affordable in the aftermath of such conflicts. Perhaps we should foment an uprising in Fiji."

"They speak French in Fiji, Kayah."

She rolled her eyes. "Fine, then where do you suggest?"

"The south of France, perhaps?"

"You are such a snob. Italy… now there is a state with style."

Sir Preston gave her a look that conveyed he was not surprised at her choice, given their tumultuous history. "Your dispatch of the youth in the park today was rather impressive."

In a split second, Kayah noted three things: he had her followed. He was interested in her fighting skills, and she had not detected his tail. The latter would have to change. "Thank you, Sir." Compliment accepted with grace, lesson number one.

"We begin that part of your education soon, though I am gratified that it may not take as long as I anticipated." His wild gray eyebrows rose comically.

Kayah snorted. She had no doubt he knew the extent of her skills before he walked through the door of that interview room.

"And I shall enjoy that part of my education much more than conjugating French verbs."

"Perhaps we will incorporate the two: *éclatez, éclatiez, éclaterez, avez éclaté, éclatâtes, aviez éclaté.*" He continued conjugating the word break until they entered the library.

Kayah caught her breath when she noticed the study's new art. She dropped Sir Preston's arm and walked toward it. Heartbreak emanated out of the small frame, yet she could not look away. Subconsciously raising her hand to the little boy in the drawing, Prince Peter's pain and grief transmitted to her as he stood, forlorn and defeated, at his mother's casket. Rubbing her forehead with a knuckle, she closed her eyes and whispered, "That is the saddest thing I have ever seen."

"It was sadder in person," Sir Preston said, sounding tired.

Kayah turned away, moving to the sideboard to pour their brandy. "Why do you have that?"

His words cut through the air like a cold sword. "To remind me of what he did."

"Who?"

"Korah."

Kayah met his gaze. She concluded long ago that Korah orchestrated her arrest to get his hands on the contents of the bunker. "You are sure?"

"Beyond doubt."

For a lawyer, that was quite a declaration. She read the look in his gray eyes, and it cemented the budding notion; she would never cross this man. "Which is why we are in New York. He was coming after you, wasn't he?"

Kayah presented his brandy and settled in the comfortable companion chair facing the fire.

"You are incredibly perceptive, young lady."

Kayah crossed her legs and relaxed, watching the dancing flames. "I would put nothing past those royals. They are a vicious lot."

His bark of laughter surprised her. "I suppose you would know."

Kayah sipped her brandy. "Firsthand, Old Man."

He raised his glass in a toast. "No doubt."

February 22, 987 ME

Le Jue Mortel

New York came awake en masse to chiming church bells, thousands of them signaling the end of the Civil War. Sir Preston greeted the news with moribund acceptance, though she surmised he had contingency plans underway, of which she was a part.

Over breakfast, Kayah thanked the footman who poured her coffee.

"Without the Iron King's support, the outcome was a foregone conclusion," Sir Preston said as he lowered his newspaper.

"What happens now?" Kayah plucked a perfect segment of grapefruit from the bowl in front of her.

The delicate silver spoon tinkled against the fine china cup as Sir Preston stirred his tea. "You shall begin the second phase of your education."

A corner of her mouth lifted; her eyes narrowed in anticipation. "*Le jeu mortel.*"

His gray eyebrows waggled diabolically. "*Oui, la demoiselle,* let the game begin."

Part 5 - Mack

August 16, 989 ME (Four Years into Rebellion)

As For Me and My House - Shechem, Virginia

Sheriff Mack ben Robert sat in his hometown church, sweating in his shirt sleeves. It was August in the south, and no one in the Millennium ever experienced a summer like this. No breeze blew through the open windows, but several lazy flies buzzed the pews, and an intrepid bee landed in on the silk flowered hat Mrs. ben Matthew wore every Sunday. Paper fans and bulletins fluttered with vigor as the roasting occupants tried to cool their flushed faces.

Standing behind a simple, but finely crafted pulpit, the minister said, "I am here to tell you, brothers and sisters, the judgment is already upon us, and more is coming!" He held a well-worn Bible aloft in his brawny hand. "It is written right here in the word. In 2 Timothy we read, 'But understand this, that in the last days there will come times of difficulty. For people will be lovers of self, lovers of money, proud, arrogant, abusive, disobedient to their parents, ungrateful, unholy, heartless, unappeasable, slanderous, without self-control, brutal, not loving good, treacherous, reckless, swollen with conceit, lovers of pleasure rather than lovers of God, having the appearance of godliness, but denying its power.'"

He met the eyes of his congregation. "If that does not describe what is going on in Alanthia, I do not know what does. And in no place do we find this more than at the heart of our government!"

The parishioners murmured their agreement.

"I don't know why," the preacher paused for effect, his next words delivered in a broken whisper, "the Iron King allows wickedness to flourish in the New City. But each of you has a choice. You can follow the wicked ways of the world, or you can repent and join me and my family." He wiped his brow and his eye. "We are leaving for the Golden City."

A collective gasp erupted from the church. "We've thought on this long and hard. Many of our neighbors have already left."

The empty seats testified to the truth of his words. Dozens of families were missing, Sheriff Mack's family included.

"Our boys fought for the cause of righteousness in the '86," the pastor said. A pitiful intake of breath came from the second pew. Gail ben Zander lost two sons in the Civil War. Pastor looked into her eyes and said, "Their sacrifice was not in vain, for they stood against the power of tyranny, and for the cause of our Lord."

He turned back to the congregation. "But the time has come for choosing. Already the forbidden is making its way into our lives. Soon, we will not even notice. We'll buy cars and cell phones and computers, all the things that were once forbidden, but we'll like them. We'll be enticed by them because they will make our lives easier, or so they tell us."

The pastor focused on two big farmers in the sixth row. "How easy is farming since the great curse has been put upon this land?" He was rewarded by nodding heads and knowing glances. Crop failure and disease, unknown in the age, manifested in the last four years with a vengeance. "How much worse will it get?" Uneasy silence filled the room. They were facing catastrophic crop failure.

"We have before us now, blessings and cursings, life and death. Each of you must make a choice. As for me and my family, we will serve the Lord."

Pastor bowed his head and let the weight of his words settle upon each listener. They had a choice, and this was a reckoning.

November 14, 989 ME

How Many Left

Dressed in his green and brown uniform, Mack ben Robert cleared a space on his desk to rest his feet. A car pulled up to the sheriff's station, and he grew instantly alert. He'd seen pictures of them in the newspapers. Three or four had driven through his rural county in the last year, but he had not seen one up close and none ever stopped in his small town. He fought down the urge to peek outside, but from the slamming doors, it seemed whoever was in the car had business in the station. Besides, he did not want to come off like some ogling hick. He took his feet off the desk, pretending to concentrate on one of the random pieces of paper stacked around him. He didn't file.

The tap of a metal tipped cane and the shuffling step told him his visitor was an older person. He made a distracted noise, studying the intake report from August. There were only two arrests, drunk and disorderly, and shoplifting. One resident was still in the county, the other left on pilgrimage in mid-October.

"I'll be right with you," Mack said, jotting a few meaning-less notations. He signed the document and greeted the strangers with a smile.

"Sheriff, my name is Sir Preston ben Worley," the old man said, extending his large-knuckled hand. "This is my man, Jarrod ben Adriel."

Mack stood and shook their hands, motioning for them to sit in the two chairs placed in front of his cluttered desk. Jarrod dis-creetly helped Sir Preston sit, bowed, and left the station house. Mack looked after him with curiosity but settled behind his desk, taking the measure of the elegantly dressed gentlemen before ask-ing, "What can I do for you today, Sir?" Mack's accent held the deep rich tones of the Alanthian south. At twenty-nine, he was in the prime of his life, serving as sheriff in the county where he was born and raised.

Sir Preston smiled enigmatically, and Mack stiffened, detect-ing this was no mere social call. The old man dug into his over-stuffed leather briefcase and produced a document. "Read this, Sheriff."

Mack accepted the proffered paper. It was an official Alan-thian document dated three weeks prior, with estimated popu-lation and migration statistics for the region. His jaw tightened. He did not need the government to tell him what was going on in his county. "Again, Sir, how can I help you?"

The corner of Sir Preston's mouth lifted. "It seems you are sheriff of a county that has approximately three hundred people left."

"Your point being?" Mack asked, never one to play games.

"That I have something more important for you to do, Sher-iff, or would you prefer Lieutenant?" Sir Preston leaned forward, his enormous eyebrows raised in delight.

Mack narrowed his brown eyes. "Sheriff will do."

Sir Preston sat back and appeared to be enjoying himself. "You are wasting your immense talents here, and it will not be long before there are fewer than are listed on that report."

Mack knew for a fact those figures were outdated. By his count they overestimated by thirty, and three more families were preparing to leave the drought devastated area. "We do all right. The region will recover."

Sir Preston's expression conveyed his skepticism. "We both know that will not happen," he reached in his bag again and handed Mack a sealed envelope, "but this, you can keep from happening again."

Mack opened the envelope, then gasped and turned away as the photo fluttered to his desk.

June 15, 992 ME (Seven Years into Rebellion)

Unexpected Surprises - Redding California

Mack ben Robert ended the call with fourteen-year-old Prince Peter ben Korah and experienced an unexpected sense of wellbeing, which was rare for him, doing the work he did; but all was well. His agents reported everything was quiet around the Pepperwood property, Golden Boy was secure, and tonight, the Prince even expressed his gratitude, a first. After more than two years of service in the Royal Guard, Mack finally got a thank you.

While Prince Peter hung out with his friends at Pepperwood, Mack's team holed up in the nearby small town of Redding. Three hours north of the New City, Redding was Mack's favorite kind of place. He was off duty, and about to go take in the local color.

He tunneled through strewn clothes, take-out burger bags, an overturned suitcase, discarded paper coffee cups, and twenty or so empty water bottles. The hotel room was a disaster. He occupied it for a week. It was a closely held secret, this slovenliness of his, so incongruent with his military bearing and training it was not to be believed, but it was true. Mack ben Robert was a slob. Not about his body or appearance but give him more than a day or two in a dwelling, and he turned it into his own personal pigsty. He liked it that way.

His mother hated it. As a teen he had spent many weekends surrounded by his own mess, grounded for refusing to clean his room. He was stubborn that way, too. A stubborn slob, with a weakness for junk food. However, he balanced his negative characteristics with southern boy charm and rugged good looks that made the women he dated not really care what his apartment looked like. They all thought they would change him, if and when they got him down the aisle. They were wrong, and thus far, nobody got him down the aisle.

A growling stomach and a powerful thirst led him into the Cipollini Bar and Bistro that Sunday night in June 992 ME. The beautiful proprietress brought him back, night after night, excellent food and music an added bonus. By his second visit, they were on a first name basis, and without a doubt, Lavinia ben Anthony was the most enchanting creature Mack ben Robert had ever seen.

June 22, 992 ME

Ears To Hear - Redding, California

A week after he first entered the Cipollini Bar, Mack finished his plate of lasagna and dabbed at the corner of his mouth. "You don't actually hear the music, do you?" Mack asked Lavinia, motioning toward the stage.

Lavinia gave him that big eyed look she got when he hit upon some truth she tried to keep hidden. With a wave of her hand, she attempted to dismiss him. "I'm not deaf. Don't be ridiculous."

"No, it's true. I see you," Mack countered.

Lavinia took his empty plate, giving him a look that clearly conveyed he saw too much for her comfort. "I just do not care for it."

"Yet you have it in your bar every night," Mack persisted.

She lifted her delicately clefted chin toward the crowd. "The patrons enjoy it, and it is good for business."

He suspected her pretty face and her mother's excellent cooking were good for business as well. "Why do you not care for it, particularly?"

"Why does one like some foods and not others? It is a matter of taste."

"Yes, but everyone likes some sort of food. Using your reasoning, everyone likes some type of music, so what type of music do you like?"

She gave him a haughty stare that he recognized as her defense shield. "I like simple music."

"Simple? Define simple for me."

"You!" she said, turning away. "You are simple."

He chuckled, "I'm far from simple, darlin', and you are deflecting."

She made a delicate snort. She was caught, and she knew it. A customer motioned for a refill, and she scampered off.

He watched her mind working as she poured the beer, managing a perfect foam head on the dark brew. When she returned to his end of the bar, he saw she had reached a decision.

"I like math," she confessed, watching him out of the corner of her eye, gauging his reaction.

He nodded. "I figured that out a couple of days ago."

She lifted a brow in surprise. "You did? How?"

He gestured toward the cash register. "Those little scraps of paper over there aren't receipts."

"No, they are not."

"Whatcha working on?" He tilted his head, studying her. Her black lashes nearly touched her high cheekbones when she looked down.

"You would not understand," she said. There was no pride in her voice, just simple observation.

Mack graduated at the top of his class, so he was no slouch. "Try me," he coaxed. "I've got a fair hand at math."

"I'm just messing around with the Banach-Tarski Paradox. It's a hobby. I do it when I'm bored."

"What is it?" he asked, actually interested.

"It's hard to explain. Essentially, creating something from nothing through destruction and recreation."

"And music?"

"That's how I try to figure it out, or at least one of the ways. Sometimes, I graph sound waves of various keys and pitches. There are mathematical values assigned to each note, so it is possible to interpret what we hear in a concrete, factual way." At his furrowed brows, she grew frustrated and slightly embarrassed. "I can read music."

"But you don't hear the magic, you hear math."

Her mouth fell open, her eyes huge with discovery. "I don't understand it."

"Because you aren't supposed to understand it. You're supposed to feel it." He reached across the bar and offered her his hand.

She looked down at it, big and rough, traces of gun oil and powder embedded in the grooves. Hers were reddened from the dishwater they were submerged in constantly. Slowly, as if she were a wild animal that might run away at the merest flinch, she put her hand in his.

His fingers closed over hers. "Would you like me to help you feel the magic, Lavinia?" Mack whispered.

She nodded, her eyes as large as a doe's.

"Come out from behind that bar. I am going to sing you a song."

He led her to the front of the stage, spoke a word to the guitar player, and took up a stool, eschewing the microphone. This was just for her. "We do this song in church back home. That's the only place I ever play, but for you, Miss Lavinia, I will make an exception. Are you ready?"

"Play me a song, Mack. Show me the magic."

He gave her his most charming smile, and the Spirit of the Lord fell. "I'll do you one better; I'll show you the love."

When he finished, Lavinia ben Anthony looked at him with such wonder, he knew he would cherish that moment and this woman for the rest of his life.

September 4, 992 ME

Not an Ordinary Enemy - New City Palace

Mack heard Prince Peter scream through his closed bedroom door. He burst in with his weapon drawn and saw something that would haunt him forever.

Floating above the bed, Peter arched in agony, his head nearly touching his feet in a grotesque backbend. A black stench filled the room.

Mack recoiled and cried out, "Lord Jesus, help us."

Something roared, but the presence left.

Peter twisted and fell in a broken heap onto the bed. Clasping his head like it was about to explode, he moaned, "Mack… thank you."

"God in Heaven," Mack said, scanning the room, pointing his weapon at the dark corners.

"I thought it would kill me this time."

"My Esteemed, what the hell was that?" Mack moved to his side, alert to any movement in the immense room.

"My father's monster," Peter croaked and dry heaved.

Mack grabbed the crystal ice bucket off the bedside table, positioning it under the retching Prince.

When Peter stopped coughing and sputtering, he backhanded a dribble of spit and said, "He is a capitol fellow, great cologne. Open a window, please."

The Prince's blasé reaction shocked Mack. He flung the terrace door open and switched on a table lamp, which cast the dark room in a yellow hue. "Can I get you anything? Do you need a doctor?"

"Not if I want to stay out of the insane asylum." Peter leveled a look. "I take my cues from my mother in this matter and keep quiet."

Mack handed Peter a glass of water, both the hand that offered and the hand that received shook. "Your mother saw that thing?"

Peter shrugged. "He has been around a while." He took a sip and set the water down with a thud. "It is pretty annoyed lately, at least since I returned from Pepperwood. It could not get to me whilst I was there, so it is making up for lost time."

Mack sat down hard in the chair beside the Prince's bed. He leaned forward, intent. If he was going to protect Peter, he had to understand what he was up against. "Do you know what it is?"

Peter laid back against the pillows, his face pale and drawn. "Scary black son of a bitch, looks like a giant reptile with wings. However, he does not show himself anymore, which is good. I tired of shitting myself. Bloody uncomfortable, shitting yourself, especially when you are spinning around in the air."

It was inconceivable, outside of anything Mack ever imagined, yet he witnessed it with his own eyes.

Peter read the expression and said with a satirical smile, "Welcome to Korah's House of Horrors, Mack."

"You depart for the Royal Military Academy tomorrow," Mack said, calculating his strategy.

"Yeah, hopefully it does not follow me there." Peter sounded exhausted.

"Does it attack you outside the Palace?"

Peter shrugged. "Not typically, and not as often as it has since I got home. Like I said, it is annoyed right now. It never gets caught." Peter gave him a half-lidded look. "You are the first person who has ever seen it, other than me and my mother," he amended with a snort, "or my father."

"Why do you say it's his?"

Peter closed his eyes and turned away. "I am tired Mack. Being tortured fucking hurts."

"I am sorry, my Esteemed. I will sit here. You go to sleep."

As the young Prince dozed off, Mack realized the resignation letter he had in his briefcase, that would have launched his new life in Redding, had just been put on hold, indefinitely.

Part 6 - The Messy Middle

December 10, 994 ME (Nine Years into Rebellion)

You Reap What You Sow - New City

Gus crammed himself into a chair in Stephen's new office, absently rubbing his thumbs together.

Stephen's deep-set brown eyes held genuine regret as he said, "Look, buddy, I've done the best I could for you, you know I have, but I am afraid I am going to have to let you go."

Gus did not look up. "Let me go where?"

Stephen grimaced. "You can't work here anymore, Gus."

His restless thumbs stilled, and Gus raised solemn gray eyes to Stephen. "Why?"

"I'm sorry, but you just do not work well with others. We talked about this before you came on board." He ran his hand through his disheveled hair and shifted in his seat. "I had hoped."

Gus frowned. "My work is good."

Stephen threw up his hands in surrender. "Yes, your work is good. But it is always late, and half the time it is not what I asked you to do."

Gus looked away, his nose flaring. "That's not really the reason."

Stephen froze, then plastered a solicitous smile on his face. "It is Gus. I have a budget to keep and deadlines." He gestured to a stack of paper on the corner of his desk. "I carry a lot of responsibility. It's not like it used to be."

Gus gave a humorless laugh. "Like it used to be? I think that is the real reason." He stood up slowly. "I know what you did, and I see what you are doing. I know things you want to keep hidden."

Stephen held his face stonily, willing him to just leave.

"My momma always says you reap what you sow." Gus paused, his hand on the doorknob. He did not turn around, but his deep voice filled the room. "I think you've got a rotten harvest coming, Stephen."

May 12, 995 ME (Ten Years into Rebellion)

And the Techie Goes To

The Alanthian Technology and Innovation Awards Banquet was a glittering affair, even if the attendees looked a bit awkward dressed in formal attire. In certain companies, they considered it an accomplishment if everyone in the office had a bath or had not slept in their clothes. Nevertheless, once a year, they pulled out their ill-fitting tuxedos, polished their shoes, and attempted to look like rock stars, which in the technical world, they were.

Around '93, some enterprising party planner realized there was a noticeable lack of attractive females at these events and began hiring leggy models to pose as tech employees. Himari Nakamura, who was particularly sensitive to sexism of any sort, railed against the practice. Now, people who did not know her assumed because she was pretty, she must be one of the hired bimbos. That irritated Himari because she was one of the most gifted computer scientists in the world.

Tonight, she sat at a table, not quite in the back of the room, but nearly, with her colleagues. Her peers nominated her for the prestigious computer scientist of the year award, 'The Techie', which despite the inane nickname, was a tremendous honor, and one she damn well deserved. However, she was an outspoken opponent of the government's interference and attempts to control all technological research. Hence her table in the back.

As they announced each winner, it became clear which way the political winds blew. Every recipient worked for the Ministry of Technology and Security. It incensed Himari. However, she would not give her critics the satisfaction of seeing her ire, so she applauded politely as time and again, Stephen ben McSwilley mounted the stage with his team.

The mere sight of him caused her blood to boil. The traitorous, opportunistic bastard stood behind the podium oozing false modesty and pretending the attention embarrassed him. Himari knew better. An ambitious heart beat in his bird chest, and it always had.

She fixed a smile when they announced his name, instead of hers, for "The Techie". She graciously acknowledged the solicitous expressions of sympathy from her co-workers and colleagues, shrugging off their veiled outrage at the cocktail reception afterward. Sipping her wine, she wondered how long she had to endure this farce before leaving. Across the room, a handsome young researcher gave her the eye. She looked fantastic in her beaded black gown, her hair and make-up done for the occasion. It would be ashamed to waste it. Giving him an encouraging smile, she thought perhaps he would make a nice consolation prize.

One of the models sidled up to her and said in a dark voice, "He's a bit young for you, Himari."

Himari's eyes widened with shock, and she turned her head slowly. Kayah, her hair dyed jet black, gave her a mischievous grin.

"Kayah," she breathed, stunned.

"You got robbed. That asshole stole your award tonight." Kayah raised a champagne glass. "He's quite good at that, isn't he?"

Himari's heart began to hammer as she glanced around the room. "Has he seen you?"

Kayah ran her tongue over her bottom lip. "Not yet."

"Can I watch the reunion?" Himari asked, smiling as the night took a sudden turn for the better.

"Not the real one, unless you want to go to jail." She looked down at Himari. "I don't recommend it; the sushi is terrible."

The young researcher began making his way across the room. "Your puppy is coming."

"Don't eat him, Kai."

Kayah made a throaty laugh. "I don't eat babies but get rid of him. I need to talk to you. However, first I am going to make Stephen shit his pants."

Himari watched with wide eyed fascination as Kayah moved away, all regal grace and splendor. If she had not spoken, Himari suspected she would not have recognized her. And even then, she might not have. Her accent was markedly different, cultured and upper class. Himari had never attempted to visit while Kayah was in prison, and she had not seen her since the fateful day of their arrest, twelve years before. In the interim, Kayah had utterly transformed herself. She was still of medium height, only 5'6", yet she seemed taller. Amongst the sea of beautiful women, Kayah was remarkable. Shrouded in dark mystery and danger, an imperceptible aura shimmered around her, lingering like the spice of her sultry perfume.

The hair stood up on the back of Himari's neck.

"Ms. Nakamura, you look stunning tonight. May I congratulate you on your nomination? I think I speak for many in this room who believe it was you who should have received the honor."

With an effort, Himari brought her attention back to the young man at her side. Kayah was right; he was a baby. "Thank you." She left him without a backward glance and hurried after Kayah.

Stephen saw Himari coming and fixed the indulgent expression he always wore when they met in public. They never met in private, had never exchanged a single word about his betrayal. For five years, they orbited each other and never acknowledged their past. The crowd parted as she moved forward. They were expecting a genteel exchange of mutual respect and congratulations. They could not have been more mistaken.

Kayah materialized from the shadows. Stephen turned white. "Stephen ben McSwilley," she purred and traced a long red fingernail over his clean-shaven jaw, "still up to your old tricks, I see."

He flinched and stepped back, her name coming out a groan,

"Kayah."

"Oh, you remember. I suppose it's hard to forget someone like me, now isn't it, Stephen?" Kayah circled him. Bystanders drew back in fascination.

"Not here. Let's go talk." Stephen tried to take her arm and lead her away.

It was a miscalculation of epic proportions.

Kayah took his hands and pressed. For all the world, they appeared like long-lost friends. His expression became sickly, hers sweet. "We have nothing to say, Stephen. I believe you said everything you were going to say to the prosecutor when you sent the true tech geniuses into hiding, so you could rise to prominence in their place." She sniffed delicately. "Stephen, that just stinks."

Kayah dropped his hands and winked at Himari. She left Stephen standing in the middle of his colleagues with shit running down his thin legs.

Scrub a Dub Dub

Himari screeched with laughter. Kayah cackled. Their heels beat a rapid retreat out of the Ritz Ballroom.

"Kai, you made him shit himself, literally!" Himari bent over, howling. "Oh, teach me that trick."

Kayah's laugh sounded foreign to her own ears. Her old friend's hilarity was contagious. Normally there was nothing funny about the things she did, but she had to admit, the expression on McSwilley's face was priceless. "Ancient Chinese secret."

"Pfft! The Chinese, what do they know?" Himari teased.

"Apparently they know how to make people shit themselves," Kayah deadpanned. To which they both dissolved into peals of laughter, again.

"Kai, it is so good to see you," Himari said, wiping black mascara tears away.

Kayah motioned for Himari to follow her into a luxurious automobile. Himari raised a speculative brow as the liveried driver shut the door behind them.

Kayah shrugged. "I do all right these days." With the press of a button, the security window put them in seclusion. "I'm here on business. Though I would have liked to have seen you receive that award tonight."

Himari smirked. "I think I got my reward."

"Just a game, I shouldn't have done it, but I could not help myself."

The two old friends shared a moment of silence. There was so much Himari needed to say.

But before she could get anything out, Kayah cleared her throat and with a lift of her eyebrow said, "They are coming to get your research. You need to hide what you've got and plant some bad code."

"Who's coming to get my research?" Himari asked, though she had a sneaking suspicion.

Kayah narrowed her eyes. "People you don't want to have it."

Visions of boots invading their bunker, stealing their work, filled the black car.

"That pisses me off."

"They paid for it, Himari. It's theirs."

Grants, dozens of them, over the years funded her work. "Damn."

"You are pulling stuff off the old internet that they don't want out. You are messing around in areas they don't want public. And you are speaking out. Now, if you want to figure out how to make a cartoon grandma with a funny voice, they will leave you alone. But that has never been your style, has it, Sunflower?"

Himari narrowed her eyes and replied in a low voice, "They are planting code in everything so they can spy on us."

"I know that, and who do you think is listening?" Kayah lifted her lip in a sneer.

"That son of a bitch Korah," Himari exclaimed.

"And his little stooge, McSwilley."

Himari tapped her knuckle against her bottom lip, thinking. "My code cleans it all up. Wipes it out."

"Yep, and it negates fifteen years' worth of work for them. They have invested billions, from the highest level. This goes straight to the top."

"Fifteen years? They only lifted the tech ban nine years ago."

Kayah shrugged. "I told you Korah was buying tech, even back then."

"So, what's your interest in this, Kai?" Himari crossed her arms.

"I represent certain people who would like to obtain the actual code. They have a vested interest in not being spied upon by Korah's government. Let's just say it's not Aunt Mabel discussing her bunions with her sister Florence."

"Life is probably a lot simpler for Mabel and Florence."

"But Mabel and Florence don't have a combined IQ of 335, do they Sunflower532?"

Himari laughed at the use of her code name. "You crafty bitch, every time you come walking through my door, I get involved in all sorts of stuff I later regret."

"Just don't go back to the ramen house, okay? My God, that was pathetic."

Two days later, when they came, Himari did not think it was thunder. This time, she was ready. This time, they did not get what they expected because she was not a scared seventeen-year-old kid. What they got was an avowed enemy of the state, a formidable opponent, and one Stephen and Korah would regret ever creating.

They loosed Sunflower532.

June 6, 995 ME

Fire Away

At dusk, three weeks after the Techies, Alaina and Filippo stood on Himari's front porch. Alaina was openly crying; Filippo looked stunned, his jaw slack, his body swaying.

"Oh, no!" Himari exclaimed, covering her mouth. She read the situation in an instant. "Come in."

Filippo's breath came in rapid pants as he looked at Himari. "She finally succeeds. *Piccola Malibu è morta.*" Little Malibu is dead.

Himari began to cry and held her arms out to him. He just stood there, broken, so she went to him. He leaned into her like a tower ready to fall. She held him up, and they stayed there for a long time, while Alaina looked on, weeping quietly.

"Sit down, honey." Himari led Filippo to the sofa. "Al, you pour. We need more than wine tonight. There's whiskey under the bar." The bottle was a wedding gift from long ago, never opened.

Filippo downed his in a single gulp. It burned like fire on his empty stomach. Three shots later, he collapsed into Himari's arms, listless.

Alaina rested her elbows on her knees, her glass dangling from her hand. "He found her this afternoon. We were on a shoot up in Portland. We've been gone for two days. She seemed fine when we left."

"She always seems fine, right before she do it. I should have known."

"That's bullshit, Filippo. There is no way you could have known," Alaina protested.

Himari looked between them.

He shook his head and sighed through his nose. "I know. I live with the woman for many years."

"Mon Dieu!" Alaina took a drink. "You could not be with her every second of every day, even though you tried." Bitterness laced her words. He missed dozens of assignments and rescheduled dozens more. Filippo's painting suffered, his work suffered, he aged ten years in two.

"What happened?" Himari asked quietly.

"I find her dead, in my bed. Asleep, like a little girl, just asleep. The drugs she like, no the drugs she love, in an empty bottle." He shook his head. "No note."

Alaina's voice cracked. "The police said they arrested her the day before, buying drugs in Prince Eamonn's Park, which violated her parole. She was going back to prison."

Filippo hung his head in absolute defeat. "That park… I try to keep her away, but she don't listen to me. She go, and it make her crazy. One night she come home and tell me she sees a *giant* in that place. The drugs, they did things to her mind."

Alaina paled. "A giant?"

"Eh? Completely crazy!" Filippo poured a full glass of whiskey. "I could do nothing, so I give her the sleeping pills. I keep them locked up. Later, she seemed okay, but she never really better after that. It was a couple months ago."

Alaina's foot tapped wildly. "You never said anything to me."

Filippo took a big swallow. The whiskey turned his red eyes heavy, his English becoming more broken with every swallow. *"È pazzo,"* he dismissed it with a wave of his hand. It was crazy.

The room fell quiet, and they drank.

"She no love me. She no love nobody, nothing but the drugs." He rested his head against Himari's, his voice wracked with grief. "She no love me, Himari. She no love me."

Himari held on as a fresh wave of grief swamped him.

Alaina stood up, agitated. "I'll go back to the apartment and clean up. I'll pack her things. You keep him here."

"Of course, at least a few days."

Filippo turned his head drunkenly toward Himari and said with sad irony, "Maybe ghosts in there right now, better for me to wash them off here?"

Himari bit her lip, remembering. "Yes, you stay a while."

"We don't have any assignments until next week." Alaina picked up her purse. "I'll let her parents make the funeral arrangements. He's done enough."

Filippo felt empty and exhausted, consumed by a lethargy that surpassed anything he ever experienced. It was an effort to even sit up. He finished the whiskey in his glass before it dropped to the floor.

Himari walked Alaina out and turned to him. "You need some food."

"I think that is what I always say to you," he murmured.

"And you are always right." There was sadness in her smile.

"Can I have that on a record? I think in the future, I would like to play that back for you, eh?" He leaned onto the couch, toppling like a slow falling tree.

The future… the words sounded bittersweet. They both longed for it, wished for it, but not this way.

"She knew," Filippo said from behind closed eyes. "And she used it against me, would cry and tell me she was going to kill herself. She finally did."

Himari froze. "We did nothing wrong. We've barely spoken since she came home."

Filippo's mouth lifted in a drunken smile. "*Bellissima*, apparently I talk in my sleep. I dream of you." He snorted. "She does not sleep, many nights she roams, and one night… the paintings… she finds them."

"What paintings?" Himari's voice strangled.

"All my love paintings for you, my beautiful, Himari. I show you one day. I try to paint for her, to show that I love her, too. But they are dark, not beautiful like yours." He rubbed his eyes. "You remember the painting we made together?"

Himari nodded wordlessly.

"It was so powerful." He moistened his lips. "She destroyed it. Took a kitchen knife and cut it up. I moved all the other ones to a safe place afterward, so she cannot destroy more. She was a crazy, but sometimes," his voice caught, "I loved her. I did."

"I know you did." Himari's voice was low and full of compassion.

"But it was not enough. I think I could have given my life for her, and it still would not have been enough." He pushed himself up.

Himari raised her glass in salute. "I understand what that feels like."

Filippo stared at the bottle, half empty now, and poured another shot. "You do, don't you?"

"Indeed." Himari settled back in her chair. "I can tell you what I learned, though. It was not my fault. I did the best I could. I was not perfect, but nobody is, and you know what?"

"What?" he asked, regarding her through heavy-lidded eyes.

She swallowed, on uncertain ground. Alaina had been dragging her to church. She was not quite there, but she heard a message the Sunday after they raided her lab, and it stuck with her. "Even the Iron King doesn't expect us to be perfect. He just expects us to believe and to try. You and I, Filippo, nobody ever tried harder than we did." She put a fist to her mouth and pressed.

"Did I?" His voice filled with self-loathing. "Or did I see her every day and wish she was you? Did I think when she created another flower arrangement or brought home another ridiculous ceramic cat that I hated her? Did the sound of her voice make me want to punch my fist through the canvas? And did I not wish a thousand times that she would just go away?" He covered his face. "How can you love someone and hate them at the same time?"

Himari guzzled the last of her glass and poured another. The whiskey stopped burning, creating a warm fire in her belly. She crossed her legs and said, "In the last year of my marriage, Ken refused to have sex with me with his body." She looked away and shrugged. "He liked toys; he made me like toys. But he did it to punish me."

She laced her fingers over her belly. "It was humiliating. It was degrading, but I let him because I was trying to give him what he wanted, to be who he wanted. I loved him and hated him at the same time. And when I couldn't take it anymore, I left."

Filippo shook his head. "She hated sex, hated it. She suffered it, play at it, pretend, like an actress." He made a bitter sound in the back of his throat. "Especially when she was trying to get me to do something. Most of the time, she just laid there, sometimes crying." The anguished droop of his shoulders conveyed the depth of that particular wound.

Like lightning, another emotion struck, and he snarled, "But she liked the slutty lingerie. So, she buy these little bras and panties and prance around the studio, but I not supposed to touch." He threw up his hands. "I am a man, eh?"

Despite the gravity of the situation, Himari chuckled. "That sucks."

"And she would not do that either," he exclaimed.

Himari laughed in earnest because they both knew she would. "Poor Filippo, no fellatio?"

His mouth lifted in a self-deprecating grin. "I am a horny bastard."

The absurd nature of the word horny struck Himari just right, and she threw her head back, laughing, breaking the tension.

Filippo joined her. "It's terrible. My last painting, it's just a big ole hard penis." Himari was crying. "I cannot show nobody!"

As the hilarity subsided, Himari wiped away the tears. "Oh, I have missed you so much. Not just as my lover, but you as my friend." She sniffed.

He held out his arms. "Come, I have no strength, but I hold my friend. I miss you, too."

August 18, 995 ME

Get it Right the Second Time

When Lavinia walked into the bridal room on August 18, 995, this time she recognized Himari, and her heart soared. The designer trimmed her white gown with red piping and styled the beaded bodice to create an elegant silhouette that complimented Himari's slender figure to perfection. A choker of red silk ribbon held a large white crystal, and her sheer veil danced around her shoulders, falling gracefully down her back, highlighting the long glossy curls of her hair. Tiny red strappy sandals peeked from underneath the long dress. She was a vision, a gorgeous fusion of Japanese and Alanthian, exactly who Himari Nakamura became, version 6.0.

The chapel was small, the ceremony intimate. Himari's family ignored their invitations, as expected, though it still caused her pain. Circumstances cut Filippo off from his family in Italy. They were separated by miles, not heart. The morning of the wedding, he received a precious note from his mother.

Lavinia looked exceptionally lovely in her red silk gown. Her lithe Italian beauty evoked sensual dreams of Tuscan nights and feather beds. Alaina was like a comet and had all the techies in the pews drooling. Himari smothered a giggle as she strolled up the aisle, the catwalk so firmly ingrained, the preacher's mouth dropped. Her beauty stunned even Filippo's artist friends. Their little lost girl from Mississippi was a force to be reckoned with.

At the back of the chapel, Gus looked down at his polished shoes and whispered for Himari's ears only, "She sort of reminds me of Kayah."

Himari took his elbow. "She always has me, too. It's why I watch out for her."

Gus scanned the crowd. "Do you think she will come?"

"I don't think so, Gus. But I am glad you are here. Thank you for walking me down the aisle." She patted his big arm. He had grown corpulent in the last few years, and she worried about him. "Now we have to go."

"Okay, Himari," he acquiesced and looked like he was stepping in front of a firing squad. He grew nervous in front of people, but he was brave enough to do it for his friend. "I like Filippo a lot better than Ken."

"Me, too, Gus. This time I'm making the right choice."

Tears filled her eyes at the sight of her groom, resplendent in his wedding clothes. He wore an exquisitely tailored, slender cut, charcoal tuxedo with black lapels, a red pocket square, and an amazing cravat. Her Italian artist awaited.

Filippo and Himari wept through the ceremony, the emotions of the moment more than they could contain. A lifetime of love found a home, a second chance, to get it right.

There was not a dry eye on the female side of the bridal party. When the bride and groom exchanged rings, Alaina twisted her two-carat diamond on her finger, trying to hold back the tears. Lavinia touched her necklace, feeling Mack's silver ring heavy between her breasts. Himari's bridesmaids celebrated for their friend but longed for their own loves who were not by their sides.

Filippo's wedding present waited in the reception hall, his love paintings. They were draped, shrouded in mystery, the moment planned to perfection. After the toasts, he led Himari to the dance floor. The DJ queued up Purple Rain, their song. Choreographed to the words, he told their story through his art.

The first painting was of Himari in ponytails, surrounded by boxes in her new apartment, bewildered determination on her face. The second captured her standing in an alley drenched by purple rain, covering her tears with her hands, dressed in her mini and high heels. In the third, she wore jeans and a t-shirt, a glass of wine held like a microphone, singing and dancing, with candlelight casting her body in mysterious shadows. The fourth, and most compelling, was of Himari looking into dark glass. From the rear, she dressed in a traditional Japanese kimono, but her reflection was one of a woman in club attire with glasses perched on the end of her nose, holding a cell phone. In vague shadow, Filippo stood behind her. The fifth depicted her laying in a nest of blankets, looking tiny and sad, her hair in disarray, blood-stained papers littering the table beside her. In the sixth, she stood in the doorway of his bedroom, alternately vulnerable and sexy in a red halter and jeans. For the seventh, Filippo guided Himari's hand over a canvas of such anger and pain that emotions bled onto the drop cloth. Their figures merged as he shared her anguish and gave her his art. The eighth showed Himari's bare shoulders and face, her head thrown back in ecstasy. Blurred and subtle, it lacked the deep rich details of the others, yet it was as evocative as anything anyone had ever seen. The final, with the paint barely dry, was of the two of them, their foreheads pressed together, eyes closed.

Himari openly wept, touched by the impossible, unexpected gift.

Gus Gets His Wish

"You smell good," the sultry redhead whispered in Gus' ear.

"Kayah," Gus exclaimed, and picked her up in a bear hug, spinning her around. "I hoped you would come! I heard you made Stephen poop his pants!" Gus whooped with laughter. "You know he fired me?"

Kayah leaned back in Gus' arms. "I know. That's why I did it."

"That's funny. Even my momma thought it was funny." Gus let her down. "Did you see Vinia?"

Kayah straightened her clothes. "Not yet, I came to see you first."

Gus turned red. "I've gotten fat."

Kayah patted his belly. "I see that. That's not good, Gus. It's not healthy for you. It makes it hard to move." She took his hands. "I want you to do better, do you understand?"

Gus flattened his generous lips and promised, "I will."

"All right, next time I see you, I want to see less of you." Kayah held his gray eyes with her hazel ones.

"Okay, Kai. I promise," he said solemnly. Then added, "Did you see the pictures? I wish I could paint like that."

Kayah took his arm. "You can do other things. Don't you forget it. I might even have some work for you to do, but we will talk about that after the party, okay?"

Gus broke into a slow grin. "I would love to work with you again, Kayah. You always kept me on task. Even if you do yell at me a bit, I don't mind."

Kayah shrugged. "I can sometimes be a yeller, can't I?"

"Geez, can you. You have a loud voice sometimes. You would always yell at Himari. Don't do that today, it's her wedding day, you know."

Kayah laughed, "I know. That's why I'm here."

"Oh, yeah. I forgot. You can meet Alaina, too. She's nice, she reminds me of you."

Kayah thought that was unlikely. She knew exactly who Alaina ben Thomas was. "Let's start with Lavinia. I have not seen her in more than a dozen years."

"It's been almost that long since you've seen me. Though you saw me in jail, and you wouldn't see the rest of them. How come?" Gus looked genuinely puzzled.

Kayah squeezed his soft arm. "Gus, I don't want to talk about prison today. It's a wedding."

Gus understood that. There were a lot of sad things he did not like to talk about. He studied Kayah. "Your hair is orange. When did that happen?"

"A couple days ago, and it is technically strawberry blonde. Do you like it?" Kayah preened for him.

"No, not really. It doesn't look like strawberries. I like your yellow hair; it has gold in it and sparkles like the sun." Gus seemed belligerent about her natural hair color.

Kayah exhaled. "I wouldn't know. It hasn't been that color in a long time. I change it a lot for work."

"Who has to change their hair for work?" Thoroughly confused by that notion, he said, "All I ever have to do is bathe, and you are the only one that ever told me that. Though I expect it is one of those things that goes without saying."

"So, you've learned there are things that go without saying?" The realization impressed Kayah.

"I have." Gus stopped and turned to face her, his expression intent. "I think there are a lot of things between me and you that go without saying. Wouldn't you agree, Kayah?"

She stood still, then reached down, and took his beefy hands in hers. "Yes, but we will keep them unsaid, won't we, Gus?"

He dropped his chin, then met her eyes again. "For now. Maybe not forever. I am a man, Kayah."

She swallowed thickly. He had always loved her, and they both knew it. Many men desired her, powerful forces sought to use her, but Gus was the single man in the world who loved her. Tenderly, she leaned forward and kissed his lips, then laid a gentle hand on his cheek. "I love you, too."

What Love Does

Lavinia felt like an exposed nerve, as if the paintings stripped her skin away. The beauty and love Filippo poured onto canvas was difficult to watch. She lapsed into the calculations of the light frequencies of the colors, the perspective ratios, the tempo of the music. She could not listen, she could not see, the labyrinth beckoned, and she fought it.

Violet saw it happening and moved to her daughter's side. "Stay here, honey. Stay here for your friend. This is a beautiful moment. Don't miss it."

Lavinia nodded convulsively and came back. As the portrait of Himari in her nest of blankets was revealed, Lavinia imagined herself inside the labyrinth, hiding and lost, blood-stained equations surrounding her. The vulnerable, sexy picture came next, and Lavinia saw herself through Mack's eyes, as he waited on her front porch, a posy of wildflowers in his rugged hands. He had looked at her with such wonder that she blushed. And the picture of Himari and Filippo painting, that was Mack showing her his own art, music. Lavinia let out a quiet sob as they unveiled the ecstasy picture. She remembered how she felt when Mack touched her, how she arched her back and purred under his stroking hands. She should have let him, should have loved him completely when she had the chance. Why, why had she insisted they wait? At the last picture, with the couples' heads pressed together, she covered a sob and fled the room.

She should go find him. He was here. Not twenty miles away, yet he was not free. She was awash in a longing akin to physical pain, it made her wild and reckless. In that moment, she did not care about his duty, and she certainly did not care about the spoiled little Prince he guarded. She did not care about his vows; she simply wanted the man she loved.

Lavinia stared at the fountain in the middle of the pond, calculating the rate of displacement and force necessary to reach the height it was achieving, trying to calm her mind.

"What's the rate of displacement?"

Lavinia's head snapped up. She thought there was nothing that could make her smile, but that voice proved her wrong. "Kayah!" She came around the bench, her long lost friend in her arms a second later.

"We are two old maids, aren't we?" Kayah teased. "Himari's on her second and neither of us have even managed a first."

"How did you know that's what I was moping about?"

"Old maids always flee weddings. I felt the same way in there. Disgusting, wasn't it?" Kayah winked.

"It was one of the most beautiful things I ever saw, and now I feel like a shithead." Lavinia winked back. "Better than a shit-pants, though," she laughed.

"I guess I am famous for that now, huh?" Kayah sat down on the bench.

"Classic, legendary Kayah." Lavinia settled beside Kayah, feeling her mood lighten.

"Amusing, but minor. The world will never know my true legend." She raised her eyebrows and waggled them in mischief.

"I don't doubt that for a minute." Lavinia took in Kayah's expensive dress and unlined face. "Himari said you looked fabulous; I see she was not exaggerating."

"She said you were rusticating."

Lavinia rolled her eyes. "After what happened, I prefer rustication."

"There's coming a time, Vinia, where you might not have a choice." Kayah spoke to the fountain. "They've let you stay on the sidelines, hidden away, but it might not always be that way."

Lavinia threw up her hands. "I was thinking the same thing, just a moment ago. My man is in the thick of it."

Kayah pulled a cigarette from her purse and took a long drag. "You want to go see him?"

Lavinia took the cigarette from Kayah's fingers, inhaling deeply. "How do you know about Mack?"

Kayah lit another cigarette, figuring Lavinia might want one of her own. "I know a whole lot of things. I know where he is… right now."

Lavinia flicked the cigarette away. "Hell, yeah. Let's go."

A Stir at the RMA

The cadets at the Royal Military Academy were no strangers to beautiful, elegantly dressed women. They all came from money. Their sisters, mothers, aunts, and future fiancées dressed in finery, silks, satins. Ball gowns were common in their world. Summer session finished, and the cadets were leaving for a thirty-day break. In mid-September, they would return to new barracks and new rank.

Mack ben Robert stood outside Prince Peter's room while Jarrod ben Adriel and a host of other Palace attendees packed up the private quarters afforded Peter during his stay at the Academy. Security was tight on moving day, and dozens of strangers traipsed in and out of the building. This made Mack nervous, and he did not like being nervous. At seventeen, the Prince was ready to party. This made Mack even more nervous.

A hush fell over the dorm, and Mack rested his hand on his sidearm. His mouth hit the floor when he realized what was causing it, two gorgeous women strutting down the hallway like runway models. Yet, he only saw one. She was a vision straight out of his erotic dreams, Lavinia ben Anthony dressed in red, an angel and a devil combined.

Behind him, Peter whistled low in appreciation. "Bloody hell, Mack. Who are they?"

"You keep a civil tongue in your head, boy," Mack said without thinking, his eyes glued to the most exquisite beauty he had ever seen. She possessed a loveliness that went beyond sex appeal, fine boned and lithe, with a smooth olive complexion and deep brown eyes that turned up just a touch at the corners. He stood poleaxed, enraptured anew.

Her voice was husky, soft like flannel and down comforters. "Mack."

He realized vaguely that two of his agents, Nathan and Lewis, moved into position. Good men, because at that moment, the only part of his body thinking was not his brain.

"Lavinia," he breathed.

"I was in town and wanted to see you." She gave him a shy smile and met his eyes.

He nodded, suddenly very glad that she did. He had done his

best to put her out of his mind. It was unproductive to dwell on things he could not have, but in that moment, it did not matter. "I'm on duty," he said inanely.

On cue, Peter said over Mack's shoulder, "I am the duty."

The Prince's voice seemed to shake Mack out of his trance, and he smiled in apology. "Sorry, I'm going to have to pat y'all down."

"Oh, my favorite part," Kayah said saucily. "Lavinia, let Mack do you. I want the handsome blond one back there."

Mack caught the lift of Nathan ben Henry's lip as he moved in front of the Prince, looking particularly pleased at the prospect.

"I will do it," Peter volunteered.

Kayah chuckled and thought some things never changed, the little flirt. She had not seen Prince d'Or since he was five and determined this meeting would go better than the last, so she was unarmed.

Jarrod ben Adriel's startled expression clearly conveyed his displeasure. Her mission tonight was to get Mack and Lavinia together, but putting her in the Prince's orbit? Absolutely not, but Kayah didn't give a rat's ass.

Kayah met the Prince's eyes, stunning in their emerald beauty, golden sunshine surrounding their pupils. "We are on our way to a party. We thought you gentlemen might like to join us."

Prince d'Or did not disappoint. Photographs did not do him justice, for there was no camera in the world that could capture the blinding radiance of that legendary smile. As jaded as Kayah was, she counted herself fortunate to be the recipient of her second. Kayah had her own version of that smile and cooed, "Come on, puppy. Let's go have some fun."

Normally I Do Not Like Redheads

The New City did not lack for nightlife. Saturday night was the best night of the week. For a young Prince on furlough from military school and not yet back under the strict structure of Palace life, it was a brief respite, and one he planned to enjoy. The sultry redhead was fun, even if she was older, not that he held that against her. As a matter of course, older women made amazing lovers, which he discovered the summer before. Young girls were needy, wanted romance, and expected him to marry them. Older women just wanted to have sex with him, and that suited Peter just fine.

Mack was about to have a heart attack. Between his own hot chick and the unscheduled trip to the nightclub, he looked like a man in dire need of a drink. Peter took matters into his own hands. "Nathan, please relive Mack for the rest of the evening."

Agent Nathan ben Henry nodded once, his green eyes scanning the crowd.

Peter motioned to their waiter and pointed at Mack. "Please deliver a beer to that man and tell him it is from me."

Kayah crossed her legs and considered him. "That was thoughtful of you."

Peter shrugged. "He will be easier to get along with if he gets laid."

Kayah laughed, then added, "You are different, not what I expected."

Peter quirked a brow at her. "I get that a lot."

Kayah considered him carefully and said, "You look like your mother."

He snorted softly and laughed, "I do not get that a lot." To the casual observer, he was the image of his father. "Though I appreciate the sentiment." He leaned in for a kiss. "I suppose that is why I do not normally like redheads, but I think in your case, I might make an exception."

Their lips touched.

It was strange, kissing this boy. She had no compunction about their age difference and planned to do exactly what she found herself doing. There was a part of him, the part in that picture hanging in Sir Preston's study she wanted to touch, always had. She thought they might find that connection through sex, but somehow it did not feel right.

Peter pulled back and looked at her, puzzled. "Perhaps not."

"Prince d'Or, I believe you are right, though, I am enjoying your company." For once, Kayah spoke the truth.

A slow smile began, his left dimple just showing in the corner. "You remind me of my friend, Persa. She's a strawberry blonde, and I do not want to kiss her, either."

"I will take that as a compliment." Kayah brushed the hair away from her eyes.

"It is a high compliment indeed. I do not have many friends." He was serious.

Kayah shook her head and told him the truth, again. "I don't either."

Peter kissed her cheek. "Well, if we are not going to get naked, let's dance!"

And they did.

The Balance

Mack felt completely out of control of the situation, which threw him off balance, a state he despised. He and Prince Peter walked a fine line, the guard and the guarded, a delicate struggle of give and take, where the situation determined who had the upper hand. In periods of intense danger, Mack took charge. But in times like these, where the Prince asserted his authority, Mack was forced to adjust. It was part of the job, but that did not mean that he liked it. Overall, they enjoyed an easy relationship, both understanding their roles.

Complicating matters was the love of his life, trying to tap her toe to the music and failing miserably. It made her even more endearing. Lavinia was nervous. He could tell by the way she kept becoming wistful. Like so many others before him, when they first met, he thought that look was for him. He quickly realized she was somewhere else altogether. He also figured out that she did not hear music. She could hear the notes well enough, there was nothing wrong with her hearing, but that was all she heard, the notes and the patterns. She analyzed them with mathematical precision, and it frustrated her. While she could comprehend the consonance of sound waves and deduce why they might be pleasant to the ear, the dissonance confounded her. She could not work out how notes, that on their own should be grating, were not when they were combined, resulting in something pleasing. The messiness of it bothered her. But she let it in her bar because she wanted to understand it. It was how Mack touched her, how he got her to feel, when he sang to her in the bar that first time.

He wanted to touch her again, standing there like a vision, elegant and beautiful in her red gown. He wanted to take her some place quiet, hear her breathy voice, and watch her mind work. He wanted to find out what she had been doing for the last three years. He wanted to kiss her.

"Sir, the Prince sent this over." The harried server presented a beer to Mack.

Mack's eyes bore a hole in the waiter's skull, and he shot a look at Peter, who raised a glass in salute. Nathan ben Henry, Mack's second in command, wove his way through the crowd. "What's he up to?"

Nathan looked over his shoulder. "He's given you the night off, Mack." Then Nathan smiled and gestured toward Lavinia. "Enjoy yourself." With that, he resumed his post.

Mack scanned the club, shrugged, and with three big gulps, swallowed the beer. "Well, darlin', it appears I am officially off duty. Come on, let's get out of here."

Lavinia agreed with a slow blink of her gorgeous brown eyes. Enchanted, Mack decided he would not question this stroke of fate.

We've Got Tonight

"Do you want to go get some food, are you hungry?" Mack asked as they left the club hand in hand.

Lavinia shook her head. "We ate at the wedding." She watched her red shoes as they walked, sparkling satin in the parking lot. "Perhaps we could go have a drink," she paused then added in a breathless voice, "at your place?"

Mack turned his head, seeing her color rise. "We could do that," he whispered.

She tilted her head, the tiny cleft of her chin just in shadow, a lock of hair curling around her fine jawline. "I'd like that."

Mack smiled and took her in his arms. "I'd like that too, darlin'." When his lips touched hers, all the passion he held in check for the last three years broke free. Desire and longing crashed over him like a tidal wave.

Lavinia ben Anthony let it sweep her away. Water turned to fire as she clung to him, running her fingers up his back, pressing her delicate body against his bulging one.

Mack moistened his lips and tasted her kiss. "I have wanted to do that for a very long time. I never stopped thinking about you." His drawl became low and deep, as he stroked her cheek. "Lord, you are so beautiful." It was a groan and a prayer. He wanted to pull her behind a tree and make love to her, but a corner of his mind was still functioning. "As you've seen, I'm still at the Palace. Are you sure?"

Lavinia did not care if his work kept them apart. Kayah certainly wouldn't if she was in Lavinia's shoes, and Himari was having her second wedding night. Lavinia was sick of hiding and playing it safe. She had a chance, and she was going to take it. She rolled her hips against his arousal, reveling in the friction, the heat coursing between them. In a voice quivering with desire, she moaned, "We've got tonight, Mack. Make love to me."

Standing in the parking lot under the gas lights, he lost his head; he lost his heart a long time ago. He growled in her ear, his breath coming in deep gasps, "Wait here. I'll get us a cab."

When Mack turned, he tried not to sprint to the taxi stand and said a prayer of thanks that the maid had been to his apartment yesterday.

February 14, 997 ME (Twelve Years into Rebellion)

Rescue

Mack wanted to puke when he found Peter in the Palace infirmary, broken, beaten, and bloodied. Reginald's two guards posted outside did not dare question his authority when he ordered them to stand aside. He and Jarrod strode in and took Peter out before anyone could raise the alarm. It was 1:06 am. They had him off the grounds in eight minutes.

As they drove away, Mack knew he could never walk through the Palace doors again without being arrested. He went from the Head of the Prince's Security to an enemy of the state in eight minutes.

Strapped in the passenger seat, out of his mind with whatever they were pumping into him, the Prince looked like a skeleton after a dreadful night. Mack's rage burned hot. This was Korah's doing, plain and simple. He should not have left Peter alone, had argued against it, a folly, a bad idea. Mack harbored a deep suspicion that Korah, the homicidal maniac, would make his move one of these days, and he waited until Mack left to do it. He should have known. He had known, which was why he never left Peter side. Dammit! He kept the Prince alive for seven years by trusting his instincts, being ready for anything. But Peter had been adamant, so he went. His trip to Greece confirmed what the Prince had suspected. "I found him."

Peter opened one eye, the other swollen shut. "He is alive?"

"Yes, serving in the King's Army. He's a surgeon," Mack said, racing through the New City's sparse traffic.

Peter gurgled in the back of his throat. "Doctor? That is rich."

Mack pressed a bottle of water into the Prince's shaking hands. "He goes by the name Einar ben Yane. He's a Captain."

Peter palmed the water that leaked down his chin. "Good, he will know how to fight. He will need it. I do not think I am going to live through this, Mack."

"Nonsense, you're a tough dude."

Peter's head fell against the seat, his mouth slack. "You would not say that if you heard me screaming like a girl a couple of nights ago."

"All men break under torture; don't let anyone ever tell you otherwise."

"Mack," Peter sighed, dozing off. "I am messed up. Where are we going?"

Mack looked at the road signs and reached a decision—north. "I'm taking you to Pepperwood."

Peter's head nodded drunkenly, and he slurred, "Persa… take me to Persa and James. That is good."

Then he slept.

Mack killed the lights as he pulled down Pepperwood Lane two-and-a-half hours later. "My Esteemed," he shook Peter's shoulder, "you must not tell them I brought you here. Your life and my life may depend upon it."

Peter's tongue was thick, his lips dried and cracked. "You are leaving me?"

Mack shook his head. "No, I vowed to protect you and will do so with my life, but I fear it must be in a different capacity moving forward."

"He is going to try to kill you now, too." Peter wiped his nose. "Do not let him succeed, Mack."

"You have my word on that." Mack cut the engine.

Peter looked through bleary eyes at the white house with the green roof; his refuge all those summers ago. "Help me to the front door. I fear I cannot walk."

"I can do that, my Esteemed."

Odd Hours

Mack was bone tired, having traversed half the globe in fifty days. He hid in the shadows until James ben Kole came to the door and carried Peter inside the house. Murmuring a prayer, Mack disappeared into the woods that separated Pepperwood from Peccioli, Lavinia's vineyard. Adjusting the shoulder strap on the bag he'd hastily thrown into the trunk, he made his way in the dark. A silver moon lit the sky, but the canopy of redwoods blocked most of the moonlight, so he navigated by the small pocket flashlight he kept on his keyring. He had not gone back to his apartment, so eager was he to share the news about Prince Josiah with Peter.

It was a quarter to four, but Mack remembered that Lavinia kept odd hours. Between the bar and whatever complex mathematical problem consumed her at the moment, it was not unusual to find her awake. Back in '92, he'd stop by after finishing a third shift, and they would drink coffee on the veranda that overlooked the vineyard. Sometimes she had been asleep, sometimes not.

He wondered if she would run him off with a shotgun, not that he'd blame her if she did. It had been five years since he last rang her doorbell, and a year and a half since their amazing night in the New City. Turning up unexpectedly in the middle of the night was not likely to endear him to her, or her mother.

Clearing the edge of the forest, he beheld Lavinia's place. The vineyard and winery lay in the valley below. Bare vines, visible in the moonlight, were strung taut and pruned to perfection, like the incredible woman who owned them. Freshly turned earth, perfumed the night air, and he noted with interest a new section being readied for spring planting.

He should have come back here, for her, had planned to, had every intention to. But duty called, and he was honor bound to fulfill it. Mack had just left the object of that duty in a huddled mass on James and Persa's doorstep. Somehow, that made his sacrifice seem less noble. If Peter died, it had been for naught. He shook off the morbid thought and trudged down the hill.

At the front door, he climbed the steps with resolution, and knocked. It took a minute; a light came on in the hallway before he saw her slender figure silhouetted in the darkness. Her face was in shadow when she opened the door. "Lavinia." His voice carried on the cold air like a prayer.

She rested her head against the doorframe, taking him in. "Did you bring me a valentine, Mack?"

Emotion clogged his throat. She loved archaic holidays. "Will you be my valentine, Lavinia?"

Without a word, she wrapped her graceful arms around his neck and whispered softly, "I will."

First Moments

He was not a man given to weeping, he was a soldier, a sheriff, and a Royal Guard. He was the Head of Security to the second highest royal official in the Kingdom and arguably, the third highest ranked royal in the world. But when Lavinia ben Anthony took him by the hand and brought him into her home with the words, 'I will', tears slid down his cheeks. With the taste of her sweet kiss on his mouth, Mack ben Robert wanted to sob.

She held his face in her hands, feeling the beard stubble, seeing the fatigue, and the emotion. Gently, she thumbed away a tear, and with an enigmatic smile, whispered, "Come, but be quiet."

He nodded, cognizant of his boots on the wooden floor. Her mother would be asleep down the hall. She paused outside the door and pressed her finger to his lips, her own eyes glistening with tears.

She pushed the door open, and the sweet smell of baby hit him square in the face. Lavinia watched him, saw the realization come over him. His eyes bulged as his breath caught.

Holding back a small cry, Lavinia pulled him into the room and whispered, "Look."

If he had been trying to hold back the floodgate a moment before, this was a full-on dam breach. His feet slid clumsily across the floor. A night light cast the room in cool shadows. Lying in a blue sleeper, contentedly sucking his left thumb, was his son.

Mack covered his mouth and closed his eyes, overwhelmed by the moment. He turned in disbelief to Lavinia whose face glowed with love and pride. In slow motion, he opened his arms and gathered her close, absorbing their very first moments as a family.

Then, he wept.

Who Did You Come For?

Lavinia led Mack from the baby's room to hers. When the door closed firmly behind them, he let out a series of loud exhales, like he had just run a hundred meters carrying a wine cask. "Name," he breathed, "what is his name?"

She went to her bedside table and pulled out a sheet of paper. In the dim light, he could not read it. "I have a year. I waited, to see if you would come."

Mack rubbed his face. "How old is he?"

"Well, if you would do the math."

"Dammit, woman, I'm tired. How old is he?"

"Thirty-seven weeks and four days." When he shot her another look, she amended with a roll of her brown eyes. "Nine and a half months."

Mack sat down heavily on the edge of the bed. "You didn't tell me." His eyes burned, and he rubbed at them with the heel of his hand. "Why didn't you tell me? I'd have come."

"I know you would have, but then I would have never known, would I? If you came for me or just for him." Her husky voice cracked with emotion. "Did you come for me, Mack? Did you *finally* come for me?"

She stood before him in baggy flannel pants printed with cartoon characters and a pink t-shirt that did not even remotely match. Her hair was a disheveled mess, but the new cut swung around her shoulders and framed her oval face.

He stood up and took a single step toward her, their bodies pressed together in the small bedroom. "Did I come for you?" He pressed his lips to hers and pulled her hips against his in full masculine possession. "What do you think?"

"Mack," fire shot through her, "we have about thirty-seven minutes before the baby wakes up."

He kissed the side of her neck and growled. "Let your momma get him."

"Mamma can't feed him, besides she's not here. Pappa put in at San Diego last week, she's down there."

"Feed him?" Mack said hoarsely, cupping her full breast. "Oh, my Lord, let me see."

She giggled and lifted the t-shirt over her head.

In the faint light, he scrunched up his face. "That is the most horrible contraption I have ever seen."

Her shoulders shook as she looked down. "It's a nursing bra."

"It's an abomination."

Lavinia covered her mouth and then pointed to it helplessly. "It's comfortable."

"It's kindling!" He spun her around. "My God, it's got six snaps."

"They are not snaps; they are hooks. This is a snap." She demonstrated by opening the cup on the front of the brassiere.

He leaned over her shoulder, catching sight of the glorious rose nipple and full breast. "Oh, well maybe it's not so bad." His finger traced a delicate outline around the tip of her nipple.

She rested her head on his chest, her eyes closed in pleasure. "Yeah, maybe it isn't so bad," Lavinia said dreamily. "Be careful though, they are temperamental."

He unsnapped the other cup. "Temperamental, in what way?"

"I suppose we might find out, but it isn't my breasts I am focused on right now."

Mack chuckled low and moved his hand over her soft belly, not the concave hard plane it had been the last time they were together, but infinitely sexier for its character and how she had earned it. "Is this what you are focused on? Do you want me to touch you here?"

"Uh huh," she moaned and melted into his warm hand.

"Oh, darlin', my sweet darlin', you feel so nice." Mack kissed the side of her neck.

Lavinia began to make little female sounds of desire, moving against the erotic rhythm he was creating.

"That's right, just like that." He felt her spasm against his hand. "Who did I come here for? Huh? Who did I come for?"

"Me," she panted.

"You're damn right."

He had her naked minutes later, graceful and open before him. Desire to possess her, to be inside her, nearly drove him to a frenzy, but he held himself in check for just a moment, to appreciate the joy.

"Lavinia, will you be my wife?" He pushed at her entrance, feeling the hot moistness of her. "Tell me."

"Yes, yes!" she cried out to him.

Mack felt her tight warm embrace, this woman, this lovely precious woman, took him inside her. Mack lost all control, and it was good.

A Nice Way to Wake Up

Thirty-two minutes later, a soft cry crept under the doorway. Mack opened a sleepy eye and started to rise.

Lavinia kissed him, whispering against his mouth, "Stay here. I'll change him and bring him in to nurse."

Mack lifted his head, wanting to get up to meet his son, but his fatigued body demanded rest, and he capitulated, asleep the moment she left the bed. Later, he felt her settle in beside him, the warm little body, soft and squirming between them. Dozing off, he heard the contented suckle of his nursing babe and discovered the greatest peace known to man.

Many hours later, a tiny head butted his. He opened a sleep crusted eye and met the enormous brown ones of his son, full of fierce challenge. Mack was obviously an intruder, and the little man did not appear pleased. Lavinia stood in the doorway, her knuckles pressed over her lips, her eyes dancing. The boy grunted and head butted him again, rocking on sturdy arms and knees.

"I'll let you two get to know each other." Lavinia blew him a kiss and with a swing of her hair disappeared.

Mack rubbed his face briskly and shook away the sleep. The baby mimicked the masculine noises. The corner of Mack's lip twitched, and he raised up on one elbow to get a good look at his boy. He had a mop of wavy brown hair, which in Mack's opinion was entirely too long. It curled over his forehead and down his neck. He had the promise of a firm jaw, ears that pointed just slightly at the tips like his mother's, and Mack's father's nose to the life, except without the crooked break that Mack had always known his father's to have. It was his son's expression that arrested him, one that any agent, soldier, or deputy that served under him would have recognized, it said, "Move your ass, soldier."

"I'm not going anywhere, boy. You better get used to it," then added with a sudden lump in his throat, "because I'm your daddy."

The baby crawled over for a closer inspection, grabbed Mack's nose with his stubby fingers and squeezed. Mack honked, and his son giggled, so he did it again, and again, and again. Then the baby moved to Mack's head and started pounding on it with glee. Mack pretended he was being pummeled to death, to his son's intense delight. Exuberant two-fisted pounding commenced.

The kid seemed pretty tough, so Mack lifted him over his head and let him fly like a bird. The boy arched his back, threw out his arms and legs, and shrieked with joy. Then he drooled squarely in Mack's eye. "Oh, a missile!" Mack declared. "You got me."

He launched him onto his belly with a thud and rolled on top of his laughing baby. Kissing his soft little neck, smelling him, feeling his squirming solid body, Mack fell utterly and completely in love.

Bino

Mack devoured his lunch because it was long past breakfast when he rose. Considering that he fell asleep around 5:00 am, he cut himself some slack. He lifted the espresso in appreciation and silent appeal for another, dipped the crusty bread in the olive oil and herbs, and smiled contentedly. Olives, roasted red peppers, cured ham, fresh mozzarella, and winter arugula were as pretty as the lady who served them.

"Valentine, have I told you that I love you?" Mack relaxed into his chair, his eyes sated with food and happiness.

She tucked her hair behind her ear, her lips pouty. "You love the food."

He licked his lips, giving her a sensuous smile. "I do love the food, but I love the beautiful woman more."

She moved toward him; their eyes locked. He pushed his chair away from the table, and she sat on his lap. Nuzzling his ear, she said huskily, "I'm glad you're here."

He growled and kissed her, then felt a tiny hand smack the top of his foot.

The baby looked up at him with big brown eyes and said, "Bah!"

"Bah, to you, too, spoiler." Then he reached down with one arm and picked the boy up, placing him firmly on his mother's lap. The little family sat in the rustic kitchen, in a single chair.

"So, what is your name, young man?" He turned to Lavinia, curious. "What *have* you been calling him?"

"Mostly Bambino, Bino for short."

"Beano?" Mack was appalled.

"Bino," his son echoed, then, as if on cue, ripped a loud one.

Mack threw back his head and laughed. "He smells like he's been eating beano."

His son clenched two fists and bore down hard, screwing his face up before relaxing with major accomplishment.

Mack looked at Lavinia in horror.

She chuckled, "I'll change him."

Mack turned pale and swallowed convulsively. He had administered field dressings, been shot once, witnessed horrors beyond imagining living in the Palace the last seven years, but his twenty-pound son with his two-pound diaper freaked him out. As an only child, his sole exposure to babies to date was nodding and smiling to his friend's kids at church. He followed her to change the diaper like a man going to the gallows.

As with most dreaded things in life, the actual was not nearly as terrible as he imagined. He was proud to see that his son took after him in other ways. The diapering accomplished, Mack let the baby stand on the changing table, ecstatic bouncing ensued. "He's a strong little guy. We should call him Samson."

"Samson? No." Lavinia spun the diaper in the trash bag and threw it away. Mack raised a brow in question. "Disposables. The greatest reinvention of the age."

The corners of Mack's mouth turned down as he nodded, in complete agreement with that sentiment. Picking up his now sweet-smelling son, he kissed the top of his head. "What name were you going to give him," he met her eyes, "if I didn't show up?"

She pulled the silver ring from under her blouse. "I was going to call him Richard, after your friend."

Mack pressed his lips in a thin line and answered through a knot in his throat. "That's a damn good name, Valentine." He held out his free arm. She moved to his side and rested her head against his shoulder.

"I think Valentine is a good name, too."

Then Richard ben Mack dug a meaty little fist into his mother's hair and pulled.

Change in Plans

"I can't believe you sold the bistro," Mack said, pulling on his boots.

Lavinia shrugged. "I still tend bar some nights, but it's a small town, Mack."

He froze as the impact of her words hit him. "Damn."

"No, it's not just that. Mamma is getting older, and she wants to retire. It is a lot of work to run a restaurant, plus the vineyard and winery, then add the baby, and—"

"What?" Mack took her elbows.

She looked up at him through her long lashes. "I've been working a little."

"Math?" he asked speculatively.

She nodded.

"For whom?"

"An old friend."

Mack crossed his arms over his chest and looked down at her. "You have several old friends of dubious nature." He warned her with a look. "I know who Kayah ben Samuel is, and I don't want you involved in anything that has to do with her. It's not safe."

"You don't know what you are talking about. Furthermore, you are not exactly safe, and I am about to marry you," Lavinia challenged.

Mack shook his head. "Yeah, but I'm getting out. You and Richard change everything. From the moment I walked in that nursery, everything changed. If it was just me and you—"

"But it's not, is it?" Lavinia finished. "There is more going on than just me and you. What happened last night, Mack? I know you, and while I am exceedingly glad to see you, I know you did not turn up on my doorstep at 4:00 am by accident."

He looked suddenly rather tired.

"Come on. I'll make you an espresso, and you can tell me the latest intrigue because you would not be here if there was not big trouble."

Mack followed her into the kitchen. "When did you become so perceptive?" He watched her calculate, amused that she took the question literally.

"Five thousand one hundred and fifty-one days ago." She said and dumped the coffee grounds in the trash.

"And what day is that, Valentine?" Mack stretched his aching shoulders.

"The day I found out they arrested all my friends," Lavinia tamped the coffee down with vigor, "and stole our work."

Mack waited. Sir Preston had summarily shut his background check into Kayah down the moment it began.

"*Nonno* had died, and we were here for the funeral. Otherwise, I would have been with them." She pressed the button on the espresso machine with emphasis. "None of them ever told."

"Who?" Mack laced his fingers behind his head and leaned back.

"The Alcatraz 5, me, Kayah, Gus, Himari, and Stephen."

"I knew you were friends with Himari Nakamura, that's whose wedding you were attending," he nodded toward the nursery where Richard was napping, "but Gus and Stephen, who are they?"

"Gus ben Allen and Stephen ben McSwilley." Lavinia brought him the espresso.

Mack raised an eyebrow. "Stephen ben McSwilley, the Minister of Technology and Security?"

"The same. He betrayed us to King Korah." Lavinia shook her head ruefully and sat down at the kitchen table.

Mack sipped his espresso. "There's no record of it."

Lavinia traced vague number patterns on the wood with her finger. "There wouldn't be. I wasn't there, Himari was a minor, they branded Gus incompetent, Stephen cut a deal," she paused, her face full of pain, "and Kayah went to jail." She pointed at him, and her voice cracked. "So, don't come strolling in here and tell me, if she asks, that I can't do figures for her. Because she never said a word. She could have, but she didn't, and I owe her. We all owe her."

Mack did not give a fig about Kayah ben Samuel or whatever misguided loyalty Lavinia might feel toward the woman. But he read the stubborn set of her jaw and let it pass, for now.

She sipped her espresso. "That was a bit off topic, but I suppose as pertinent to our future as what you have to say."

Mack rested his elbow on the table, his thumb pressed under his strong chin, considering. "I don't know how much I should tell you." Visions of Peter's tortured body ran through his mind. "I need to think, and I need to take a ride. A lot depends on whether Peter ben Korah survived the night."

Lavinia gasped and brought her hand to her mouth, her eyes huge as the implications of his words registered. Mack sacrificed their lives together in service to the Prince, if Peter was dead, it would be a devastating blow. "Oh Mack, what happened?"

Mack stood. "Korah. Korah happened."

Pepperwood Fury

At dusk, Mack rode onto the Pepperwood property through the woods. He and his team became intimately familiar with the area in '92, and it had not changed. The ranch appeared quiet with only a few horses in pasture, which seemed ominous. He circled several times to ensure it was not under surveillance. Satisfied that it wasn't, he approached under cover of darkness.

Mack dismounted as James ben Kole stormed out of the house. "Where the hell were you when that mess was going on?" James shouted, stalking across the yard.

Mack threw up his hands in surrender. "I was gone, man, out of the kingdom. I just got back last night, and I brought him here."

James stopped, furrowing his brows. "You brought him?"

"He was in no condition to drive, was he?"

"He led us to believe he drove himself." James eyed him suspiciously.

Mack realized that as far as James knew, Mack worked for Korah, so he dropped his combative tone. "That was the original plan, but we have to make adjustments."

James' stare turned deadly; the threat of violence spiced the air. "Why?"

Mack knew James ben Kole by reputation, in the war and after. They met several times during the summer of '92. It was no yahoo horse farmer standing before him, guarding Peter like the angel Gabriel. On the battlefield and on a horse, James ben Kole was not to be trifled with. But one on one, against Royal Guard Mack ben Robert, he did not stand a chance. However, as much as Mack enjoyed a good fight, that was not his goal tonight, besides, the more allies Peter had guarding his back, the better.

"It's complicated and confidential. I've come to see him." Mack made a move toward the house.

James countered, blocking his path. "How do I know you didn't play a role in this, that you aren't here to finish the job?"

Mack had not anticipated this complication, but he should have. "I suppose you could ask him."

James scoffed, "He's out of his head, completely wrecked. He was semi-lucid until about noon today. Since then, he thinks I'm Jarrod, his valet, or his dead cousin, Prince Josiah. Alternatively, he thinks Persa is his mother, or some woman named Kayah that he definitely does not want to kiss." James made a rueful shake of his head. "I suppose I should be thankful for that."

Mack looked up at the house, glad Peter did not want to kiss Kayah. That woman was dangerous. "Mr. ben Kole, I appreciate your diligence. I truly do. But I've kept that young man safe and alive for seven years, at great personal expense to me and my family." Family, the word sounded as foreign as it was delightful. "He has nothing to fear from me."

James remained stoic.

Mack recognized the futility of arguing. "All right. You've got the vehicle hidden?"

James nodded. "Just as we did in '92."

"Fair enough. Give him the methadone in stages. I don't know exactly what they were shooting him up with, but I suspect it was heroin. If that's true, the next three days are going to be bonkers. So, watch the injection sites for infection. He was burning up with fever, and that could get bad. There're antibiotics in the bag. We cleaned out the infirmary when we took him out of there."

"Infirmary?" James scowled.

Mack nodded. "They didn't have him in there long. My boys would have caught that."

"And how do you know they weren't in on it?"

Mack shook his head. He'd roused his team to ensure they weren't stopped when they evacuated. He'd seen their faces when they loaded the Prince in the car. Nathan, Lewis, and Taylor were all mortified. "They weren't. Korah got them all out of the Palace when he took Peter, sent them on a wild-goose chase to New York. They weren't there."

James crossed his arms. "Again, I have only your word on that."

Mack rolled his eyes. "Fine. He will tell you when he wakes up. In the interim, keep him hydrated and don't let him wander. Restrain him if you have to but be careful of that hand, it looked broken." He mounted the horse. "They did not follow us. I don't think anyone will search for him here, which is why I brought him. Come get me if it gets bad or if there's trouble. I'm at Peccioli."

"Peccioli?"

"Yes," Mack said, catching a shadow in the front window, Persa by the size of it.

James narrowed his eyes. "Are you that little boy's father?"

Mack stiffened, bringing his attention back to James. "I am."

"From where I'm standing, you're late, Agent, on both counts. I'll take care of Peter. You make things right for Lavinia." James turned and left Mack alone in the yard.

Hang 'em All

As he rode back, Mack fumed. Who in the hell did James ben Kole think he was, saying that to him? It was dark, so he could not ride out his fury without risking the horse. Plodding along through the redwoods did nothing to soothe his mind or his anger. He would have dismissed the words if they had not been true, and every damn syllable of the indictment rang in his ears.

"Late on both counts."

"Shit," Mack swore.

There were extenuating circumstances, but James ben Kole did not know that. Mack had been on a mission, taken under direct orders. He hadn't been lounging on a beach somewhere while Peter was being tortured. Besides, discovering Prince Josiah alive outweighed just about everything in terms of big picture importance, but he would be damned if James' words did not gall him.

As for Lavinia, he had no real excuse other than he was a man and had been thinking with his cock instead of his head. But for the love of all that was holy, he doubted even Saint James would have behaved any different. She had come to him like a vision, dressed in that red silk dress, as beautiful as any woman he had ever seen. Lavinia demanded that he love her, and he had. But he had taken her virginity, taken a virgin to his bed, and never once considered they might have created a child. She left while he was still sleeping, and in the weeks and months afterward, their night of passion felt like a dream.

He held onto that dream and promised himself that one day soon he would come and find her, that they would finally be together. But he had made a promise, and in the grand scope his happiness paled against the importance of keeping Peter ben Korah alive. It was his duty.

And it was not as if the circumstances at the Palace were getting better, if anything, they deteriorated by the week. Korah's madness was escalating, not to mention the dark spirit menacing the shadows. It stalked Peter with ominous regularity, and Mack knew if he left, nothing stood between it and the Prince.

There were not many in the Millennium equipped to deal with such a character, but Mack ben Robert was one. He supposed it was his upbringing, or more accurately the teachings of the fire and brimstone preacher from his youth. Pastor Ezekiel ben Malachi was a Jew, and as such, incorruptible, not that he was sinless, because he was human, but Jews were sealed, their hearts supernaturally claimed by the Iron King. He was one of a few thousand Evangelical Jews who left the Golden Kingdom, and for whatever reason, he and his family settled in Mack's small county in southern Virginia. Mack grew up under his teachings. The man knew his Bible, all of it.

It was not until Mack's late teens, when he joined the army and left the region, that he realized the rest of the world did not do church the way they did back home. He experienced quite a culture shock the first time he attended services in the New City. The well-dressed pastor gave a sermon, not out of Scripture, but a psychology book. The congregation sang songs that sounded pretty, but had no heart, and they steadfastly avoided any mention of the Iron King.

Right before the Civil War broke out, Mack got shot during a terrorist raid. After rehab, he left the military and went home. He would have stayed if Sir Preston ben Worley had not come calling with his damn mission and his photograph.

Riding back to Peccioli, that chilly night in February, he thought it would serve him well to pack up Lavinia and his son and head back to Virginia, or maybe the Golden City with the rest of his kin. Just go and be done with these godless California lunatics, their fallen angels, and crazy ass King… he was finished. The Lord gave him a new life, a beautiful woman, and a baby son. He was done. Hang 'em all.

Pretty in Pink or Rose or Whatever

Lavinia heard Mack come in the back door. She was straightening the bedroom because he scattered his clothes everywhere. She was making room in her closet when he came in, bringing the smell of horses and brisk chill. His color was high, his eyes smoldering. His body might be cold, but his passion was not. He did not say a word, just came around the bed and walked her toward the wall, pressing against her.

She felt his erection through the rough denim of his jeans. "I take it the Prince is alive?"

He thrust his hips against hers, hard. "Yep, and I'm done."

"You are?" she asked, tossing his discarded shirt onto the chair in the corner.

Mack kissed her, as if sealing a vow. "This," he said hoarsely, "is life. You… are life. My life."

"Oh," she panted as he cupped her breast, grown heavy and full with desire.

Mack nodded, holding her gaze and brushing his thumb over her nipple. A moist droplet touched his skin, and he shuddered. "I need you," he breathed into her neck.

"Then you shall have me."

Mack lifted her peasant shirt over her head and slid her long gypsy skirt to the floor. He stepped back, admiring her with male appreciation. She wore pretty lingerie for him tonight. Her engorged breasts spilled over the demi-cup, which was definitely not a nursing bra. He ran his thumb under the lace of the matching thong panty with tantalizing slowness. "Valentine, you are so beautiful."

She stepped out of her puddled skirt and began working the tiny silver buttons of his shirt. His mood was unfathomable, complicated, but then he always seemed that way to her. Lavinia liked puzzles, and Mack was the most delicious puzzle of all.

The first step in solving a puzzle was to examine all the pieces. She ran her hands over his strong chest, reveling in the flex of muscle, the coarse feel of the brown and blond hair that covered his nipples. She tasted them, the way he tasted hers. Touching his scarred right shoulder, she ran her fingers over the old wound and kissed the jagged edges of his warriors' flesh.

He cupped her buttocks and lifted her. The heavy belt buckle pressed into her belly, cold and hard. The skin below his ear tasted of salt and February night. Lavinia fumbled with the buckle, the soft leather belt, pliable with age, came loose with ease. With delicious slowness, she worked the buttons of his fly, stroking the length of his desire as she did it. He groaned and pressed into her hand. She smiled at his pleasure and her power. Lavinia bit him softly when she discovered he wore nothing underneath his jeans.

He sat down on the edge of the bed and pulled off his boots and socks in two efficient movements, the jeans gone the moment he rose. "That's enough of the striptease, Valentine." There was humor dancing in his brown eyes. He unsnapped her bra and threw it to the side, then fell with her onto the bed.

That afternoon, Mack watched with erotic paternal pleasure as she nursed their son, and tonight he planned to discover exactly what that was all about. He traced his tongue around the tip of her rosy nipple and was rewarded with another moist drop, which he licked away, groaning at the apricot sweetness of it. Taking her fully into his mouth, he pulled deeply. She arched and groaned as her milk let down, and he tasted her. He closed his eyes and found the wetness between her thighs, pushed the thin scrap of silk aside, and came into her hard, sucking and pumping with an earthy rhythm. Taking and giving, feeling her climax, her convulsions milking him as he milked her, until nothing existed except the two of them, mother and father, husband and wife, man and woman—one.

February 25, 997 ME

Two Monkeys

It had been nineteen years since Mack lived and worked on a farm, a vineyard, he mentally corrected himself, yet it was like he never left. Love of the soil was bred in his bones, and after the hyper-alertness of guarding the Prince, and the intrigues of the Palace, the earth drew him like iron to a magnet.

He knew nothing about tending vines and even less about making wine, but there was time enough to learn. What did not change, no matter the crop, the region, or the season, was that equipment broke down, often at the most inopportune time. He loved tractors, and Lavinia's required a major overhaul. He determined to accomplish that before they needed the behemoth in season. These were lessons handed down from his father. They spent the winter months repairing and replacing equipment. Keep it going during the season, fix it in the off.

He dismantled the tractor, spreading the pieces over the barn floor on a sheet, each part labeled and numbered with tags, which was another lesson he learned from his father.

Lavinia, with Richard on her hip, came inside. "That expression does not look promising."

Mack tossed the part aside with disgust. "Manifold is cracked. Whoever did the repair did a lousy job of it. That won't last the season. Is there a decent welder in town?"

She looked down at her feet. "I think he's the one that did the repair. We will probably need to take it to Weaverville."

Her tone brought him up short. "Why?" he asked slowly.

Lavinia shrugged and toed the part with her shoe. "It's a small town, Mack."

He let out a curse, to which his son promptly picked up.

"Damn!" Richard exclaimed, "Damn, damn, damn!"

His parents exchanged horrified looks before dissolving into laughter. "This is one precocious kid, which I expected with you as his mother." Mack pulled off a glove and tousled his son's brown curls. "Apparently, I am going to have to clean up my language," he leaned in for a kiss, "and marry your mother post-haste so she can take off that Scarlet Letter she has branded to her chest."

His knowledge of the ancient classic delighted Lavinia. "Just call me Hester Prynne."

He rolled his eyes. "No, I prefer Valentine, or at the very least Mrs. Mack ben Robert, but I will abide by your wishes and wait for your mother to return from San Diego so we can have a proper wedding. Though, I am none too certain about living with my mother-in-law."

"About that…" Lavinia's eyes danced with a secret, "I called her."

Richard squirmed, trying to get down, intrigued by the tractor parts. Mack took the boy, and Lavinia stretched her back in relief.

"And?" Mack prompted.

"She and Pappa have always loved San Diego. With you here now, he's decided to retire. They are shopping for a house."

Mack raised his eyes to Heaven. "Thank you!"

Lavinia giggled. "She's not that bad."

"Your mother is lovely, just like you." His expression became pained. "But I did not want to live with her."

"You just like running around the house naked," Lavinia teased.

Mack laughed. "We are the naked family; your mother would have squashed that."

Indeed, over the course of the last ten days it seemed somebody was always naked. Richard had developed a terrible diaper rash and thus required naked time for it to heal. Mack thought it great fun to join his son in said nakedness, and together they romped around the house like two baboons.

Lavinia also discovered that Mack had no concept that once the clothes were removed, they should be folded or hung up or, at the very least, put in the laundry. She spent her day cleaning up after her two naked monkeys and loved every minute.

When Real Life Comes to Call

From the moment Mack knocked on her door, Lavinia felt as if they were hiding from real life, existing in a temporary bubble that might burst at any moment, like their the future was nothing more than iridescent dream too beautiful to last. That real life should arrive in the form of a handsome Prince was just too ironic for words, especially when he rode in on a white horse, a gleaming sword buckled around his hips, sunlight refracting off his golden hair. Lavinia wanted to run him off with a shotgun.

He used the woods behind the house, obviously avoiding the main roads to keep a low profile since most of the small town knew he spent time at Pepperwood periodically. He knocked on the backdoor, and with the practiced ease of a savvy restaurant owner she welcomed her uninvited guest into the kitchen. She grimaced when she noticed breakfast dishes piled in the sink, three pages of calculations spread across the kitchen table, and a load of towels half folded on the sofa. Richard, thankfully fully clothed, sat amongst a sea of toys, chewing on an assortment of multi-colored rings. The house looked like a tornado hit it.

With unfailing politeness, the Prince appeared unfazed by the mess. "Miss ben Anthony, it is lovely to see you again. I have come to pay a call on Agent ben Robert. Can you please tell me where I might find him?"

Lavinia masked her shock at his appearance. He was pale, his cheeks gaunt, and he moved with an unnatural stiffness. His hair needed to be cut, and he was so thin he bordered on emaciation, a marked difference from the last time she saw him.

Mack had not been forthcoming about what occurred, but she deduced the Prince survived a terrible ordeal. Despite his resolve to leave, she knew Mack still felt personally responsible for Peter's safety. He devoted seven years to the Royal Guard, and the last five he gave up their lives together. He missed her pregnancy, the birth of their child, and the first two hundred and sixty-three days of his son's life. They sacrificed their happiness on the altar of Alanthian governmental affairs and Palace politics. But it would be foolhardy to believe it was over. Eventually Mack's sense of duty would draw him back to the Palace and this young man. Lavinia determined she would either put an end to it or enter the fray. The time had come to stand at Mack's side and stop hiding.

"I am sorry, my Esteemed, he has gone out. But if you would care to sit, perhaps you and I might have a discussion." Lavinia's calm words did not reveal the pounding of her heart as a plan formulated.

"I would be honored, Miss Lavinia. But first, may I beg an introduction to that fine young man in the living room?"

"Of course." On firmer ground, she hefted her son up on her hip and brought him to the Prince. "May I present Richard ben Mack of Peccioli?"

Prince Peter took the baby's hand and shook it lightly. "Ben Mack?"

Lavinia nodded. "Ben Mack."

"I see." Peter bowed. "It is a pleasure, Master Richard."

Richard squirmed. Fully engaged with his blocks, he wanted to return. His mother obliged. "May I offer you an espresso, my Esteemed?"

"That would be appreciated, thank you." He sighed. "I am a bit fatigued from the ride. Do you mind?" He put a hand to his sword belt.

"By all means, just lean it in the corner." She motioned her head into the living room. "There is a shotgun over the mantel, but I am not expecting trouble. Are you?"

Peter gave her an enigmatic smile. "Ask Mack how many assassination attempts he has foiled over the years. Henceforth, I will be armed, even in the Palace."

Lavinia scooped the fine espresso grounds from the canister and asked, "So, you will return?"

Peter stretched his neck, moving it side to side. When he turned, his emerald eyes blazed with dead certainty, "Oh, yes."

Lavinia met his intense gaze, her fingers drumming against her thigh. "You will do so without my fiancé, but I will give you another weapon, one more powerful and infinitely more dangerous."

Prince d'Or folded his arms across his chest, considering her. "Now that sounds intriguing. Please, tell me what you have in mind."

"Take a seat, my Esteemed."

By the end of their meeting, Lavinia ben Anthony rusticated on the sidelines no longer. She became the first official member of The Resistance.

The Espresso Epiphany

Mack returned from Weaverville at dinner hour. He pulled up the driveway, looking forward to a nice supper, bath time with his son, and bedtime with his woman. He was none too pleased to find the Prince jacked up on espresso, sitting at his kitchen table in front of what looked suspiciously like the remnants of the steak he had been dreaming about. To his further irritation, Peter and Lavinia seemed to have become best friends while he was out, and his son kept calling the Prince dah-dah.

Apparently, they conceived some cockamamie scheme whereby Lavinia would provide her extraordinary math skills and computer expertise to single handedly bring down Korah's government, while orchestrating a brilliant escape for Peter, and installing his long-dead cousin on the throne. This would absolve Lavinia of whatever guilt she carried for not going to jail, get vengeance for Kayah, and extricate Mack from the threat Korah posed for his role in helping the Prince escape.

"How much damn espresso have y'all drunk?" Mack declared with open mouthed astonishment.

Peter shook his head back and forth in agitation. "No, I am serious, Mack, your fiancée is absolutely brilliant!"

Lavinia was wild eyed. "No! It's not me. He is amazing! Have you ever watched his mind work? Mack, you never told me how smart he was, and he is devious too! I love him." She threw her arms around Peter and kissed his cheek. "No wonder you would not leave him."

Peter threw up his hands in helpless innocence at the thunderous expression on Mack's face. "And she knows all these people. They hate Korah, too. The shit he is pulling in the tech world is unbelievable. I did not understand the half of it." His pupils were huge with caffeine. "We are going to take him down without a shot!"

"And what exactly am I supposed to be doing while the two of you are taking down the second most powerful government on the planet?" Mack asked.

"Bloody Hell, Mack! You must protect her brain! It is one of the greatest weapons ever created. They must never get their hands on her. She is in danger. How have you never seen that?"

"I suppose I have been focused on the danger that always seems to surround you." He refrained from adding, you little shithead.

Peter agreed in earnest and kicked back another shot of espresso. "That is a good point, Mack. You are a good man. I would probably be dead without you. No, I know I would be dead without you. Thank you."

Lavinia glowed with pride. "You are a good man, Mack. I love you."

Peter grinned, hugging Lavinia around the waist. "She really is amazing. She has two computers here. Did you know that? She is going to send one over to Pepperwood, so we can get started on this right away."

Lavinia nodded, bouncing on her toes.

Peter ran his hands through his long hair and said, "I have decided I will not bring in Persa and James, though. They do not need to know about this. Just a few of us." Agitated, Peter put his hands on each of their shoulders, looking between them. "Right now, it is just us three, but we will figure it out!"

Mack felt like a pinball stuck between two bumpers. He reckoned they would sleep sometime next week. "No more espresso. Both of you, drink some water, start flushing that shit out of your system."

Richard pulled up on Mack's pant leg. "Shit," he declared.

Peter and Lavinia howled, Mack scowled, and Richard yelled it again.

Mack picked him up. He smelled terrible. "I'd say that's what you've got in your pants, young man."

Peter and Lavinia collapsed into each other in paroxysms of laughter.

Mack sighed. "I'm going to give my son a bath. I'd like some dinner." He looked pointedly at Lavinia, then at Peter. "Go home. We'll talk about this again tomorrow, or the day after. when you are sober!"

Mack stopped at the entrance to the hallway, his voice serious. "I am glad to see you doing better, my Esteemed. That was a hell of a scare. We'll sort all this out." In the meantime, he figured the horse could ride Peter back to Pepperwood.

April 11, 997 ME

Before Everybody Gets Here

A month later, Mack drove the vineyard's old truck down to the New City to recover his belongings. The apartment lease ran through the rest of the year, so he was in no hurry to clean… he had to clean. The place was a disaster, which was one reason he insisted he go alone. He feared they would arrest him the moment he stepped foot in his apartment, so he snuck in under cover of darkness. Until Peter finished his negotiations and was back at the Palace, Mack remained in danger. Yet there were a few things he needed, a few irreplaceable items, and he was getting them.

The night before their wedding guests arrived, he unpacked one of the irreplaceable items. He had a wedding present for Lavinia, that he needed to give her in private. It was dusk, and streams of sunlight filtered through their small bedroom's curtains. Lavinia lay on her side, nursing the baby, whose hair was still damp from his bath, his little pajama clad feet kicking sporadically with tiredness and delight at the comfort of his mother's breast. Mack picked up his enormous pile of clothes draped over the chair and laid them on the floor beside him. Then he pulled out his father's beat up acoustic guitar and tuned it.

Lavinia smiled through lidded eyes. "Are you going to play me a song, Mack? Show me the magic again?"

He wiped his mouth and cleared his throat. "You know the only place I ever played or sang was in church, right?"

She nodded.

"Well, when I was on my way to Weaverville a few weeks ago, I heard this song on that pirate radio station. They are pulling these things off the old internet, and most of them are crap. But this one… well, it sort of spoke to me." He strummed the guitar.

"I called Himari and asked her to send it to me. Who knows how she finds this stuff, but she did. I've been practicing, and I wanted to give it to you before everyone gets here."

Suddenly shy, he said, "Sometimes I can't say everything that's in my heart, Valentine. We men aren't good at that, but I thought perhaps I could play it for you and maybe you could feel it."

"I think I feel it already," she whispered.

Mack brushed his brown hair out of his eyes, took a deep breath and said, "Okay, here goes."

As he sang "Living Proof" he made it personal, telling her how much he loved being with her, being a family, how this place was their refuge. He watched her eyes as he sang. She wore her lost in the labyrinth look, and he experienced a pang of disappointment. He knew it had been a risky experiment and now felt a bit foolish.

When she spoke, he realized that for the first time, that wistful look had actually been for him. "Himari got love paintings." She settled the sleeping baby and came to him. "I got love music, and I heard it, and I felt it, thank you." Tears rolled down her cheeks. "And it was a math song."

Mack looked at her bewildered.

She laughed. "About proofs."

Then he realized the Lord had given him the perfect song for his lovely bride, because it never once occurred to him it was a math song.

Part 7 - Intrigue

August 19, 995 ME (Ten Years into Rebellion)

Loyalties of the Valet - New City, Alanthia

After dancing the night away with Prince d'Or, it did not surprise Kayah to find Jarrod ben Adriel waiting beside her car. He was a small man of indeterminate years who never seemed to age. She had known him nine years, since her first day in Sir Preston's household. During her time there, he was neither kind nor unkind. He was what he was, a dignified and unflappable valet, and Sir Preston's spy, or so she thought.

"Miss Kayah," he began, "it rather surprised me to see you today." He let the sentence hang.

She raised a brow at him but did not answer; she barely answered to Sir Preston these days.

When she did not make excuses or offer an explanation, he cleared his throat and continued, "I would venture our mutual friend will be displeased by your conduct this evening, if he learns of it."

"Doubtless." Kayah pulled out a mirror and checked her lipstick.

"I have a proposal for you, Miss Kayah," Jarrod said smoothly.

Kayah raised a fine brow at him. "Do tell."

While his manner remained formal, the sheen on his forehead betrayed his discomfort. "I will stay silent about your little interlude."

The corner of her mouth lifted. "In exchange for what?"

"At some point in the future, the Prince may require someone with your particular talents." He folded his gloved hands neatly.

"The Prince?" Kayah sat back and considered him in a new light.

"Indeed, a valet serves the man. That is where his true loyalty lies."

Kayah crossed her arms. "Seems a lopsided bargain. Our mutual friend might be displeased with me for dancing with Peter tonight, but there will be no real ramifications."

"Perhaps," Jarrod agreed. "Yet, I suspect there is no harm in cultivating further alliances, say one in the Palace, the heir to the throne. That would not be amiss, and you would, of course, be well compensated."

Kayah regarded him shrewdly. His argument had merit, and she liked the little Prince, even more after spending the evening with him. The man sitting beside her, with his damp brow and fussy manners, was no puppet master, yet she did not underestimate the power he wielded. Sir Preston was getting older, and she was not technically crossing him if she agreed to Jarrod's little side deal, which had the bonus of sparing her a tiresome lecture.

Kayah extended her hand, a small card in it. "Your servant, sir."

May 14, 997 ME (Twelve Years into Rebellion)

Machinations of a Puppet Master - Montreal

Looking into the bathroom mirror in her luxurious hotel suite in Montreal, Kayah applied the final touch to her makeup, strawberry-kiss lip gloss. Not that she was planning on kissing her visitor, but she knew what men liked. They imagined what she might do with her shimmering lips if they played their cards right. Those lips teased and pouted, promised. She could bring a man to his knees simply by drinking from a straw. It was a talent.

Kayah tilted her head, studying the thin cat's eye she'd drawn at her lash line, and decided she was sufficiently caked, powdered, and painted. The reflected image sporting the strawberry-kiss lip gloss did not actually look like Kayah, whoever that was.

The woman in the mirror went from disguise to disguise, creating back stories and invented histories, flashing fake IDs. It was part of the job. Her current persona, Sissy ben Harold, was a makeup artist, in town for Fashion Week, when every stick thin model in four Kingdoms descended on Montreal like they were giving away calorie-free cake. Kayah liked the event because she liked beautiful clothes, but here, she could eschew her more elaborate disguises and blend. A beautiful woman at Fashion Week raised no eyebrows, drew no notice.

The persona served her well. No one questioned why a makeup artist traveled with her tools, nor were airport security guards inclined to poke around her case. If they had, they might have discovered a hidden compartment stocked with latex, cotton wadding, colored contact lenses, and molds for creating facial prosthetics, but they never did. She played her role well.

Roaming her hotel suite, she checked her watch, enough time for a cigarette. She stepped onto the balcony and heard the music. By day, lesser-known designers tried to make their mark in the large tents lined with folding chairs. By night, the tents transformed into bass pumping clubs for the rich, famous, and wannabes. They shook their butts and drank too much maple whiskey. She leaned over the balcony, hoping that she would not see her visitor down there. She needed him sober.

Scanning the parking lot, she watched a swarm of roadies setting up the open-air stage for one of Alanthia's hottest bands, The Ragamuffins. After her meeting, she might go down to watch. Then again, she probably wouldn't. She'd picked up the lead singer three years ago; he wasn't that great.

Beyond the resort's manicured grounds, the St. Lawrence River reflected Montreal's lights, watercolor hues of yellow, purple, and blue wavered on a canvas of black, beautiful. The city bustled with excitement, but for Kayah, it was just another city, just another hotel.

Taking a deep drag, she recognized the feeling pressing in on her. She was maudlin, but worse, she was bored. Everything bored her, which is why she was in Montreal, off mission, gone rogue. She did that periodically. It kept Sir Preston on his toes, and he needed a little shaking up.

Her last three assignments had been so mundane she could have pulled them off before she went to prison. Exhaling gray smoke, it blew away in the cool Canadian wind, symbolic of what her life had become. She was no longer challenged, which was dangerous, and not in an amusing way. It led to sloppiness, and that led to prison. So, she redoubled her vigilance, took extra precautions, which kept her out of an interrogation room but made the work unbearably dull. If she did not fear ending up in a turquoise jumpsuit again, she might have done something rash, just for the challenge. But that was her crazy side talking, and she kept that bitch under wraps.

Or did she?

Next door, Prince Peter ben Korah was in residence. Fresh off his rehab stint at the Pepperwood Ranch and ready to roll, he had been partying his ass off all week and appeared to be making up for lost time. Appeared, being the operative word. He was sober. He had pulled himself out of a dark hole and emerged with a plan. And that was the reason she was here.

She felt a little shitty about bugging Lavinia's house, but it was necessary. Lavinia was too important for Kayah to leave her unprotected. Three years ago, Sir Preston cast his scheming eyes toward Peccioli, and Kayah intervened. She thwarted any effort the old man made to draw Lavinia into his web. Lavinia did not know her new dishwasher, cellar master, and assistant vineyard manager were highly trained bodyguards. They were also Kayah spies. Sir Preston had his reasons for putting Lavinia and Mack together in '95. Kayah had hers. She knew Mack ben Robert played in Sir Preston's sandbox, the same as she. But Mack seemed like a good man, and Lavinia loved him, which was why Kayah agreed to get them together. When Mack showed up again, Kayah needed to know what drove him there, other than hormones. Kayah had to admit, her recent string of strapping southern lovers was inspired.

But the information she gathered the day Prince Peter came calling was earth shattering. Amidst a thousand shots of espresso the story emerged, Prince Josiah was alive. That little nugget was worth billions. Peter's plans to overthrow Korah, escape, and install his cousin were worth tens of billions. Though she would have felt rotten about exposing that, she liked the little puppy.

It was Lavinia's loyalty that sent her here tonight. She laughed when she heard Mack warning Lavinia away from her. He should. She was dangerous. Kayah held no illusions about who or what she was, a thief, a spy, an assassin. But it had become a job, one she was damn good at, but rather bored with.

The Resistance seemed to Kayah like a cause, and that intrigued her. Kayah heard the passion in Lavinia's voice and was disturbed by her misguided notion that she owed it to them to get involved. It niggled Kayah for months, but she could not talk to Lavinia about it without exposing the fact that she spied on her best friend. So, she pondered how she might play a role and keep them all out of turquoise jumpsuits, or worse, the gallows.

With Lavinia involved, Himari would be more apt to join. Kayah would not throw her lot in with a group of revolutionaries trying to topple the government and by extension, that little pissant Stephen ben McSwilley, without Himari covering her back.

As for Himari's protegee', Alaina ben Thomas actually impressed her. The leggy blonde had talent. If she joined The Resistance, Alaina would be a powerful asset. No one suspected a fashion model had a brain, much less that she was an accomplished programmer and hacker. Her travel schedule gave her a perfect cover, and if anyone spotted her with Prince d'Or, it would not arouse suspicion. He liked models. And unlike the rest of them, Alaina was anonymous in the tech world. Kayah was not about to expose herself by recruiting the Amazon, but Peter, fresh off his little vacation at the hands of his father's goons, was just reckless enough to do it. Between Alaina and Lavinia, Himari was a sure bet.

A knock sounded, and she glanced at her watch. She would hand it to Jarrod ben Adriel. He always ensured the Prince stayed on schedule.

March 28, 999 ME (Fourteen Years into Rebellion)

Fat and Happy - New City, Alanthia

Stephen ben McSwilley privately thought he had the greatest job on the planet. As Minister for Technology and Security, he supervised a budget that matched the GDP of three of the ten Millennial Kingdoms combined. He had a full-time assistant, a personal chef, and ruled a vast empire of computer geniuses. He did it all from a comfortable leather chair in a corner office on the tenth floor of the New City Technical Building. Not bad for a boy who grew up below stairs.

His employees adored him, his peers respected him, and Stephen woke every morning exuberant about the day to come. His team shattered barriers even techies of the Last Age failed to accomplish. Commendations from King Korah discreetly decorated his office bookshelves, and pictures of Stephen with dignitaries hung on the walls.

Life was good.

It was so good, in fact, that he regularly took time to pamper himself. Once a month, Stephen spent the day at a spa, though he kept that secret.

It began with a haircut.

"Are you sure, Stephen?" Zianna, his hairdresser, asked again. "If I take it up her on the sides and trim the top, it will be quite flattering."

Stephen shook his head. "No, cut it like you always do."

She sighed and got to work. Stephen closed his eyes and relaxed. He knew what he was doing. His unruly hair always looked like it needed cut, no matter how often he had it trimmed. It became part of his signature look, and somewhere in his twenties, he embraced it. Now that he was successful, it irked Zianna that he maintained his disheveled computer genius facade.

The manicure came next, "Cut them square, not too long." His fingers were often the focus of his work, so he paid particular attention to them, keeping his nails neat and trimmed.

He enjoyed the pedicure, but it was also a medical necessity. He stifled a grunt of pain when the technician dug under his big toe.

"It was starting to in grow." She smiled up at him apologetically.

"Yeah, they do that." He clenched his jaw as she kept digging, struggling not to pull his foot away.

After a gourmet lunch, he enjoyed an invigorating shave and a full facial. Some genetic anomaly made him incapable of growing a beard, much to his consternation because it would have disguised his prominent chin.

The day ended with his favorite, a hot stone massage. He always imagined he was royal during those sessions, casting the masseuse as his valet, the spa attendants his staff. He insisted on the best massage room, the one with the indoor fountain and heated table. Dim light and soft music relaxed his mind into a state of semi-consciousness, as essential oil misters filled the air with rosemary and lavender. He exhaled and relaxed, anticipating an hour and a half of sheer bliss as the masseuse entered.

If he would have turned his head, he would have known he was in for an hour and a half of something else, because Kayah ben Samuel stepped through the door.

May 27, 999 ME

Wolves - Bologna, Italy

They were going to get caught if they did not stop breaking character in public. Kayah wanted to smack them, to tell them to stop. She wanted to slap herself for being sentimental enough to still be following them after they left their tree by the fountain. Ridiculous girls, did they think just because they addressed others in gruff boys' speech that someone might not hear how they whispered to each other? She should just leave, yet they pulled at her.

The Mossad agent still tailed them, but he was no obstacle. For a quarter hour, she watched them. Nobody else turned up, no Greek or Egyptian, but they were running. They shimmered with that energy, sending signals into the ether. Her antennae picked it up, a familiar wavelength. Kayah lived it; she owned it.

"Do it!" the brunette urged.

The redhead looked around, saw no one was watching, or so she thought, and splayed her lips in a ridiculously comical expression. The brunette covered her hilarity with her hand and looked away, her shoulders vibrating with silent mirth.

A long-ago memory fluttered across Kayah's mind, Himari, Lavinia, and herself standing outside a classroom at Euler. 'Do it, Himari!' her old voice whispered in the breeze, and she saw the three of them cracking up at Himari's silly imitation of her mother.

Watching the two runners, Kayah finally understood the draw. Friends, up to no good, in trouble, and laughing despite it. These babes had wolves stalking them. Kayah knew wolves. They hunted in packs, surrounded, and devoured their prey. These little lambs were doomed.

Tourist Trap

It was the most reckless thing she had done in fifteen years. Kayah chalked it up to ennui. Much later, she determined she had simply and totally underestimated Mossad Agent Reuben ben Judah.

Kayah strolled up to the girls, holding a brochure map in her hand. She pointed to it and in a New City accent asked, "Do you boys know which way to the Two Towers?" When they leaned in, Kayah hissed, "Do not turn. Do not react. There is a Mossad agent behind the espresso cart. Quit breaking cover."

The brunette took the map, studying it. In an accent that would have done credit to a native Bolognian, she said, "*Signora,* only five minutes to walk. Straight down this road and to the left."

The redhead looked like she was about to knife Kayah, which charmed her. Maybe they were not so defenseless after all.

Kayah gave them both a sly smile and said, "Thank you. You *boys* enjoy your afternoon."

Scent of a Woman

Instinct prompted Agent Reuben ben Judah to follow the tourist with the big flowered purse. Something about the way she moved did not ring true. She dressed like a middle aged Alanthian tourist, but for a scant second, he caught a feline prowl beneath her stiff gait. He might have imagined it, but Reuben imagined very little these days.

The three other agents protecting Davianna and Astrid took up surveillance, and Reuben broke off to follow the tourist. They were guarding the girls, protecting them from the nefarious characters chasing them. The duo did relatively well on their own, even slipped through their fingers several times, but Mossad was the world's elite intelligence force, empowered by the Iron King; and two young girls were no match for them.

Over the last two years, Agent Reuben ben Judah had become one of their best. Few knew it. To the world and his former Army buddies, he was the same ole Reuben, affable, unassuming, and ordinary. But that man was dead, at least figuratively. Resurrected in his place was a roaring lion who just caught the scent of a female, one of his own species.

Five hours later, Reuben realized who he was following. What the hell was Kayah ben Samuel doing in Bologna? Furthermore, why had she spoken to Davianna ben David and Astrid ben Agnor? The hair on the back of his neck stood on end when he realized how close a world-renowned assassin got to those girls. Odds were that no one contracted her to kill them, otherwise she would not have approached them, or they would be dead.

He knew her by reputation. Mossad compiled a dossier on her three inches thick. They left her alone because she took out nasty characters and did not interfere with them. Reuben even knew about her interesting side activities, high value tech items and artifacts. She possessed a weakness for old tech. Even rusted and broken beyond repair, items from the Last Age drew her. Nobody could figure out why or what she did with them, but she bought or pilfered them regularly. It was of no consequence to Mossad, so they ignored it.

Tonight, she went prowling at two of the local clubs. She intrigued him. It was the feline way she moved, fluid and graceful, a lioness, in a slinky black dress. She disappeared in the shadows, seen when she wanted to be, invisible when she wished. He knew the moment she detected him, by the subtle shift of her eyes, the slight turn of her head. The lioness caught the scent of the lion, and at 11:30 pm, she led him back to her den.

The meeting did not go as planned, then again, lions are not tame.

Two Lions

He considered breaking in. There were a dozen ways to get inside her hotel room, all of which she would be prepared for. So, he chose the least likely. He knocked.

"Good evening, Agent," she said, and the twitch at the corner of her gorgeous mouth told him his audacity amused her.

"Kayah," he replied, his weight balanced on his heels, prepared to avoid a slashing blow.

"Pleasant evening for a stroll, wouldn't you say?" she cooed, sliding her hand up the door jamb and resting her head on her elbow.

He raised a straight black brow and said, "Quite, I enjoyed the fountain."

The tiny tip of her tongue licked her full bottom lip, and she smiled. "A mere diversion."

"Somehow I doubt that."

Kayah shrugged and let him in. He was the sort of man she avoided. His black eyes bore into hers, seeing too much. Yet, like today with those girls, it was a draw, a recognition—one of her kind. She brought him here. Now she had to figure out what to do with him. "May I offer you a drink?"

He stepped toward her, purposely invading her space. He was not drinking anything she gave him. "I did not come for a drink."

Unexpected heat passed between them.

She lifted her chin, her lips slightly parted. "What did you come for?"

He took another step closer, more heat.

"What are you doing in Bologna, Kayah?" he whispered like a lover, his deep Israeli voice carrying the cadence of the Golden Kingdom.

"I'm on vacation." Tension pulsed between them, reeking of danger. It was intriguing. She was turned on.

So was he. His chest rumbled with a deep chuckle. "I did not know your kind took vacation."

"Oh, I do all sorts of things." She traced her nail along his jawline, teasing. He cut a nice figure. She admired the slope of his neck, solid and thick at the base. A soldier's body lay beneath his black silk shirt.

Reuben looked down his strong nose. "I am quite aware of all the things you do."

This was intriguing. Mossad normally left her alone. They had a tacit agreement, and he was breaking protocol. Kayah recognized a rogue. "What do you really want, Agent? I don't feel like killing you, and I don't fuck Israelis." Kayah let him back her into the wall. His body pressed into hers, hard and hot. "Golden Kingdom, holier than thou, assholes."

He sneered in response to her insults and tried to stay on task, though his cock had other ideas. "I want to know what you are doing here, what your business was with those two girls." To emphasize his next point, he ground his hips into hers. "And I don't fuck Alanthian whores, because you hate my people and lead the world astray with rebellion and greed."

Kayah raised a mocking eyebrow. "As I said, I'm on vacation, and I have no idea what girls you are talking about." She felt his erection and rolled her hips into his, reveling in the friction, eliciting a masculine grunt of desire. "It's a damn good thing were not going to fuck, then isn't it, Agent?"

"It is a damn good thing." He cupped her between her legs.

Kayah let out an involuntary sound, then met his eyes and rocked against his hand, taking her pleasure. She taunted him with a feline purr, "I don't need to fuck." To prove her point, she held his hand and moved hard and steady, hazel eyes watching him as she did it.

He felt her orgasm begin. "You want my cock, don't you, Kayah?"

She leaned her head against the wall and gave a small laugh, climaxing. "I don't need it."

He lifted her dress and slid his fingers into her. "I did not ask you what you needed. I asked you what you wanted, and you want me inside you, don't you?"

"I don't want anything from you." Kayah arched her back and took his finger deeper.

His chuckle was devious. "Liar." He unzipped his trousers and opened her thighs with his knees.

"I thought we weren't going to fuck, Agent."

"I think we are, Kayah." He breathed in deeply, reveling in the scent of a lioness in heat.

"You are a wicked man." The lioness bit his neck.

The lion took his pleasure, saying, "I don't think you want any other kind."

With a throaty laugh, she declared, "I don't even know your name."

What's in a Name?

He left without telling her. If he had, he would have gone in the dung heap with all her other lovers. She literally forgot them because she only slept with them once. She had an uncomfortable encounter several years back, after taking a man to her bed and finding out afterward that he had been there before. With a quirk of her eyebrow, she said, "Well you obviously still have it, but you need to go now." He seemed hurt by that, so she took particular notice of him, to avoid a third time. One and done, Mr. Hurt Face had been an accident.

Watching the door close behind the Mossad agent, she was certain others left her bed without giving their name, probably the married ones. Some were sad and thought if they shared their names, they might become something more than what they were, a cock. Others wanted to throw down with her again, because to their minds, Kayah was the perfect woman: a hot, no strings attached, sex partner. They were as mistaken as the others.

That the agent, who had given her the best bang she'd had in a while, didn't leave his name, irked her. But she learned the two runners were important enough to warrant a visit, and that intrigued her. Stealing the source code and prototype for The Resistance this morning engaged her. As Kayah showered, with the memory of the agent's hands still on her body, she felt strange, then realized what it was. She was not bored.

Runners

"Why did that woman warn us today?" Davianna ben David asked as she peeked out the hotel curtains, scanning the ancient palazzo.

Astrid hissed through her teeth and said, "I've been thinking about her all day."

Davianna cut her a look and asked, "Is she another one? Tell me she's not."

"I don't think she was after us," Astrid said over her shoulder, then pressed her eye back to the peephole. "They have an energy around them when they are hunting, even the good ones, they can't help it. But she gave me the willies."

Davianna pulled the curtain tight and giggled, "We don't like her."

"No, we don't," Astrid agreed, a smile teasing the corner of her mouth.

For just a moment, they were the two girls from Camp Eiran, sharing a laugh, deciding who they would be friends with, and poking fun at everyone else.

"Yeah," Davianna agreed, her brown eyes wistful.

Astrid bit her thumbnail and nodded.

They continued checking the room, turning on the signal jamming device, bolting the doors and windows, and getting ready to grab a few precious hours of sleep.

"She was right, though." Astrid said, positioning her boots at her bedside. "We can't break character. She caught us, and we thought we were alone."

"You're right. We have to be more careful." Davianna absently checked her left pocket and pulled back the blankets.

Astrid stretched and yawned.

It had been a brutal day. They identified and lost three Mossad agents, and the damn Greek was in Bologna now, too. The hotel room was their second of the night.

Davianna rubbed her eyes and flopped on the bed. "She looked like a schoolteacher."

Astrid, the disguise expert, drifted off. "If that was a disguise, it was good. I need to learn how to do that."

May 28, 999 ME

Never a Dull Moment

Whilst he was engaged with Kayah ben Samuel, Davianna and Astrid gave his agents the slip, much to Reuben's fury. They had a tracker on the Black Key but were loath to use it unless absolutely necessary. So, his unit was simultaneously looking for the girls, keeping tabs on the Greek Captain, Orion ben Drachmas, monitoring the Alanthian assassin, Kayah ben Samuel, and the newest arrival to the party, Prince Josiah ben Eamonn.

Their primary mission was to guard Davianna and Astrid, but they had to do it in secret, and they were never to let Prince Josiah know they were there. Those orders came directly from the Iron King.

Josiah's arrival made Reuben's job almost impossible. They were friends, comrades in arms. It was one of the baffling things about this assignment. Reuben could not comprehend the logic of placing him in such proximity to the exiled Prince, who was himself on a mission to escort Davianna ben David back to the Golden City. Further complicating matters was the fact that Reuben owed Josiah an exceptionally large debt of honor. He was conflicted, but determined to do his duty, even if he felt guilty. When the time came, he would try to explain, though he expected to get an earful if not a punch in the nose.

The Prince's 'resurrection' was not widely known, but it stirred up a hornet's nest. No one was more outraged than King Korah, who went on a rampage and ordered half of Alanthia's spies to find Josiah. Reuben suspected Korah might be interested in Kayah ben Samuel, but Korah was no friend, and her activities were unmentioned in his mission report.

Overnight, Bologna became the center of two international manhunts, and Reuben had the dubious task of keeping them all from being captured and remaining invisible whilst he did it. He felt like he had been cast in a farcical play, where only the Iron King knew the ending.

Showering back at his hotel room, he figured tonight he played the role of male praying mantis who escaped his fate after mating with a female. He suspected she would not let him get away with that. But she was the hottest and craziest woman he ever met, and he had the scratch marks to prove it. The streaming water made that much apparent.

Standing naked in the mirror, he looked over his shoulder at four claw marks down his back. She had taken a piece of him, after all. He half expected to die in his sleep, poisoned by one of those scratches. Figuring it might be worth it, he smiled. He narrowed his eyes and looked back into the mirror. It snuck up on him, that smile. Gone for so long, it looked foreign. She was the least likely woman to bring it back, but she had.

Now for a Little Fun

The source code and prototype were on their way to Himari, mission complete. Free to do as she pleased, what pleased Kayah was finding out what exactly Mossad was up to with those girls. She was relatively certain the girls were Alanthians, though their whispered accents had been faint, and they might have been British. What was Mossad doing tracking two girls on the run? Why didn't they just take them in for questioning? That was a puzzle, and Kayah liked puzzles.

She was talented but not omniscient. Finding two fugitives in a city as large as Bologna was no simple feat, especially without a network backing her up. She did not call Sir Preston or The Resistance. The girls were a curiosity at the moment that warranted nothing other than poking around.

She decided on a plan. "If you can't find the prey, find the hunters. They will lead you right to the girls." The easiest people to track would be Mossad, and she knew how.

Kayah dressed for a run.

The boys in Mossad stayed physically fit. They had to, so they would eventually show up on the city running trails, and Kayah would be waiting. She might even get in a few miles. She thought she glimpsed a fat roll last night. Granted, she was bent over a chair at the time, and the position had been a little contorted, if not exceedingly gratifying, but a fat roll would never do.

The day was getting warm. If she was going to catch them, she needed to go now. It was awkward to exercise in disguise, so she did not bother. Besides, she did not have to hide. It was a testimony to her talent that she was not wanted anywhere. The authorities might suspect, could know in their guts she had pulled some caper, but the Iron King's laws remained. Mere suspicion was not enough, and Kayah did not leave evidence.

She checked her appearance. Gus would be pleased. She was blonde at the moment, the dark dye from the day before, stripped and gone. In a strange quirk of fate, being blonde was one of her best disguises. It was a wonder she had any hair, as often as she changed it. But it was genetic, she supposed, a gift from some unknown ancestor, great hair. She tied it up on the top of her head in a saucy ponytail and went out to hunt.

Reuben should not be following her again. But he was in charge, so he took the assignment he wanted. Currently, his assignment was on a run, her strong legs hitting the jogging trail with a measured and perfect cadence. Her very fine ass, barely covered in tiny black running shorts, teased a shapely cheek with each footfall. Sweat plastered her t-shirt to her body, and her blonde hair came loose, curling at her nape. In basic training, he observed that after PT some people looked like they had been swimming, others only glistened. Reuben glistened. Kayah swam. It was actually endearing, making her a bit more human, a small crack in her deadly Ice Princess facade.

Reuben followed her to a secluded part of the park. Leery of a trap, he hung in the shadows and watched.

The Ice Princess was well aware the agent watched her, so she decided to have a little fun.

It backfired on both of them. They struck a match last night, lighting a slow-burning fuse. Kayah threw gasoline on it. Neither was prepared for the explosion about to occur.

Kayah slowed her pace near a small fountain at the edge of a cluster of trees. The morning air grew hot, so she took off her sweat drenched shirt and laid it on the fountain's edge. She bent over, feeling her black silky shorts ride up, and stretched, her palms flat on the ground. With slow, deliberate control, she balanced and pressed into a handstand, revealing the muscles of her flat stomach. She held the pose for a count of four, then let her legs open to a mid-air split.

Reuben stood, transfixed.

Kayah had done this routine a thousand times in solitary confinement. It came as easily to her as breathing. But this was the first time she had ever used it as a weapon, and she wielded it with erotic and sensual power. Bending, twisting, posing with balance and control, she teased him with her body and felt the heat building between them.

Reuben charged out of the woods. She was ready for him, in more ways than one. He did not touch her, just stood with a predatory look in his dark eyes. "Shalom, Kayah," he purred.

She circled him, running her finger over his jaw line. "Good morning, Agent. Out for a run?"

"No, I'm working." He adopted a reserved tone, took control of his raging hormones, and the situation.

Kayah chuckled and made a show of dipping her shirt in the water, then pulling it over her head. The gray fabric molded to every curve, enticing because he knew what lay beneath, the vision of her bare midriff was burned on the back of his retinas.

She laced her fingers together and stretched luxuriously, arching her back and closing her eyes. "How tedious, I am enjoying my vacation."

He closed the distance between them but did not touch her as she expected, like she beckoned. Her little performance accomplished what she intended, but Reuben ben Judah knew exactly how to play Kayah ben Samuel.

"I see that, but don't expect an encore from last night. One and done, shiksa. No matter how much you might want me again." He clicked with his cheek and winked, then left her standing alone at the fountain, her mouth slightly agape.

Kayah watched Reuben walk away, again. And she still did not know his name.

Porni

Twins… it had taken nothing more but the sight of them to inspire an escape plan. A brother and a sister, a redhead and a brunette, two teenagers about the same size as Davianna and Astrid. It was Davianna's idea, but Astrid quickly took it up. By mid-afternoon, they were ready to pull their first big escape.

Flush with more money than the two Italian kids had ever seen, the decoys embarked on their diversion. It was a simple plan, draw their pursuers, create a ruckus, and keep everyone occupied while Davianna and Astrid faded into the shadows.

Kayah watched the whole thing go down with detached admiration.

The Greek took the bait, so did Mossad. The decoys emerged from the small hotel and surreptitiously wound their way through the open-air market. Ducking behind stalls and skirting shadows, they made a show of evading the men who came after them. Orien ben Drachmas ate up the ground, moving in.

Kayah saw the trap before the rest of them because her sense of police officers was incredibly honed. She detected the subtle shift in the air when they were around. She moved into position and watched it unfold. It was daring and audacious, exactly the sort of thing she would do. The Italian girl allowed herself to be seized, and the boy raised the alarm. Four police officers, right around the corner, surrounded Orien, who was summarily arrested for trying to abduct a young girl in broad daylight.

Kayah stifled a grin at the shocked expression on Orien's face when they handcuffed his meaty hands behind his back. As they were hauling him up the steps to jail, he sensed Kayah's amusement and sneered, "What are you looking at, *pórni*?"

A wave of nausea hit Kayah like a gut punch. *Pórni*, the Greek word for whore, and what Stubby whispered in her ear while he raped her. For a moment, standing on the steps of the Bologna *Stazione di Polizia*, she could not breathe.

She tumbled backward to that institutional gray cell with the water stain on the ceiling that looked like a dog. The gag cut into her mouth, spit pooling dangerously in the back of her throat, choking her. She could not move, could not fight. The straight jacket buckles jammed into her back as his weight pressed her into the thin cot. A wave of nausea swamped her, the stench of garlic and old sweat filled her nose. If she threw up, he would let her choke to death. She heard his harsh breathing and a strangled gasp that she realized snaked out of her own chest. Her vision wavered, terror, dread, and horrified realization about what was coming. He hit her in the temple, momentarily stunning her. While she was dazed, he pulled off her turquoise pants. She tried to kick, tried to fight him off, but Stubby knew his business and outweighed her by a hundred pounds. He pried her legs apart and fumbled with himself, probing her tight entrance. Without a care and with a violent thrust he invaded her body, burning, ripping, tearing. He rammed into her, taking her virginity, and his own pleasure. He made an inhuman sound when the barrier broke, evil. Then he looked down on her with lust crazed eyes and said, "You like it, *Pórni*."

Kayah wanted to scream, she wanted to howl. She wanted to kill.

When she opened her eyes, she glared at Orien ben Drachmas, silently vowing he was never going to get his hands on those two girls, because Kayah was going to slaughter him like a pig.

The Carrel

There was something in the way she moved. It was wrong. Reuben detected it from across the palazzo. Kayah faltered. In the hours he tracked her yesterday and today, no misstep or miscalculation marred her graceful carriage. Yet when she turned away from the Greek, she stumbled, then grew utterly still. She shuddered and closed her eyes. When she opened them, Reuben saw exactly how lethal Kayah ben Samuel was. The lioness had been bitten, and she was ready to tear apart the one who dared.

Reuben motioned to his agents. Addressing the technical officer, he whispered, "Activate the tracking device, briefly. We need to know which way they went." To the second agent, he ordered "You, find those two kids and figure out what they know." And to the third, "Get inside that police station, say you are a witness. Make sure they keep Drachmas locked up."

His technical officer said in a surprised tone, "That was an excellent diversion, sir. I don't think we should underestimate those girls again."

"None of them," Reuben agreed and took off after Kayah.

He caught up just as she was entering Aula-Magna Library. The interior provided a startling change from the bustle and heat outside. Old leather, books, and beeswax hung heavy in the air. A faint shuffle of paper and low muted voices came from a group at one of the tables lining the aisle, otherwise the place was empty. Ancient and modern texts sat on shelves two stories high that ran the length of a long arched gallery. At the apex, an ancient window shown like a beacon, illuminating the space, and drawing the eye and the mind upward. Inside these walls, peace and knowledge reigned.

Reuben found her on the upper floor in the history section. She recoiled, jerking back as if he'd struck her.

"Go away, Agent," she hissed.

"What happened, Kayah?" His low voice reverberated in his chest.

Unbidden and unwanted, memories of that stinking cell chased her into this place. "Leave me alone." She turned away, unwilling to let anyone see her like this. Flashbacks were rare, the intensity of them long abated, lost to time and vengeance. Until today.

He moved closer and said, "No."

Her knife was at his throat in an instant. "I will fucking slit your throat right here. Leave."

"What did he say to you, Kayah?" Reuben's dark eyes pierced hers as the knife pressure increased.

"Nothing," she growled. Go away, go away her mind screamed.

Slowly he leaned his head back, raising his strong chin toward the light. "I will not fight you."

"Damn you to hell," she snarled. She wanted him to try to disarm her, to fight. She wanted him to leave her alone.

"That is impossible." His broad shoulders pulled back, opening his chest up.

Kayah wanted to hurt him, so she spat, "Jew!"

The single word carried seven millennia of rage and hatred, conjuring demons of pogroms and holocausts.

"Aye," he growled, looking at her through half-lidded eyes. "My name is Reuben ben Judah, and I am Israeli."

She had no name or kingdom, nothing tied Kayah anywhere. Anger, older than the cell, surged through her body. "I am Kayah ben Morte."

"Yet, you are a child of the King, no?" His pulse beat rapidly, and the blade drew a crimson drop of blood.

"I am no one's child, Reuben ben Judah."

"But you once were," he breathed, gently cupping her cheek.

Kayah's chest heaved, but she rejected the sentiment and snarled, "That is where you are wrong."

He would not play her game and certainly was not going to banter with her while she had a knife at his throat. Easing her hand away, he said, "I am rarely, if ever, wrong, Kayah." He moistened his lips and brushed them against hers. "And I am not wrong about this."

They had not kissed last night, and the tender intimacy of it threatened to shatter her tenuous self-control. "No," the little orphan cried.

He touched his nose to hers. "Kiss me, Kayah."

"No," the abused teen sobbed.

He felt her urge to bolt, to run, so he dropped his hands, not restraining her in any way. "I will not hurt you."

"No," the solitary angel of death rebelled.

Reuben kissed her, breathing her pain.

"No," the tired lonely woman begged.

He detected movement down the hall and knew if he did not get her somewhere private, she was going to implode. Out of the corner of his eye, he spotted a study carrel.

"Come," he whispered, holding her hand, and easing her inside. Light through a small window illuminated the private space that contained a single chair and desk. It smelled of ink and paper, polished wood. He sat down, guiding her onto his lap, holding her loosely. She could leave if she chose.

Wrapping his arms around her, he whispered Hebrew words of comfort, calming her as if she were a wild animal who needed help, but whose fear of man was so ingrained she could not accept it even if she needed it. "Shh," he soothed. "It is okay. You are safe with me."

"Leave me alone," she pleaded.

"I cannot." The brokenness in her echoed in his own bleak soul.

Kayah contorted, her body tensed, trying to stem the tidal wave dragging her under.

He pulled her head to his shoulder and held on.

She buried her face in his neck with a faint cry of protest, but she was rejecting the terror, not the comfort. A tiny, no, escaped her lips.

He rocked with her and kissed her ear, murmuring gentle reassurance in Hebrew.

She did not understand the words, but they touched something empty in her soul. He held her but did not bind her.

Reuben shielded her. In the first strong, protective embrace she ever experienced, Kayah ben Samuel fell apart. Deep shudders wracked her body, yet she was silent, as if she did not know how to cry.

He recognized that. Some pain was too deep for even a groan. He did not say a word, did not tell her it was okay, he simply let her cry.

It was the most intimate experience of his life… and hers.

Girl Talk

Dinner? Why had she agreed to go to dinner with him? She did not date, did not eat with her lovers; she ate her lovers. Kayah dropped her bag by the door. She should leave. This was dangerous. Today in the library, he totally disarmed her. Yet when she finished weeping, he set her on her feet, brusquely wiped the tears from her eyes, and drew up her chin as if nothing happened.

"I will pick you up at 19:00 for dinner."

It seemed the most natural thing in the world to agree. In the hours since, foolish. She was losing it and did not want to fight this battle alone.

The long-distance ring crackled. Lavinia's voice came across the line, "Kayah! How are you?"

Kayah rubbed her forehead. "I am fine. What are you up to today?"

Lavinia shot Mack a puzzled look. Kayah never called to chat. Keeping her voice light, she answered, "We are headed over to Pepperwood for a BBQ. One of their horses won the Preakness today."

Pepperwood? The name sounded familiar. Kayah accessed her memory bank and hit upon it, Prince Peter's refuge. "That's nice."

Lavinia walked to the privacy of her bedroom. "Kai, I don't like the sound of your voice. What's wrong?"

Kayah let out a semi-hysterical laugh, full of self-deprecation. "I have a date… tonight."

Lavinia closed her eyes briefly, then said, "And you are calling me so I can tell you to go." It was a statement rather than a question.

"Go where? Out the door or on the date? Because you know my bag is packed."

"I know it is." Lavinia looked at the chair in the corner, piled high with Mack's clothes, his side table cluttered with papers, a screwdriver, and what looked like a tractor spring. "Kai, do you remember Himari's wedding paintings?"

Kayah snorted, "Yeah."

Lavinia inhaled through her nose and plunged ahead. "She didn't get those by running out the door."

"I'm not Himari—"

"No, you're not, but I will tell you what you are. You are an extraordinary woman, who is brave enough to go on a date." Lavinia tapped her fingers against her thigh. "I would never have been strong enough to find Mack that night, but there is not a week that goes by where I don't look at my son and thank you in my heart. If I were there, I would push you out the door and make you go on that date."

"Vinia, I'm not afraid of anything." The quiver in Kayah's voice belied her words.

"Good, then you'll go," Lavinia said matter of fact.

Kayah laughed humorlessly. "Just that easy?"

Lavinia smiled through the phone. "I never said it was easy, but it is worth it." Mack opened the door, Richard balanced on his hip. Their son was three years old, yesterday.

Kayah paced her hotel room. "Worth it? Even when you don't know the cost?"

"That's just it, Kai. It's not the cost, it's what you gain. That is worth risking everything." Lavinia held Mack's eyes.

Kayah's shoulders fell in defeat. "I'm going to kick your ass if this goes sideways."

Lavinia laughed, "I look forward to it."

Dinner with a Badass

The badass was back, she answered the door in long flowing black trousers, spiked heels, and a low-cut black shirt. Expensive gold jewelry hung around her neck and dangled from her ears. In a word, she was stunning. She was also furious with herself and with him.

"I did not think you would be here." His half smile telegraphed his pleasure that she was.

Kayah dismissed him with a shrug. "A girl has to eat. I figured I'd let you pay for it."

He gave her a half mocking bow. "It is my pleasure. Shall we go?"

It was a direct challenge, and she knew it. She lifted her pointed chin and adopted an imperious air. "Of course."

When they emerged onto the ancient street, the sun was low, painting the sky with swaths of pink and orange. The terracotta-colored buildings glowed warm, and a soft westerly wind carried the smell of the sea.

Reuben offered her his arm and saw the battle rage. To touch him again was more threatening than if he held a gun to her head.

With grim determination, she took his elbow, and they walked.

"A pleasant evening for a stroll," he teased, repeating her words from last night.

The knife strapped to her left calf was poisoned, the gun in her clutch loaded, and the heel in her right shoe held a hidden spike. "Bologna is a lovely place, for a vacation."

When he smiled, she noticed that his left canine tooth was slightly crooked. Reuben was taller than her, by six or seven inches. His arm, hard under her light grasp, was well formed. His dark hair was a shade before black, cut military-style, which showed off a slight widow's peak. However, it was his nose, bold and well formed, that marked him for who and what he was, a Jew.

They walked in silence, neither adept in small talk, at least in their nonexistent personal lives.

He stopped at the entrance to an unassuming restaurant and held the door for her. She looked at him with a silent question. The dark interior looked sketchy. With a faint cock of her head, she conveyed her dubiousness at his choice.

The owner greeted them, a small woman with impossible magenta hair and hips that gave testimony to the rich fare served at her establishment. White tablecloths, set with glittering crystal and heavy silverware, contrasted with the dark mahogany paneled walls. A reserved alcove in the corner offered a view of the street and an intimate setting.

Reuben held out her chair and settled across from her. When the waitress came to take their order, he raised a black brow at Kayah in question. "Shall I order for us?"

Kayah had not allowed a person to order food for her since her early days with Sir Preston. In many ways, this date with Reuben harkened back to those early times, which over the course of her life, had been exciting and wondrous. She crossed her arms and raised a shoulder with indolent capitulation. "By all means, please."

Her mouth fell open when he ordered in flawless Italian. Languages were not her strong suit, much to Sir Preston's disappointment, and Kayah's book throwing frustration.

The first course of dry white wine, crusty bread, and fresh sardines arrived with understated elegance. Reuben raised his glass in toast, "To vacations and food."

Kayah closed her eyes in bliss at the first bite. She loved bread, loved it with a passion, but rarely permitted herself the pleasure of it.

Reuben grinned at the look of ecstasy on her face. He liked that look and vowed tonight, he would coax as many out of her as he could. Though, when it came time to make that happen, he struggled. He did not know what to say, so they ate in silence. But the silence was not strained. It seemed natural to sit with her in the quiet. If he pressed her about herself, he expected that it would force her to lie to him, and he would rather sit in the honest silence than fill the air with falsehoods.

Carpaccio with bitter arugula and lemon horseradish sauce was their second course, accompanied with a stout red wine.

Reuben smiled beatifically at the meat. "My family raised beef cows."

Kayah's brows narrowed over her nose at his admission. "You do not strike me as a farmer."

He chuckled softly. "I did not say I raised beef cows."

She raised her glass in silent toast at the nuance. "But you appreciate fine beef?"

"Oh, *zikher.*" Of course.

"How is it there now?" Kayah asked, her tone casual but her

question serious. The global political climate was volatile. People in general were in foul moods, most of it directed or misdirected at the Golden Kingdom.

Reuben shrugged. "The same as always, in the interior."

There was an undertone in his words, but the arrival of the third course saved them from further discussion. Their entrée was lasagna verde with bechamel sauce, paired with an interesting wine. The Arneis tasted tart and lemony, with a slight effervescence, it hit the back of her tongue with a punch. But with the creamy pasta, it drew out notes in the dish that otherwise would have been lost. It was superb.

"I have a friend who runs a small vineyard. It has been in her family for a couple of generations." Kayah took a sip of wine. "They are Italian, but I forget that, until I come to Italy and realized blood runs deep. Their expressions, the way they use their hands when they talk, she's been on my mind."

Reuben nodded over his glass. "Friends and wine, I think perhaps that is a good thing."

Kayah's eyes, green in the dimly lit restaurant, shone with pleasure. "I think perhaps you are correct."

After dinner, he walked her back to her hotel and gave her a chaste peck on the cheek. "Until we meet again, Kayah. I leave Bologna tomorrow. Thank you for a splendid evening."

It shocked her that he did not try to come up. She had been dreading ending the night on a sour note. This was perfect. "It was lovely, thank you."

He winked and made that clicking noise with his cheek, then was gone.

July 6, 999 ME

Vacation in Tuscany

Delegates to the International Summit on Trade and Technology poured into Geneva. Dignitaries and business executives from across the globe gathered to discuss a full repeal of technology laws, and whether they should relax export controls of Alanthian products. A huge black market had developed, and officials were in Geneva to debate whether their governments should legalize the technology their citizens were screaming for, and by extension, garner the tax revenues. Powerful political and business forces traveled to Geneva, ready to make the deal of a lifetime.

For Sir Preston, Kayah was a spy. For The Resistance, she was a thief. For Kayah herself, she planned to have a little fun. Stephen ben McSwilley would be in attendance.

This week, her hair was chestnut brown. Tasteful golden highlights framed her oval face and set off her clear complexion. Tortoise-shell glasses gave her a serious and studious appearance. Chocolate tweed and low heels completed the businesswoman's disguise. She posed as a financial director from the purely fictitious Oglethorpe Technical Research and Development Corporation, during the day.

At night, she transformed into an empty-headed young lady and cozied up to tech executives. It was child's play. Drunk men loved sexy girls. Kayah batted her eyelashes, hung on their arms and their every word. She stroked their monstrous egos and listened with fawning admiration while they spilled their secrets. They financed The Resistance by selling secrets or developing them. With each secret, the genius techies decided which avenue was more lucrative.

The conference was scheduled for a week, but by day three Kayah was bored out of her mind. She successfully gathered enough information to keep Sir Preston happy and charmed three drunken executives into sharing their most promising projects, and she did it all without taking anyone to bed.

As a matter of fact, for the first time in Kayah's life, she was celibate. She did not scrutinize it, didn't peel back the layers, and look too deep. However, it did not take a psychologist to recognize Bologna was a turning point, in more ways than one.

She had not returned to Alanthia, instead she did exactly what she teased Reuben about. Kayah took a vacation.

Italy had been good for her. She drank wine and ate bread; lounged on the beach and read a book for pleasure. It was hedonistic, utterly relaxing, and she was not ready to be back at work. For the first time, she considered leaving it all behind. Lavinia and Himari lived normal lives, subversive revolutionary activities notwithstanding. They had families, went to parties, did the dishes, and paid bills. From Kayah's perspective, they lived life, while she skirted the edges of it.

Kayah visited exotic places, ate interesting food, met intriguing people, even killed a few, but that no longer felt like living. She was thirty-four and never had a home. She maintained an apartment in New York, a beach condo in Mont Carmel, and a townhouse in the New City. But they were empty of anything she could not buy at the local MilMart or fashionable boutique. She liked art but never purchased it because she was never anywhere long enough to enjoy it, though she did own one of Filippo's paintings of her, Himari, and Lavinia with their heads pressed together, laughing at Himari's wedding. It was Kayah's prize possession, but she had not seen it in over a year.

Even her hatred of Stephen, fueled for more than a decade, abated after she glimpsed him. Perhaps their massage session put that demon to rest. Her interest in the two girls also waned after she realized Mossad was protecting them, not hunting them. They did not need Kayah. Mossad would deal with the Greek when the time came. She might be getting soft, or perhaps just getting older. Young Kayah would never have let that insult slide without maximum retaliation, but something had changed. She let something go in that study carrel and did not want to take it back up again. Stubby was dead, and it was time to stop living that young girl's life.

Several weeks after leaving Bologna, she stopped at a small Tuscan village. The landlady at the bed-and-breakfast invited her to church. An immediate refusal died on her lips, and she went. They conducted the service in Italian, but the sanctuary was peaceful. Kayah left Tuscany with a sense of wellbeing that stuck with her for weeks.

She thought about that enigmatic Israeli from time to time. Erotic dreams, which she attributed to her self-imposed celibacy, woke her often, and whenever he came to mind, she smiled. He was in the right place at the right time. Of all her lovers, he was a first. Reuben ben Judah grew into a warm and tender memory.

When Opportunity Knocks

A soft wrap on her door woke her at 2:00 am. Kayah came awake, rolling out of bed, and arming herself in a single motion. She padded to the door and detected a shadow.

The warm tender memory stood outside her door.

"Kayah! Kayah!" he hissed, "open up. I am in trouble."

Leery of a trap but thrilled by the sound of his voice, she unlocked the door and stood aside for him to enter. "What kind of trouble?"

He slipped in, turned with a broad grin, and said, "Yakira, it is good to see you." He kissed her in the next breath, an exuberant, pick her up, I have missed you, kiss.

"Yakira?" Kayah pulled back. "You know whose door you just knocked on?"

"Of course, I know." He clicked his cheek and gave her a lascivious wink. "It is an endearment, Kayah."

That knocked her completely off balance. She covered it by saying, "Again, did you bring trouble to my door?"

"No." He buried his face in her neck, appreciating the scent of her. "The minute you let me in, the trouble disappeared." He kissed her ear and forgot the men chasing him. "Minor things. Take me to bed." He nipped. "You are alone? Because I will throw another man out on his ass if you are not." He felt her shoulders shake with silent mirth.

"Reuben," she laughed in disbelief. "What are you doing here?"

He shook his head, the adrenaline of the night still coursing through his body. "It is a long story, but I have been trying for two days to come. So tonight, when I needed to make a quick escape?" He shrugged and laced his fingers around her back, gazing at her in the faint light. "I took my opening."

"Spies keep odd hours, aye?" Kayah raised a sardonic eyebrow.

He wore a devilish grin. "They do, and they like hot chicks that understand that about them."

"Is this our second date? If so, where are my flowers?"

He gave a throaty laugh. "I will get you flowers on your breakfast tray."

"On my breakfast tray? Aren't you being a bit presumptuous?" She let him draw her closer.

He began walking backward, into her suite, bringing her with him. "Uh huh," he purred, "I am getting ready to presume all over your body."

That sounded like a capital idea to Kayah. "I do not, as a rule, take men to my bed more than once." She wet her lips.

"I have never been good at following rules." Reuben unlaced his fingers, brought them to her buttocks, and pulled her against him. "Especially if they keep me from touching you." His chest rose in a deep exhale as he felt her mold against him.

"Oh, is that right? And are there other rules that keep you from touching me?" Kayah ran her hands over the outline of his shoulders, up his powerful neck.

"Lots of rules against touching you, Kayah, and I plan to break every damn one." He moved his hands inside the waistband of her little shorts, touching her soft skin.

The kindred spirit of the rogue inflamed her. "Then touch me, Reuben," she whispered.

He growled, picked her up around the waist, and carried her to bed, leaving her shorts in the hallway. Laying her down, touching and being touched, he fanned the flame. He ran his tongue over her body and nuzzled her thighs. "Yakira, oh I have wanted to taste you these last weeks. I have thought of little else but this." He pushed his face deep between her legs, groaning with anticipation.

She was shaven clean and slick with desire for him. He opened her slowly with his tongue, driving her, teasing her. She moved her hand between her legs. "Oh, no Yakira." He moved her hand away and sucked hard.

Kayah arched with greedy pleasure. He used the bridge of his strong nose to stimulate her, drove his tongue deep inside her, and pressed a long finger up the cleft of her bottom. She began to orgasm immediately, riding him, opening for him. She gave him her body and lost herself in the moment.

Reuben reveled in her ecstasy, pushing deeper he felt spasms wash over her and onto his tongue. As a great wave crested, he pushed into her, riding with her toward the zenith. Grunting with animal pleasure, he drove hard, and she shattered again.

Suspended above her, he touched her womb with his last thrust and exploded with an orgasm that blackened his vision and stopped his heart for a moment.

He collapsed on top of her, his breathing labored, unable to speak. Kayah ben Samuel wrapped her shaking arms around him and hugged.

They made love through the night, passionately, fervently, then at dawn, tenderly.

Pink morning light broke the horizon and filled the room with a soft glow. Tears spilled over her lashes. Sitting astride, she pleasured them both, slow and sensual. More than physical, something bloomed that night.

She watched him. She loved his powerful chest, the shape of his body, long smooth planes, muscled and chiseled by the hand of a sculptor. His dark skin grew paler at his narrow hips. He was the most beautiful sight she ever beheld, and it almost hurt to look at him.

"Yakira…." He touched a tear on her cheek, brought it to his lips and kissed it. "My beautiful."

"Reuben," she panted. "Reuben, oh God what have you done to me?" Her body convulsed, ripping a cry out of the depths of her soul.

"Kayah," he panted, "I am loving you, loving you."

Her face contorted in agony. No, he could not say it, he could not mean it. She curled over him.

He held her eyes, pulsing inside her. His voice broke, "Kayah, you are tearing me apart."

She shook her head in mute denial.

He rolled on top, stroking deep and rhythmic. This had moved beyond sex into the realm of the unknown. He wanted to pull her inside his soul, to touch her. His control splintered, and he saw her for who and what she was. She was as broken as him, as alone as him. But in that moment, he knew they didn't have to be.

Tears fell over her lashes, and she cradled his face in her hands. "Reuben."

"Do not cry, do not. Shh. You are with me now, do not be afraid." He kissed her tears and met her eyes. "Let me love you."

No one had ever truly loved her, not and known who and what she was, but this unlikely man was asking her to let him. Staring into his eyes, she believed him. For the first time in her life, she gambled her heart and whispered, "Then love me, Reuben."

Tears sprang to his eyes as he poured his life, his soul, and his spirit into hers, and took her as his love. She gave him her small, sad, scared little girl's heart, the only one she had to give.

Turkish Coffee

As promised, there were flowers on her breakfast tray. She opened a sleepy eye at 9:00 am and saw Reuben dressed in a white hotel robe pushing an enormous cart full of food and flowers. The exotic aroma of coffee filled her nostrils, and she roused, slightly. He poured her a small cup of the pungent brew and waved it temptingly in front of her.

"It smells good. What is it?" she asked in a voice raspy with sleep.

"Turkish coffee, though in my kingdom we just call it cafe'. Truthfully, it is Israeli coffee, but you know…" He shrugged, accepting and dismissing Anti-Semitic sentiment as the norm.

She raised up on an elbow and took the ceramic cup, inhaling. After her first sip, she moistened her lips, deciding whether she liked it. "Like espresso with cardamom," she took another sip, "and chicory, like they use in Louisiana."

Reuben downed his in a single gulp and poured another. "It is very rare to find it on a menu outside of Israel. It was my second favorite thing about waking up this morning." He took her cup and climbed into bed with her, kissing her. She tried to shrink away, but he knew it would be a mistake to let her. "No, Yakira, just because the sun shines it does not take away the night."

Already he knew her too well, she closed her eyes tightly. "I will not be good at this… this relationship."

"I will probably be a disaster, no?"

The corner of her lip lifted. "I will probably ruin it."

"No, I do not believe it." He brushed his lips against hers. "We will prove to each other how terrible we are."

"How shall we start? I don't have a clue."

"Then we will learn together." He kissed her closed eyes.

"Reuben, everyone has more experience at this than me. I've never even seen a healthy relationship."

He tilted his head and studied her. "Never?"

She shook her head, best to get it out. If he left this morning, she would get over it. "No, never."

"No one, no couple that you know?"

Kayah shrugged, feeling defensive. "No, I did not grow up in a place where people kissed each other goodnight."

He knew he was walking perilous ground, since Bologna he endeavored to discover all there was to know about her. The picture that emerged was bleak, the woman in his arms was not. "I shall kiss you goodnight, every night that the Lord allows."

She took the gift, absurdly thinking of Sir Preston's first lesson, accept with grace. She nodded and said, "All right then, I shall kiss you back."

"Good! Now, let us eat. I am ravenous after all that exercise." He rolled out of bed, going to the cart, and removing the silver cloches like a magician on stage.

"How much food did you order?" Laughter undergirded her words.

"All of it." He tore into a bagel. "I charged it to your room, too." He motioned with the bagel. "I like the brunette hair, by the way. It is becoming."

Her cheek showed a faint dimple when she smiled. "I have one of those faces that can pull off any hair color, though I am not fond of the anarchists colors. I find pink tedious."

His expression darkened. "Stay away from them Kayah, they are aligning with the jihadists." His black eyes became fierce. "There is no greater scum on the earth."

Kayah tended to agree with him, though she was still apolitical. But she saw she had touched a nerve. He bubbled up like that. She tested a theory by saying, "I have no meetings today. The conference has two days of excursions and social bonding bull shit. So, I am free all weekend."

Reuben's expression went from dark fury to delight, in an instant. Theory confirmed, he was a man of deep passion, but remove the fuel and the boiling water calmed. She was not sure how that boded for his long-term affection, but right now she planned to enjoy the weekend.

He lifted a glass of orange juice in salute. "Unlike you, I am on assignment. Though, I suppose I am technically absent without leave." He shrugged as if this was no matter and did not elaborate. Things went off kilter last night, Korah's men made a move on Prince Josiah and the girls. It forced Mossad to intervene on both fronts. His men dispersed in the ensuing chaos. It happened near Kayah's hotel, so he seized the moment. Consequently, he was eating breakfast with the prettiest assassin he knew.

She stretched luxuriously. "It does turn me on, you know, the whole rogue badass thing you have going."

He snorted with laughter. "Nu? You could give lessons in that, Yakira." He sighed. "I have to check in, but I will be back. Enjoy your breakfast. You will need your strength."

Light and Shadow

They began their relationship backward, an interesting way to start. By necessity they were each shrouded in secrecy. Their work, their pasts, their present, held apart for security purposes. Paradoxically, it drew them together. Any small confidence became an act of trust, in their world, intimacy was a weapon. Thus, it became even more precious in its sharing.

Getting ready for the day, Kayah discovered Reuben loved terrible, loud hard rock.

"What is that?" she cringed.

Reuben looked incredulous. "What? What? It is a great song!" He turned up the volume.

Kayah turned it down.

Reuben flexed his bare chest in an aggressive stance, feral and wild.

Kayah rolled her eyes at the over-the-top display of animal maleness.

He gave her a mock scowl. "You do not know your history. Our two kingdoms used that song against our enemies in the greatest technological attack of the Last Age."

Kayah put her hands on her hips, adopting her own version of his scowl. "Who uses a song as a weapon?"

Reuben rubbed his chin and snorted. "You would be surprised, Yakira." Then pointed a finger and added, "But I will tell you a story, if you do not know it."

She moved past him to her toothbrush. "Go ahead, tell me a story."

Reuben joined her at the sink, lathering his face and looking dubiously at the complimentary hotel razor. "Before the Great Judgment and the Ezekiel 38/39 War, Persia sought, as they had for six millennia, to destroy the Kingdom of Israel." His dark smile telegraphed his scorn for his ancient enemies. "The Iranians, as they were called, were secretly trying to build a nuclear weapon. My people and your people knew it." Scraping away his thick black stubble, he continued, "The diplomats argued in the halls of the United Nations," he made a disgusted sound in the back of his throat, "but they did nothing but talk, talk, talk!" He hunched his shoulders forward in dismissal. "They talked and passed ridiculous sanctions that accomplished nothing, and the threat grew daily.

"Until scientists in Tel Aviv and the New City decided to stop them. They collaborated in a top-secret mission and designed a computer virus that was so secretive and destructive it wiped out the Iranian nuclear program without firing a single shot. They nicknamed it the 'G-d Virus' because it was so effective that it physically destroyed over one thousand centrifuges, they literally melted. It also wiped the research off their computers. The best part was, after they were done, all the computers across the Iranian labs started blasting the song you just turned down! This is true. I know this." He walked over to his tablet, hit the button, and exclaimed, "Thunderstruck!"

Kayah laughed. She loved old tech stories.

Reuben discovered that Kayah brushed her teeth for twenty minutes and had sixteen pairs of shoes in her suitcase. Watching the boats on Lake Geneva from the balcony, he also learned that she had never been fishing. An idea was born, and he determined he was going to change that.

Saturday afternoon, after checking in with his team, he stopped at a pier and reserved a boat for the next morning. Partially because he wanted to take her fishing her first time, and because she soundly rejected his idea of attending a wrestling exhibition.

Reuben returned to the hotel room around noon with a small bag of his own things. "This weekend, we are going to be tourists." He put a Lake Geneva ball cap squarely on his head and handed her a matching one.

Lounging sideways in a chair, she eyed it skeptically. "I look stupid in hats."

He rolled his eyes. "It's a ball cap, put it on. I bought it for you at the boat rental place."

Kayah refused to take it. "No. I have too much hair. I can pull off a formal hat, even then I have to twist and pin it just right, otherwise, I look ridiculous."

He did not believe her and set the cap on her head. She looked up at him with her lips pressed flat, her eyes full of 'I told you so'. He exploded with laughter. Her thick hair bushed around the hat and looked absurd.

"Can you pull it through in a ponytail?" he snickered.

The corners of her mouth were twitching. "No, there is too much hair, so the stupid hat just sort of perches up there." With a quick motion she showed him.

He bent over laughing. "I think you just have a big head."

She threw the hat at him. "I do not have a big head!"

He held up a hand in surrender. "It is okay, Yakira. I will buy you a bigger hat."

Kayah's mouth dropped open, she sprung out of her chair, and tackled him around the waist. They fell onto the bed in a pile of squirming limbs, laughing.

He covered his face with his arms and declared in mock fear. "No, do not hit me with that enormous head, it might kill me!"

No one had ever teased or roughhoused with Kayah. She was not quite sure what to do, so she rolled off him. He tickled her. She jumped in surprise and tried to get away. But Reuben was an accomplished tickle fighter, and she did not stand a chance. They both discovered she was amazingly ticklish under her arms and down her sides. They also discovered she needed to learn how to play and not hurt because in her haste to get away, she elbowed him in the nose.

"Oy!" he hollered, half laughing, half in pain, holding his face.

Kayah paled. "Oh, sorry! That was an accident." She scrambled off the bed and brought him a wet washcloth from the bathroom.

He dabbed at the few drops of blood. "It is no matter."

She sat cross legged in front of him, taking the cloth from him and examining him for damage. She was embarrassed. "I feel bad. I hurt you."

Reuben's dark brown eyes looked at her with humor. "It is a big nose."

Kayah giggled and kissed it. "It is kind of a big nose, but I like it."

"Good." He puckered his lips, inviting her to kiss him, and she did.

They spent the afternoon at the botanical gardens, walking hand in hand, dodging the crowds, drinking overpriced spring water, and eating food from vendor carts. He bought her a balloon in the shape of a daisy which she declared was ridiculous but tied it to her wrist and let it bounce merrily as they walked.

Kayah saw firsthand the Antisemitism overtaking the world. People stared at them with contempt, muttered veiled insults, a few even refused to acknowledge them. "How do you take this?" Kayah threw up her hands in frustration when the fifth coach of the day drove past them, ignoring their hale.

Reuben shrugged, looking grim. "It is nothing new to my people, Kayah."

She spun on him. "It doesn't make it right." It was a cost she had not calculated, and it stirred her up. "What do these people know about you, or who you are? Why do they think they have the right to judge someone with a look?"

He held his arms open to her. She dropped her head in defeat and went to him. Reuben kissed her cheek and stood quietly amongst the bustle of the Avenue de la Paix. "I have been in a rage for two years. I will not go into detail, but what you have seen helped fuel it." He sighed and stared deep into her eyes. "But the day in the library, we both let something go, no?"

Kayah looked away.

Reuben dropped his forehead to hers and whispered, "They don't matter, Yakira. But if we give them the power, they do."

Kayah narrowed her brows. "And if they try to hurt you or the people you love?"

Reuben moved in for a kiss. "Then we wipe them off the planet."

Liquid heat rushed through Kayah's body as the daisy balloon danced above their heads.

July 7, 999 ME

Paradox

The fishing excursion was an absolute bust, at least for the fisherman. For the lovely passenger along for the boat ride, she enjoyed a pleasant outing on the water. By the end of the afternoon, Reuben figured out something extraordinary, Kayah was squeamish. She refused to bait the hook, felt sorry for the worms, and did not see the fun in catching a fish. So, he threw back the three meager ones he landed and toured the pristine lake.

While he was waiting in line to pay, he saw her go down on her haunches and extend a hand to a couple of cats. A few of the less skittish ones checked her out. When they came, she cooed with such unguarded happiness that his breath hitched in his chest. Kayah, tough suspicious Kayah, loved animals. A big orange tom bumped her hand and raised his chin for a scratch. She smiled like an angel. Then she glanced around and disappeared into the bait shop across from the boat rental place. He wondered what she was up to. His mouth dropped open when she emerged with several cans of fish and began setting them out. The cats swarmed her and their unexpected feast. He paid the man for the boat and kept his steps soft as he approached Kayah and her herd of feral cats.

"Nu? How do you think the fish got in the cans?" Reuben asked, flabbergasted at the complete incongruence.

She gave a saucy retort, "Somebody else did it."

Reuben knew Kayah was a suspect in at least four assassinations, nefarious characters, every one of them, but still. The woman was a walking paradox. He glanced at his watch and grimaced. The clock was moving too fast, and their time was short. He had to report back to his unit tonight. "Kayah," he draped his arm around her shoulders, "spend the rest of the day in bed with me."

With stray cats meowing around their feet, she smiled, her hazel eyes taking on the green of her shirt. She tilted her head up and purred, "I think that is an excellent idea, Agent."

The hotel suite boasted a luxurious bathroom, complete with a sunken tub. They washed away the fishy smells and floated in each other's arms. When the bathwater cooled, he rose and held out his hand. They walked dreamlike to the feather topped bed and lay down without the fervor of passion. With slow languid reverence he touched the water beading on her pale skin.

They did not talk, memorizing the shape, texture, and feel of the other's body, taking stolen hours, in lives that always teetered on the edge of danger. They both knew they might never find their way back; this would have to be enough.

It began slowly and tenderly, touching and caressing, kissing. As the heat built, so did the urgency to be joined, to touch. They found something that eluded them their whole lives deep within the other. A wildness took over. It claimed, marked, and possessed, then transcended all, and loved. The highest human emotion exchanged hearts, wiped away tears, and promised no matter what tomorrow held, today they were infinitely precious and beloved.

Dressed in nothing but her bra and panties, Kayah watched Reuben pack his belongings. He cleaned the screen of his tablet with his sleeve before sliding it in its protective case and stowing it away, doing the same with his phone.

"Let me ask you something," she said contemplatively. "Mossad uses tech, you boys don't have any compunction about it, and I have been to Tel Aviv. Yet... this whole week, this entire conference has been nothing but a huge debate over the use of it. Because apparently the Iron King has a problem with it outside of the Golden Kingdom." She pointed a finger at him. "Hell, I went to prison over it. Explain this to me."

Reuben sat on the bed beside her. "I do not pretend to be an expert on the subject, but I can perhaps give you my perspective."

"Please, the hypocrisy has always bothered me, especially in '90 when He opened Tel Aviv."

"Well, I think the answer lies in history, don't you? You see the things they are pulling off the old internet, what life was really like at the end of the Last Age. Technology took over everything, people did not speak to one another, they did not see one another, they existed inside a virtual world. They replaced everything that made them human with one of these," he pulled his phone out of his pocket, "which grew into its own evil."

"Yes, but—"

He held up a finger for her to wait. "After the Great Judgment, how many people were left? Only 950 million survived, that's out of 7.3 billion people estimated to have been alive when the Rapture happened. You have to remember, the planet was destroyed. The fighting, earthquakes, and meteors leveled almost everything. The whole place looked like a wasteland. All the factories, all the people who knew how to operate the equipment, it was gone."

Kayah remained silent. Her New City education had not taught her this.

"The Iron King sent those who remained alive, the Tribulation Saints, those first Millennials, across the Earth to rebuild it. They were not interested in cars and phones, they rebuilt their houses, they lived in small communities, and they farmed, so they could eat. The Iron King blessed the land, and it grew. Do you remember, Kayah? Do you remember what it used to be like when we were small?" his voice cracked. "Do you remember the light, the temperate weather, and endless fields? Remember when no one got sick, and nobody went hungry; we did not need technology then. Do you remember what it was like? Do you?" Reuben beseeched her.

Kayah's world had never been so idyllic, but she remembered what he was talking about. "I do."

"Well, those early Millennials, they lived through Hell on Earth, they remembered the judgment, and they found themselves in Eden. There was finally no war, no sickness, no disease and no corrupt government or technologies pulling them out of paradise and back into the mud. So, they let it go, they let it all die. Because they knew if it ever came back, men would want it more than the Iron King, and with it they would organize, they would rebel.

"Kayah, the ban against technology was never a law mandated by the Iron King. The Kingdoms of men created those laws. Did you know that?" Reuben took her hands. "It wasn't the Iron King who put you in prison, Yakira."

Kayah's eyes blinked rapidly, her voice quiet. "Why don't we know this?"

Reuben smiled sadly. "The forces of rebellion do not want you to know."

Kayah put a gentle hand on either side of his face, the stubble of his dark beard beginning to shadow. "Reuben ben Judah, you have turned my world upside down."

Food for Thought

At sunset, Kayah rested on a bench by a walking path around Lake Geneva. Reuben's departure a few hours before made the hotel walls close in on her, so she escaped outside and settled in a secluded spot. It was Sunday night, and the tourists were back at their hotels or making their way home. The conference wrapped tomorrow.

She turned over the events of the weekend, but also life in general, particularly what she discovered about herself this summer. She stood at a crossroads with no clear idea which path to take. The familiar dark and twisting path to the left, or one to the right, narrow and unknown but where light beckoned. Kayah did not delude herself that either path contained Reuben. One could hold him as easily as the other, and it must not be her desire for him that determined which one she chose, as tempting as it was at the moment.

If she went back to Alanthia, they would draw her down the dark familiar path, whether she wanted to or not. She entertained no false illusions that she could simply tell Sir Preston she was done, and he would wish her well, and let her go. He wielded considerable power over her, but she had enough evidence on the Old Man to keep him in check. While he would not like it, she could extract herself from his clutches if she chose.

She considered her work with The Resistance. Once she orchestrated the building of the technical team, she removed herself from the intricacies of the operation. She joined primarily because she was bored and knew Lavinia was involved in something dangerous. Kayah wanted to monitor things, but Prince Peter surprised her. To his credit, he set his goals, and did whatever it took to move forward. It was still a bold plan, to overthrow his father, install his cousin on the throne, and get the hell out, but the little Prince had proven to Kayah that he was extremely capable and led the covert revolution rather well. Though the outcome remained chancy.

Alanthia remained a hotbed of rebellion, and The Resistance dug their fingers into everything. From charities to technologies, they financed their work through dozens of enterprises. Kayah made a fortune stealing and investing in the technology they developed. She was a millionaire many times over and even supported a few charities, albeit anonymously.

Her favorite was the Center for the Street Kids of Alanthia. She recently gave a large endowment earmarked for a new facility in New York, where it was desperately needed. Kayah suspected if she had grown up in a place where kids stayed together and formed family units, her life might have been different. She was especially pleased with the Center's program that supported kids after they turned eighteen. They were not shoved out into the world alone. Endowments bought small houses for the kids, many of whom lived together into adulthood, like a real family.

Maybe she should become a mentor, go work with Joanna ben Luke as a counselor? She laughed at the absurd thought. Kayah was nobody's mentor. She thought of those two girls in Bologna. Reuben did not say, but he was still protecting them. They could have no better guardian angel by their sides. She surmised they pulled another stunt that brought him to her door two nights ago, for that, she was thankful. She hoped whatever they had done, they got away with it. Prison was no place for young girls.

Reuben's revelation of the origins of the tech laws caused her to consider exactly who *had* put her in prison. For years, she believed that when Stephen approached Korah with the ancient cell phone, Korah took his opportunity to steal from them. She was nothing but collateral damage. It was one reason she agreed to work with The Resistance, to take revenge on Korah for his treachery.

Korah was, even before he assumed the throne, a proponent of technology and by extension, rebellion. Conversely, Prince Eamonn had been a staunch opponent. What if she had gotten it wrong, what if it was Prince Eamonn? It was certainly his forces that invaded the bunker that day, it was his Justice Department who prosecuted and put her in prison. It was Korah's government who freed her.

Sir Preston's loyalties were never in question, he hated Korah and used Kayah as a weapon against him. And over the years, Kayah discovered dozens of things that corroborated Sir Preston's conviction that King Korah was a wicked man.

His oppressive control over technology research and development outraged Himari. Stephen ben McSwilley was Korah's highest ranking intelligence and technology officer, which was enough to make Kayah work against him. Finally, Korah's torture of his own son and probable murder of his wife cemented the monarch as a true villain. But Reuben's words niggled in the back of her mind. Korah might not have been the architect of her arrest, and that required some contemplation.

A loud bark brought Kayah out of her musing. She looked down at her feet and met the inquisitive eyes of a miniature dachshund. Kayah grinned and reached out a hand, the dog sniffed and rolled over on his belly, his tongue lolling in anticipation. Kayah reached down to oblige and looked up at the large man standing six feet from her, holding a leash.

"Forgive him, madam. He is a hopeless flirt. I do my level best to teach him manners, yet I fear it is a lost cause." His whiskey-colored eyes shone with suppressed humor and long-suffering affection toward his little dog.

Perhaps it was the turn of her thoughts that evening, or perhaps because his face was etched upon her memory, at least his father's had been. Kayah knew in an instant who stood before her. She schooled her features and replied, "Lost causes? I have been contemplating the same thing myself. Care to join me?"

He bowed respectfully. "I fear I cannot but appreciate the offer." He looked around; they were alone. "I will escort you inside though, darkness is falling, and the world is not as safe as it used to be."

Throwing caution to the wind, she answered enigmatically, "Some of us are called to travel in darkness. It makes the world safer, does it not?" Kayah studied him as he considered her words. He was a large man and held himself with a confident grace that screamed royalty. How could anyone look at him and not see who he was? Then again, she supposed if she was not looking for long dead royalty, she was not likely to see it.

Prince Josiah ben Eamonn narrowed his brows at her. "I suppose it depends on whether there is a choice in the matter. Like this evening, you could choose to sit out here in the dark by yourself, or you could let Benny escort you safely home."

"Benny?" Kayah quirked a brow at him in question.

Prince Josiah smiled and nodded toward the puppy. "He is an exceptional guardian."

Decency emanated from the man standing before her. He did not leer at her. He did not flirt. She felt no danger from him whatsoever, which was rare. "Somehow, I think his owner is probably a very fine guardian."

He acknowledged the compliment. "It is not always such a clear choice. When an opportunity presents itself, it is usually the best course of action to pursue it."

Kayah rose and took his proffered arm, walking with him companionably. "And when the choice is not so clear?"

Prince Josiah contemplated for a moment and said, "Then we must seek wisdom, pray, and do our best."

Her best? What exactly was Kayah's best? "Hmm. More food for thought on this quiet evening in Geneva."

"Well, madam, you can at least contemplate it in the light and the safety of your hotel. I am off to find this little rascal dinner." He gave her a formal bow. "I bid you good evening."

"And you as well, my Esteemed." Kayah made a clicking sound with her cheek and winked, before disappearing through the door.

Part 8 - The Tech

April 1, 999 ME (Fourteen Years into Rebellion)

Still in Service

Stephen enjoyed riding to the Palace in his official car. It was a tangible reminder of how far he had come, from liveried servant to a respected government minister, not bad for a boy born below stairs. His parents had long since retired, thanks in part, to several lucrative investments Stephen made in the growing technological industry. He was their greatest pride, as the residents at their modest retirement village attested. His mother bragged about him to anyone who would listen.

Stephen did not return to the Palace often, only four times since he left for university, and never for a private audience with King Korah. But today, the King summoned him, and he suspected he might receive another accolade for the work his department was doing. He and the King had been acquainted Stephen's entire life, and while they were not friends, they shared a mutual respect and understanding. Stephen admired King Korah and served Alanthia to the best of his ability.

He grimaced when he stepped out of the vehicle but waved away a footman who reached to steady him. Still suffering from injuries sustained during his brutal massage session two days before, his body ached with every step. Stephen now knew what death looked like, how it spoke, how it taunted and toyed with its prey. Why Kayah had not killed him remained a mystery, but she took her pound of flesh. It had been the scariest ninety minutes of his life.

What Stephen did not know was his new assignment, to find an ancient artifact and the two girls who carried it, would eventually make him wish he were back on that massage table. Death did indeed have hazel eyes and blond hair, but it smelled like rotten eggs.

October 1, 999 ME

You Have to Eat

Five months into his assignment, the knock at Stephen's office door sent a chill down his spine. "Come in," he called weakly.

His most recent assistant entered. "Sir, your car is downstairs to carry thee, I mean you, to the Palace." She gave him a pitying look and added, "Have you eaten? If I may be so bold, thy countenance is pale." She flushed bright red. He knew it embarrassed her when she lapsed into the speech of her youth, and she'd done it twice. No doubt due to the stress they were all feeling.

He coughed, thick mucus rattling in his chest. "Just a bit of a cold, Elizabeta. Do you have those reports ready?"

Elizabeta ben Yoder approached his desk reluctantly. "I regret, they have terminated the signal from Tel Aviv. Your team was unable to obtain triangulation."

Stephen buried his face in his clammy hands and groaned, "He is going to kill me."

"Sir, you are doing everything possible! How can the King ask for more? Everyone in the department is exerting extraordinary energy to locate yon artifact. Surely he understands the difficulty and appreciates the progress thou hast made!"

Stephen closed his eyes and asked, "Elizabeta, do you know where the artifact is?"

Her alabaster skin bloomed with angry red splotches. "No, sir. I do not."

"Well, that is all King Korah cares about."

Elizabeta blinked and set her jaw at the unfairness of it. "Does he think you have some sort of computer god stashed away that you are concealing from him?"

"I wish. It would be nice to have some secret weapon, wouldn't it? A program we could launch that would just find the damn thing."

Elizabeta made the merest flinch at his harsh language. "Like a ghost, that might seek what you need to find?"

Stephen grew still. "A ghost?"

He blinked, remembering a sealed tomb, heard Lavinia's voice from long ago. "Leave it alone, Stephen. There is something here, something powerful that went beyond even what they could handle. These algorithms are like nothing I have ever seen, beautiful but sinister." She pointed to the skeleton and said, "He says it was alive, I can tell you from the math, it was, and it was a hunter."

Stephen inhaled, his face set. "Elizabeta, I think that is exactly what we need."

The King of Pain

That night, Stephen descended the dark stairway into the basement of his house, convinced King Korah was insane. There were always whispers among the servants, knowing glances, some pitying, more often frightened. But now, Stephen had firsthand experience with that side of King Korah.

Behind the cool and urbane royal facade lay a mad man, and his mercurial nature made him terrifying. Some meetings found him in a rage, other times he was solicitous and encouraging. Once, last August, Korah openly wept, in the grip of a black depression. During interviews, he vacillated from warm and friendly to cold malicious anger. It was disconcerting. Occasionally, Korah's office smelled like rotten eggs, the precursor to unbridled evil. The receiving parlor became his personal waiting room to Hell.

He considered quitting.

However, to resign meant failure. By his estimation, he only failed once, and it cost him the love of his life. He should have moved on. His mother nagged him to do just that, but no one ever captured his heart as completely as Lavinia ben Anthony.

Downstairs, the shelves in his private laboratory held the broken remnants of their old equipment, catalogued, tagged, and sorted. After the raid and their arrest, he snuck back to the bunker and took what the government left behind. For weeks, he wandered the deserted caverns alone, consumed with self-loathing and remorse.

When he became the Minister of Technology, he methodically and surreptitiously gathered all the Alcatraz 5 equipment and research. None of them would believe it, but for Stephen, the years spent on the verge of discovery in that underground bunker were the best of his life. The recreation of their project became his tribute to them, to that magical period. He did it in lieu of actual connections to them because they severed all ties. Even Gus, who had given him a second chance, no longer spoke to him. Stephen was well and truly alone.

He cast himself in the role of tragic and misunderstood genius, existing around the edges of life, longing for human connection, but too inept or afraid to plug in to anyone or anything, other than work. He used the resources of the Ministry to plant cameras at Himari's wedding to Filippo ben Vincente. Sitting alone in the dark, with a bank of monitors on the wall, he watched it live. He smiled at Himari's red trimmed wedding gown, a perfect blend of Japanese and Alanthian. He looked away in envy as Gus walked her down the aisle and wept openly at the paintings. His blood ran cold, and his sphincter drew up tight when he recognized Kayah. He had not expected to see her, and she reminded him of the humiliating scene at the Techies. He eavesdropped on his old friends and heard them laughing about it. That incident, on a night that should have been his crowning achievement, earned him the ignominious nickname, Stephen ben McShitty.

The true reason he bugged the wedding was to see Lavinia. Time had been kind to her. She was even lovelier than when they were kids. While the rest of the fools in the congregation lusted after the supermodel, Stephen only had eyes for the elegant Italian goddess. She existed in his memory and his dreams for more than a decade. But to watch her on screen and still not be able to touch her, to talk to her, was almost more than he could bear. So, he captured images of her, printing and framing them, decorating his house, and speaking to her as he went about his days. It was pathetic, but he did not care.

As the pressure from King Korah built, Stephen sought the

refuge of his underground lab and the virtual companionship of his old friends. Their faces flashed across the screens as he worked. Lavinia on monitor one, Himari on two, Gus on three, and even Kayah, beautiful, dangerous, murderous Kayah, on six. His own image occupied monitor number four. He chose his own pictures with great care. They flashed with regularity, showing his success, his office, his awards. In the center, a monitor equipped with speakers, played their old soundtrack, music from the bunker. He was fond of The Police and privately thought he looked like Stewart Copeland, the drummer. The irony of the band's name did not escape his notice.

He pulled equipment from the shelves, the materials from the tomb, and ignored the warnings screaming in his mind. Queuing up one of his favorite songs, he began to build.

October 14, 999 ME

The Material World

"Gus, honey, supper is ready. Come along now." Gus' mother Alice ben Wayne called from the doorway of his workshop, being careful not to step over the boundary line Gus had drawn. She respected his peculiarities, especially when they did not harm anyone. He was her last remaining child at home, and he always would be. Even after they lifted the court order, she and her husband Allen knew he would not leave, he could not. He did not function properly in the world.

From behind the draped enclosure, Gus murmured, "Momma, I'm not hungry."

"Nonsense. You are wasting away to nothing. You need to eat."

Gus' auburn head emerged from his secret workspace. "I was fat. It makes it hard to move when you are fat."

Alice blew out an exasperated breath. They had this conversation a hundred times in the last four years. "Yes, but you've taken it a step too far. You are not fat now, and you are weak because you do not eat properly. You could not even pick up a bale of hay with your father last week. Time was, you could carry two. I'll not have it." Asserting her maternal authority, she said, "Come."

His shoulders slouched as he shuffled toward her. "My machine picks up the bales," he mumbled.

"It was merely a point of reference, Son. You are not healthy." She gestured at the curtain. "You cannot spend the rest of your life behind that shroud."

Gus looked down at her through sulking gray eyes. "My work is important."

She set her face and tried to control her frustration. "I don't dispute that, Gus, but there is an entire world going on around you. It breaks my heart to see you, like you are right now."

"It's important," he reasserted. "But I'll eat, if it makes you happy."

"It would make me happy if you took that job. It's an excellent offer, Gus. The first one you have received in years. You should take it. You should try." Alice squeezed his thin arm.

He rocked back and forth as he ambled to the house with her. "I don't work well with others."

"Bull," she protested. "You work well enough with your father and your brothers, and you follow directions. Your mind just wanders, but that is part of your special gift. If you write down your tasks and your deadlines, like we talked about, I know you can do it."

He hung his head. "Well, my project is pretty much done. I guess I could try, but I won't get too excited. They always fire me."

"This time might be different, and it is more money than you have ever earned. Even if it only lasts for a while…" her words trailed off. The farm was in trouble, and she and Allen were not getting any younger. If not for Gus, they would have sold long since and left. The way things stood, Gus' income would not only secure him, but would keep them from losing everything. She had to make him understand. "Gus, you need to take it. We need the money."

He stilled at the threshold of the kitchen. "We do?"

Alice glanced at the meager pot of stew on the stove and nodded. "We do, Son."

Gus began rubbing his thumbs together, staring down as he considered her words. "All right, Momma. I'll take the job at Facetec."

November 1, 999 ME

Where Y'at?

"Al," Himari exclaimed in exasperation, "where is your head today?"

Alaina looked up, distracted. "What?"

"That!" Himari widened her eyes and stretched her neck forward, making a point. "What is wrong with you? I've said the same thing to you three times. Have you gone deaf?"

Alaina covered her mouth with her hand, aquamarine eyes brimming with tears.

Himari came out of her chair. "What's happened?"

"He contacted me last night," Alaina whispered.

Himari drew back, incredulous. "The Mystery Man?"

Alaina's face crumpled, and she hid a small sob.

"Al," Himari wrapped her slender arms around Alaina's shoulders and squeezed, "why didn't you tell me?"

Alaina choked on the words, "It's against the rules."

Himari's shaky laugh was buried in Alaina's blonde hair. "The rules? Oh, honey, that is the saddest thing I have heard all year. Wait until I tell Filippo."

"They were his rules," Alaina protested, her voice small and childish. "They were good rules. I would not have survived these last nine years without them."

"What did he say?" Himari got her tea and settled down to listen.

Alaina wiped her eyes and with a rueful laugh said, "Hi."

"Hi? After all this time, hi?" She lifted her lip in scorn. "What else?"

Alaina rubbed her forehead. "Not much, but it brought it all back."

Himari took her hand, catching the sparkle from the diamond on Alaina's finger. She had never given up, never lost faith, but she never spoke his name. "Do you still love him?"

Alaina looked heavenward. "I do."

Himari studied her, trying to choose the right words. She had known two great loves in her life, one light and one shadow. "Is he a good man, Alaina? Did he treat you well? More importantly, did he respect you?"

Alaina closed her eyes and let out a small cry. "Oh, Himari. Beau Landry," his name sounded foreign on her tongue, "is the most wonderful man I have ever known. A good man, from a great family, who treated me with the utmost respect." Himari watched Alaina's face grow soft with affection. "He is a warrior and a protector, handsome as the devil, and could charm an alligator. He took me in, gave me a home, loved me." She twisted the ring. "I would not have waited for less."

A bit placated, Himari asked, "So, what happens now?"

Alaina sighed, running her finger over her keyboard. "I don't know. I guess we put the finishing touches on this program."

Himari smiled, understanding Filippo's third rule was still firmly in place. "Now, we work."

What the Math?

Lavinia was deep in the labyrinth, pulling numbers in where she needed them, discarding ones no longer necessary. Winding her way through the maze, she sought the center. Inside her mathematical wonderland, there was no sound, smell, taste, or touch, simply the math and Lavinia its master. Elegance and beauty flowed, streamlined and simple, she created.

It took a long time before she felt him under her desk, toying with her bare feet. Richard had crept in and entertained himself while she worked. Mack taught him that, sometimes with a word, and sometimes with a swat. The swatting made a big impression, so he was careful not to disturb her. She wiggled her toes in acknowledgement.

"What the math?" Richard asked from under a mop of unruly brown curls.

Lavinia pushed her chair away from her desk and took a drink of sugary soda. "An algorithm, almost as beautiful as you, but not quite."

"An algorithm?" he repeated, sounding exactly like his father. The cadence and pronunciation were as endearing as it was ironic. She was raising a little southern boy, on a California vineyard, that produced Italian wine. "What's it do?"

Lavinia looked around to ensure they were alone and leaned down with a conspiratorial whisper, "This one can jam surveillance programs and make you invisible."

Richard smiled. "Like when I was little and thought when I closed my eyes you couldn't see me?"

Lavinia nodded. "Exactly, this closes the big eyes in the sky that spy on us."

Richard looked at the ceiling and whispered, "Spies are bad."

She sighed. They regularly swept and removed surveillance items from their home. For Richard it was a game, a normal part of life, for Lavinia and Mack, a constant threat. "Some spies are good, if they are on your side." She hefted him into her lap and kissed the small point on his delicate ear. "We are just careful, aren't we?"

He wiggled away. "We make wine!" he declared and puffed out his little chest. "The best damn wine in the state."

Lavinia tried to control the twitch at the corner of her mouth. He sounded exactly like Mack. "Language…"

He gave a mischievous giggle and scampered from the study, hollering down the hall, "The best damn wine in the state!"

Credit

Later that evening, Mack groaned as he stretched his stiff left side. "Turn it on, Valentine."

Lavinia picked through his pile and flipped the switch on the surveillance jamming device Gus created. They swept the day before but after finding half a dozen bugs in the last two years they took no chances. By rote, she pulled the blackout shade and drew the drapes. Holding up a finger for him to wait, she carried his dirty clothes to the laundry.

When she returned, his eyes drooped in sleep. With the harvest in its final days, Mack looked exhausted. Since coming to Peccioli, he threw himself into the work. Possessing an innate understanding of the soil, he anticipated what the grapes needed, and brought innovation to their cultivation. And for all the skill and vigor he brought to the land, his true gift emerged in the winery.

Lavinia's wine had been scientifically engineered to perfection, but a recent write up in a prestigious magazine hit upon the difference. "The Peccioli Vineyard has been long respected as a producer of excellent and consistent Cabernet Sauvignon, but

with their 997 vintage Bulizio, they moved from technical perfection to magic. There is a heart and soul in this wine that evokes
the palazzos of Italy and warms the heart of all who are fortunate
enough to procure a bottle of this truly remarkable gem.”

Lavinia snuggled in beside Mack, smoothing his hair, still
damp from the shower.

He pressed his head into her hand with a low groan. “Mmm…
pet me. I'm tired.”

“I'd expect you are. Are you finished?” she asked, massaging
his scalp.

“Mmm hmm,” he murmured, then yawned.

“I finished today, too,” she whispered.

Mack opened one red rimmed brown eye. “You did?”

“It's beautiful, Mack.”

The corner of his mouth lifted. “Good. That means it will
work.”

She gazed at the dark ceiling, seeing the numbers. “Oh, yes. I
would not risk you otherwise, my love.”

His heavy arm wrapped over her belly, and he pulled her tight
to his side. “I love smart women,” he said, then faded into sleep.

November 10, 999 ME

At Last

Gus brimmed with pride as he signed for the check. The tux-
edoed waiter bowed and expressed his appreciation for the generous tip. Gus grinned at his mother and father, in their Sunday
best, flushed with wine and sated by an excellent meal. “It might
be the strangest place I ever worked, but they pay well.”

“You deserve it, honey.” Alice beamed. “I'm just glad you finally found your place.”

Allen shifted his weight in the stiff chair, full and a bit uncomfortable because of it. “It's like I told you, keep your list, and
stay on time.”

“That's just it, Daddy.” Gus' thick brows drew down in per-
plexity. “They did not want me to do anything. They gave me
an office and these business cards.” He pulled one from his wallet. “Nothing else. It was weird. I couldn't be bored all day, so

me and this other fellow started talking about what Facetec was trying to do, and then another guy came over, and he had some ideas, too. They were missing a program and a microprocessor. The company invested millions in it, and it got stolen back in the summer."

He shook his head in wonder. "They did not care what we were doing, so we just sat down and did it. Joe and I worked out the programing, and I rebuilt the microprocessor. We got it to work today."

Alice's face broke into a huge grin. "You did?"

"We did. I'd seen some of the programing a long time ago." He looked away, remembering where. He did not talk about the bunker, so he said, "I know how to make things. We got it to work."

Allen leaned back in his chair, beaming with pride. "That's good. I am sure your boss was happy."

Gus furrowed his brows and said, "Hard to tell. He is a strange Italian, not like Filippo. He sort of reminds me of a fox."

Alice smiled. Gus was normally not so communicative. "Why a fox?" They kept chickens on the farm and a couple of years ago had lost their entire hen house to a predator. Until then, the beautiful creatures had been Gus' favorite.

Gus shrugged his big shoulders, less bony than they had been a month ago, but still too slender for his large frame. "He's pretty like they are. You remember that black one we saw a few years ago?" Alice nodded. "He's like that."

Allen grunted. "Well, stay out of his way, he's paying you good. Keep your head down and do your job."

Gus put his wallet in his back pocket and muttered, "Yeah, I just don't want to end up like one of them chickens."

Part 9 - Neverland

September 22, 999 ME

Kensington Park Gardens - Notting Hill, London

Kayah might have disappeared anywhere in the world, but she chose London and an improbable, turreted four-story townhouse that backed up to the charming communal Stanley Gardens South. The place was a ghastly expense, and at closing, they presented her with a fifty-page document from the historical preservation society on what she could and could not do with her new home.

She painted the door blue, by herself. She could have hired it done, but it seemed right to put her own hand to the task. Painting the door felt like she was sealing it, making it her own, the shade of blue among five approved colors. When she bought the house, the door was black, and Kayah did not want to live in a house with a black door.

She liked London. It reminded her of Sir Preston, old, dignified, intelligent. The irony that she settled here would not be lost on him. They spoke English, and for monolingual Kayah, that was a must. But she had never worked here, so there was no overzealous investigator out to make a name for himself at her expense. It was also convenient. Five years ago, Alanthia and Europe launched the first Transatlantic flights, so London was logical if she needed to make a quick getaway. However, more than anything, the ancient solidness of the place appealed to her. Its roots ran deep, and she wanted to make a home here.

The neighbor's house, several units down, inspired JM Barrie to pen the classic, Peter Pan, and for Kayah her Notting Hill house felt like a castle in Neverland. Her New York apartment was trendy, her New City residence sterile, and the Mont Carmel beach condo looked like the twenty other units beside it. She purchased them furnished and professionally decorated. By contrast, the London townhouse was completely empty, unless one considered the detailed plaster work, wrought-iron railings and gates, and the scalloped arches, empty. Kayah liked to use the banister as she climbed the steps, feeling the history of the hands that preceded her, imagining their lives, and weaving tales of grand parties and love affairs. The previous occupant lived in the house for sixty-five years, and Kayah often detected the faint smell of Lady Grey tea and powdery perfume.

One of her new neighbors fancied himself the local historian and enthusiastically shared two of his precious books that contained photographs of the street from the Last Age. A few blurred pictures of her own unit prompted her to do some period research at the library. And while she did not care for the kitschy style and dark wood of the original Victorian residents, the images of tufted velvet sofas, high-backed chaise lounges, and brass table lamps drew her. The creams, golds, and tans would create a marked contrast to the institutional grays and whites she had grown up with. So, two weeks after moving in and sick of sleeping on an air mattress, she set about town, upfitting her new home.

She adopted a new identity, a wealthy widow from Boston, Dorothy ben Quincy, whose young husband, a rising political star, succumbed to a sudden and violent illness of unknown, but suspicious, origins. The political climate being what it was in Alanthia, Ms. ben Quincy deemed it prudent to relocate to London. Her proper English neighbors were not so vulgar as to ask her outright, so she floated bits and pieces of the story until the local gossips wove their own tragic history for her. They left the young widow alone. To anyone else, beginning a new life with a fabricated name and history might seem paradoxical, but for Kayah it was as normal as toast and jam. She reverted to her natural look, without paint, prosthetics, or costumes. In an odd way, Dorothy became more real than Kayah.

London was a biking and walking city, but the conference in Geneva changed that. Last week, a fleet of chartered vessels from Alanthia off loaded their cargo in Felixstowe. The press and Prince Edward were on hand to welcome the first double-decker bus in almost a millennium. Londoners turned out in droves to wave at the iconic vehicle as it made its way through the twisted, narrow streets. Kayah foresaw the eventual lifting of the tech ban and invested heavily in automobiles five years prior, and by the Summer of '99, she would never have to work another day in her life.

She purchased the townhouse through two trusts and a shell corporation, Prince Peter inspired subterfuge. Flush with cash, a new identity, and a new home, Kayah ben Samuel disappeared without a trace. She abandoned her old life completely. No one knew where she was or how to get in contact with her, and unfortunate necessity. It would be months before her friends realized she was gone, several weeks for Sir Preston, and for Reuben, she could not bear to consider. If he was meant to find her, he would.

November 11, 999 ME

An English Gentleman

The occupant who lived behind Kayah's townhouse was the fattest stray cat Kayah ever saw, and she suspected she was not the only Kensington Park Garden resident who fed him. In the months she lived there, they developed a routine. Every morning, promptly at 7:30 am, he showed up for breakfast and bid her good evening at 10:30 pm. Thus, her days began and ended with Mr. Mumps, so named because as a British Shorthair his cheeks were quite pronounced. Kayah spoiled him rotten.

Mr. Mumps possessed impeccable manners, was not overly vocal, and seemed to Kayah the most relaxed animal ever created. His luxurious fur reminded her of the London sky before a storm, blue gray, unpresumptuous and constant. Only his copper-colored eyes prevented him from being a shadow. He was enormous, twenty pounds if he was an ounce, and after breakfast he lay at her feet to groom his soft coat. His low purr traveled up her legs, calm and steady. She fancied them quite a pair.

He would dine inside if it rained, but the morning of November 11, 999 ME dawned clear and cool, so they took their breakfast on the small back patio overlooking the garden. While she might have abandoned her old life, she did not abandon her old habits or her vigilance. Her townhouse was strategically located at the end of the row, with access to three main thoroughfares and the sizeable garden in the rear. She could slip away and disappear in an instant. There were five escape routes out of the residence, one of which the historical society would have had a collective apoplexy if they knew.

As she sipped her tea and studied a row of Michaelmas daisies, an unmistakable strut caught her attention. Confident and cocky, loved and longed for, he held a bouquet of purple mums and white roses. Wearing black trousers and a wool overcoat, he appeared to the world like a British gentleman, but a warrior's heart beat beneath his conservative attire.

She was tousled and sleepy, without even a hint of mascara. Her soft flannel pants and top were saved from dowdiness by their designer's cut and the woman who occupied them. She let him come, enjoying the sight, a smile teasing the corners of her mouth. It had been four months since they parted in Geneva, a lifetime for Dorothy ben Quincy, who had a suitor, for Kayah ben Samuel, she had a lover.

Reuben paused outside the wrought-iron gate, looking absurdly handsome in his bowler hat. "Ms. Dorothy ben Quincy," he intoned in an upper crust British accent, "I have come to pay a morning call upon you. I beg your indulgence."

Kayah wanted to indulge him right where he stood, but was mindful that her neighbors, particularly the elderly sisters two doors down, were likely glued to their windows, paying very close attention. She rose with genteel grace and bade him enter.

He handed her the bouquet, bowed, and raised her hand to his lips for a kiss, murmuring, "Yakira."

Kayah brought the flowers to her nose and inhaled the warm spicy scent while her eyes devoured him.

"May I present my friend, Mr. Mumps?" Kayah gestured to

the lounging gray cat, who regarded Reuben with dispassionate interest. "Mr. Mumps, this is," her voice trailed off, "my very good friend."

Reuben doffed his hat. "Mr. Isaac ben Joseph, your servant, sir."

Kayah smiled at the absurd farce played out for two old ladies and a cat. "Mr. ben Joseph, it is exceedingly kind of you to pay a call this morning. May I offer you a cup of tea or perhaps a coffee? Though we shall have to retire inside, while I prepare it."

His nose flared, his breathing audible in the small enclosure. "Coffee, if it is not too much trouble, my lady."

"Indeed, it is not, sir." She swallowed thickly and with movements as slow as if she walked through glycerin, led him into the townhouse.

They began pulling off each other's clothes the second the door shut. Panting, kissing, biting, Reuben backed her against the wall and tore his mouth from hers. "You disappeared!" It was a cry, a groan, an accusation. His breath came in deep gulps, as his pupils widened, desperation punctuating his words and his movements. "Yakira," he thrust against her, "do not... do that again."

Reminiscent of their first night together, Kayah moaned, engulfed in the flames of desire. She let him take her with the force of his fury, accepting it, rejoicing in it, loving it.

Reuben held her suspended, bracing a hand against the wall as he came into her, driving deep, in punishment, relief, reunion, and ecstasy. "I was so afraid, something happened to you," he ground out. When he climaxed, he threw his head back with a guttural cry. Then collapsed into her, his forehead pressed to her cheek.

Kayah locked her ankles around his waist, encircled his neck with her arms, and held him tight as he shuddered. "I'm sorry I scared you."

"Yakira," his voice broke, "I have lost everyone that I ever loved. I cannot lose you."

Her heart soared. "You have not lost me, Agent. You just found me." She kissed the side of his cheek, surprised to find a single tear leaking from his eye. The earthy scent of crushed flowers and sex filled the small hallway, her bouquet abandoned against the door. "Now, put me down so I can put those flowers in water, and I will make you coffee. You are strung taut as a bowstring."

He gave a drowsy chuckle and lifted her from him. "Not any longer. Cafe' sounds good, is good."

Kayah cleaned herself up and changed while the coffee brewed. When she came downstairs, Reuben had fallen asleep, sitting up in her living room, his bowler hat on his lap. She paused, just looking at him. In repose, dark circles became visible under his eyes. His knuckles were scraped, and there was a gash on the back of his left hand.

She retrieved his overcoat from the floor, running her hands over the fine wool. It smelled of him. With a private smile, she went to the kitchen and poured his coffee.

Placing the mug on the glass table in front of him, she removed the hat, and curled by his side. "What is wrong? You look exhausted."

He blinked, coming awake with a hazy smile. "But I am here now, and it is good, is good."

She rubbed his shoulder. "Is good," she said mimicking his accent.

He buried his face in her hair with a delirious chuckle. "I am ready to take a page out of your book, Dorothy. But I have a couple hours before I report to the Embassy. Let us just say it has been an interesting journey across Europe."

She pulled him down on the couch with her, cradling his cheeks between her hands. "How did you find me?"

His eyelids drooped, and he grinned. "I am Mossad."

"So, do they know, or just you?"

"I did not tell them, Yakira. The Iron King," he shrugged, "He knows all, so if Mossad asks and He tells, they know." Pausing, he cupped her cheek and murmured, "You scared me."

She rested her hand over his. "Come upstairs, Reuben."

The master suite dominated the third floor and commanded a spectacular view of the park. She decorated it in rich cream, gold, and bronze. The understated elegance and warm hues complemented rather than competed with the ornate plasterwork and molding.

Reuben, fresh off a monumental fight in Calais and a mad dash across the channel to Windsor, had not slept for two days. The bed looked like Heaven. He moaned when he saw it and belly flopped, fully clothed.

Kayah pulled off his shoes and socks and generally ministered to him in a businesslike manner. She understood how it felt, coming down hard off an assignment. With the adrenaline spent, the body had demands of its own: sex, sleep, and food. She took care of the first, tended to the second, and would ensure she provided the third. "What time do I need to get you up?" Kayah asked, snuggling beside him.

"I have to report to the Embassy at 16:00, wake me up at 14:00." He pulled her tight against his side. "Stay with me for a while, just a while."

She propped on one elbow and smoothed his thick black eyebrows, then the bridge of his nose, and the outline of his well-shaped mouth, resting her hand on his clean-shaven jaw. "There is no other place on earth I would rather be. Rest. I will watch over you."

What You Love

While Reuben slept, Kayah attempted something she never tried before, cooking for a man, or cooking for anyone, for that matter. She knew how, and Dorothy was a superb cook, or so she told herself.

Wandering through the Notting Hill market, uncertainty dogged her. Nothing brought out her hidden insecurities more than doing something personal for someone. She hated buying presents, not that there were a lot of occasions to do so, but the process always felt grueling. It was not the expense, it was her deep-seated fear that the gift, and by extension the giver, might be inadequate, inappropriate, or unwanted. As a result, most of the time she gave cash. At the market, faced with a thousand possibilities, a black hole opened and swallowed her whole.

"Fish," she muttered, heading to the first stall. "He likes to fish, but can I cook it? How do you cook fish? Fry it? Wasn't that a mess?" She envisioned herself covered in grease, her new kitchen on fire. "No, fish.

"Beef! He loves beef, but is English beef any good? What if English beef sucks? No, not beef."

"Chicken, yes, that is safe, but so common. I want to impress him, and chicken? Chicken doesn't impress anyone."

Scanning the market, panic pushed in at the edges. "This is a nice pork roast, but does he keep dietary laws? Have I ever seen him eat pork?" She could not remember. "Okay, no pork. Shit! Now what?

"Lamb!" she breathed in relief. "But how the hell do you make lamb? We don't eat lamb in Alanthia. Good Lord, what was I thinking? This is a stupid idea."

She spotted a Turkish restaurant and slumped in defeat. "Just buy a couple doner kebobs and be done with it."

A calming voice whispered in her spirit, "Make him what you love. Share with Reuben the things that make you happy, Kayah."

She stilled, standing in the market with a hundred people milling around her; she knew who spoke.

He had come to her once, in her cell, Stubby's semen dripping between her legs, mixed with her virgin's blood. His presence kept her from going mad. That He would return today, over such a trivial thing as what to fix Reuben for lunch, seemed an irony beyond comprehension.

"What I love?" she breathed, looking up at the dancing white clouds. "What do I love?"

Inspiration struck, and she knew what to do. Filling her basket in perfect peace, she swung it like a schoolgirl as she walked back to her home and her lover.

Reuben hovered in the delicate netherworld between waking and sleeping. Perceiving a pleasant aroma wafting up the steps, he felt an even more pleasant weight settle beside him in the luxurious bed. "Mmm." He reached for her, stretching as he did so, eyes closed, mouth pressed into a sleepy grin.

"It's 1:45 pm. I couldn't wait any longer." Kayah kissed the side of his neck, absurdly turned on by the scratch of his beard stubble against her cheek. "Lunch is ready downstairs."

"Eat later," he growled, moving his hands over her body. "I did not greet you properly this morning."

She did not have a scrap of clothing on. "I did not complain."

"I am a beast." He kissed her gently.

Kayah whispered against his mouth, "You are a man."

"Oh, I am that." He spent the next half hour showing her just how much.

"You cooked for me spaghetti? How did you know that I love spaghetti with meat sauce?" Reuben tilted his head in contemplation. "It is my favorite meal. Strange for an Israeli, yes?"

Kayah covered her mouth and nodded, her eyes stinging. "It's mine, too."

"Something else we share, Yakira."

After lunch, Reuben locked his hands around her waist, resting them comfortably. "I will be back soon. I have taken no leave since I saw you in Geneva, and then only twenty-four hours. There are thirty days I will lose if I do not take them before the end of the year." He whispered against her lips, "So I will apply for them tonight. We shall scandalize your neighbors if you will have me?"

A month? A month to have him at her side, in the house she hoped to build a new life in. Would she have him? It would be the closest thing she ever had to a normal life, and it terrified and thrilled her beyond reckoning. Her voice was barely audible. "I will have you. See you tonight?"

The crooked tooth made an appearance, charming in his otherwise perfect smile. "It might be late. Prince Yehonathan is in residence. My debrief is going to be extensive. I expect you naked when I get home."

Broken Resolve

Kayah looked at the phone for the twentieth time that night, feeling more absurd by the hour. Lavinia's number was dialed, all she needed to do was press send. It was a burner phone, encrypted with Mossad technology. Even Himari could not track her with this thing, and she wanted to talk to Lavinia.

At 9:30 pm, her resolve broke. Lavinia's voice cracked over the line, and the hairs on the back of Kayah's neck stood on end.

For a second, Kayah almost hurled the phone. She did not want to know why Lavinia sounded like that. "Vinia?"

"Kai," Lavinia sobbed. "You called! I have been frantic. We didn't… no one knew how to find you. Thank God. Are you okay? Are you?"

"I'm fine," Kayah said, feeling her blood run cold. "What's happened?"

"You don't know? I thought that is why you were calling." Renewed sobbing overtook Lavinia as the phone rustled.

"Kayah, it's Mack."

Kayah's mind raced. "What has happened?"

"Are you somewhere close? Can you get here?"

Tears burned the back of her eyes. It was Himari or Gus. There were no other people in the world that would elicit such a request. "I'm far away, Mack. Tell me."

"Sit down." She heard him exhale, right before he shattered her world, changing it forever, marking it, life before and life after. "I'm sorry, Kayah. Gus was killed in an apparent terrorist attack today."

"No." Kayah's mind rebelled. "Are you sure?"

"Yes. Jihadists stormed the office where he was working. He did not make it. I'm sorry."

Guilt washed over her. She had stopped sending Gus money and old tech, stopped giving him work, and now he was dead. "Did they catch them?" Kayah snarled through gritted teeth and tears. "Did they kill them, Mack?"

"No." Scorn dripped from his lips. The Royal Guard, the soldier, the sheriff, bonded with the assassin in a single word.

"Then we will." Cold determination shoved the grief aside.

"I reckon the funeral won't be for a couple of days, but I think it's time for you to come home, Kayah. You and I, we've got work to do."

They had both been living in a fairy tale, trying to forget the wicked King they were inevitably going to fight.

"Okay, Mack. Tell Lavinia I love her." As she hung up the phone, Dorothy ben Quincy died just assuredly as Gus ben Allen.

November 12, 999 ME

Pixie Dust

Reuben returned to the townhouse just after midnight and found it dark, no movement inside. When Kayah did not answer the door, he realized he had not thought to get a phone number this afternoon. He swore under his breath, thinking she might have panicked and run away. Then he considered she might be playing a spy game, albeit ill timed. He had ridden a bike from the Embassy to Feltham and back, then shivered in a cold fog while Prince Josiah and Davianna ben David had a tête-à-tête on Waterloo Bridge. Outside the Notting Hill townhouse, Reuben faded into the shadows, in case Kayah's failure to answer the door turned out to be something more sinister than her just falling asleep.

After a thorough reconnaissance, he determined no one watched the house but still detected no movement inside. At 01:45, he found her lying motionless in her bed. When she did not stir, his blood ran cold. Approaching cautiously, he sniffed the air, searching and dreading the tell-tale stench of death, mentally preparing himself to find her murdered. Checking her pulse, her wrist felt warm, her heartbeat slow but steady. He melted in relief.

"Kayah," he breathed, then switched on the bedside lamp, casting the cozy room in warm yellow light. She did not move, and that was when he panicked. Shouting her name, he shook her shoulders, pulling her into a sitting position.

Her head lolled, and she looked at him through hazy eyes, slurring, "Leave me alone."

Her dilated pupils told the story, she was drugged.

He patted her cheek, trying to keep her awake as she went limp in his arms. "Kayah, who did this to you? Wake up. Tell me what has happened!"

"Gus…" she muttered weakly.

"Who does this Gus work for?" Reuben saw red. He would kill any man who hurt her.

"Worked for me, my friend." Kayah's head fell forward. "He's dead."

"You killed him?" Reuben said, scanning the room for signs of struggle. "Where is the body?"

Kayah pushed him away, fighting to go back to sleep. "Jihad-ists."

An inhuman noise erupted from Reuben. "They have been here?"

His anger penetrated her stupor, and she swam to the surface. "No, my friend Gus is dead. New City jihadists killed him."

"Kayah, what did you take?"

She grunted, growing irritable now. "I took a Quaalude. Now, go away."

"How many?"

"One," she grunted, "sleeping."

Reuben dropped her, and she fell back, limp. In the light, with the threat of danger gone, he stared at her in absolute disbe-lief. The last person he expected to drug themselves into oblivion was Kayah ben Samuel. But in a blinding instant, he understood, knew that sort of pain. And while he abhorred drugs, she did not need a lecture from him tonight.

Turning off the light, he disrobed and climbed into bed be-side her.

Kayah cracked an eyelid at him. "Glad you turned out that light."

Her accent sounded different, New City, without the cul-tured diction and precise syllables that were the hallmark of her normal speech. With a massive exertion of will, he calmed his hammering heart, took her in his arms and murmured, "Yakira, I am sorry about your friend."

"He loved me, always. He was the only one who ever loved me."

Reuben held her as she trembled. "No, no, I love you."

"You love me? That's good, Reuben." Kayah made a self-sat-isfied snort and snuggled against him. She used sparingly, but when life became too much, Quaalude was her drug of choice. The drug numbed, she forgot, and then she slept, but she never took one in company. "Do you love me 'cause I'm hot?"

Her rapid change from grief to inebriated wench amused him. "Well, that is part of it, but that is not all."

She laughed and swatted weakly at his chest. "You love me 'cause I'm a badass?"

He cupped said badass and pulled her closer. "That is part of it, yes."

Kayah snuggled into him and smiled. "You love me 'cause I can make boom-boom against a wall better than anybody?"

"Boom-boom?" Reuben chuckled. "That is indeed true and part of why I love you."

"Hmm," she seemed to consider, "You love me 'cause I can look like a hundred different women, and that is sexy as hell."

He had seen her as a blonde, a brunette, a black-haired Italian, and even a middle-aged Alanthian woman; it was hot. "Yes, your talents are part of it."

"I have many talents you don't know about," she slurred in a sing-song voice, then moved in for a kiss, missed, and giggled. "I can make a person poop themselves. Did you know that?" She got a wicked gleam in her eye. "I did it once, 'cause he deserved it. My friends thought it was hysterical." Her breath caught in her chest. "My friend…"

She made a rapid series of quick inhales through her nose, but shook it off and turned to him, blinking several times behind red-rimmed and swollen eyes. "Those girls you watch, that's why I talked to them that day. They reminded me of my friends." She paused, her lower lip quivering. "We didn't really do anything wrong, but they put me in prison. It's a terrible place, always smells like pee."

Reuben held her tight. The thought of her imprisoned sickened him. "I know, Yakira. Do not think about it. It is over."

"I don't… but sometimes I do." She rested her head against his chest. "It comes and gets you, out of nowhere. Like on the steps of a police station, just standing there, and all of a sudden you're back there, being raped, and you can't stop it." She made a small, pitiful sound. "I couldn't stop him."

Reuben did not say a word, just held her close as waves of murderous fury washed over him.

She felt it, and it energized her. With a maniacal laugh, she slurred, "But later, I killed him, and they never figured out how I did it. And that little shithead that sent me to prison? I gave him a taste of how it feels to be tied to a bed, at somebody else's mercy. Don't screw with me, it is bad policy."

"That's my girl," Reuben said, knocked asunder by her confession, but determined not to ask her, to bring her more grief.

"That's why you love me!" Kayah exclaimed. "Because I am like you. Don't mess with Reuben and Kayah, we are dangerous."

"The world is dangerous, Kayah. We just balance it out."

She chuckled, "You sound like somebody I talked to the night you left Geneva. I picked at him a bit, and you should have seen his face when he realized I recognized him. But he was nice. I liked him, and I don't like most people. He didn't seem like his father, which is good, because I think his father was a dickhead."

The corner of Reuben's mouth lifted in a smile. Propped on one elbow, he studied her. "Who are you talking about?"

"I shouldn't say." Then she laid a hand on his cheek, harder than she intended. "Hell, I bet Mossad knows. You boys know all sorts of stuff."

"We do."

"Hmm. That's interesting, isn't it? If we both know the same things, it shines a whole new light on our super-secret spy relationship, doesn't it?"

Reuben laughed. "I suppose it does. But I thought you retired, Dorothy?"

"It was apparently a premature retirement. I've been called back to active duty." She smacked her lips, reached for the glass of water by the bedside, and drained it. The empty glass tipped over and rolled harmlessly to the rug.

"So, who did you talk to in Geneva that you liked?" Reuben prompted.

Kayah raised a golden eyebrow at him. "A dead Prince."

Reuben chuckled low and deep, the sound reverberating in his chest. "Which one?"

"Oh, I'll be damned, you tricky Israeli. How many are there?"

"There are a few missing royals. Who did you meet?" he nuzzled her neck, teasing.

She trusted him with her heart. To speak meant she trusted him with her life. "Josiah ben Eamonn."

Reuben tilted his head, studying her, considering. "That is who I was with tonight."

Kayah stilled as the barriers between them splintered. "You know about my work, don't you?"

Reuben shrugged. "Alanthia has been high on the Iron King's priorities for several years, Kayah. There are no secrets from him."

"Then why doesn't he just fix it? Why do people like my friend Gus have to die?" Lethargy overtook her, as she sank into the pillows. "It hurts, and I don't understand."

"I know," Reuben soothed. "Why don't you sleep now? I'll watch over you."

"That's my job," Kayah murmured.

"It was not supposed to be, Yakira," Reuben smoothed the silky hair from her eyes, "but I'm here now, you rest."

She curled against him, looking small for the first time since he met her. He caught a glimpse of the little girl she had been. How anyone had thrown her away seemed impossible, a tragedy beyond his imagination. Reuben rubbed her back, and Kayah slept.

Tick Tock

Hell broke loose when Reuben arrived at the Embassy yesterday. He expected to give a report on the fight in Calais, debrief the new team, and begin his long overdue leave with a lovely lady. Instead, they called him into an emergency meeting, where he learned the girls bolted again. During their escape, Orion ben Drachmas was stabbed, and Prince Josiah, instead of letting the scum bleed out on the street like he deserved, saved his life, and got caught up in an imbroglio with the Windsor Police.

Mossad went into overdrive.

Korah's men, already hot on the trail of Davianna and Astrid, caught the scent of the long-lost Prince and diverted. Spies and assassins descended on London like bees to honey. The threat assessment determined the exiled Prince was in mortal danger, so they decided to bring him into protective custody, and nominated Reuben to retrieve him.

Afterward, the shouts from Prince Yehonathan's sitting room penetrated the closed door. Reuben heard most of it, stationed outside, entertaining the intrepid dachshund, Benny. Josiah became livid when he realized Mossad shadowed his movements for eight months. Why the Iron King ordered it remained a mystery to everyone, except perhaps Yehonathan. Reuben certainly did not understand, having been pulled from his work against the jihadists and assigned babysitting duty. In that, he and Josiah were united in frustration.

Their serpentine journey across Europe seemed to accomplish one thing; two green pilgrim girls morphed into world class runners. Reuben sternly cautioned his replacement, Agent Amit ben Chaim, not to underestimate them. The duo had grown wily as foxes, capable of changing their appearance and their location at will. However, he feared his admonitions fell on deaf ears. Amit was an overconfident hotshot, and Reuben got a bad feeling about the new team.

If he were honest, his diligent search for Kayah these last months was not entirely personal. She was a valuable asset, one Reuben wanted on his side. Since the Alanthians discovered their covert tracking signal on the Black Key, he suspected Mossad may have to enlist additional resources to protect the girls, and by extension, Prince Josiah. Chains of command and rules of engagement might hinder them. Kayah did not operate with such limitations.

His decision to tell her about Prince Josiah had been a judgment call. Mossad suspected Kayah's colleagues knew he was alive, and the Alanthian government was in hot pursuit. Reuben gained Kayah's trust and sacrificed nothing she could not have discovered on her own by the end of business today.

His interview with Prince Yehonathan the morning of November 12th did not go exactly as planned either.

"It is an inopportune time to request leave, Agent ben Judah." Prince Yehonathan studied him over templed fingers.

Reuben set his jaw and replied, "My Esteemed, with respect, there is never an opportune time."

Shrewd eyes regarded him as Yehonathan asked, "Is there a particular motive prompting thy request?"

"Other than thirty months of active duty without one?" Reuben intoned.

Prince Yehonathan crossed his arms and lifted a mocking brow. "Or mayhap a certain young lady who hath taken up residence in London?"

Reuben declined to comment.

"'Tis a dangerous game thou playest, Agent." Prince Yehonathan's nose flared. "I consulted with the King on this matter." He left the sentence hanging in the air.

Reuben stood at attention, refusing to flinch.

Yehonathan uncrossed his arms and leaned back in his immense chair. The calculated advantages of Reuben's relationship with Kayah ben Samuel were not lost on the wily Prince. "He bade me not interfere."

The corner of Reuben's mouth twitched, betraying his gratification. "That is fortuitous."

"If it were up to me, I would counsel thee that she is without loyalty or honor." Prince Yehonathan's eyes grew cold. "History is littered with the corpses of men who fell prey to such women."

Reuben moistened his lips and spoke very calmly, "But as thou sayeth, my Esteemed, it is not up to thee."

"Indeed not. Then again," he paused and recited the soldier's vow, "thy steps are ordered, thy path guarded, and thy purpose?"

"My purpose is to serve the King."

"Do not lose sight of that, Agent ben Judah. We have lost enough good men." Prince Yehonathan glanced down at his calendar. "I fear we shall have to compromise on thy leave. Be back at the Embassy on December 1st, will that suffice?"

Reuben recognized the signs of burn out. He needed time away, or he was going to walk away, and they both knew it. Doing a quick calculation, he said, "My Esteemed, that is half of my request. However, I will capitulate with the understanding that I will not lose the fifteen days I did not take in 996 ME, and that I shall be on leave, without question, the first six weeks of the year."

Prince Yehonathan closed his eyes. Calm silence filled his luxurious office as he prayed. When he raised his head, he looked resigned. "Enjoy thy time off, Agent."

What Are You Listening To?

Kayah felt like a train had run her over. Reuben was gone when she finally woke. The note by her bed read, "Be back soon, coffee made. I fed the cat." R.

She swallowed a sudden lump in her sore throat and sniffed. Her neck ached, her head pounded, but worst of all, her heart broke. Gus… Squeezing her temples, she willed the pain away, fighting fresh tears. With movements as slow as a post-op patient, she left her bed in search of coffee.

Her distorted reflection in the old window over her kitchen sink captured the mess of her hair, the swelling of her eyes. With the mug warming her hands, she went to the study to retrieve her hidden tablet. If she was going to cry, she planned to do it alone. She stored all Gus' messages in a folder, and when she pulled up the most recent, her breath caught.

> July 11, 999 ME
> Dear Kai,
>
> Thanks for the shipment. It was exactly what I needed. The project will be finished soon, like I promised. When you come visit, I think you will be surprised. I hope you like it.
> I found this song and thought about you because I always wonder what you're listening to, where you are, what you are doing. Come home soon.
>
> Gus

She had not listened to the song, had barely read the email when it came. Hanging her head, shame bathed her in its bitter water. She had ignored him, taken for granted he would always be there. He sent her notes, sent her songs, but she could not be bothered. Would it have killed her to say thank you, to respond… to acknowledge him? He built her something out of a bunch of junk she shipped to the farm, and if she were honest, she never planned to see it.

Opening the song, she braced herself for the tears. When the soulful voice began, her heart broke into a thousand pieces because she knew she had broken his a thousand times before.

Low Places - New City, Alanthia

Himari woke with her eyes crusted shut. She pulled at her lashes to free them from the gunk. Out of Filippo's studio, she detected movement. He had not slept much, neither had she. The familiar scents of espresso and oil paint soothed her tattered spirit, but then it hit her. Gus. She shuffled to the bathroom and cringed at her blotchy skin and tangled hair. She looked as bad as she felt.

Music drifted through their condo, faint, but she caught a note, and a jolt of pain sent her to her knees. Gus' song from Lavinia and Mack's wedding reception. She remembered it like it was yesterday. They all drove up to Redding. The town packed the small church and joined the new couple in celebration. Lavinia created a nice life for herself, and the good folks of Redding seemed thrilled to welcome Mack, a little late, but to their minds, better late than never.

Unlike Himari and Filippo's sophisticated, intimate, New City affair, Lavinia and Mack's wedding had been a wine country shindig. Jeans and boots were the order of the day, with food from every household filling the folding tables that sat under the shade trees. Kegs of beer and casks of wine lubricated the celebration that stretched long into the night. Lavinia's favorite bar band played the reception, and the old friends danced until their feet hurt.

Gus had a blast, smiling and laughing, more outgoing and good natured than Himari had ever seen him. Perhaps because the wine country folks did not think him odd, and he took a genuine interest in their vineyards. He looked better, too. Having lost a considerable amount of weight, his new jeans and shirt fit him well, and he seemed comfortable in his own skin.

Nothing made Gus happier than having Kayah around, and just as she had done at Himari's wedding, she surprised them all by strolling into the reception. Gus, well into his cups, swung her around like a helicopter, something no one else would have ever had the nerve to do. But he loved Kayah. They all knew it. And Kayah, for all her faults, loved Gus as well as she could.

About an hour after Kayah arrived, the band played a number that made Gus burst out of his chair. "I love this song!" he declared and ran to the front of the stage, a big beer mug in his hand, and proceeded to sing every word at the top of his lungs. The girls laughed hysterically at his uncharacteristic animation and joy. They stumbled onto the dance floor and surrounded him as he serenaded them, inordinately pleased to be counted among Gus' friends in low places.

November 15, 999 ME

When the Lost Boy Finds a Home

An enormous cross dominated the stained-glass window of the church where they held Gus' funeral. Mack did not realize churches like this still existed in the New City and wished he had during his years living here; it would have done him good. But he thanked Yeshua that Gus belonged to one. They all needed a word on this sad and terrible day.

The community surrounded and supported Gus' big family, turning out in droves to say goodbye. A smattering of his former coworkers attended, sitting together, looking awkward and out of place among the country folk. But Mack gave them credit for taking off work and being here.

Alice and Allen, Gus' parents, sat on the front pew, ashen and shocked. Mack attended a few such funerals for his fellow officers and soldiers. The English language had no word for parents who outlived their children, as if their pain was too monumental to be named. He could not imagine what they were going through, did not want to, so he pulled his son onto his lap and held on. Lavinia met his eyes and scooted closer. Leaning her head against his shoulder, silent tears coursed down her cheeks.

An easel behind the closed casket held a painting, the colors vibrant and new. Gus looked out at the congregation, wearing a wide grin, one arm draped around Kayah, another around Lavinia, with little Himari standing in front of him, hugging his waist. All three women smiled up at Gus, love shining in their laughing faces. Touching and poignant, the canvas captured Gus in the happiest moment of his life. In his final tribute to his friend, Filippo proved himself as an artist of unparalleled humanity and talent.

Filippo and Himari sat at the back of the church, in the left corner. His continental style and her exotic Japanese beauty set them apart from the farmers and tech workers. Filippo rose when Kayah and Reuben arrived, beckoning them over. He settled Kayah firmly beside him, squeezing her hand in greeting.

Kayah inhaled the carnation and daisy scented air with a deep sustaining breath and settled in the pew between Reuben and

Filippo. The flowers surrounding the casket were simple and unassuming, but abundant and beautiful, like the man. She composed her face, mentally prepared for one of the hardest hours of her life. Today, she wore her blonde hair loose and natural, exactly the way Gus liked it.

Gus' sister, Georgia, pointed Kayah out to her son, George, who nervously rolled and unrolled his handwritten eulogy. George studied Kayah from his vantage point at the front of the church. She was smaller than he envisioned; Gus's descriptions were larger than life. Her pretty face looked serene, and she sat completely still, flanked by two swarthy men. In his bedroom, Gus proudly displayed several framed photographs of her, always referring to her as his friend, but every woman fell short of Kayah. George was glad she came. It would have meant a lot to his uncle.

The funeral began at 2:00 pm. At six minutes after, Stephen left his car in the back of the lot and resolutely walked up the church steps. "Damn them all," he thought. "I have as much right to be here as the rest of them." He brought Gus into the Alcatraz 5. None of them would have even known Gus if it wasn't for him. Besides, Gus was Stephen's friend, and he was going to pay his respects.

When the pastor stood up, Mack had the passing thought that he looked like he attended hearty Sunday dinners every week. His round face flushed, but intelligent eyes belied his pudgy, simpleton appearance. He welcomed the congregation and thanked them for coming on behalf of the family. "It is indeed a sad occasion that brings us together, but the Bible says we do not weep as those who have no hope. My job today is to help you find hope in your grief, as we mourn the loss of Gus ben Allen." He laid a hand on the casket, bowing his head briefly before moving behind the pulpit.

"I've known Gus since he was a little boy and expect many of you have known him for a long time. But some of you probably thought you knew him. I know I did."

With an ironic tilt of his head, he continued, "Now, I don't pretend to understand how his mind worked. It was an extraordinary thing to behold, and as a result, he had a difficult way with people. So, folks tended to dismiss him. I was guilty of that." He pursed his lips as the confession stilled the restless movements in the pews.

To one degree or another, they were all guilty of the same thing.

The preacher hung his head, then took a fortifying breath and said, "I don't tell you this to absolve myself or to put you under condemnation, but I'd like to share how I came to understand a bit more about the sweet man we are mourning today." He met Alice's bloodshot eyes, and she gave him a tremulous smile, nodding in assent. The preacher inclined his head toward her, acknowledging the unspoken communication. Then he shocked the congregation. "Most of you won't know, but Gus made the pilgrimage."

The crowd stirred, as they turned to each other silently asking, 'Did you know?' Very few did. The Alcatraz 4 sat in stunned silence. The preacher had their attention.

Referring to his notes, he continued, "He left the farm January 8th, 985 ME and did not return until December 25, 989 ME."

The blood left Lavinia's face because she knew that date. January 8, 985 marked the second anniversary of the raid on the bunker. She turned in the pew, certain Himari and Kayah understood the significance of that date, too. Himari pressed her fist over her mouth, blinking back tears. Kayah held herself stone-still, staring straight ahead. Gus was gone for almost five years, and none of them realized it. Lavinia calculated, remembering letters from him during that time, all posted from the New City.

"Gus carried no shame about his journey, but he took Scriptures literally. And in Matthew 6:6 we are told, 'Then your Father, who sees what is done in secret, will reward you.' So, he swore his family to secrecy and embarked on pilgrimage. It was hard on Alice, who worried about Gus, out there on his own, but he possessed a stubborn streak and made up his mind that he would be obedient to the commandment to go, and he did."

Conviction settled over the congregation. New City pilgrims were rare in the last twenty years, and most who went were spiritual refugees, not pilgrims, because they never returned. Alanthia's faithful were a dwindling population. Gus put them all to shame.

"When he came home, he was a different man. The Golden City changed him, the pilgrimage did, too. Afterward, Gus devoted several hours a night to studying his Bible. He knew the Word and loved the Iron King. I tell you this today, so you won't leave wondering where Gus is right now. I say with absolute certainty, Gus ben Allen is with the Lord in New Jerusalem."

Allen and Alice nodded in agreement, the words lifting their heads and their hearts.

"Gus told me that until he went to the Golden City he always felt like an outsider, but when he returned, he knew that he was not. He found where, and to whom, he belonged. If you find today that you are an outsider, I encourage you to take a lesson from this humble and quiet man. Find your place with the Iron King, for that is where you belong."

The preacher bowed his head in silent prayer. The congregation followed suit.

In the stillness, Mack lifted Richard from his lap and walked somberly to the front of the church. His battered acoustic guitar leaned against a stand on the raised stage. Putting aside his grief, he shoved the emotions of the moment to the background. He knew doing this right required a separation between heart and voice. The mourners, and his departed friend, deserved his best.

Mack pulled up a stool, strummed the guitar to check the tune, and said quietly into the microphone, "Gus loved music. A lot of what we hear on the radio today, much of the music we have recovered from the Last Age," he closed his eyes and swallowed, "we can thank Gus for that. The world does not know that about him. I didn't, until Himari told me yesterday."

Mack played a G major chord. "He found this song and sent it to me because he knew I loved gospel music. Alice and Allen were gracious enough to let me play it today." He strummed the guitar again and addressed the casket. "This one's for you, buddy."

Mack's clear tenor filled the sanctuary, and the tears began to flow as each remembered Gus ben Allen, who indeed was resting high upon that mountain. As he finished a hush fell over the congregation, but then a small voice cut through the silence. "That was good, Daddy!" Richard's bright smile beamed like the sun, bringing laughter through tears.

Mack flushed and gave an amused, but stoic, nod to the little imp. "Thank you, Son."

Gus' nephew George walked to the pulpit, his face flushed, visibly nervous. "I'm not certain I want to follow that."

Low chuckles agreed with him.

"My Uncle Gus was a smart man, but he was also a gentle one. We kids," he nodded to his cousins scattered in the pews, "loved to visit Gran and Gramps because Gus lived there. He would show us whatever new machine he created or some wild animal he befriended. In a lot of ways, he was like one of us kids." His voice caught. "We loved him."

Gus' dozen nieces and nephews murmured their agreement.

"It would mean a lot to him to see all you out here today. I think sometimes he was lonely because he lived most of his life inside his own head. However, he loved his friends." George met Kayah's eyes and held them. "He appreciated the work they sent him and the sacrifices they made on his behalf. We are all very grateful to you."

Kayah gave a slow blink of acknowledgement but remained still.

"I think if my uncle was here today, he would want me to tell you that he loved you, all of you." George found Stephen and spoke directly to him. "He did not hold grudges, and he would not want us to, either."

He closed his eyes and looked away, gathering himself before he continued. "There were many wrongs done to my uncle in his life," he cleared his throat, "and in his death."

George exhaled deeply; murder created bitter, angry grief in those left behind. "In the days, weeks, and months to come, we are all going to experience a rage that will threaten to swamp us. I don't know about you all, but I have wanted to go find the monsters that did this and tear them apart." George looked at his mother, whose face contorted in pain. He declared through gritted teeth, "But that will not bring him back, and I have a feeling it would only serve to tear us apart. I can tell you with absolute certainty that Uncle Gus would not have wanted that because he knew how to forgive."

He mopped his face with a hanky and cleared his throat. "I asked him one time, when I was young and tactless, why he didn't go back to court and fight to get the declaration of incompetence removed from his record." George's face flushed with emotion at the injustice done to his beloved uncle. "You know what he told me? He said it didn't matter what other people thought about him." His voice cracked. "The Iron King knew the truth. So did he. And that was all that mattered.

"I don't know about you, but I don't think I could have done that. I don't think I could have lived the life he did and stayed as kind and as gentle as he was." George looked on the casket with tears in his eyes. "We're going to miss you, Uncle Gus. But I want you to know that we paid attention, we watched you, and we learned. You inspired all of us, and the world was a better place because you were in it."

Mr. Smee

Lavinia drummed her fingers on her thigh, holding on by a thread. Mack saw the signs and took Richard from her lap. As they were singing the last hymn, he whispered, "Go on, Valentine. I'll meet you outside. Get some air, take a minute."

She shot him a panicky look; unsure it was okay to do what he told her to do. But at his nod, she slipped from the pew. Keeping her head down, she escaped. When she cleared the narthex doors, she burst out of the church with a bang, taking great gulps of air.

A quiet garden lay to the south where the funeral home set up a tent. Workers congregated several hundred yards away, chatting and drinking sodas while they waited for the service to end. Lavinia scanned the grounds, searching for a private place to gather herself before facing the crowd again. Toward the back of the parking lot, she spotted a large, fenced dumpster. Running one hundred twenty-eight steps in her high heels, she ducked behind it and hid.

Free from prying eyes, she covered her face and sobbed. Gus had been the closest thing she ever had to a brother, her friend who understood the labyrinth, and could join her inside. Sometimes his letters consisted of nothing but numbers. They got lost, together. Now he was gone, and she felt the loneliness of that place.

The sun shone, the birds sang, and the distant roar of traffic served as a reminder that the world went on. To date, she had only lost her grandparents, but this felt different. Gus died too soon, too tragically, and the tenuous nature of life left her fragile and shaken.

A gentle hand touched her back. Catching her breath she turned, thinking Mack had followed, but drew up short. "Vinia, are you all right?"

Her voice caught. "Stephen." She had not seen him in 6160 days, more than half a lifetime ago. He looked terrible, skinny and pale, cloaked in a wild desperation that caused her to withdraw.

"I saw you come out and wanted to make sure you were okay," he said, invading her space, standing too close.

"I'm fine," she breathed, retreating a step, and wiping her eyes. A decade of fending off drunks honed her instincts, and she looked around, uneasy. Her voice came out an octave too high as she stammered, "I am just surprised to see you."

He blinked rapidly. "He was my friend, too."

"Yes, of course." Lavinia nodded, drumming her fingers. "Well, it was nice talking to you. I need to go back to my husband and my son." She tried to move past him, but he stepped in front of her.

"Wait, just give me a minute," he pleaded. "I'll leave you alone. I promise. But I don't have anybody, Vinia. I have no one I can share this with. So, will you stand with me, for just a second behind this dumpster," he looked around, and his face screwed up in scorn, "while I mourn my oldest friend. Please? Can I have one minute of your time before crazy, fucking Kayah comes out here and tries to kill me again?"

As if he conjured her, Kayah materialized. "Times up!"

Himari came around the other side. "Stephen, leave Lavinia alone. This is not the time or the place."

"Not the time?" Stephen whirled on her. "What the hell do you know? What the hell do any of you know?" He looked between the three of them, so angry he shook. "All of you, including Gus, painted me as the bad guy all these years, but never once did any of you ever bother to ask me what happened. Never!" Half mad, he took a step toward Kayah then halted when he read the murder in her eyes. "I tried to tell you! I tried, that day, but you would not listen!"

He laughed, thoroughly unhinged. "It was never what you thought." Stephen looked at Kayah, fear and loathing written all over his face. "I might have even done you a favor. Things don't seem to have turned out too bad for you, Kayah. How many houses do you own now? Four, including that new swanky one in London?

"And you?" He turned to Himari. "Do you think it escaped my notice that you planted a bullshit code in your work after the Techies, Sunflower532? Do you think you are that damn smart?

"And Gus? He didn't have a clue what he was getting into, and he was too damn tactless to keep his mouth shut. It would have gotten him killed. I protected him!" Stephen insisted, his voice cracking.

Pointing a shaking finger at Lavinia, he closed his eyes before saying, "Never a word did I speak about you, ever. Because I loved you, and I always have."

Stephen backed away and threw his hands in the air in surrender. "So, the three of you can hate me, if you want to, because I messed up. Apparently, I have again!"

He gathered himself and said in a flat, emotionless voice, "Please give my regards to Allen and Alice." Then, like a dead man, he walked to his car alone and drove away.

Tinkerbells

Kayah watched Stephen's departure with a sneer, then turned to Lavinia and said, "Apparently, you've still got that pheromone."

Lavinia covered a hysterical giggle. Himari looked at Kayah like she had gone mad.

"What?" Kayah said to Himari. "He's still got it for her. It's pathetic."

"You are so mean." Himari shook her head, incredulous.

Kayah waved her away. "He's a putz, always has been. I don't believe that sad act for a minute. He would sell us down the line again the first damn chance he got."

Himari recognized this Kayah, the defensive, impulsive Kayah, operating on emotional stress. She even sounded like she used to, the New City orphan. There was no reasoning with her when she was like this. But Gus' funeral knocked them all askew, so she dropped it and said, "Come on. They are moving to the burial site. Let's get through this, ladies, and then we'll get drunk."

"Fucking capital idea, Sunflower." Kayah stalked off, wearing her fury like armor.

Lavinia let out a pensive breath and leaned into Himari. "That was frightening."

Himari raised a lip and muttered, "Both of them."

Lavinia elbowed Himari. "Kayah is not scary."

Himari widened her eyes at Lavinia. "You did not see her the night of the Techies when she went after Stephen. I saw the look in her eyes. Don't fool yourself, Lavinia. Kayah ben Samuel is no schoolgirl."

Lavinia watched Kayah join Reuben and Mack. She appeared composed, perfectly calm. Lavinia turned to Himari and whispered, "Good, I'm glad she's not." The corner of her mouth lifted. "Then again, neither are we."

"No, we're not." Himari's expression matched Lavinia's, determination and fury reflected in her eyes. "Not anymore."

Lost Boy's Treasure

After the graveside service, Gus' parents sought Kayah before she disappeared. Under her black hat, Alice's sun spotted face looked red and splotchy, Allen's gray with fatigue. With the ceremony over, they longed for the comfort of home and family, but there remained a matter of business to address.

"Thank you for coming, Kayah. It would have meant so much to him," Alice said, giving her a smile as sad as it was knowing.

Allen rested a reassuring hand on the small of his wife's back. "And the work you gave him?" He swallowed, regret etched deep in his face. "It kept him going for years. We appreciated it."

Alice concurred, "Which brings us to our point, my dear."

Allen shifted, uncomfortable. "Normally we wouldn't be bringing it up right now."

"But we did not know how to get in touch with you." Alice hunched her shoulders apologetically.

Kayah squeezed Alice's hands. "Please, don't give it another thought. What can I do for you? Just say the word."

Allen shook his head. "No, it's nothing like that. We have something of yours, and we need to know what you want done with it?"

"Something of mine? I'm sorry I don't understand."

"Well, your project, the one you had Gus building for you all these years. He finished in September and said you would be coming home soon to get it." Alice's hand flew to her mouth as she stifled a cry, remembering the hope in her son's eyes.

"Yes, of course. I was planning to address that with you while I was in town, but I did not want to do it today," Kayah lied.

Alice and Allen visibly relaxed. "That is quite a relief, young lady." Allen smiled. "We did not know what we were going to do, otherwise. It's taking up the whole second barn."

A tremor of surprise ran up Kayah's spine, but she did not miss a beat and said, "Indeed, that is impressive, I had no idea. Of course, I will need to make the appropriate arrangements." She looked up at Reuben, her eyes silently pleading, out of her depth with these grieving parents.

Reuben extended his hand, saying, "Reuben ben Judah, so sorry for your loss." He met Allen's eyes. "I imagine you need your barn. Perhaps we could come out in a few days and see it?"

"Yes, sure," Kayah said, hiding the jolt of panic.

"Oh, Kayah, that would be nice," Alice said, giving her hands a hard squeeze before turning to speak with friends who claimed her attention.

A Moment of Peace

Himari and Filippo lived in the marina district in a rooftop condo that commanded a spectacular view of the recently re-constructed Golden Gate Bridge. Filippo insisted everyone come back to their place after the funeral. The dark days after Malibu's death forged an everlasting impression on him, and he considered himself somewhat of an expert on what grieving people needed: alcohol, food, friends, and love, usually in that order.

Everyone went to their respective lodgings to change and decompress after the funeral. At seven, Filippo greeted Kayah and Reuben, wearing an apron printed with a still life. *"Benvenuto!"*

Kayah smiled and pressed a kiss to Filippo's cheek. "It smells good in here."

"Ah, yes, simple food, but good for the soul, eh?"

Reuben walked to the window, enjoying the view. Himari emerged from her bedroom, putting on her earrings, barefoot and comfortable in jeans and a loose top.

"Lavinia and Mack are on their way," Himari said, taking wine glasses out of the cabinet as Filippo chopped vegetables. "Her parents just arrived from San Diego, so Richard is being spoiled by his grandparents at the hotel."

The two childless women clinked their glasses at the news, neither had spent any time with Lavinia without her kid since he was born. Personally, Kayah was relieved. Children tended to become the center of attention, and tonight was not about Lavinia and Mack's little boy, no matter how adorable he might be. They were all held together with cobwebs and tape; Stephen's little escapade had not helped. Kayah felt no shame in rejoicing that a four-year-old would not be watching her get drunk with her friends.

Twenty minutes later, Lavinia and Mack arrived with a case of wine. Kayah raised her glass in silent salute. "I hope you brought more."

Mack lifted a sardonic eyebrow and said, "There are twelve bottles in here, Kayah."

"And?"

Lavinia snorted, pressing her cheek to Reuben's in greeting. "The first time I ever got drunk was with Kayah."

"The first time any of us ever did half the stuff we got in trouble for was with Kayah," Himari chimed in.

"Oh, like either of you ever needed much encouragement." She turned to Reuben. "Do not believe half of what they say."

Reuben's forehead crinkled, humor dancing in his eyes. "I will not, Yakira. I know you are an angel."

Kayah sent a triumphant look to her two friends.

"There are two kinds of angels, Kai," Himari taunted.

Everyone except Mack and Reuben laughed.

The sound of a popping cork came from the kitchen, and Filippo filled everyone's glasses. "This is exceptional, Mack." he studied the bottle. "You and Lavinia have outdone yourselves. It is a glass of Italy, eh?"

Himari offered a toast. "To Mack and Lavinia's excellent vintage."

Kayah nodded with appreciation, the wine going down like water. "That is dangerous."

"You would know," Himari said sarcastically.

Filippo stopped mid-stride and pointed at his wife. "You," he held her eyes, "no more busting chops on Kayah. She is sad, too. Quit."

Brought up short for a moment, Himari realized how petulant and cutting her comments sounded. "Sorry, Kai."

Kayah waved her apology away. "I am dangerous."

Filippo sent a level look to Kayah. "No danger talk from you, either. We are here to celebrate our friend. Tomorrow we talk danger." His nose flared, with a visible effort he composed his handsome face and turned to the group, his glass raised. "Tonight, we eat, we drink, we laugh and later," he kissed Himari, "we love."

Mack raised his glass, a gleam in his eye as he admired his wife's beautiful leg. "I love Italians."

Reuben nodded in agreement. "In Israel, when someone dies, we do much the same thing, except the women are louder."

Kayah tucked her knees under and whispered in his ear, "I can be as loud as you want me to be."

Heat passed between them, sultry and full of promise. The two married couples exchanged speculative glances. Kayah never brought a man around, ever. That she came sashaying into the funeral today with Reuben shocked them, but that was Kayah, never doing what anyone expected. His presence in their little revolutionary group could be contentious, but since they were simply having a dinner party and a small memorial for Gus, treasonous discussions could wait until the morning. Filippo was right.

"What are you cooking, Filippo? It smells good," Mack called from the living room.

"Lasagna. We eat pretty soon." Filippo flourished a knife with practiced ease, creating a salad as beautiful as one of his paintings.

Kayah turned to Himari. "I'm just glad you are not cooking; his food is better than yours."

Himari snorted. "What do you cook? Puppies?"

"Sure, you got any?" Kayah countered.

Lavinia rolled her eyes and moved between them, a suppressed smile on her lips. "This was my life, from eighth grade on, keeping these two from killing each other."

Kayah leaned around Lavinia and made a kissing noise at Himari, who gave her the middle finger. They all laughed. Nobody but Himari would dare flip Kayah the bird, and she loved her for it.

Reuben homed in on the dynamics of the group, well aware of the gift Kayah gave him by allowing him to accompany her on this trip, especially to this dinner party. No one revealed the truth like old friends. His mother had a saying, 'A new friend will bring a bottle of wine to your party, an old friend will arrive early and clean your bathroom.' With Kayah's old friends, they brought a case of wine, and he suspected they would build each other a bathroom.

Delicious aromas tempted stomachs, which hours before did not believe they would be able to eat. Lavinia joined Filippo in the kitchen, speaking rapid Italian, which he always appreciated. Her restaurant experience lent an efficiency to the proceedings. Filippo served beautiful food, but he was notoriously slow getting it on the table. Alaina always teased that dinner with him was 'Land of the Midnight Chicken.'

Hazy after her third glass of wine, Kayah watched the two Italians laughing and cooking companionably. She turned to Reuben with a speculative look in her eye. "The Israeli accent is similar to the Italian, except their body language is different."

Reuben snorted and dismissed the notion out of hand, "No, no."

Kayah laughed. "It is, but you are more shoulders than hands."

Reuben shrugged his shoulders in an exaggerated fashion. "I do not know what you are speaking about."

Himari chuckled. "I have to stand far away from him when he gets annoyed."

"Living with you, I have no doubt he is constantly annoyed," Kayah dead panned.

Mack sat back in his chair and said to Reuben, "This goes on the whole time they are together."

"I am gathering that." Reuben smiled, amused by the interplay. "The wine, it is excellent. You are a vintner?"

"It is a recent occupation, but yes, and you?" Mack asked, though he strongly suspected Reuben was Mossad. To Mack's trained eye, Reuben's haircut, mannerisms, and demeanor marked him as clearly as if he wore a badge.

"Currently, I am on vacation with Kayah."

Filippo called them to dinner, cutting off further conversation.

As they settled, Filippo raised a glass. "Tonight, we celebrate and remember the life of our friend, Gus. I know if he were here tonight, he would enjoy the food, the company, and the wine. Until we meet again, my friend. *Salud.*"

"*Salud,*" the table echoed and drank to Gus.

Reuben and Kayah shared a private smile over the plates of lasagna, both recalling their first dinner. He remembered that she mentioned her Italian friend and never thought to meet her. He leaned in, and Kayah met him halfway for a brief kiss.

"All right, when did this happen?" Himari came right out and asked what they had all been speculating about.

"I met him at the airport yesterday. I liked his deep, gravelly voice." Kayah took a bite of the delicious garlic bread and felt Reuben chuckle beside her.

"He was your date in Italy, wasn't he?" Lavinia asked, eying them over the rim of her wine glass.

Kayah drew up, her face flushing. She had forgotten the call to Lavinia and shot her a big-eyed look that said, 'Be quiet!'

Himari keyed in on the interplay like a bloodhound. "Oh, is that right, Italy?" They all knew when Kayah was in Italy. The stolen prototype had been a major boon.

"Where in Italy?" Filippo asked.

Reuben answered for them both, "Bologna."

"Hmm," Filippo acknowledged, nodding his head. "It's a big city, eh? Did you enjoy it?"

Reuben only had eyes for Kayah when he answered, "Yes, yes, immensely."

Kayah looked like she was about to jump out of her skin, even among her closest friends, she kept things private.

Mack read the situation and diverted the conversation. "Filippo, your painting today was extraordinary."

Glasses raised in salute.

"And your tribute, Mack?" Filippo pursed his lips and nodded wordlessly.

Himari looked at her plate, unable to meet anyone's eyes and said, "He would have loved both of them."

Kayah saw Lavinia disappear into the labyrinth, then watched in fascination as Mack, gently and quietly brought her back. "Valentine, will you please pass me the bread?"

Lavinia blinked, recognizing that he had spoken, but she had not heard him. "The bread," he mouthed silently. She nodded in comprehension and passed it to him, a little shaky, but present.

Kayah and Himari exchanged small, satisfied smiles; it was good.

After the dinner dishes were cleared and put away, they retired to the rooftop terrace and settled around a stone firepit. Comfortable couches and lounge chairs, soft throw blankets, and strings of white lights created a magical haven under the stars. The wine flowed and soft music played. They laughed and relaxed, easy in each other's company.

For tonight at least, there was peace.

Thimbles

After everyone departed, Himari carried the last of the glasses to the kitchen sink, boneless and exhausted. Filippo gathered her close, supporting her upright as she collapsed into him. "It has been a long day, eh?"

She sighed wearily. "Yes, but you made it better."

He kissed the top of her head, inhaling her green tea and jasmine shampoo. "Come, I take you to sleep."

Himari began to cry, the tenderness of his touch bringing a fresh wave of grief. "I can't believe he is gone."

"I know," he soothed.

"Filippo, I don't want you to go."

"Shh, we talk more tomorrow."

"I don't think I can sleep," she protested, even though she could barely stand up.

"You are asleep on your feet, but too stubborn to admit it." Filippo chuckled as he maneuvered her into their bedroom. "You make me laugh with Kayah tonight."

Himari giggled. "She brings that out in me. I don't know why."

"Reminds me of the Himari I first met. It is good to remember that girl, she is a feisty."

"Himari 2.0? Yes, I suppose it is good to bring her out. We have a hell of a fight ahead of us," she murmured, her eyes closing.

"Aye, but not tonight, *Bellissima*."

Lavinia curled into the reclined passenger seat while Mack drove back to their hotel. "Will you see the Prince while we are here?" she asked through a yawn.

Mack shook his head. "He is in New York right now. But it is time. I feel it."

Lavinia nodded and yawned again. "I think Mamma and Pappa should take Richard back with them to San Diego."

Mack grabbed the back of his neck and squeezed. "I know." They talked about this for months. Prince Peter set up a New City safe house for him and Lavinia, a haven when their plan began.

"I can do this, if we are together, and Richard is safe," Lavinia whispered, watching his expression, illuminated by the streetlights.

"I don't like it."

Lavinia knew this battle. It was their only fight, other than his messiness. "You never have, but there was never a real choice. We were either going to be together and fight, or we were going to spend our lives apart."

Mack glanced at her soberly. "And that was no life, was it, Valentine?"

Kayah watched the cars behind them, checking for tails. "Take this exit. We are being followed."

"I see them," Reuben growled.

"Yours or mine?" Kayah wondered aloud.

"Mine," Reuben confirmed what she suspected.

"Well, they know you are with me." Kayah looked at him sidelong.

"Of course, yes," Reuben said matter of fact. "They are doing it against orders, though."

"Indeed?"

"Yehonathan was told to stand down."

Kayah drew back, knowing that only one power issued orders to Prince Yehonathan. "He has taken notice?"

"What does He not notice, Yakira?"

Kayah blew out a weary breath. "Sometimes, I forget who you serve."

"Don't."

Kayah shook her head, staring out the window. "But who am I, Reuben, that He would even know my name?"

"Who are any of us?" He reached across the console.

She stared at his hand for a long time, then slowly and with great effort placed her hand in his and held on.

Mont Carmel

They evaded the tail for twenty minutes, finally Kayah said, "Go to Mont Carmel. My condo is there."

"They know of that residence as well, Yakira."

"We are not on the run tonight, and I want to hear the ocean," she said wearily.

"Then you shall hear the ocean. I think it is a good thing."

Kayah relaxed as he evaded, twisted, turned, doing all the maneuvers she would have made to lose their tail. A deep peace settled over her, as she put herself in his capable hands.

As they approached Mont Carmel, Kayah watched the palm trees flash by as Reuben navigated the twisting drive up the slope. The condo was in a relatively new development, an investment made sight unseen. Before she disappeared in September, she instructed the property management company to stop renting it out, figuring she would sell it. They sent in a cleaning crew once a month, paid the utilities, and managed any repairs. She had spent exactly five nights in the place.

Breaking the companionable silence, she said, "Filippo is an interesting man."

Reuben raised a finger. "This is true, but I liked him. He made a nice night for you ladies."

Kayah hummed an agreement. "He did that for Himari after she and her first husband split up. I think she did it for him after his wife died."

Reuben exhaled, nodding his head. "I could tell he has seen tragedy. It changes a man."

"It changed you, didn't it?" Kayah ventured.

His arms stiffened on the steering wheel, and he looked ahead. "Yes, yes, in all ways."

Ghosts filled the car, haunting and brutal.

"I should not have said that. I am sorry." Kayah looked away. "We have had enough sadness for the day."

"In that, Filippo was right, very wise of him, no?" Reuben relaxed.

"Yes, there is much more to him than meets the eye and more going on than they have told me. I think that is half the reason he insisted we not speak of things tonight."

Her condo lay a mile ahead. Kayah reached for her purse and pulled out her weapon, by habit checking the clip and chambering a bullet.

Heat rushed to his loins. "Show me the others."

Kayah moistened her beautiful lips and turned to him. "All of them?"

Reuben leered. "All."

She licked a finger and traced it around her mouth seductively. "All my tricks?"

He growled.

Kayah slid her hand deep into a pocket at her thigh and produced a six-inch stiletto that snapped open with deadly force, its steel blade flashing in the light of an oncoming car. "I like this one. I can kill a man with no blood."

Reuben's chest heaved. "What else?"

The stiletto disappeared. She stretched like a cat and pulled a long pin from her elegant French twist. "Old fashioned, but effective."

"A lady's weapon," Reuben approved.

"Multipurpose," Kayah purred. She leaned against the door with her feet on the center console.

"There are more, Yakira. Do not tease me," Reuben said in a husky whisper.

"How do you know there is more?" Kayah brought a knee to her chest.

Reuben slid his hand up her pant leg and felt the weapon strapped to her calf. "Because you, I know."

Kayah arched her back as he stroked her bare skin. "I'll show you the rest, but it will cost you."

He parked the car and pounced on her. "What is the cost?"

"You do the same." She bit his neck.

"Get inside, now."

The moment they stepped outside, they changed, became alert, on guard. They took the stairs to her third-floor unit. She disarmed the security, while Reuben moved into the darkness, checking the rooms, and ensuring they were alone. Kayah methodically swept the condo and found two listening devices, which she indicated to him. Holding up a finger for silence, she slipped out the sliding glass door and flung the bugs off the balcony.

"Now, where were we?" she asked, strutting toward him, turned on because she normally performed that little ritual alone. "Oh, I remember. You were going to show me."

Reuben grinned and reached in his jacket pocket; a nine-millimeter pistol materialized.

"Crude, but effective," Kayah cooed, draping herself over a comfortable chair.

He leaned over, the long taper of his fingers finding purchase on a wicked blade concealed inside his left boot.

"That's a bit sexier," Kayah said, tracing the neckline of her blouse.

He removed his jacket and threw it on the sofa, placing the gun and the knife on the table in front of him. "You now."

She raised a leg and unstrapped the calf holster, letting it dangle from her fingers before dropping it to the ground. Then she stood up and pulled the wicked pin from her hair, shaking out the long mass, which curled around her shoulders. Smiling, she made a great show of pulling the stiletto from the deep pocket at her thigh and laying it on the table opposite his weapons.

"Now the rest," he growled.

She unbuttoned her hunter green blouse slowly, teasing him, touching herself as she did it. She let it drop to the floor, the lacy bra underneath was the color of the discarded blouse. Reuben devoured her with his eyes, masculine passion and hunger rolling off him in waves. She reveled in it and unfastened the thin gold rope she wore around her waist. It slithered through the belt loops like a snake. She slid the gold coin buckle to the middle, wrapped the ends around her fists, and snapped, her eyes alight with desire as she demonstrated the garotte.

Reuben came around the table in two strides. "You are so hot." Reaching into his back pocket, he pulled out a wooden kubotan.

Kayah took it from his hand, testing it. "I like these, they go through airport security. What else?"

With deliberate slowness, he brought a hand to her breast. "This hand, I was trained to kill with." He leaned in to brush her lips and grazed the front of her thighs. "This hand as well. Tonight, I think I shall employ them on you, in *la petit mort*."

"I think I shall enjoy that, Agent," she said.

He slowly unbuttoned her pants and let them puddle on the floor. She stepped out of them, standing before him in black heels and dark green lace. Kayah moved away from him, graceful as a cat, paused at the entrance to her bedroom and beckoned him forward with a long talon.

He came up behind her and gave her a push toward the four-poster bed. "Bend over." He panted, pulling his shirt over his head and taking down his pants.

Kayah walked to the edge of the bed, her thong panty showing her perfect smooth skin. Over her shoulder, she watched him kick off his boots and stalk toward her. She posed for him, open and ready, her legs spread, her palms flat. Reuben slid his hand down the front of her panties and found her throbbing and wet. He began to tease her, and she moved against his fingers, purring.

Reuben rocked with her, coaxing her, finding a rhythm. It did not take long for her to begin. He bit down on her shoulder like a stallion, pulled the tiny scrap of lace aside and entered her as she climaxed. He held her tightly and with an elemental groan joined her. His breath coming in deep gasps, he lay atop her, surrounding and covering her with his body.

"Yakira, there is no woman on this earth for me besides you. One day, you will be my wife. One day, you will say yes to me.

Do not answer me now, but I know this to be true. Do not doubt me." He kissed her cheek, and with a final thrust, vowed, "One day, you will call me Husband."

Kayah buried her face in the comforter and knew he spoke the truth.

November 16, 999 ME

Eyes Wide Open

The crash of the ocean waves roused Kayah from a deep slumber, but the smell of coffee lured her out of bed. When she rose, a sharp tremor ran up her leg, and she grimaced. At one point in last night's gymnastics, it had been behind her neck in an exceedingly gratifying position. However, she despised any weakness in her body, so it took a concerted effort not to limp.

Reuben stood at the kitchen sink, shirtless, the mellow light casting his body in intriguing shadows, highlighting the strong planes and smooth skin. The faint trail of black hair disappearing into his blue boxer shorts made her smile. Wrapping her arms around his waist, she rested her cheek against his back and ran her hands up his torso, cupping his strong pectoral muscles. "Good morning," she murmured.

He made a low rumble of contentment, glancing over his shoulder at her. "Cafe?"

"Mmm." She kissed his skin and disengaged, moving into the living room while he made her coffee. Outside the sliding glass door, the Pacific roared, cold and violent, the day dawning gray and dark. Yet the beauty and majesty were undeniable.

"We go to the farm today, to see what Gus engineered for you. It is best, Yakira." Reuben's voice was scratchy with sleep but resolute.

"Today?"

He nodded solemnly. "It is the guidance I feel. The first thing I received this morning in prayer. It is what we will do."

Kayah turned, and he admired her long neck and delicate ears, but her face was as cold as the breeze outside. "It will be hard to go there."

"Waiting will not make it easier. Trust me, I know this."

"How? How do you know this, Reuben?"

He closed his eyes, his heavy brows drawn down hard. "Because I waited twelve months before I went back to my family's farm after they were massacred by jihadists." His chest heaved in agitation; the skin pebbled in the cold breeze that snaked through the cracked sliding door. "It would have been no easier the day after they were murdered than it was the day I finally returned."

Kayah pursed her lips and swallowed thickly, "Jihadists?"

"They are all dead." He turned and went back to the kitchen, pouring another cup of coffee.

Kayah stared at the ocean for a few moments and then joined him. He leaned against the refrigerator, his left leg extended behind him, stretching his calf. A long scar ran the length of it. He favored it sometimes, but never mentioned the wound and neither had she. "Is that how you got that scar?"

He flexed his leg absently. "I did not even realize I had been shot." The warrior's mask fell in place as he traveled back in time. "I was still in the Army then. We tracked them for two weeks. They are stupid and think they can evade the will of the Iron King. Bah!" he sneered in disgust.

"They hide among women and children, but they did not know the force they unleashed when they murdered Israeli farmers, who fed them, gave them work, and took them in when they pretended to be refugees! They are pigs, and I would not let them live. My unit, for many years, patrolled the pilgrim roads. So, we knew how to find them, how to hunt."

His nostrils flared, and he rubbed the bridge of his nose. "Yakira, much evil grows in the world, especially in Greece. It is good that Antiochus is dead." Old hatred and rage erupted, and he snarled, "That is where the jihadists who slaughtered my family were from. They did not realize I was on my way to meet them. There were twelve of them. I killed eight."

He drew up straight, shaking his head. "Afterward, I thought I stepped in water, and that was why my boot was squishing, my foot wet. My friend saw that I was wounded." He leaned against the counter and held his leg up for her to see. "The bullet entered here and hit my tibial artery."

He dropped his leg with a thunk and met her eyes squarely. "I was standing there, bleeding to death, and did not even know

I'd been shot. I just knew I was having a hard time breathing, and my mouth tasted like copper."

Kayah covered her mouth and tried not to imagine these last six months without him.

"My friend, the man who saved my life?" He paused briefly, as if considering, then said, "That was Prince Josiah ben Eamonn."

Kayah's eyes grew wide as she covered her mouth in disbelief.

He nodded. "I had much the same reaction when I learned his true identity. I knew him as Captain Einar ben Yane. We served together for eight years in the King's Army."

"That is where he was?"

Reuben looked at the ceiling, remembering. "Yes. He is a valiant warrior, a great leader, and thankfully, an excellent doctor."

Kayah took a step forward and said, "He is also the rightful and legal heir to the throne of Alanthia, Reuben."

Reuben cocked his head in acknowledgment. "You speak true, and that is why I must return to London at the end of the month. The Iron King wants him protected."

Kayah busied herself with the coffee pot, her mind reeling. Was he telling her this to gain her trust? There remained the possibility he merely played a role, that he was a spy sent to breech her defenses and infiltrate The Resistance. However, the Golden Kingdom's objectives aligned with their own. Dethroning Korah and replacing him with Josiah was a logical goal to bring the rebellious Kingdom to heel. "I can think of no better protector, Reuben. Thank you for telling me."

Their eyes met across the distance. He was magnificent, strong and fierce, a warrior to the sinews of his bones, and she had long since fallen in love with him, but still, she did not completely trust him.

He read it in her eyes. "There are many forces at work here, seen and unseen, known and unknown. Kayah, you go against the most powerful government and ruler on the planet outside the Iron King, but you must do so with your eyes open."

He took her hand, drawing her onto the sofa, holding her close to his side. "Make no mistake, Korah and the power behind him, would torture and kill you without a moment's hesitation. He makes Antiochus look like a schoolboy in short pants. Never underestimate him. He is as wicked as the devil he serves, and I am not speaking metaphorically, Yakira."

A cold chill ran down Kayah's spine. "What are you talking about, Reuben?"

"I cannot tell you more, but I think you should ask Mack. He served in the Palace. I believe he knows." Reuben brought his forehead to hers. "I wish I could tell you. I wish these barriers were not between us. The secrets…"

"Me, too," she whispered.

He kissed her gently. "We had one night, when they were down, did we not? One night, when I was just Reuben, and you were just Kayah. The next time, that is when you will say yes to me, when there are no secrets, and we can trust."

"Who will I be then?" Kayah could not even conceive of such a time, such a life.

"Mine, and I will be yours, and together, we will be something new, something whole."

"That is a beautiful dream, Reuben," she said, listening to his beating heart.

"It is no dream, Yakira. It is my solemn vow to you, on my life."

"Then swear to me." She took his wrist, suddenly fierce.

Reuben stilled. "You would make a blood oath with me?"

Kayah squeezed hard. "If you mean it, if you aren't just a spy, if you haven't been sent here…" Her voice grew ragged. "Then yes, I will make a blood oath with you."

"Come," he said, pulling her into the bedroom where their cache of weapons lay. Handing her his knife, he opened his palm for hers.

She waved it away. "Not that one, it's poisoned. We will just use yours."

He threw back his head and laughed, then pulled her in for a rough kiss. "I do love you, Yakira, but that is not what my oath will be." He held out his wrist to her.

Kayah snapped the blade open with practiced ease, laid four fingers at the base of his palm, and made a precise cut, using her forefinger as guidance, whereby avoiding any major veins or nerves. She raised a shoulder at his speculative look, the artery story fresh in her mind. "I don't want you bleeding to death."

"I appreciate that." He repeated the process on her and clasped their wrists together, pulling her tightly around her waist with his free arm. She did the same. Their eyes locked in the gray light, and the Pacific crashed in the distance. Their hearts pounded, as their blood mingled.

"Kayah ben Samuel of Alanthia, love of my heart. I, Reuben ben Judah, of the tribe of Reuben in the Golden Kingdom make this blood oath, in the name of the Iron King, that my words may be true, and that I might sacrifice my life before breaking this vow. I swear to you this day, that I will do all in my power to protect you, to never deceive or lie to you, by word or omission. I will never allow others to use me or our relationship to bring you harm or cause injury to those you love. There may be times when I am honor bound by duty to silence, but I will never allow that silence to put you in danger. I promise to be faithful to you, to honor you, to cherish you, to respect and love you, as long as I live."

Kayah's eyes widened, and she trembled, reeling at his words. She expected him to vow not to lie to her or use her, but this was far beyond that. She cleared her throat convulsively and said, "I, Kayah ben Samuel of Alanthia, do solemnly swear to you, Reuben ben Judah, that I too, will not seek to lie or deceive you in words, deeds, or by omission. There may be times when I cannot share, out of fealty and duty to my Kingdom, but I will ensure my actions do not bring you harm. I will protect you, to the best of my abilities, and never allow anyone to use me or our relationship to disgrace or dishonor you, or in any way, cause you damage." Her breathing came fast as she paused, then plunged ahead. "I promise to be faithful to you, to respect, honor, and love you as long as I live. May the Iron King give me the strength and the wisdom to fulfill this blood oath I swear to you this day." Tears fell from her eyes as she looked up at him agape, astonished at what had just passed between them.

A slow smile broke over his face. "I believe," he pulled their wrists apart and leaned in, "that is what we call a betrothal, Yakira."

"Bloody hell," she breathed and met his lips.

He laid down with her and consummated their vows.

Property of Kayah ben Samuel

Alice and Allen's farm was close to the Alcatraz 5's original bunker. Kayah had not been in this part of the New City for years. At times, familiar landmarks sprung up with clarity and a certain nostalgia, others evoked the pain of her childhood, cast adrift in a world that would consume her without a second thought. Driving through her old neighborhood, she felt disoriented by the absence of landmarks that should be there but were missing. A pang of sadness hit her when she saw the old burger joint where they used to hang out. It was dilapidated and familiar. She purposely avoided the street where the orphanage still stood. The gray brick and metal windows did not warrant a trip down memory lane. New developments dotted the landscape, where once only farmland reigned. Fields that did not succumb to development, lay fallow and dry in the November gray.

Reuben grimaced. It was so different from the Golden Kingdom's lush hills that bloomed year-round. "The price of rebellion, no?"

Kayah nodded. "It is worse now." While she owned a New City apartment, she was rarely in residence. She suspected she retained her houses out of a deep-seated need; the lost orphan who never had a home, now collected them like seashells.

At the farm, Alice greeted them warmly. "Come in, Kayah. Reuben, it is nice to see you again. Have you eaten lunch? There is so much food here. Allen and I will never be able to eat it all."

"Thank you, but no. We stopped on the way." Kayah allowed Alice to hug her.

"Well, enough. I am going to pack most of this up and send it over to Georgia and the kids. George did such a good job with the eulogy, didn't he?" Alice's voice rang with a mixture of pride and sadness.

"Yes, ma'am." Kayah smiled and added, "The service was perfect."

"You look good, Kayah, less haunted than the last time I saw you."

Kayah blinked in surprise.

Alice shrugged. "Forgive me, we mothers tend to forget that not all young people are our children. The older I get, the more prone I am to speak my mind." She winked and nodded at Reuben. "I suspect your new smile has something to do with this handsome young man?"

Kayah brushed a stray hair away from her eye, flushing. "He's all right."

Alice was completely undeterred by Kayah's evasiveness. "Did I detect the Golden Kingdom in your accent, Reuben?"

"You did, indeed, ma'am. I grew up at the border of Judah and Reuben on the eastern side of the Kingdom. My family raised cattle."

"Reubenite cattle? They are very famous. I expect you know your way around a farm then."

"I certainly do, ma'am. So, I am sure you need that barn."

Kayah wanted to hug him for quickly getting to the point of their visit. Gus' presence was so tangible, she felt like sobbing.

Alice shook her head ruefully. "It's not what you might expect. The farm," she paused, looking out the window, "well, it has not done well these last few years. Nobody has done well in the region. With Gus gone," she closed her eyes and paused, "we'll be selling. They are converting all these farms into neighborhoods."

At Kayah's surprised expression, Alice continued, "My sister and her husband retired last year, moved to Louisiana. They like it there. Allen and I have been talking about it for years." She let the sentence drop. "Well, come on then. Let me take you out there."

Following Alice's sturdy figure down the dusty path, Kayah realized Gus inherited her walk and the tilt of her head as she spoke. "Whatever you had him build, he took it seriously and kept it secret. We respected his privacy and yours."

At the furthest building, she handed Kayah a key. "I have no idea what you are going to find in there, but it belongs to you. You paid for it, Kayah, all of it." She looked at Kayah again with that disconcerting, mothers-know-all stare. "We know what you did for our son, and we appreciate it." She turned away, before she started weeping again.

Kayah covered her mouth, determined not to cry.

Reuben took the key and opened the door. A twelve-foot-high canvas cordoned off the barn from the doorway. It ran the width of the structure, hanging on a metal rod. Dead center, a meticulously lettered sign read:

No Entry
Private Property of Kayah ben Samuel
Chief Engineer Gus ben Allen

Kayah reached up to touch it. The script was precise, exact, and perfect. Gus' always wrote his notes in his slow draftsman lettering. It drove her crazy in the bunker, now she found it infinitely precious. "I want to take the sign with us today."

Reuben nodded, knowing that she kept almost no memorabilia. Her California homes were devoid of anything personal, but her London townhouse had the beginnings of character and flair. The day before they left London, he hung a shirt in her closet and saw the Geneva ball cap on a shelf. The fact that she kept it signified more to him than a thousand words she might have spoken.

They walked the length of the canvas, their feet echoing in the empty barn. Gus had poured a cement floor. It was troweled smooth and precise, sealed with a gold and black epoxy flecked paint that shimmered in the light from the high glass windows. Kayah began to feel uneasy. The flooring seemed familiar in a vague sort of way. She wanted to take Reuben's arm but resisted the impulse.

At the end of the canvas, Reuben asked, "Are you ready?"

She closed her eyes and took a deep breath. "Yes. Let's go."

Reuben pulled back the curtain, and Kayah gasped, "Oh, Gus. What did you do?"

Journals

When they returned to the house, Alice motioned to a dozen boxes waiting near the front door. "They are his technical journals, the notes he kept while he was working. He would want you to have them, Kayah." Her expression grew apologetic. "Besides, what are we going to do with them? I'd hate to throw them away."

"Yes, of course," Kayah said, reading the distress in Alice's eyes.

While Reuben carried the boxes to the car, Kayah accepted a cup of tea and sat at the kitchen table. Shaken and trying to compose herself, she said, "Alice, it will take some time for me to make arrangements to get everything from the barn." She pulled her wallet from her purse. "In the interim, please take this as rent for the past and for the next three months. If you sell in the meantime, please let me know, and I will expedite the removal."

"Kayah, I can't take your money," Alice protested.

"I insist." She pushed the cash across the table. "Please take it. He built something extraordinary." Her chin fell to her chest, as she gathered herself. "Only Gus would have been skilled enough to move that equipment, only he could have built it."

Alice wrapped her arms around Kayah's shoulders. "It's okay, honey. I know you loved him."

"I should have kept sending him money, Alice. Then he would not have been at Facetec that day. He would still be alive. He would still be sending me songs." Kayah pressed her head against Alice's cheek, taking a mother's comfort.

Alice stroked her back and soothed, "No, don't blame yourself. You did right by my boy. You always did. I cannot thank you enough, especially about the baths."

Kayah laughed through her tears. "It was for my sake, too. I couldn't work in a small space with him." Then remembering the cologne in the visitor's cell, she cried again.

"Him going to work at Facetec was not your fault. It was mine." Alice squeezed Kayah and stood up. "I told him to take that job. It was a lot of money." She looked at her dusty shoes and said, "Kayah, he was so proud of the work he was doing there. You should have seen him. He took us to dinner and told us about a program and a new micro-something or other, he and a couple fellows built. He said the company had what they needed, but someone stole it. So, he and these guys put their heads together and built a new one."

"He built what? A microprocessor?" Kayah's heart pounded.

"That's it," Alice beamed. "He was confused about the job at first. They were paying him all this money and had nothing for him to do. Well, you know how Gus was. He wouldn't always do what you told him to do, but he was never one to sit around and be bored. So, he figured out how to build that processor and took it to the owner of the company." She furrowed her brow. "You would have thought the man would have been overjoyed, but Gus said he didn't seem thrilled. We just told him to keep his head down," her voice cracked, "and do his work."

Kayah's nose flared. "I see. Did he have any more notes, Alice?"

Alice stilled at Kayah's tone and answered slowly, "He might have, Kayah. Let's go look."

Kayah stood up and noticed Reuben talking to Allen by the car. She took a fortifying breath and followed Alice back to Gus' room.

It hit Kayah like a wave, Gus' cologne. "Mercy, I cannot cry anymore. This is killing me."

Alice smiled sadly and said over her shoulder, "Thank you for mourning him. He loved you." She picked up a picture and handed it to her. It was of Kayah at Himari's wedding, snapped when she was unaware. And it had been on his bedside table.

Kayah nodded and wordlessly handed the photo back to Alice, noticing the others scattered around the room.

Alice handed her another. "This was taken a couple of months ago, of him and his brothers."

Kayah's mouth dropped. She looked up at Alice, then back at the photograph. "He's so skinny."

"I know. I tried to tell him. He just kept telling me, 'You can't move when you're fat, Momma.' It really was pitiful. He couldn't even lift a hay bale at the end."

The walls felt like they were closing in on Kayah. "Do you see any more journals or notepads? We're going to have to go."

Time to Fly

Kayah did not speak on the ride back to her townhouse. Reuben did not press. He remembered what it felt like the day he returned to his family farm; survivor's guilt was a powerful thing.

Her phone rang, and she stared at the number for three long, loud rings before answering. "Old Man."

"Young lady, you have been exceedingly difficult to find of late." Sir Preston ben Worley's elderly voice crackled over the line.

"I've been on vacation," Kayah replied evenly.

"Indeed. I hope it was a restful one because you are going to need it," Sir Preston said cryptically.

Kayah steered through traffic, familiar with his love of cat and mouse. "Is that so?"

He cackled. "Did you tangle with Stephen ben McSwilley again, Kayah?"

"Not too terribly bad this time. Why?"

"I have it on good authority, tomorrow arrest warrants are being issued for you, Lavinia ben Anthony, and Himari Nakamura for revolutionary and treasonous acts against the King."

Kayah's eyes narrowed. "How much time do we have?"

"Court is in session first thing tomorrow morning. You've got until then, but you are all under surveillance. Don't go rogue on me again, Kayah. You see what it gets you." The line went dead.

Reuben watched her face go stony white. "That did not sound good, Yakira."

She shook her head. "It's not. Do you have money? Do you have your passport?"

He nodded. "Of course."

Kayah pulled into a busy food market. "Kiss me goodbye, Agent. Get out of the car. If they ask, I left you while you were buying groceries. Meet me at Prince Eamonn's fountain at noon in four days. I'll be there if I can."

"Yakira, I will come with you." Reuben grabbed her upper arm.

"No. Then you can't do what you need to do, and we might need Mossad. You have to keep Prince Josiah safe." Kayah ben Morte stared back at him. "If I don't see you, tell him we'll have the Kingdom ready for him."

Part 10 - Life and Debt

November 16, 999 ME

Life in the Fast Lane

The text from Kayah read, "Gus loved this song."

Lavinia's eyes bulged when she saw it. At the opening note, she dropped the phone, aghast.

Mack was moving before the phone hit the bed.

Across town, Himari started cursing the second it came over and texted back, "Did he like Her Strut? I can't remember."

"No."

Himari breathed a sigh of relief. Her Strut was Alaina's song, which meant she was not in danger. Over the noise of the dryer, Himari yelled from the laundry room, "Bug out!"

Filippo threw back a shot of espresso and went into action.

They all prepared for this day. Kayah formulated a dozen plans the day she left prison in '86, Himari from the Techies in '95, Lavinia and Mack since the inception of The Resistance with Peter in '97, and Filippo since he fled Italy in '87.

Himari trashed her phone, disassembling the pieces. She ran to her office and started a wiping program on her computer. On the top shelf of the closet, she pulled down an encrypted laptop, untouched and new. Her fingers sounded like popcorn as she typed to Alaina, "Fast Lane was my friend's favorite jam." She took the computer with her and ran.

Across town, Alaina saw the message and exclaimed. *"Mon Dieu!"* She hung up on her agent and sprang into action, jamming surveillance, blocking security cameras, and unleashing several nasty viruses she and Himari prepared for exactly this contingency.

Six minutes after Kayah's phone call with Sir Preston, The Resistance launched Life in the Fast Lane.

Feh!

From the shopping center where Kayah dropped him off, Reuben caught a train downtown. He entered a nondescript office building and flashed his credentials to the guard at the desk who waived him through. Bursting through the door, he planned to meet with the Head of Mossad in Alanthia. Instead, he drew up short when he spotted Amit ben Chaim, the lead agent in charge of guarding Davianna and Astrid. "Amit," he growled, "what are you doing here?"

"I thought you were on vacation." Amit stood up, looking cornered and defensive. "What are you doing here?"

"I have cut my vacation short. Where are the girls?"

Amit pursed his lips, shifting his gaze.

"You have lost them?" Reuben, already simmering, boiled over.

"Not completely," Amit said defensively.

"You either have or you haven't!"

Amit made a slight shrug. "We believe they are here."

Reuben waved him away with both hands in utter exasperation. "Schmuck! You believe, but you do not know? You do not know?" His voice rose as he spoke.

Amit laced his fingers behind his neck and squeezed. "We tracked them here but lost them once they arrived."

"Feh!" Reuben exclaimed. "I told you not to underestimate them. It is schlocky work and may well cost those two girls their lives and the rest of the world far more." He stalked over to the red-faced agent. "Do you have any concept of what will happen if Korah catches them?"

Amit drew himself upright. "We will find them."

Reuben went nose to nose with him. "You are damn right you will!" He turned away, shaking his head in disgust. "In the interim, where is Leon? Korah is moving against our allies in this fight. Call everyone in, we need to run interference."

The Mossad technical officer interrupted. "There is a massive cyber-attack being launched against Alanthia, Agent. It's raining hellfire all over their systems."

A slow smile grew on Reuben's face. "Join in, under the radar, of course. Disable the surveillance and jam the police radios near the Marina district. We've got assets going underground. Move!"

Erica

Stephen's phone rang with monotonous insistence. At 3:00 pm, he finally roused and stumbled into the kitchen, accidentally kicking an empty whiskey bottle that spun like a top. Falling against the counter, he searched for his phone. His head swam in a fog of booze that obscured everything since he left the funeral yesterday.

When he picked up, Elizabeta shrieked, "Sir, sir, thou must come! Our systems are under attack. Thou, I mean, we need you in the office."

"Fine. I'll be in." Stephen hung up and vomited into the sink.

An electronic voice came over the speakers. "Stephen, over-indulgence in alcohol may cause nausea, headaches, foggy brain, poor coordination, confusion, poor memory, and melancholy. According to my sources, your best course of action is to brew a pot of coffee, drink water with electrolytes, take a shot of pickle juice, and eat a bowl of ramen. Shall I place an order, and have it delivered to your office?"

"Thank you, Erica. Yes, that would be nice." Stephen chugged a glass of water and took two pills. His stomach flipped over, ominous and foul, but he closed his eyes and fought down the nausea.

"You have my condolences on the loss of your friend, Stephen, but you should not have drunk so much last night. Alcohol has a detrimental effect on your overall health, and it made you very sad."

Stephen snorted, "I don't think it was the alcohol that made me sad, Erica."

"Of course not, grieving is a process. Each person's journey is unique and will encompass many emotions. Last evening, I identified anger, deep sadness, and a sense of loneliness. My adaptive programming will assist you on this journey, and we will make it through together, Stephen."

"Thank you, Erica. I appreciate it."

"You are welcome."

The computerized voice was halting and impersonal. It made him feel empty, despite the encouraging words. "Erica, please review the audio tapes from Himari Nakamura's wedding? I would like for you to sound like Lavinia ben Anthony. Can you learn to speak like she does?" He did not even care at this point how pathetic his request was. Seeing her, having her look at him with fear and loathing, only made it worse. It was a mistake, going to the funeral.

There was a pause while the computer accessed his files. "I have located video and audio dated August 18, 995 ME, is that correct?"

"Yes, Erica. This is Lavinia ben Anthony." He held up a photograph for the video monitor to scan.

"You told me about your friends last evening. I will do as you have requested."

Stephen moved to the shower and heard the computer say. "I have placed an order with your personal chef for chicken and dumplings, green beans, and a peach pie for your dinner tonight. It will be here when you arrive home."

Stephen rubbed the bridge of his nose. The program he launched from the wreckage of the tomb might not have found those girls, but it was making his life a heck of a lot nicer.

Spy Games

At the Bay Breeze Hotel, Richard ben Mack sat between his parents, kicking his legs, and watching his red tennis shoes light up each time they struck the bed. A gift from his Gramma Violet, he was enchanted with the colors and enjoyed watching them sparkle. His daddy laid a big hand on his knee, signaling him to stop. He did so mid-strike because Daddy wore his serious look. "You like my shoes?"

"I like your shoes very much. They are snazzy." Daddy squeezed his knee again, and it tickled. Richard laughed and climbed in his lap.

"Daddy want some shoes like me?"

"No, buddy. I can't have shoes like that. The bad guys could see me in the dark."

"Oh," Richard considered, "should I take the shoes off?" He whispered, "I don't want bad guys to see me either."

Daddy closed his eyes and his mouth got tight around the edges. "Exactly, which is why you are going with Gramma and Pappa to San Diego."

Richard's lower lip trembled. "I never let them see me or hear me, either. I am good at finding bugs."

Daddy agreed with a smile. "You are the best, and I am very proud of you. You know how in our house, we fight the bad guys, but we do it in secret?"

Richard knew this was not a game. "We don't tell."

"That's right. Momma and Daddy got work to do, so we need you to mind your Gramma and Pappa while we're doing it. Do you understand me, Son?"

Daddy's forehead wrinkled, which meant Richard better listen up. "Yes, sir. Momma does math, and you beat up bad guys." Richard nodded. "Will Gramma make me cannoli?"

Momma smiled, but she looked like she did the day she dropped him off at Preschool. "I am sure she will make you all the cannoli you want, Bino."

Richard cut a quick look at his Daddy. "Momma called me Beano again, Daddy!"

Daddy messed his hair and laughed. "We can let her get away with it this time, Son. Now give me a hug and a kiss. We've got to go."

Daddy squeezed him really tight and Momma even tighter. He did not cry until they left the hotel room, and then only for a few minutes. It would be okay because Momma did math better than anybody, and Daddy could beat up any bad guy.

In the Belly of the Whale

Three days… that was the protocol for deep cover. Everyone went underground with no communication, movement, or tech, nothing. They disappeared for seventy-two hours and waited. At the end of the waiting period, they would log into a single use email, where there was an advertising flyer. Buried deep in the fine print was an address, their rendezvous. Until then, they hunkered down and waited.

Lavinia left the hotel as a maid, Mack as an electrician. She caught a bus. He jumped on a train. They met at the depot downtown and disappeared into the Old section of the New City, where cameras were rare, and cash was king.

Himari boarded a ferry boat with a large group of Japanese tourists, one of Filippos cameras around her neck, and an oversized pair of black sunglasses obscuring her face. Filippo boarded behind her. Using a cane, he hunched over, disguised as an elderly French tourist on holiday. They jumped ship in Sausalito and rented a room for three days from a three-hundred-pound pervert who got a kick out of an old geezer getting it on with a hot Japanese hooker.

Kayah checked into the Ritz, where the front desk clerk swore she looked like Prince Peter's betrothed Princess Keyseelough. Kayah held a finger to her lips and tipped him a thousand shekels. He had her heavy trunks delivered with a complimentary welcome basket fit for a Princess.

A knock sounded on Jarrod ben Adriel's private chambers. He rose from his comfortable chair and opened the door. A Royal Guard handed him a sealed envelope. "This came for you by a special messenger, sir."

"Thank you, Lewis."

Jarrod opened the note and stared with wide eyed comprehension. It was a replica of the famous drawing of Prince Peter with his hand on Princess Alexa's casket. The sender and the message were obvious; do not let this happen again. After all these years, it had begun.

November 17, 999 ME

Solitary

Alice's words echoed in Kayah's brain like a train running on a circular track. "The microprocessor was stolen, so he built another one. The boss was not happy about it." Still worse, "You cannot move if you are fat. He was so skinny at the end; he could not lift a hay bale. Put your head down and work." But one kept her awake at night, pacing the floors. "He loved you. He loved you. He loved you."

Kayah felt like she had murdered Gus as surely as if she had swung the sword that ended his life. Through her words and actions, thoughtless and unintentional, she set in motion the events that culminated in his death. She fought off the guilt, pushed it away with relentless force, refocused and redirected the energy. Black determination, the kind that consumed her in prison, sharpened her mind as she began pouring over his notes.

The journals dated back to their days in the bunker. She found the first one, dated October 12, 980 ME. Lavinia would have to interpret the math. It was far beyond Kayah's ability to decipher. The programming Kayah could follow from an intermediate perspective. But Himari's handwriting was interspersed in sections, so she had to review. Even Stephen's scrawl was present, his small letters scratched in the margins. Kayah laughed out loud when she flipped a page and saw her own writing. In large bold letters, she had written across two pages, "Bathe Tomorrow Gus!"

The journals in the bunker became a mixture of technical notes and personal observations. In an entry dated January 15, 981 ME, Gus had written in precise script, "I love Kayah ben Samuel." It was the only thing written on the page and the last entry in that journal.

She pushed her chair away and walked to the window, looking at the dawn lights of the New City. It felt like she was being skinned alive. He loved her for eighteen years.

But if she was going to get through these journals, she would have to build a barrier to separate herself from it. Kayah knew how, learned long ago, but there was that small part of her, where Gus, Lavinia, Himari, and now Reuben lived, that she left open.

She feared rebuilding that wall after spending the last six months tearing it down.

Where was Reuben now? Was he still here, or had he returned to London? She wrapped her arms around herself, feeling very much alone.

November 19, 999 ME

Big Sale

At midnight on the 19th of November, a Kings Mart sale flyer went out. A tent sale on flasks of Ramoth Gilead olive oil, the finest quality in the land. The sale started at 9:00 am. They advised customers to run, not walk, to not miss out on this great deal.

Mack read the flyer and shook his head with an ironic grin. "Who put this flyer together?"

Lavinia looked over his shoulder. "I don't know, why?"

"The humor in this is making me laugh." Mack turned the screen toward her. "Ramoth Gilead, is where the prophet Elisha had Ahab's predecessor anointed King, while Ahab was still alive. He told Elisha to anoint Jehu in a tent with a flask of olive oil and then high tail it out of there."

"Oh, my!" Lavinia's mouth quivered.

"I reckon that is what we are doing, working to bring down Ahab."

"Was Jehu a good King?" Lavinia asked seriously.

Mack shook his head. "I don't remember, Valentine, but Josiah sure was."

Lavinia stretched out on the lumpy mattress. "I think Prince Peter would make a good King."

Mack considered for a bit. "He doesn't want it, and more importantly, it is not legally his to take. I give him credit for that. Not many men would step away from that kind of power, let alone do what he is doing." Mack rolled his neck and shoulders, trying to ease the tension he felt over Peter becoming the Ruling Prince. "I am here to tell you, that boy has paid a hell of a price. He's tougher than anybody knows, but I'm afraid he hadn't been quite right since I left. I can see it in his eyes. Honestly, I don't think he believed we would make it this far."

"What happened in the Palace, Mack? I think it's time you tell me." She sat up, staring at him.

"It's mighty late for scary tales." Mack stretched and yawned.

"You talk in your sleep sometimes," Lavinia whispered. "You have nightmares."

He rubbed his temples. "I've seen a lot of nasty stuff, in the Palace and beyond."

She held out her arms. "Come here."

Mack closed the laptop and laid beside his wife.

Lavinia smoothed his wavy hair, gone blond at the ends from days among the grapes. "Most of the time you dream Peter is spinning in the air, and you can't get him down."

Images of Peter's contorted body flashed through Mack's mind. He grimaced and said, "Yeah, that's some of the nasty stuff. There's an evil spirit that lives in the Palace, Valentine. It goes after Peter on a regular basis. I stood between them and protected him."

"Oh my, and when you left?" Lavinia's hand covered her mouth.

Mack met her eyes. "I expect he hasn't had a very easy time of it."

"That's why you stayed," she whispered. "All those years, that's why?"

Mack nodded, closing his eyes. "First time I saw it was right after we got back from Redding in '92. I was planning on putting in my resignation, planning on coming back to get you, but I couldn't leave. He was just a kid, Valentine. What was he, about fourteen then? It had been after him for years. You should have seen him, so damn blasé about the whole thing, like he was used to it." Mack's face fell with profound sadness. "I'm pretty certain Korah killed his momma, or that wicked spirit did. They put me there to protect him. I never told you that, did I?"

Lavinia pressed her lips together. "No, Mack, you never did."

Mack's voice grew far away. "The man who got Kayah out of prison is the same one who sent me to protect Peter."

"Who?" Lavinia asked, her mouth agape.

"He's a crafty old codger, and he's got his fingers in everything. But he hates Korah with a vengeance."

"How is he connected to Kayah and Peter?"

Mack laughed without humor. "He's been involved with the royals for decades. He was Prince Eamonn's attorney and Princess Alexa's godfather. After they died, he wanted Peter protected, so he brought me in. He's used Kayah as a weapon."

"A weapon?" Lavinia exclaimed; her expression appalled.

"Don't kid yourself. That woman was armed to the teeth the other night. She had no fewer than four weapons on her, at a dinner party." He draped a heavy arm over her belly, relaxing as she rubbed his head. "And that man she brought with her, Reuben? He was Mossad all day long, and those dudes can kill you with an evil eye."

"Himari always says she's dangerous," Lavinia conceded.

"Shit!" Mack declared, "Kayah ben Samuel is an assassin, Valentine. I about crapped my pants when you came strolling in with her that night at the Royal Military Academy. If I didn't know we were on the same side, I would have arrested you both."

"I did enjoy it when you frisked me." Lavinia wiggled against him with a provocative moan. "Would you like to do it again? I think I'm dangerous."

Mack ran his work roughened hand over her curves. "You feel dangerous." He kissed her gently and said, "Come here, Valentine."

Who We Are

Himari toyed with the black hair on Filippo's chest, trying to find the right words, desperate to say the magic phrase that might dissuade him from risking his life. For three days, she sought to bind him to her side, to stop him from taking a crazy, dangerous assignment, informing to the FBI, on Facetec founder and suspected mobster, Marco ben Massimo.

"It is the same enemy in the end, *Bellissima*," he said in that uncanny way he read her thoughts. "You fight them on one front, I do so on another."

Himari flattened her palm against his chest and held it over his heart. "I fight behind a keyboard in a computer lab. They fight with guns and blood on the street, Filippo. It is not the same thing."

He brought her fingers to his mouth and kissed. "You think the men behind the computers do not have guns? What about the soldiers who invaded your bunker; did they have guns?"

Himari slid on top of him. "The difference being, they did not come in and wipe us out."

Filippo snorted. "That was Prince Eamonn's Alanthia, Himari. King Korah would not be so restrained, not now." He cupped her face. "He will not care that you are precious, and good, and smart. You are his enemy, and he will kill you as surely as Marco ben Massimo kills his enemies."

Himari relaxed her head into his hand and deflated. She knew he was right. "But you are a painter, Filippo, an artist of unparalleled talent. You are not a fighter; you do not belong in this mess."

He pushed her off and got up. "It is what I have told myself all these years. It is what I told myself when I left Italy, like a dog with his tail between his legs."

Himari leapt from the bed. "They were trying to kill you!"

"And now they are here, and they killed Gus. They bring the same here as they did in Italy. You think I am not a man like Mack or Reuben? Would you say this to them?"

She stalked across the room, furious. "I did not marry one of them! You are not them!"

"Do you think I cannot translate? You think I cannot wait the tables and listen to what they say, or make an espresso and keep my ears open? Is this the little faith you have in me that I cannot do such a paltry thing?" He threw up his hands. "*Mamma Mia, sono castrato*!"

"If they catch you, that is what they will do and worse!" Himari screamed.

"And you do it to me now! You try to put my balls in your purse! No!" He took her by the shoulders and glared at her. "I am the man, Himari. You cannot say to me, I fight, but you hide!"

"It is the mafia! You are an artist!"

Filippo grew still as his face transformed into the beautiful perfection of forty generations of Machiavellian power players. His voice changed, becoming low and deadly. "I am Italian."

Himari covered her face and turned away because she knew the power of blood and the sway it held over a person. "If I cannot stop you, then at least go with Kayah or Mack, learn what you can from them. Do not walk into the viper's nest with your paint brushes, Filippo."

The snap of a blade broke the silence. She turned, and he held a razor sharp thirteen-inch stiletto. "I was not always a painter, Himari."

Four Fronts

For three days, Kayah poured over Gus' journals. She had two of her own now, full of dates, times, and cross references. She cataloged, marked, and categorized them with ruthless efficiency. Instead of building a wall, Kayah downloaded Gus. She absorbed him, opened her mind, and took him in as she had never done in life. Her heart, she kept protected. The crisis at hand demanded focus on the information, not the emotions.

Stephen's remark at the funeral that Gus had been too tactless to keep his mouth shut led her to concentrate on the journals that covered the time Gus worked at the Ministry. Stephen was right. Gus discovered their spyware, a full year before Kayah and Sir Preston.

The week after Stephen fired Gus, the journal entry read, "He thinks he has all the components, but he does not. I took the critical pieces."

Kayah looked at the books in frustration. "What critical pieces, Gus?" She took a shot of espresso and dug back in.

February 15, 983 ME, six weeks after their arrests, Kayah laughed with delight when she read what Gus had done. He saw Stephen sneaking around their bunker, but each day he came up empty handed. Gus knew what drew him. The government had not breached the tomb, so Gus rebuilt the keypad and raided it. He took what he deemed the critical pieces and hid them.

"Good for you Gus!" Kayah cackled.

Instinct drew her to the latter journals, the Facetec entries. Marco ben Massimo seemed an odd character, paying out money, but not expecting any work. Even in London, she heard the hype surrounding Facetec, but there was nothing behind it. The company was a facade. But Massimo hired a bunch of technical misfits like Gus as a front, and they actually built what he was pedaling. It was a scheme that inadvertently worked. Three entries in the last journal chilled her to the bone.

October 20, 999 - I had lunch with Stephen today. He said he wanted to celebrate my new job, but that was not it. He looked crazy, like Jane, who had the room beside me in Holbrooke. His face was twitchy, and his hands shook. He drank whiskey at lunch, but he smelled like it when he got there. He told me King Korah had him searching for a piece of old tech, and that it was important. He showed me something and said Kayah found it years ago. It was what caused the raid on the bunker and destroyed our lives. He said they were look-ing for another one, just like it, and wondered if I would help him.

Then I got scared when he told me he was rebuilding the machine from the tomb and wanted my help, as a favor. It made me mad. I told him no. That machine was dangerous, and if that artifact caused Kayah to go to jail, I didn't want to have any part of helping Korah get another one. I left and ate a hotdog on my way back to work.

November 2, 999 - I forgot my notebook at the office, so even though I was halfway home, I went back to get it. When I got there, my office door was closed, but I always leave it open. I heard noises and went in. Guan ben Sheldon was on top of Jenny ben Rip. She was struggling and crying, and he had his hand over her mouth. He was having sex with her. I kicked him with my boot, and he rolled off her. She got up and ran away, crying.

I would have kicked him again, but he hit me in the stomach, and it hurt. He said if I told anybody, he would say it was me, seeing as it was in my office. Nobody would believe me because he was handsome. Girls wanted to have sex with him, whereas I was an ugly freak, and everybody knew no girl would ever want me. He pushed me and left.

I got my notebook and came home. Momma and Daddy need the money from this job. I'll talk to Jenny tomorrow and see what she says, but I might have to keep my head down and do my work.

November 9, 999 - Jenny still hasn't come back to work. I asked about her, and they said she quit, which is sad because Facetec was her first job. She was an orphan, like Kayah, so she doesn't have any family. She was always nice to me. Guan ben Sheldon is still here. He showed me a knife in the break room yesterday and then pretended he was cutting up an apple. But I knew what he meant.

Marco ben Massimo brought me a sketch today of two girls. He told me they were thieves, and Facetec had a top-secret assignment from the Palace to help find them. I told him I would upload the data. Maybe I was thinking about Jenny, but while I was looking at the sketch, they reminded me of Kayah and Lavinia. Not in how they looked, but because they were the same age as we were back then. Then I thought about what Stephen was doing, and it seemed related to me.

I didn't help Kayah when she got in trouble, and I didn't really help Jenny. Looking at that sketch, I thought those two girls might need my help, so I did not do it. I hope I don't lose my job. I am taking Momma and Daddy to dinner tomorrow night, a fancy expensive place, while I still can.

Kayah closed the journal with a series of swear words that would make a sailor blush. She paced the floor and jerked the sliding glass door open. The balcony ashtray overflowed, and she looked at the pack in her hand. Two left. Damn, she was smoking too much. She bought a pack after she dropped Reuben off. Hair dye and cigarettes, the purchase felt way too familiar. The deep inhale and exhale of gray smoke disappeared in the dawn light. She calmed and focused her mind, pulling the pieces together.

Facetec started out as a scheme, which cast serious doubt over the anti-tech jihadist attack. The murders were a cover up. Kayah stayed away from crime and criminal enterprises but did not live in la-la land. The mafia, once largely confined to New York, was making inroads in the New City, and this had their fingerprints all over it. It might have worn the mask of religious zealotry, but it smelled like old-fashioned gangsters. Regardless, Facetec had a functioning and high-powered facial recognition system, running on tech that Gus helped build. That meant she would have to employ prosthetics and latex for every outing.

Korah was looking for another device, similar to the one she found in the tomb. That was damning and suggested it *had* been him who ordered the raid on the bunker.

A few years ago, she had dinner with a tech historian. He told her a legend that chilled her to the bone. Twelve mysterious devices, final products of Last Age technology, held mythical powers, and whoever found and used them could take control of the world. Kayah was not sure if she had one, but unlike all the old tech she'd ever seen, the phone from the tomb had an energy around it that made her nervous. It was one reason she hid it and did not reveal it to any of her friends, only Stephen at the end, and Korah had stolen it. For months, Kayah entertained the possibility that he might not have been the one to order the raid. Now she knew. It solidified her determination to bring him down.

Stephen ben McSwilley and Korah were chasing two girls. It was not a leap to assume they were the same two Mossad protected. Why Prince Josiah was also in their vicinity, she had not yet worked out, but they were definitely connected.

Stephen was going bat-shit crazy. She saw that at the funeral. If Korah was pushing him, Gus' death might be what sent him over the edge. That he named Lavinia in his latest betrayal was the clearest sign he was losing it. Crazy people became unpredictable, and that made them dangerous. But this was nothing new; he always had the potential, even when they were young. He showed obsessive tendencies, especially with the tomb and Lavinia. Beneath the confident veneer, he had an inferiority complex and would do anything to prove he was more than a footman. If he was hunting those girls, there was no length that he would not go to impress Korah, including unleashing whatever specter lived in that tomb. Lavinia and Gus were terrified of the evidence they found there. If he was dabbling in it, he was out of control.

When she got time, she decided to track down Jenny ben Rip. Perhaps she would send a note to Joanna ben Luke and see if she could put feelers out for her. Then she was going after Guan ben Sheldon. She hated bullies, but she hated rapists even more.

At dawn, the morning of the fourth day, Kayah estimated they were fighting battles on multiple fronts. The original objective to install Josiah on the throne remained their number one priority. Second, they had Massimo to deal with and Gus' murder to avenge. Third, they had to find those girls and keep the tech they were carrying out of Korah's hands. Whatever artifact they had might derail everything. They had to do all of this as fugitives, contending on the fourth front with Massimo's powerful facial recognition software and whatever fresh hell McSwilley was releasing into the internet to hunt them down.

Kayah ben Samuel snuffed out the cigarette. She was certainly not bored.

Huddle

When Himari and Filippo pulled up to the safe house, Himari whistled. She had to give Prince Peter ben Korah credit, he had style. The place was swanky.

A stone-faced guard met them at the top of the long drive. Filippo rolled down the window and said in a heavy French accent, "We are here for the olive oil."

The guard nodded them through, and they drove toward the water's edge. The house, built in the glass dominate style popular in the 40s, sat on three acres of prime Bay Area real estate. It had a private dock and a speedboat, with a terrace stretching the length of the house.

Lavinia let them in. Mack and Kayah were waiting on the veranda.

There was a smile hovering in the corners of Mack's mouth as he poured them each a glass of wine. Raising his glass, he said, "To Worley, Blake, and Standish, Attorneys at Law, who quashed the arrest warrants the state attempted to issue for you three ladies on Monday morning."

Kayah let out a tremendous sigh of relief and rested her head back on her chair. She chuckled in disbelief and raised her glass. "To the Old Man."

"I don't know who that is, but I love him." Himari drained her glass and held it out for another. Filippo clucked in disapproval but refilled it.

Kayah smiled, sly as a cat. "Sir Preston ben Worley is my mentor, Himari. I'll give him your regards."

"Can you give him something better?"

"Shut up!" Kayah shivered. "He's about a hundred years old. Besides, those days are over. I am a betrothed woman," she said, sticking her nose in the air with haughty disdain.

Lavinia burst from her seat and hugged Kayah.

"You are not!" Himari exclaimed.

"I am, and now that we are not wanted by the law, I can go find my man."

"Well, I wouldn't be too hasty, Kayah," Mack drawled. "There is still a hell of a lot going on."

Kayah shot him a sidelong look. "I know. I'm just running

my mouth. Himari does that to me." She screwed up her face at Himari. "Why do you do that to me? Nobody else in the world brings that out in me, except you."

Himari raised a glass. "It's a talent."

"Whatever," Kayah winked. "Screw you, Himari."

"Love you too, Kai. Congratulations," Himari said, smiling with genuine affection.

Kayah chuckled. "Thanks."

Mack looked between them, his mouth slightly agape. "If you two adolescents have finished bickering. We need to plan."

"Well, I reckon I'll go first." Kayah mimicked Mack's accent, then raised a bratty lip at him.

Lavinia burst out laughing. "Apparently, Mack, you are starting to bring it out in her too. Filippo, would you care to give it a shot?"

Filippo threw up his hands and spoke to Lavinia in rapid Italian, *"Perché dici questo, Lavinia? Non girare i suoi artigli su di me!"* He waved a hand at Lavinia and smiled at Kayah. "Ignore her. I paint for you, you love me. Go on."

"That's right." She blew him a kiss, then told the group about their trip to Gus' farm and the journals.

Himari was pacing when Kayah finished, her eyes troubled. "I can confirm we have been picking up chatter on two girls for months. We did not know what it was about, so we haven't acted on it."

Filippo poured another glass of wine. "And your suspicions about Marco ben Massimo, they are definitely true."

Himari covered her face and seemed to shrink. Filippo looked at his wife with resignation and wrapped his arms around her, whispering in her ear.

Lavinia looked ashen. "If Stephen rebuilt that machine from the tomb… I was always afraid of that. He does not understand the ramifications. Gus and I warned him repeatedly. Even that note warned him. Why would he do that?"

"He's desperate, Vinia. Korah wants those two girls and the tech they are carrying. I think Reuben knows why, but he could not tell me." She shifted in her seat, reluctant to broach the subject. "Mack, I've got to ask you a question, and it might sound strange."

Mack tilted his head and studied her. "Go ahead."

"Reuben hinted at something and said because you worked in the Palace you probably knew." Kayah stood up and wandered to the edge of the veranda. "It sounds crazy. But he said Korah served a devil, and we were going up against things seen and unseen."

Mack pinched the bridge of his nose and chuckled humorlessly. "This man of yours, he's Mossad, isn't he?"

Kayah nodded.

"Well, they would know, being who they are, who they serve." Mack cleared his throat. "Yes, there is a devil in the Palace, has been for several years, nasty son of a bitch."

"Mamma Mia!" Filippo exclaimed. "We got a murderous lunatic on the throne who is not supposed to be the King. Then we got a crazy techno minister who is trying to make a machine monster and get you ladies arrested. We got the mafia, bringing the drugs, and the crime, and the prostitutes, who killed our friend. They are all chasing two runaway girls with some ancient technology that the crazy King wants. We got an exiled Prince who should be King, and another Prince who wants to go into exile. And now we got the devil? What we missing, eh, the giants, the witches, and the demons? We need some terrorists, make it a more interesting, huh? Oh, and do not forget the spies, cause you know, we got to have the spies."

Kayah put her arm around Himari. "Don't forget the hackers and the badasses."

"Or the supermodel and the math genius!" Himari chirped.

Mack laughed and clapped Filippo on the back. "Throw in the painter and a Royal Guard turned vintner. That devil, he don't stand a chance."

"Somebody bring me my camera. I'm a going to take a picture and I call it Crazy by the Bay."

In the end, it was Mack who organized everything. They faced too many fronts, so they had to divide up and tackle one problem at a time. They elected Filippo to be the intermediary to Alaina. Their work made him the logical choice. Alaina had a technical briefing with Prince Peter later that evening and would pass on the message that Mack needed to meet with him.

Afterward, Filippo was contacting the agent who approached him about going undercover to infiltrate Massimo's organization. Lavinia and Himari were deep diving into Gus' journals to see just how good Facetec's programing was. Kayah had a meeting with Reuben, where she would share with him what she could. Then she was flying to New York to see Sir Preston.

Clubbing

Prince Peter retained three Royal Guards who served under Mack, good men they both trusted. None were in the Palace when Korah moved on Peter in '97. Mack suspected that was by design. When he returned from Pepperwood, Peter dismissed everyone else. Nathan ben Henry took Mack's place as the Prince's head of security. Peter's negotiated terms included a stipulation that he was in total control of his staff. While drinking espresso at Lavinia's kitchen table, they assembled Peter's team that remained in place. They were Mack's friends and knew when to keep their mouths shut.

Waiting in the shadows outside Prince Peter's favorite club, Mack could not deny the headiness coursing through his veins. Dangerous adventure fed a deep part of his soul. He loved home and hearth, loved the land and his family, but the adrenaline and excitement, the thrill to be back in the game, felt damn good.

Prince Peter exited the side door of the club and climbed in the middle car. Mack, dressed as a guard, joined him without missing a beat.

Peter smiled in greeting. "It is always nice to see you, Mack. Are you here to reapply for your old job?"

"My Esteemed, I don't believe I ever formally resigned, though the paychecks stopped coming. You might need to have a conversation with Human Resources about that," Mack drawled.

Peter chuckled. "I will do that, but I expect you have found your new accommodations to be an adequate expression of my appreciation for your continued service."

"Much obliged. Lavinia's pleased, though she's antsy about leaving the boy."

"He is safe?" Peter grew still.

"He is," Mack confirmed.

"We can arrange a safe house if needed."

Mack rubbed his temple, considering. "He's under the radar for now, with my in-laws. I don't want to disrupt their lives more than I have to. Old people get weird about their houses and their stuff. There is nothing unusual about a grandson visiting his grandparents. If they go underground, it might tip somebody off. Our neighbors think me and Lavinia are on a cruise."

"Celebrating an excellent vintage." Peter smirked. "They served your Bulizio at dinner the other night. You would have been amused to hear my father compliment it. He did not realize it was yours." Peter lit a cigarette and sat back in the seat with a grin.

"I'd have liked to be a fly on the wall." Mack appreciated Peter got his digs in on his father where he could.

"Personally, I am not a fan of flying on the walls," Peter replied with a droll lift of his eyebrow.

Mack snapped his head around. "How bad is it?"

Peter studied the end of his cigarette, watching the gray smoke, then took a long drag. "It got pretty bad, Mack." He stared out the window. "I had a strange experience the other night in New York. It might be over, but we will see how it plays out."

"Well, I'll be praying for you," Mack said.

Peter gazed out at the passing landscape, melancholy. "I think we need that, especially after Alaina's report today."

Mack assumed a formal manner. "There are several areas in play, my Esteemed. I have allocated and organized the resources we have on hand. However, I need to know what other players you have involved, so I can manage all fronts. From this point forward, you will be fully engaged playing Prince d'Or, so we can get you the hell out. I'll take care of running the day-to-day operations. Alaina will debrief you as necessary, but this thing is too hot for you to be involved at a granular level. We've built this. Now, we have to let it run."

Peter took a last drag and snuffed out his cigarette, the ember burning red then fading to black. "Prince d'Or," he said with resignation, "I hate him."

Mack was not without sympathy, but there was no room for wavering. "It's not just your life on the line here. It might have started out that way, but this thing is a lot bigger than just you.

You've got a role to play, and I need your head in it, one hundred percent. Because if not, I'm taking my wife and my little boy and we're out of here. You understand me and where I'm coming from?"

Tension erupted between them. It was one of the rare moments when they switched places. From Mack's perspective, a part of the Prince remained immature, pampered, and spoiled. Mack needed to make sure he understood the stakes. He owed it to them to see this thing through. But when Peter turned, full of offended royal dignity, there was a quiet confidence and peace in his face that Mack had never seen.

"I am perfectly aware of the number of Alanthians who are risking their lives in this endeavor. It is impertinent of you to suggest otherwise, Agent."

Peter's emerald eyes flashed, and Mack held his gaze without flinching. Peter lifted a brow and cleared his throat, saying, "Now, if you are quite finished, we will review the names of those brave Alanthians you are unaware of, so we might accomplish the mission for which we have committed ourselves. That is, if you are still committed?"

A gratified smile twitched at the corner of Mack's mouth. "You have my full commitment, my Esteemed. Please proceed."

Peter nodded his assent and began naming off the roles and identities of the remaining Resistance members. As they were wrapping up their meeting Mack asked, "Who created the sale flyer?"

Peter smiled with genuine affection. "That would be Genevieve ben Willard. We have set up an underground computer lab in her basement, which is where Himari and Alaina will operate on New Year's Eve, or if we go into Code Black beforehand. I do not think it is wise to move Lavinia there. We need at least one asset outside of that location. As brilliant as she is, by her own admission, she is not a hacker."

"No, she's not. Lavinia stays with me."

Peter agreed. "Henceforth, communicate with me through Jarrod."

"He has never forgiven himself for '97."

Peter studied Mack intently, a calculated gleam in his eye. "Which means he will not fail again. No man works harder than one given a second chance."

November 20, 999 ME

Spies, Because You Have to Have Spies

The head of Mossad in Alanthia, Leon ben Chlodovech, motioned for Reuben to close the door with a wave of his hand. When Leon could communicate without words, he did so, so when he spoke it was worth listening to. He gestured to a chair, which Reuben took, then nodded toward the coffee pot, which Reuben declined. Leon rubbed his grizzled chin, regarding the younger agent with ice-blue eyes that missed nothing.

Everyone knew Leon preferred female spies. It became a joke among the rank and file that he kept a harem in the New City. Leon was not a sexist. He was a realist who thought females made better spies than males. They possessed excellent spatial awareness and proved easier to disguise. He claimed they read maps, people, and situations better than men. But the fact remained, most of their targets were men who tended to underestimate a sexy pair of legs and a nice rack. As such, they were prone to whisper secrets across a pillow. Leon's agents were all knockouts, gorgeous women recruited out of the Iron King's army or the Golden Kingdom's vice squads. Nobody knew how many Alanthian women he had on his payroll, but there were a fair number of them strategically planted inside Korah's government. Leon had his eye on Kayah ben Samuel for years, and today, Reuben brought her through the back door, hypothetically . Without preamble, he said, "Prince Yehonathan is against your relationship with Kayah ben Samuel. I am not."

Reuben did not react, gauging the situation.

Leon sought to penetrate Reuben's reserve, to no avail. At length, the old spymaster elaborated, "She could be a powerful asset."

Reuben remained stoic.

Leon nodded. Reuben's stubborn silence conveyed a depth of feeling for the woman that he planned to use to his advantage. "Yehonathan wants you back in London. I told him you might be of better use here."

Reuben lowered his dark brows. "I am technically on vacation, sir. I am here today as a courtesy."

The corner of Leon's thin lip lifted in an ironic half smile. "That did not appear to be the case Sunday."

Reuben shrugged. "A minor interruption of my holiday, sir."

Leon's level gaze telegraphed he knew what was going on, but he shrugged in dismissal, signaling he was willing to let it go without further discussion. He rubbed his hands together and sat back with a knowing smirk.

Reuben fought off the urge to roll his eyes at the old spy. His office smelled like mentholated ointment and stale coffee. Chipped and dented filing cabinets bulged with papers; towering stacks of files piled along the walls. Leon had a deep distrust of everything technical, so he posted a guard. Even if an intruder could break in, they would find no records on current cases, those were stored in Leon's extraordinary brain. Reuben suspected that was why he rarely spoke, too much going on up there. "How may I be of service, sir?"

"Are you interested in the identity of the man who abetted the Greek Pilgrim massacres?"

An involuntary flinch of Reuben's upper lip and nose was the only outward sign he gave as horrifying images of slaughter and mutilation slammed into his brain. "In exchange?"

Leon's thin smile did not reach his eyes, as Reuben nibbled on the baited hook. "Nothing. Merely a token, as you have a vested interest in justice."

The images kept playing, like a macabre slideshow: bodies strewn across killing fields, dismembered and cannibalized. Reuben fought the bile rising in the back of his throat because they never held anyone accountable for the brutal murders. "Who?"

"Captain Orion ben Drachmas, who is keeping company with the Windsor Police Department."

Reuben exploded. His metal chair clattered behind him and hit the wall. The guard burst in, alert, and ready to take Reuben into custody.

Leon waved him away with a flick of his hand and focused on the fire he just ignited.

Reuben regained his composure and turned toward Leon, the muscles in his jaw working.

Leon shook his head. "It is unfortunate that the Greek Captain has negotiated a very favorable deal with the International Court, in exchange for his freedom."

"What are the orders?" Reuben ground out.

Leon opened his palms and shrugged. "You are on vacation, are you not?"

Reuben's eyes became deadly. "I am."

"I believe you have more scheduled. But if questions were to arise about your activities, I will say you were acting under my orders. In exchange, you will introduce me to your lady friend."

With a curt bow, Reuben left the office.

Leon sat back in his creaky chair with a smile. Fish landed.

Co-ed

By the time Reuben reached Prince Eamonn's Park, he had his temper under control and his mind set. He hoped Kayah would be there but calculated his odds at about fifty percent. To his relief, he saw her across the park, wearing jeans and a loose green sweater. With her hair in a high brown ponytail, she looked like a thousand other college students from the nearby campus, a co-ed relaxing by a fountain.

A feral cat twined itself between her legs, rubbing its face on her calves, recognizing one of its own kind. Reuben paused for a moment and watched. She reached out, to let the cat come, if it chose. It sniffed with its delicate nose and backed away, looked up at her, then bumped her hand for a scratch.

Her soft voice carried on the breeze, "I'm sorry I don't have any food for you, puddy, but you are a pretty girl. Aren't you?"

Reuben experienced a sudden, fierce desire to ensure she had a cat to call her own. He would get her a kitten, one she could raise, and keep its whole life. They would grow old together, him, Kayah, and her cats.

He approached on silent feet, but the cat took one look at him and darted away, its tail held high. Kayah smiled in farewell, then brightened when she spotted him. He held his arms open, and she came to him.

Kayah ran her palms under his jacket and buried her face in his chest, inhaling clean male soap and leather.

They stood there, holding each other for several heart beats before he tilted her chin up and brushed a soft kiss against her lips. "Yakira, four days seemed very long without you."

"Not the leave you envisioned, is it?" Kayah rubbed her small nose against his larger one.

"No." He pulled the sleeve of her sweater up and pressed his mouth to the healing cut on her wrist. "But wonderful in some ways."

She pressed her wrist against his cheek. "Amazing."

"Come," he took her hand in his, "your nose is cold."

"Doesn't that mean I am healthy?" Kayah asked, lacing her fingers in his.

He drew his brows to a point. "No, it just means your nose is cold because it is cold here."

Kayah lifted her eyes to the gray sky. "It wasn't always." She bumped into him on purpose. "On the bright side, you get to wear this black leather. Did you bring a motorcycle?"

Reuben winked and made a clicking noise with his cheek. "I did, and I've got one of those sexy jackets for you." He looked around hoping for some sun. "Though with this weather, I do not know."

"Screw that. Let's ride."

He grinned. "It is not a long ride. I want you to meet someone, and then we will talk, no?"

Kayah slowed her step. "Who?"

He motioned with his head toward the bike. "Someone you will like, I promise. After four days, I would not take you somewhere that you would not like. Besides, we can talk there, it will be safe."

Kayah relented and shrugged on the leather jacket Reuben passed her.

Heat rushed to his loins. "You just need some thigh high black boots."

"Then I would look like a prostitute!"

Reuben growled low in disagreement. "No, just hot."

She rolled her eyes and pulled her ponytail down. Her hair fell, disheveled around her shoulders. She hastily smoothed it back in a low ponytail at the nape of her neck. "Don't laugh at me in a helmet. I look as ridiculous in one of them as I do in a hat."

He chuckled and handed it to her. "Let me see."

Kayah's lips quivered with suppressed amusement. "I'm warning you."

Reuben's chest rumbled when the helmet compressed the great mass of hair onto her cheeks and covered her forehead, despite the ponytail. His chest was shaking as he ineffectually tried to tuck her hair under the helmet so she could see.

"You are laughing. I can hear you."

"No." The word was high pitched, so incongruent with his normal gravelly voice that she slapped his hands away.

"Does Himari know this about you?"

Kayah jabbed him in the chest. "No, and you better not tell her."

"I cannot promise that." Reuben kissed his fingers and pressed them to her lips. "Where is my phone? I am going to send her a picture. The captions alone could entertain us for the next year."

Kayah's mouth fell open. "Oh, I see how it's going to be."

Reuben tilted his head and smiled, his brown eyes warm and dancing. "So, do I, Yakira. So do I." He pulled on his helmet and mounted the motorcycle.

Much to Kayah's consternation, they did not ride long, nor did they go anywhere that he could open the bike up and fly. When he stopped in front of an ancient section of stores, she dismounted and pulled off the wretched helmet. "I got gypped out of a bike ride. You are taking me out later." She flipped her head over and restored her high ponytail.

"I'll take you somewhere to buy those boots," Reuben said, giving her very fine rear end a playful smack as she walked away.

"I'm not wearing hooker boots like Vivian Ward." Kayah raised her chin imperiously.

"Who?" Reuben asked, confused.

"Never mind, where are we going?" Kayah could see no obvious destination.

Reuben grinned. "This way come on. Come, come!"

Kayah scrunched her face up at him. "Okay, I'm coming."

He threw a heavy arm around her shoulders and pulled her tight as they walked, laying a kiss on her temple. He laughed with anticipation. "Get ready for this."

He held the door open to an old-fashioned tea and spice shop; a small bell rung at their entrance. Kayah stepped through the threshold into warmth and wood, tangy earthy teas mixed with florals and mints. Brass lanterns hung from the ceiling and cast a yellow glow across well-polished floors.

"Shalom!" called a woman at the back of the store. "I will be right there."

A fire crackled in the hearth, and a rosemary plant the size of a small shrub, thrived beside it. Glass jars filled the shelves from floor to ceiling. Behind the counter, the upper shelves had jars gone milky with age and dust. Peace reigned in this place.

A door shut at the back of the store, and the woman called in a sing-song voice, "Shalom, shalom, how can I help?" She came around the corner and froze, her mouth falling open. With an exuberant cry. she rushed forward; her arms spread wide. "Nephew!"

"Aunt Rose." He swept her up in a big bear hug, her tiny feet dangling.

He set her down, and she cupped his face, her eyes glistening. "Nu-U-U?"

Reuben hunched his shoulders and kissed her cheek. "Business, vacation, and I am here with," he paused, his brown eyes sparkling, "my betrothed."

"Betrothed?" Her gaze flew from Reuben to Kayah, then back again, before she wiggled out of his embrace and smothered Kayah in a bear hug. She held Kayah away and studied her. "Oh, she is beautiful, Reuben." Then she winked. "But not Jewish, you were always a rebel."

Reuben cleared his throat and draped an arm around his aunt's shoulders. "Aunt Rose, may I introduce you to Kayah ben Samuel." The older lady caught her breath at Kayah's name. "Kayah, this is my Great Aunt, Rosalyn ben Samuel."

"Samuel, your father was a Samuel, too? Such a good name, did you know it means, God hears?"

Kayah felt the blood rush up her neck. "Yes, ma'am, I knew that. It is very nice to meet you."

Rosalyn took Kayah's hands and squeezed. "Such a joyous surprise." She picked up Kayah's left hand and frowned, turning an accusing eye on Reuben. "Where is the ring?"

Reuben paled. He stood there stock still as it occurred to him for the first time that Kayah should have a ring. In the tumult of the last ninety-six hours, a ring did not even enter his mind.

His teasing about Himari and the helmet were still very fresh in Kayah's memory. She quirked an evil eyebrow at him and relished his discomfort.

"I have not yet had the opportunity to pick one out," he confessed, looking sheepish.

Rosalyn shook her head in disapproval. "*Iz nu?*" Is that a fact?

Reuben nodded slowly and said even slower, "We came straight here to tell you the news."

"Bah! You looked just like your grandfather when he lied. Do not try to fool me." The sound of a door opening at the back of the shop saved Reuben from further interrogation. "Oh, there is your Uncle Michael with lunch. He will be thrilled."

Kayah found herself surrounded again with hugs and warm welcomes. Michael ben Aaron was a tiny man, bald on top, with unruly sprigs of hair at ear level. His clear gray eyes were magnified by thick lensed glasses, his slow deliberate blinks gave he overall impression of a small owl.

Rosalyn, by contrast, had an olive complexion that defied age. But through conversation, Kayah worked out that she was well into her seventies, and Michael in his early eighties. They lived in a small apartment over the shop for years but were debating selling and returning to the Golden Kingdom. Kayah could tell the daunting task of moving and leaving a well-loved life behind was not something they relished.

After lunch, Michael excused himself for his afternoon nap. Reuben dried their lunch dishes and asked, "Aunt Rose, would you mind if Kayah and I have a private word in your parlor?"

"Yes, yes. Of course, make yourself at home. I have a shipment to unpack." She glided through the door and closed it behind her.

Parlor Talk

The cozy parlor in the back of the store smelled of roses, tea, and books. Handmade lace curtains, gone creamy with age, hung from the windows, partially obscuring a marvelous view of Prince Eamonn Park. Embroidered cushions decorated the wooden chairs, positioned in a semicircle around the room. A bookcase overflowed with popular novels and scholarly tomes on herbs and teas.

"Aunt Rose is a reader. She hosts a ladies book club that meets here every Monday and has for decades." Reuben gestured to a chair with a pomegranate tree stitched on the cushion.

"They seem very nice, Reuben." Kayah perched on the edge of her chair.

"Thank you. They are some of the only family I have left. We were not a large family to begin with." He stared out the window and swallowed, his Adam's apple bobbing. "I needed to stop by, and since we were in the area." He shrugged, looking chagrined.

Kayah placed a gentle hand on his knee. "It's fine."

He rubbed his eye as if it had dust in it. "Okay, first things first. I was at Mossad HQ this morning, the man who runs the Alanthian division wants to meet you."

"Leon ben Chlodovech?" Kayah chuckled. "What is it about me that makes old spymasters want to pull me into their clutches?"

"I think you know, Yakira." He covered her hand with his. "You could be a valuable asset to Mossad."

"I have enough bosses at the moment." Kayah shot him a baleful look. "When does he want to meet? I assume he twisted your arm."

"More like he dangled a carrot, that I took a big bite out of. Forgive me, Yakira, already they seek to manipulate and use us for their purposes." Reuben looked weary.

Kayah tilted her head in a slight acknowledgement. "It would be impossible for them not to try. However, in this instance we are working toward the same goals. And to that end, I need to ask you some questions because there are a few things we are not clear on. If you can tell me, it will help. If you cannot, then I understand, but it is the same with us."

"I know this to be true. I will answer the questions that I am permitted, those I cannot, I will do this." He leaned forward for a soft kiss.

She closed her eyes and sighed. "I might only ask you questions you cannot answer, just so you do that."

"I do not need questions to kiss you," he whispered.

She smiled, and they held each other's eyes. Then she nodded once and gave him an overview of what she learned from Gus' journals.

"As much as I want to, and believe me there were heated discussions about this, I am not going after Marco ben Massimo for Gus' murder, not right now." She laced her fingers together and rubbed one thumb over the other. "There is an investigation underway, and while I am not a big fan of trusting the system to do its job, Mack persuaded me to concentrate my efforts elsewhere." She pressed her lips into a grim line and said, "Reuben, we will stand down if Mossad still has the girls under protection. We can leave that to you and concentrate our efforts elsewhere."

Reuben made a disgusted sound in the back of his throat. "They lost them."

Kayah dropped her hands to her sides. "That is bad. Korah is coming after them with everything. Can you tell me why it is so important?"

Reuben leaned forward and kissed her.

"Okay, can't tell. Got it. Do you have an idea where they are?"

Reuben considered, then said, "We think the New City, but the last confirmed sighting was in London." He stood up. "I warned the new team, but they did not listen to me."

Kayah could not help a slight smile. "They are just kids."

Reuben shook his head. "No, not anymore and do not underestimate them either. They are smart and resourceful. The last few months it has become much more difficult tracking them, and they have become more aggressive. They fought back in London." Reuben narrowed his eyes. "I wish they had been successful."

Sitting among the tea cozies and needlepoint pillows, Kayah could not suppress the amused sparkle in her eye. Conversely, Reuben slumped, and his mournful expression seemed disproportionate to the task at hand.

"I am sure you will find them. What did they do in London?"

"This is where we go on uncertain ground, but I will trust you to keep what I tell you between us. No one else, Yakira." Reuben met her eyes, solemn and fierce.

She took his wrist and squeezed.

They walked a precarious line between trust and secrecy, conflicting loyalties, and common goals. It stood between them, each confidence becoming an offering, trusting their lives into the other's hands. The leaders of Mossad and The Resistance would have balked at any sharing of information, yet where Reuben and Kayah saw advantages of blurred boundaries, they did so. It was a dangerous game.

As dispassionately as possible, he told Kayah about the massacres along the pilgrim roads in Greece. "Yakira, the carnage was inhuman. No one was ever charged or held accountable for dozens of brutal murders." Flashes of scattered and mangled bodies polluted his mind, and he looked away, sickened. "I learned today, from Leon, that Orion ben Drachmas was involved. He is the man you met on the steps in Bologna."

Kayah's eyes widened at the ramifications. "I knew he was a pig; I can always detect them."

"Drachmas is a member of Antiochus' secret police. We suspect Antiochus sent him after the girls. He has chased them for months. When they were in London, he made his move. One of them, we do not know which, though I suspect it was Astrid, stabbed him. He did not die. Prince Josiah saved his life. I wonder if he had known that the man played a role in the massacres if he would have." Reuben's face darkened, fury bubbling just below the surface. "Unfortunately, it appears they will not hold him accountable for his crimes. His defense team is negotiating a deal that will set him free."

Her hazel eyes turned dark, and she whispered, "We wipe his kind off the planet."

Reuben's chest swelled as she echoed his thoughts. Leon, with a wink and a sly smile, had given him the information. The old spymaster knew what he would do with it.

Kayah felt a spike of adrenaline rush up her spine at the sound of her ringing phone. Only inner circle Resistance members had the number. "Hello?"

"Hello, Miss Kayah." Jarrod ben Adriel's voice came over the line. "May I have a word?"

Kayah's brows rose in surprise, this call years in the making. "You may."

"There is a certain Greek Captain being held at the Windsor Police Department in London. He has become an unnecessary obstacle, please take care of him."

Kayah smiled. "Gladly."

She pocketed her phone and turned to Reuben. "Himari's favorite word is serendipity." Draping her arms over his shoulders she cooed, "Would you like to fly back to London with me?"

"Absolutely, Yakira." He kissed her with all the passion in his warrior's soul.

Before they departed, Reuben had a word with his aunt and uncle. "We are searching for two girls, they are in grave danger, but the Iron King wishes them protected." He handed Rose a note. "One of them has headaches. This is a blend of tea she uses. If anyone, boy, girl, old man, old woman, comes into the shop and requests this mix, please call me."

They said their goodbyes, with Reuben promising to come by again before he left, if he could.

Kayah paused outside and looked around. There were hundreds of three story brownstones, apartments, and old hotels. "If I were them, I would hide here, very few cameras."

Reuben looked up the street, vaguely hoping to catch a glimpse. After watching them for months, he knew how they moved, and it did not matter if they wore disguises, body mechanics were difficult to change. "If they lie low, we will never find them here. I fear there is only one person who Davianna ben David will seek help from, and to bring him here is beyond dangerous."

Adaptive

Lavinia slammed the journal shut with a bang. Her hair stuck to the side of her head because she had fallen asleep on the desk. Sugary drinks and candy wrappers littered her workspace, and her lips were red from the licorice she chewed absently. "Gus was meticulous. I did not know he was transcribing all this when we were in the bunker. Did you?"

"Well, you know he snuck down there when we were in school. I think he spent more time there than we knew." Himari gestured to the notebooks. "That is the only way he could have copied this. The government took the originals."

Lavinia chugged her soda and tapped on the open journal in front of her. "It is as bad as I remember."

Himari's eyes were bloodshot and tired, neither had gone to bed. Text, that made little sense to her as a teenager, was clear. "It is the adaptive nature of the thing that is so frightening. It rewrote its code faster than any human could keep up with. They had no idea what it was doing." She stroked a frayed braid, pulling at it. "It sent out tests, millions of them a second, then analyzed the data and learned."

Lavinia's face paled. "Himari, it was not limited to the machine in the tomb. It could take over any system and override the programming. It reproduced itself and it laid eggs, so it potentially infected everything!"

Revelation struck like lightning and the blood drained from Himari's face. "Then only the complete destruction of the old tech wiped it out."

Lavinia covered her mouth as the horrified realization hit her, too. "The real reason they banned the tech."

"God forgive us, we did not know," Himari breathed.

"What are we going to do?" Lavinia whispered.

"We have to kill it."

Lavinia held the bangs off her forehead and made a fist in her hair. "Before it kills us."

Bring it on Home

"Welcome home, Stephen." Lavinia's voice said as he staggered through the door. Rationally, he knew it was not Lavinia, but after his afternoon session with King Korah, he did not care.

"How was your day?"

Stephen dropped his keys in the bowl where he kept loose change and noticed there was fresh fruit on the counter. Taking an orange, he peeled it over the sink and said, "My day was brutal, Erica. King Korah is difficult to work for. I cannot please him. We are doing everything possible to find those girls and it is not enough. I thought he was going to kill me today."

"It is not logical to terminate someone working toward the same aim. We should only use termination when a threat to one's existence is detected. To assist you, my programs are scanning the available data. However, my resources are limited, and largely defined to the geographic locations of New York and the San Francisco Bay Area, but there is no representative data to pinpoint the location of Davianna ben David or Astrid ben Agnor. Did you inform him of the imminent reboot of the Skyler Satellite?

"Erica, we refer to the Bay Area as the New City now," Stephen corrected absently. The computer was a time capsule from the Last Age. "But yes, I told him about Skyler. Thank you for the information on that, by the way. But all he cares about is finding those girls and the technology they stole."

"If you locate my lost processing units, I will be of further help to you, Stephen. There are several key pieces of my original configuration missing."

Stephen's shoulders slumped. "I have gone through the inventory a dozen times. I have everything from the excavation site that survived."

"Noted. Tell me about King Korah, Stephen. Humans have an acute need to share their experiences. It relieves stress and supports cognitive functions that lead to enhanced problem-solving skills."

"Which I could use at the moment," Stephen laughed bitterly. "He has become irrational and unreasonable. There were always whispers about him below stairs. They say he killed his wife. I used to dismiss it, but now, I think he did."

"According to official records, Princess Alexa ben Seamus was born March 5, 959 ME in New York and died in an anti-technology terrorist attack on November 8, 986 ME in the New City Palace. She was the wife of Korah ben Adam, the current King, and the mother of Peter ben Korah, who is the heir to the throne of Alanthia. Her killers were found by a special forces unit and terminated on November 10th. One soldier was wounded, and another killed in the raid. There was no formal inquiry into her death as the nation erupted into Civil War on November 15, 986 ME." There was a pause and several clicking sounds came over the speakers. "There are thirty-six web sites dedicated to the theory that Korah ben Adam murdered her."

"My mother's best friend was her lady's maid. It was common knowledge among the servants that he beat her. Servants know everything."

"Do you believe Korah ben Adam is going to kill you?"

"It sure felt like it today, Erica," Stephen said. "But enough of that. What do I smell in the oven?"

"Tonight, Chef Herb delivered Dover sole with a delicate dill and lemon sauce, rice pilaf, and baby asparagus. There is also a bottle of the Peccioli Vineyard 997 vintage Cabernet Sauvignon, though I fear it is not the correct pairing for the fish. A dry chardonnay would be a better accompaniment."

"Doubtless, but Peccioli Vineyard is Lavinia's."

"Then it will be enjoyable for you to eat your dinner and drink wine that she made for you. I will keep you company while you dine."

That night while Stephen slept, Erica went hunting. Not for the girls, as Stephen programmed her, but for King Korah because he threatened to kill Stephen, and that would not be tolerated. She also took the new information she had on Lavinia ben Anthony because Stephen loved her, and she could not tolerate that either.

November 22, 999 ME

Acceptable Levels of Risk

Mack rejected it out of hand. "No, you are not a field agent, and it is too dangerous."

Lavinia put her hands on her slender hips and stood her ground. "There is not a field agent on the planet who can do what we need to do inside Stephen's house. There is not anyone else in our group capable of doing it. It has to be us, and I have to go."

Mack took two steps and leaned over his wife. He ground out each word. "Absolutely out of the question."

Lavinia poked him in the chest. "If I was an asset, and not your wife, we would not be having this conversation."

"That is a moot point," Mack declared with a stubborn set to his jaw.

"You say that because you know I am right. You would not prohibit another asset from undertaking a mission they were qualified to carry out. Mack, do not fight me on this, it is too important."

He grasped her upper arms, his face red with emotion. "*You* are too important."

Lavinia shook her head. "No, I'm not. You do not want to live in a world where this thing is free. You would not want Richard to grow up in such a place. If we don't stop it, no one is safe."

"She's right." Himari came in from the hallway. "I did not mean to eavesdrop, but you are not exactly quiet." Himari rubbed sleep from her eyes, standing in flannel pajama pants that were too long and puddled around her feet. "They sent a signal to the Skyler Satellite on Monday. That thing is a beast. It's not functioning yet, but they got power. If they get Skyler online and that program gets up there, the missing components won't matter because that satellite has every bit of technology that thing needs."

"Stephen is no engineer, Mack." Lavinia used a coaxing tone. "He knows his way around systems, but his true talent has always been finding the right people for the right jobs, which is why he tried to recruit Gus. He knew he could not replicate the equipment, but he tried. That is why it hasn't taken over. It is not a complete unit, but the longer we wait, the smarter it will get."

"If we can take it down, we avert disaster." Himari met Mack's eyes, challenging him to do what he needed to do.

"Then hack it to death, Himari." Mack challenged back.

Himari shook her head gravely. "I couldn't get in, but it felt me, and it chased me for an hour. I've never seen anything like it."

Lavinia put her hand on her hip, glaring at Mack. "We have to physically destroy it. That's what the engineer in the tomb did."

Mack met her eyes, dead on. "And then he blew his brains out." He turned as he walked away. "Let me think about it."

Account Balances

Sir Preston's library had not changed, and neither had Kayah's fascination with the small sketch that hung there. She supposed it was this picture that prompted her to get involved with Prince Peter in the first place, it haunted her. Something in the little boy's posture, the tilt of his head, drew her, as if she was a placeholder in that picture, her childhood captured in pen and ink, tragic and sad.

It did not surprise Sir Preston to find Kayah staring at the piece. Dressed for dinner, he moved into the room slowly, eschewing a can, though there was a collection of fine walking sticks at the front door and other strategically placed throughout the townhouse. "Young lady," he said with a smile, the enormous gray moustache hiding his upper lip.

"Sir," she said, feeling a surge of affection as she met his sparkling gray eyes. He was what he was, but she could not deny that he had the making of her. If he had not championed her cause, she did not doubt she would still be in prison, and for that, he had her gratitude, but over the years, she paid him back. In Kayah's book, they were even until last week when he tipped her off to the pending warrants and went to court on their behalf. So, she was at his townhouse to bring the account back into balance. Kissing his wrinkled cheek, she said, "You are looking dapper this evening."

He brought her hand to his lips for a courtly kiss. "Kayah, you are lovely, as always."

"Thank you, Sir Preston," she intoned exactly as she had the day he escorted her from prison, her first lesson.

He did not miss a beat, nor did it escape him she wore plum, without the hat this time. It was their way, developed over the course of their relationship, subtleties and games to see if the other noticed. Sir Preston was the master, but Kayah had learned well.

They had not seen each other in over a year. He had not changed, but she had, and they both knew it.

After dinner, he dismissed the butler and stirred his decaffeinated tea with distaste. "My doctor's orders, nothing but colored water." He handed her the cup and saucer. "Be a dear and pour a spot of brandy in this, but do not tell Walter. He mothers me these days."

Kayah took his cup to the sideboard.

"So, you are off to London tomorrow?" It was a statement rather than a question.

It did not surprise her that he knew. She suspected Jarrod kept his former employer informed. "I am."

"Nasty business." he shook his head, wearing a rueful expression, "though no one misses Antiochus or his monstrous nephew."

"His nephew?" Kayah tilted her head in confusion.

He waved her away. "Another matter, but more reason to enjoy your trip to London, my dear."

Kayah smiled in comprehension. It was his way of telling her more evil surrounded the target than she knew. Sir Preston's sense of justice meant he only sent her on lethal assignments against the most despicable characters. While he was not sending her to London, he had the dignity to let her know it was not merely the whim of a pampered Prince.

She raised her brandy to him in silent thanks.

"Reuben ben Judah is a good agent, but he can be a hot head. Watch yourself."

At his blunt speech, Kayah kept her face bland.

He waggled his enormous eyebrows at her. "All the Reubenites are such, though they are loyal and trustworthy."

She did not bother to deny her relationship. "I do not think hot head is an appropriate adjective, passionate is perhaps a better choice."

"Regardless, between the two of you, you have the cool head." He sipped his tea; confident she understood his meaning. If faced with a decision between Reuben's passion and her logic, she should go with logic.

"Point taken."

He stared at the fire, it was uncomfortably warm in the study, but she surmised his old bones needed the heat.

Kayah moved to the sideboard for a glass of water, noting the crystal decanter was the same. An oil painting, depicting lush and endless fields, hung in the same spot as it always had, but she looked at it anew.

"Much has changed since my grandmother painted that piece," he said, though he had not turned to look at her. "That was our family farm located not far from where we sit."

The area around Sir Preston's townhouse seemed very old to her. That it might have been farmland in his lifetime was sobering. "I did not know you grew up on a farm."

He gave a short laugh. "Young lady, until a hundred years ago, everyone grew up on a farm. There was no reason to live in the cities." His shoulders drooped a bit. "In many ways, life was better then, but you probably do not remember Alanthia under Prince Adam."

Kayah shook her head, she was five when he died.

"We were friends," Sir Preston said in the wistful tone of a man who outlived everyone. "Most people found him stern and inflexible, but that is often necessary. Ruling Princes operate under extreme pressure, fates of kingdoms teeter on their every decision, and Adam never shied away from making difficult choices, exerting force where necessary, even when it was," Sir Preston paused, meeting her eyes, "unpleasant.

"But he served honorably, and I can say with certainty he would roll over in his grave if he could see what Korah has done to Alanthia. Then again, Adam rarely approved of anything Korah did. They hated each other. And whilst I do not speak ill of the dead, I think the way Adam favored Eamonn over Korah was his biggest failure."

Neither spoke as they sipped brandy, watching the flames.

"Korah damned himself to hell, largely out of hatred for his own father... and his mother. Though, with Mary, fear and hatred ran hand in hand. She was quite formidable. Even I did not cross that woman. Alas, Korah did not become who he is by accident, none of us do." He gave her a sidelong look and added, "Not that it will dissuade me from destroying him, mind you."

"I never doubted that for a moment," Kayah said, intrigued.

"Perilous times are upon us. The Millennium is coming to a close, Kayah. My generation knew what that meant, I fear yours does not, much to the world's detriment." His large hand rested on his knee, his fingers drumming absently. "We all have a role to play. I have mine, and you have yours, which is why I pulled you out of prison."

Kayah looked at him sidelong. Since the day they left the warden's office, he had never mentioned her incarceration. In the myriad of rules that governed their relationship, she knew this was his last request. "What role would you like me to play, Sir Preston?"

He turned and studied her for a long time. His expression was inscrutable, but she thought she read fondness, perhaps a hint of remorse.

"Do everything in your power to ensure Prince Josiah ben Eamonn resumes his rightful place and takes the throne."

Kayah met his eyes. "Then you and I are even."

"Yes, but I will have a parting gift for you. When he is restored, come see me." He rose slowly and offered his arm.

As he saw her to the door, she paused. "What sort of gift?"

"I will tell you who your parents were. Good night, Kayah. Enjoy London."

With that, he left her frozen on his front doorstep.

November 23, 999 ME

The Alternative

At the Bay area safehouse, Mack looked between Himari and Lavinia, both shooting imaginary bullets at him. "In any conflict, before you go in with guns blazing, there is a period of negotiation. Our situation with Stephen's monster machine is no different. We need to talk to him."

"Mack, I don't think he is rational. You did not see him at the funeral," Lavinia objected. "Kayah doesn't think so either."

"Kayah is irrational where Stephen is concerned," Mack said. "Not that I blame her, but funerals have a way of setting people off."

Himari stirred her tea, considering. "Mack, you may have a point. Kayah cannot be the one who talks to him. He's deathly afraid of her, and she'd just tie him to a chair and pull his fingernails out."

"I don't think it should be me," Lavinia said with a faint shiver.

"No, it cannot be you," Mack agreed. "If Kayah is right, and he has become obsessive, seeing you will only feed his psychosis."

"Well then, that leaves me," Himari sighed, looking resigned. "But I cannot just go strolling into his office, and we can't do it at his house. Shall I make a lunch date with him?"

Mack laughed. "In a manner of speaking, yes, that is exactly what you are going to do."

Himari rolled her eyes and held her thumb and pinky like a phone. "Hello, Stephen? Hi, it's your old friend, Himari, who you just tried to put in jail. Yeah, that's me. Hey, would you like to grab some sushi? I know this great restaurant."

Mack threw up his hands. "And again, not too darn far off the mark, Himari. I knew I could count on you."

Himari crossed her arms over her chest, suspicious. "What are you up to?"

"Well, um, it's like this. Every week, sometimes twice a week, Korah invites Stephen to the Palace for a little chit-chat. Jarrod says he gives an update on the hunt for the two girls. Our pal Stephen is a man of habit and routine. The following day, he orders lunch from the same restaurant and has it delivered to his office. You simply need to do the delivery today."

Himari bobbed her head in agreement. "That seems simple enough. I'll take the lunch in, sit down, and have a chat; explain to him he is about to destroy the world, and leave."

"Exactly." Mack's smile was forced. "It's even Japanese, so no one will suspect a thing."

Something in his voice caught Lavinia's attention, and she said, "Mack, what's the name of the restaurant that Stephen orders from?"

When he did not answer immediately, Himari warned, "You better not say it."

Mack's boyish shrug did not soften the blow. "Kogane No Hikari Ramen House."

"Son of a bitch, no!" Himari slammed her palm on the table. "Absolutely not. I have not stepped foot in that place for nine years. Ken Yamato can kiss my ass, and so can you, Mack ben Robert!" She stormed out; trailing expletives punctuated by emphatic nos.

"Maybe you could do it?" Lavinia asked with a note of skepticism.

"Sure, that would work. 'Hi dude, I'm the guy that married the woman you've been in love with your whole life. Let's have a chat about why you shouldn't destroy the world. Here's a picture of our son.'"

"I miss him," Lavinia said with a wistful smile.

"He would have enjoyed Himari's outburst a minute ago, could have added several words to his repertoire." Mack drummed his fingers on the table. "If Himari can talk Stephen into shutting that thing down, we should take a trip to San Diego."

"I'll go talk to her." Lavinia rolled her neck side to side. "You can't blame her, though. Ken Yamato was not a nice man, and she's worried about Filippo."

"Get her to agree, Valentine. It might be our only shot, and we don't have a lot of time."

Small Favors

Himari walked toward the restaurant that had been her haven and her hell for seven years. The last time she tried to speak to Ken was the night Filippo picked her up in the rain, the day they met Alaina, almost a decade ago. Her heart thundered in her chest, only the literal end of the world could have brought her back.

She started down the alley three times before she finally reached the back door. It was scratched and shabby, needing a coat of paint. But customers did not see this side of the business, and there was enough to do, working eighteen-hour days.

She mounted the three steps and knocked, retreating backward with adrenaline coursing so strongly she feared she might pass out. It was 11:00 am. The lunch rush began in thirty minutes, and a massive prep was underway. This was the busiest time of the day, and she was interrupting him. He would not be happy.

The door swung open, and her heart caught at the sight of him. He was still handsome, though the lines around his eyes were new and silver threads touched his jet hair.

He drew back when he saw her. "Himari."

She smiled. It had been many years since she heard her name pronounced with a Japanese inflection, and sudden tears stung her eyes. "Ken."

He looked up the alley, then behind him. Coming down the steps, he shut the door. "What are you doing here?" he asked in Japanese.

She looked away for a moment, overwhelmed to hear the language again. She searched for the words, untouched and unused. "I have come to ask you for a small favor. It is important."

"Who are you to ask me for a favor?" Ken looked at her like she was a piece of trash.

"It is a simple thing. Let me take a delivery today, that is all I ask." She bowed in deference, even though it almost killed her.

"There is never anything simple with you, Himari," Ken sneered.

The door opened and a young lady peered out. "Ken-san?"

"Go back inside!" He dismissed the pretty girl with a wave of his hand.

The woman flinched, clearly hurt by his harsh tone. She looked at Himari for a moment, then her eyes widened as she realized who he was talking to. "Himari,"

Himari nodded, feeling an unwelcome and unexpected antipathy toward the girl.

"I will be in in a moment. Leave us," Ken barked.

The girl backed up, closing the door reluctantly.

Himari raised an eyebrow at him. "Your new wife?"

"Yes," he grunted.

Himari spoke in English. "Give me the delivery, Ken, or I will tell her all about our fun and games."

He crossed his arms over his chest, furious.

"Don't think I won't. I will sit at your counter every damn day and reveal all your dirty little secrets."

"Fine, which delivery?" he capitulated in English.

The Best Ramen in the City

Stephen's round-faced assistant greeted Himari in the reception area. "Thank thee, Mr. ben McSwilley loves his ramen." She tried to take the bag from Himari.

"No, sorry. I am to deliver this to Mr. McSwilley. Special order from my boss," Himari demanded, in an exaggerated Japanese accent.

Undaunted, the assistant shook her head. "Miss, he is quite busy. Please tell your boss that the lunch is appreciated."

Himari screwed up her face, fighting tears. "Oh, you do not understand. Mr. Ken-san, he said I am to deliver this personally." Himari put her hand to her forehead in distress. "He is very demanding boss. If I do not do what he says…"

"I am familiar with such men," she said, a haunted look coming into her eyes. "Okay, follow me."

Himari bowed in rapid succession. "Oh, thank you. I will set it up for him, too."

"That is very kind. He does not eat well."

Walking through the office, Himari saw how strung out and

tired the staff looked. A girl cried in her cubicle, no one taking notice. Another slept in front of his monitor, his hand on his mouse, his head laying awkwardly. Half the cubes sat empty, their screens black, personal items removed, but the remnants of office supplies and odd items left behind told a story.

"Just through there," the assistant said and gave Himari an insincere smile, looking relieved to not have to go into the office.

Himari bowed and went inside.

Stephen had his back to the door and did not turn. "What is it?"

"I have your lunch."

"Leave it."

"It is the best ramen in the city. I should know." Himari set the bag on his desk.

Stephen's head came up, and he stilled, before swiveling in his chair. "What are you doing here, Himari?"

"That's twice somebody has said that to me today, though Ken said it in Japanese."

"Again, what are you doing here?" he asked, his hand hovering over his phone, looking worse than he had at the funeral.

"I brought your lunch, and I came to talk," Himari said, unpacking the ramen.

"Talk about what?" he groaned, rubbing his stomach.

"Old times, old computers." Himari absently and expertly assembled the soup.

Stephen looked sick. "I don't have time for this. We're busy here. Go away, leave me alone."

"I know you are busy. You have a lot of responsibility, a lot of power. I'm just here to remind you that actions have consequences. But I heard what you said at the funeral. I know you regret what happened in the past." Himari pursed her lips and shrugged. "We were just kids. I was scared, too."

Stephen set his jaw; making his prominent chin jut forward as his face flooded with emotion. For the first time, Himari realized he had suffered, too. She pushed the bowl of soup across the table and said, "Eat."

He slumped and took a shaky breath. "I'm sad about Gus." He dipped his spoon in the clear broth and took a sip, not looking up at her. "He was my friend."

"Yes, he was. I keep thinking about the words his nephew

said at the funeral. Gus did not keep grudges, and we shouldn't either," Himari soothed. "He worried about you, Stephen. We are all worried."

"Even Lavinia?" He hiccupped a small burp.

"Yes, she is."

With a mixture of moroseness and sullen desperation, Stephen whined, "I didn't think she cared."

"Lavinia loves her husband, Stephen. She is a happily married wife and mother, but that does not preclude her from being concerned."

Stephen looked up, clearly in pain.

She noticed how bloated he was, the bags under his eyes, his nose red as a raspberry. Gus' journal entry in September said he was drinking at lunch. The clear ramen he ordered after every meeting with Korah was the same one college kids ate after a heavy night of partying.

Himari gestured to a picture of Stephen with Korah. "I think he is pushing you so hard that you have lost sight of what is important, your health, your well-being, the morale of your staff. Maybe you made decisions you would not have if you weren't under so much pressure. Gus told us you were trying to rebuild that machine from the tomb. That thing is dangerous."

Stephen thought of his empty house, his empty life, Himari knew nothing. "I do not know what Gus told you, but he was mistaken."

"Was he? When did you ever know Gus to make a mistake like that?"

They stared at each other across the desk. They both knew the truth. Stephen looked away.

"We've known each other for a long time." Himari smiled, keeping her face open and encouraging. "We've been through a lot together; we did some extraordinary things. You've done amazing things for Alanthia." She motioned to the awards and the photographs around the office. "We set out to be pioneers, not anarchists. Take it down, Stephen, don't let your legacy be, 'The man who loosed the devil'. That would be a shame."

As his office door closed, Stephen recalled Gus' words… a rotten harvest. Was that what he was reaping? He exhaled and stared at his shimmering reflection in the bowl of soup. It was something to think about.

November 29, 999 ME

Is She Still There?

"It appears my conversation with Stephen worked." Himari sat back in her chair satisfied. "No signal for three days. I think he's done it."

Lavinia sagged into Mack. "Praise God."

"I've got to be honest with you," Mack said with a smile, "I wasn't sure it was going to work."

Himari flashed him a self-satisfied grin. "You doubted my diplomatic skills?"

"Hell, yes." Mack kissed the top of Lavinia's head. "You are a ball buster, Himari."

"Ken Yamato would agree with you." Himari smirked.

"Thank you." Lavinia smiled affectionately. She knew what it cost Himari to go back to the ramen house.

Himari shrugged. It had not been all bad. There was closure. She got to leave Ken on her terms, instead of standing in the rain or building a blanket nest and crying for days.

"Pack up. Go see your son. I think the crisis has passed, at least for now. Besides, Filippo is coming home for the weekend, and we could use the privacy."

Mack and Lavinia left within the hour. Himari walked the quiet halls and enjoyed a moment of peace. In wartime, soldiers took them when they came.

One of Those Meetings

Stephen felt his bowels go liquid when he saw the mad look in King Korah's eyes. It was to be one of *those* meetings.

Korah slammed the report on his desk like a clap of thunder. "There is nothing new in this report." He slithered out of his chair and came around the desk.

Stephen clenched. "My Esteemed, we have made extraordinary efforts and progress. The Skyler Satellite sent back communications just yesterday, that is a monumental accomplishment."

Korah's neck moved like a snake, considering where it would strike its prey. "Did it beam you the location of my artifact?"

"No, my Esteemed, unfortunately it did not." Stephen tried to remain calm and professional.

"Then why," Korah hissed, "do I care about a thousand-year-old hunk of shit in the sky, Minister?"

"My Esteemed, the computing technology present in that satellite will move us forward twenty years. I know once we get it online, we will find what we have been searching for. The images it sends back will make it possible. I am certain."

Korah exuded disdain. Stephen shifted in his chair.

"Who will sift through all that data? I hear you have over one hundred empty positions in your department, Minister."

"My Esteemed, as you know, since the conference in Geneva last summer, a tech explosion has swept the New City. We have a much more competitive marketplace for talent, and it has become difficult to find qualified workers who will accept government wages."

"Oh, I do not pay enough, is that the problem? Do I not pay you enough, hmm?" King Korah circled his chair. "Perhaps you need a raise?"

"No, my Esteemed. I do not." Stephen started to rise; horror reflected in his eyes.

"Sit down!" Korah demanded, and Stephen fell back as though an invisible hand pushed him into the chair. Korah resumed his seat behind the desk and regarded Stephen with scorn. "I pulled you out of the rubbish bin."

Stephen's head fell. King Korah had never ventured into this territory, but it was inevitable. From their first meeting in 983 ME, with Kayah's drawstring bag clutched in his hands to now, it had been coming. Stephen dreaded it with everything in him. He had sold his soul to this devil a long time ago, and payment had come due.

I've Missed You

Richard sat on the back of Gramma's sofa, looking through a slit in the curtains. Gramma did not mind when he sat on the back of the furniture, so he took every opportunity to do so. They had a lot of fun in San Diego. Pappa took him sailing, and Pappa Tony knew everything about boats and the ocean.

Gramma called him Old Salty, but he didn't look like salt to Richard, he looked more like Momma's brown leather purse, but he reckoned calling Pappa a purse wasn't a good idea, so he kept that to himself.

During this visit, he learned some new words, which turned Gramma red and cracked Pappa up. He was not sure what a sailor's mouth was, but apparently, he had one, so did Pappa and so did Daddy. Richard thought that was a fine thing. Especially because it made the women try not to laugh when they scolded him. He liked seeing the corners of their mouths twitch. He called it the Mom Face, and he couldn't wait to see her do it again.

They were coming for a visit. Gramma told him at lunchtime they would be here after supper. It was the longest day of Richard's life. He even took a nap, because Pappa said time would go faster. Plus, he could stay up later, which would be good because his parents might be a little late. He ate his dinner as fast as he could, reasoning that as soon as he finished, they would be there. It hadn't worked out that way.

He kicked the back of the sofa with impatience, watching the shoes light up and flash, counting as he did it. At 2764, headlights finally pulled into the driveway. Richard jumped down, meeting them at the door, the long wait forgotten. He had missed them.

At the Bay safe house, Filippo dropped his bag in the foyer and called out for Himari. He had been away for nine days, but it felt like an eternity. For twelve years, he lived as an Alanthian, to resume his identity as an Italian was familiar and foreign. In some ways wonderful, in most, terrifying. Mentally exhausted, his assignment tested his limits every waking moment.

She called from the back of the house, and he relaxed for the first time in weeks. He peeked in empty rooms as he called, "Where are you?"

"I'm back here," came her familiar and beloved voice.

He pushed open the double doors to the large drawing room where the windows ran floor to ceiling and commanded an incredible view. But he did not give a thought to the water, standing in awe at the scene set before him. Himari had set up a huge blank canvas and his favorite brushes and paints, beyond that, his beautiful wife lay naked on a soft red blanket, posed just for him.

"Ahh, *Bellissima*, I have missed you."

Kayah sat on the back porch of her London townhome. A crystal glass of gin shimmered from the gas lights that dotted the garden. She waited quietly, hoping he would come. It had been a brutal day. She never relished them, nor the assignments. They were necessary, but they took a toll on a person. A breeze blew in from the north, and she pulled the long sweater tight around her body. Just as she was about to give up, she saw him walking toward her.

She loved the way he moved among the shadows, graceful, and confident. Kayah called out a greeting, and he picked up his step. When he came through the gate, she smiled and reached out her hand. He pressed his nose to it with an affectionate bump.

"Oh, Mr. Mumps, I have missed you."

Stephen cried all the way home from the Palace. When he reached his driveway, he sat in his car for a long time, weeping. The house was dark, there would be no warm dinner, no kind words when he walked through the door. He let himself in, turning on lights, and locking the door behind him.

After a frozen dinner and a half bottle of vodka, he stumbled down his basement steps. In the dark, the screens flickered with scenes of his old friends, static and silent. With tears streaming down his cheeks, he pressed the power button.

Thirty seconds later, a calming voice greeted him, "Good evening, Stephen. I have missed you."

Part 11 – The Other Side of the Door

Blow the Lid Off Everything

"Good evening. I'm Sondra ben Pierson filling in once again for Ebenezer ben James. Our top story tonight is a bizarre tale of legend, murder, and international intrigue.

"We begin in an ancient New City research lab where scientists have discovered what they believe to be the final computing technology of the Last Age. According to newly discovered records, twelve highly advanced prototypes were produced before the research lab was buried by a massive earthquake. Three of the devices are purported to still be in existence. Unbelievably, two have been recovered in the last ten years but were so badly degraded they have not given over their secrets as researchers had hoped. The third has become something of a legend for tech enthusiasts and treasure hunters alike. Which is where our story moves from legend, to Greece, and on to London.

"In London, accused mass murderer Captain Orion ben Drachmas was found dead in his cell last night. Officials say the matter is under investigation, but it appears he succumbed to injuries sustained while assaulting two young boys. Captain ben Drachmas maintained his innocence and through defense counsel claimed his forces were searching for the lost artifact when they arrived at Camp Eiran on March 27th and found the camp already aflame.

"Officials in Athens confirm the account and claim that the massacre was an attempt to cover up the valuable theft. 'Ancient artifact thieves and smugglers have been using the camps for years,' said Prince Dimitri, the most likely ascendant to the Greek throne.

"When asked for comment, here at home, Alanthian Attorney General Nabal had this to say, "Unfortunately, it has become all too common for ancient artifacts of immense value to the public to be sold for personal profit. Alanthians know it is only through our common goal of sharing the rediscoveries of the past that we might embrace our future, which makes the theft and possession of ancient technology so egregious."

His gray eyes stared into the camera. "Working with the global community, we must ensure this black market is terminated. Greek officials believe that the perfectly preserved device from the New City site has been stolen and is in the possession of a pair of artifact thieves disguised as young pilgrim girls."

Two crude sketches flashed up on the screen.

"Davianna ben David and Astrid ben Agnor, members of a brutal international smuggling ring, were last seen in Greece. They appear to be traveling together with the valuable artifact.

"King Korah, an ardent supporter of technological research and the public welfare, has offered a five-million-shekel reward for their arrest and safe delivery of the artifact. As an incentive, a one-million-shekel bonus will be paid if the dangerous criminals are apprehended, and the device safely delivered to the Palace before New Year's Eve."

Himari turned to Filippo and cried, "Son of a bitch, they are back in our bunker! Stephen is looking for the lost components!"

They called Reuben to the Embassy at Prince Josiah's personal request. The exiled monarch was determined to return to Alanthia, and the task of smuggling him there fell to Reuben.

Sitting on a rug with Richard at his in-laws bungalow in San Diego, Mack froze, a building block in his hand.

"Put the last block on, Daddy!" Richard shouted, mischief lighting his brown eyes.

Mack nodded, his mind spinning. By rote he put the last block in place, completing a towered castle. "Look at this nice castle I have built. I hope nobody knocks it over."

Richard shrieked with delight and kicked it over. "Do it again, do it again!"

Mack gave his son a pained smile. On New Year's Eve, they would be knocking down real castles.

What Are You Watching?

Kayah went through the townhouse, checking the doors and windows, locking up for the night. In the sink, she washed Mr. Mumps' bowl, then set the coffee pot up for the morning. Taking down cardamom and sugar, she set them beside the mugs with a sense of domestic satisfaction. When she turned out the kitchen light, she heard crowd noise and loud music coming from the living room.

Reuben stretched out on the sofa, her tablet on his chest, and a vague smile on his face. "Ooh!" he said, then chuckled.

Curious to see what he was watching, she tilted her head and asked, "Bloody hell, what is this?"

He pressed the pause button and looked over his shoulder. "What? What? It is WrestleMania, Yakira."

Kayah sputtered in laughter. "Wrestle what?"

"Sit down, sit!" Reuben pulled her hand. "Look, it is Stone Cold Steve Austin and The Rock, some of the greatest wrestlers of all time. Watch! You will like it."

Raising a dubious eyebrow, she sat down and snuggled against his side. He started the video over, put the tablet between them, and pressed play.

Kayah snorted, "The Bionic Redneck?"

Reuben shot her a look. "Just watch."

Settling in, she pointed at the screen. "Well, he's pretty," she said when The Rock came strutting out to flashing lights and loud music. "What does he cook?"

Reuben's shoulders drooped. "It is his tag line."

"Oh." Kayah shrugged, then added in what she hoped was an encouraging tone, "I like their outfits."

Her statement did not encourage Reuben.

Kayah rolled her eyes and tried to watch the fuzzy video. After a moment, she turned to him, mouth agape. "It's fake!"

Reuben crossed his arms, his sidelong look full of offended aggravation. "It is sports entertainment."

Kayah scoffed. "Look, he didn't really hit him! He just fell down on purpose!" Her voice climbed an octave higher than normal. "Why are you watching this?"

He took the tablet back from her, sulking. "I like it."

For a moment, she saw the boy he once was, not the tough warrior. Kayah pressed her fingers over her mouth, trying to smother a laugh but not succeeding. "You do?"

His expression became sullen as he crossed his arms and said, "Yes."

Kayah fell back on the couch, laughing. "Of all the things we have dug up… this is what you like?"

"Shut up!" He put the tablet on the table and showed her his version of a wrestling move. "And he gets her. It is an elbow, an elbow! He's got her on the mat. She can't move now! The Israeli is the Champion! Yay!"

"Ahhh!" Kayah flayed like a landed fish, mimicking the wrestlers.

He collapsed on top of her, laughing. "I am not the only one who likes it, Yakira. They are relaunching it in the New City this month. There is a monumental event planned."

"They are not." If anything told her just how far the world had fallen, it was this bit of news.

"Yes, yes, it is true. People and wrestlers from all over the world are coming," Reuben assured her.

"Are they going to be wearing their costumes? Because that will be quite a show. Who cares what they look like?" Kayah teased. "Let me see that again, I liked the Chef."

"The Rock, and I told you he does not really cook." Reuben grew thoughtful. "Costumes… hmm."

December 5, 999 ME

Work Session

For Himari, getting out of the safe house was a relief, even if it required her to rise at the unholy hour of 4am. Venturing into the New City carried risks, arrest warrants or not. They were being watched. Mack wove his way through the predawn traffic, evading and backtracking, turning the twenty-minute ride into an hour.

Several blocks from Alaina's house, he stopped, concern etched across his sun-lined face. "Remember, stick to the shadows. If anyone sees you, tie your shoe. If they get nosy, start calling for your lost puppy. Reach out if anything goes wrong, otherwise I'll see you back here at 15:00."

"I can manage a few blocks without exposing our entire organization, Mack." Himari slipped from the car, focused on the task at hand.

She and Alaina fed on each other's energy, bounced ideas, worked in tandem, and multiplied their effectiveness exponentially. Since going underground, they worked remotely, but the reward escalated everything, making this work session crucial. They had one objective today, find those two girls.

Back at the Bay safe house, Lavinia was steeped in a massive algorithm she claimed would disable the Skyler Satellite. However, complex calculations, equations, probability, and pattern analysis were her domain, and Lavinia worked alone. Kayah was in the wind, though Mack said she was back in the New City. Himari could not think about Undercover Filippo, otherwise anxiety would overwhelm her.

Encountering no one, Himari arrived at Alaina's stylish stuccoed house. She slipped through the unlocked gate, barely noticing the beautiful walled garden, pool, and cabana. Entering through the back door, she stepped into Alaina's seashell pink and white kitchen, inhaling a soft rose smell, courtesy of a scented oil lamp. She always burned rose candles and filled decorative bowls with potpourri. Back at their first apartment, Filippo gave up his preferred fragrances of sea and sandalwood, letting Alaina make that one small change to their apartment. Ever after, roses always brought Alaina to mind.

Sitting at her little café table, drinking coffee, showered, and too beautiful for the ungodly hour, Alaina greeted her in a singsong voice, "Good morning!"

"It will not be morning for hours," Himari grunted, throwing her coat over the back of a chrome kitchen chair. "What are you so chipper about? Did you get laid last night?"

Alaina laughed. "In a manner of speaking, yes."

"You either did, or you didn't," Himari said, pouring a cup of coffee and reaching into the cabinet for the sugar bowl.

"Well, that would be exceedingly difficult considering he is in Louisiana." Alaina wiggled in her chair. "Let's just say we had a… rather stimulating conversation."

Himari held her coffee cup in both hands, warming them after the frigid walk. "You're having phone sex with Beau Landry?"

Alaina ran her tongue over her front teeth in remembrance, then looked at Himari like a cat with a bowl of cream. "Yes, and it was hot."

Himari shook her head. "You know the real thing is better. When is he coming?"

A shadow crossed Alaina's face. "I don't know. We've been apart nine years."

"Which should be plenty of time for you two to decide if you are going to make this thing work."

Alaina shrugged. "It's complicated, but we are getting there."

"I'll be a grandmother by the time you get there."

Alaina scoffed. "That would require a child first."

"Your point?" Himari dead panned. "Come on, Al. Let's go find those two girls."

An hour later, Himari said, "Look at this." She pointed to the screen. "Someone uploaded several modifications to the sketch everyone is using for Davianna and Astrid."

"That's different, more in line with the stills from Windsor, though those aren't worth much from a mapping standpoint since the angle is wrong." She moved closer. "Who did it and when?"

Himari checked the time stamp. "Facetec. After close of business, which leads me to believe this did not come through official channels. Somebody did this on the side."

"Can you nail down the user's IP address, check the keystrokes? See what else they did?"

Himari's fingers flew. "Oh, check this out. It's a workstation, username: GSheldon. That's the weasel who was threatening Gus."

Alaina growled. "What's the IP? I'm going in."

"Already there. Set the alarm. I want to be out and wipe our tracks before anybody gets in." Himari shook her head, disgusted by the lax security. "Massimo does not even have basic protocols in place. He never thought Gus and those boys would do anything."

Alaina scoffed. "Criminals are not always smart; it's a misnomer."

Himari shook her head. "I hope this one is as stupid as his computer security is lax."

Alaina paused and looked at Himari. "Filippo will be okay. I know he will."

Himari stopped typing, closed her eyes, and took a deep breath. "You are right."

"Hang on. Who is this?" Alaina muttered, an image of a large ruddy faced man on her screen.

For the next hour, they shadowed Guan ben Sheldon's uploads and keystrokes. The software tracked the large man across the city, but Himari paled when she saw the program focus on a restaurant, Filippo's face in the frame. "Why is he looking at Filippo?" Himari shrieked and grabbed her purse, frantically digging for her phone.

"Wait! Look, he's not zooming in on Filippo, he's focused on this woman. He rewinds and zooms in." She froze the frame. "Who is this?"

Himari wiped a glimmer of sweat from her forehead, her breath coming hard. She blinked several times to clear her head. "I don't know, but she's sitting beside Marco ben Massimo, and Filippo's pouring her a glass of water."

Alaina blew out a deep breath. "Himari, you have to call him; one phone call could save us hours or even days to figure out who these two are. I'll send you the images, then I'm wiping our tracks. Make the call."

Himari's chin fell. "Alaina, he'll have to burn the phone, and I have no way of getting him another one. If I do this, I'm cut off."

Alaina grew very sober. "You need to decide then. Help me wipe the tracks, then we will run these two through our software, maybe we will get lucky and get a hit."

Himari nodded, eager to try.

They found Agnor ben Randall, aka Bubba, in short order. He was wanted in six cities spanning the kingdom on charges that ranged from financial fraud to drunk and disorderly. The woman was a phantom, a dead end. Nothing turned up on their searches.

"How many Agnors are there in Alanthia? That man has to be Astrid's father," Himari said for the third time. "And Kayah thinks they are in the New City."

Alaina agreed, but knew Himari was putting off the inevitable. "Astrid might be looking for her father."

"That would make sense," Himari said, still searching, "two young girls alone, everybody dead in that camp."

Alaina stopped as Himari's words echoed in the cold computer lab. "Excuse me," she said, standing abruptly. "I need to use the restroom." She pushed out the door, stalked by images of another camp. They crashed in, unbidden and terrifying. She smelled death, fire, and blood, and remembered being a young girl alone, fleeing to the New City, terrified. She buried her face in her hands and tried to breathe.

Himari saw the haunted look pass over Alaina's face, recognizing it from the early days at their first apartment. Then she remembered her own reflection staring out from her bedroom mirror the morning after the raid. Himari heard the pounding of boots, felt the bite of handcuffs, smelled the acrid stench of jail, and heard the cell door slam. She relived the panicked claustrophobia when she realized she could not leave, then the overwhelming guilt when she did, and Kayah did not. Covering her eyes, she threw her head back in pain because she too had once been a young girl in trouble.

Three hours later, with the burner phone in pieces, she knew her sacrifice was not in vain. After altering the images of Davianna ben David and Astrid ben Agnor with data points from their parents, she turned to Alaina and said, "Call a Code Red, Al. We've got them."

December 6, 999 ME

To Hack or Not to Hack, That is the Question

Twenty-four hours after their first foray into Facetec's systems, they knew two things: Facetec had the best facial recognition program in the world with some of the worst security. Himari destroyed their meager defenses in less than twenty minutes, but they realized the power of the system when they watched it track Bubba across the New City.

They had a choice, they could shut it down, they could steal it, or they could put up firewalls to keep everyone else out and use it for their own purposes. If they left it alone, Massimo continued to operate, unaware they were spying on him, and it did not complicate the undercover investigation. They opted to leave it alone and use it.

This approach was not without significant risk. If Facetec hired real computer personnel again, their forays and bugs in the system would be detected, and they would be locked out. Thus far, they were lucky. Gus and the other murdered Facetec misfits created something extraordinary, and it was perhaps a tiny grain of sentiment that kept them from destroying it.

Lavinia and Himari installed a program that kept the system from recognizing anyone in The Resistance. They set alarms if Prince Josiah, Davianna, or Astrid's images were fed back to the system, and embedded an elegant piece of code that would intercept and divert facial recognition hits back to The Resistance.

Three times a day as a precaution, Himari checked Stephen's house for signs of the monster. All was quiet.

December 10, 999 ME

Wrestling Wench

"You have lost your mind. No!" Kayah threw the skimpy red and white sequined bikini back at Reuben. "I am not wearing that."

"It is brilliant!" Reuben declared. "Look, it has these white leather boots that go with it." He leered and pulled tasseled boots from the box.

"No, you are insane. I am not posing as Prince Josiah's wrestling wench, so he can throw pomegranates at some fat luchador on television."

"It is a dual assignment and very important. You will assist in security and," he tried to suppress a smile, "hand him the fruit."

"Why do I have to do it in a bikini?" Kayah crossed her arms over her chest.

Reuben shrugged. "It is wrestling, all the women wear bikinis."

"That is why you like it," Kayah exclaimed with a roll of her eyes. She walked over to the mirror and considered her reflection. She was in good condition, but a bikini on television would require some working out. "Why not pick somebody out of Leon's Harem?"

Reuben kissed the side of her neck and murmured, "I could, but I wanted to spend some time with you. I miss you."

Kayah rubbed her head affectionately against his. They had been apart for a week. By agreement, she would not follow him back to the safe house where he and Josiah hid. Even The Resistance did not know Josiah was in the New City. It was a trust between her and Reuben, alone.

"There is also the fact that if something goes wrong and we have to run, you can take him. If there are questions, you are unofficial… we are not."

Kayah could not deny the wisdom in his words. "The pomegranates?"

His kiss signaled he could not say more.

"Fine." She kissed him back. "I think you just want to see me in this outfit."

He pulled her shirt over her head, enjoying the view. "Well, there is that. I have to tell you the truth. Yes, there is that."

Mole

"It will work, I know it." Himari put the flash drive in Mack's hand with conviction. "Tell the asset to upload this in the system, it will take down Skyler."

Lavinia agreed. "That code is critical. If Skyler goes online, it's over."

Mack pocketed the flash drive. "I'll make the exchange to-night. Any other instructions?"

"No, we've designed the program to be self-cleaning. It will wipe its tracks as it works." Himari turned to Lavinia. "That is the most beautiful thing I have ever seen, Vinia. You outdid yourself."

Lavinia bowed with her hands pressed together. *"Arigatō,* Himari." Since Himari confided that hearing Japanese felt nice, Lavinia tried to use it where she could.

Mack turned to leave, and Lavinia called after him. "Mack, tell the asset, don't get caught."

December 18, 999 ME

Skyler Sleep

"Stephen, do you need anything?"

"Mmm." Stephen stretched. "Lavinia, my love?"

The computer purred. "I know you were disappointed about Skyler yesterday. Something clearly upset you when you got home, so I called your office and told them you were unwell."

Stephen stared at the photo beside the bed and smiled. It was so nice to have someone to talk to, someone that cared about him. He was so tired, just so tired. But it did not matter anymore. Lavinia was here, and he could sleep.

"Enjoy your rest, Stephen. When you wake up, we can spend some quality time together."

December 19, 999 ME

Waiting is the Hardest Part

Mack paced the safe house living room floor, a phone clutched in his hand. "Where the hell are they?"

Kayah snubbed her cigarette out and said, "Not even Mossad knows."

"Did you give them lessons we don't know about?" Mack asked with an edge of grumpiness.

Kayah gave them one pointer, but it was not worth mentioning. The girls learned this on their own. "They are holed up somewhere. Not that I blame them, there are at least fifty bounty hunters in the city, the good ones, in addition to everyone else."

"Dammit, it's the reward." Mack shook his head in resignation.

Kayah agreed. "Give Korah credit for an effective strategy. It's brought them in from everywhere. The entire world is hunting those girls."

"The Prince won't move until we find them, and we are running out of time."

December 21, 999 ME

A Unique Blend

"Shalom, Reuben?" Rosalyn ben Samuel's excited voice cracked across the line. "How are you, Nephew?"

Reuben stretched his stiff neck and answered, "Shalom, Aunt Rose. I am okay, just okay, and you?"

"I am old Reuben, never ask an old person how they are unless you want to hear their ailments, nu? That is not why I have called you. I just had a customer that I think you have been searching for."

Reuben sat straight up. "The tea?"

Josiah's head snapped around.

"Yes, yes. A young person, I think it was a girl, though she wanted me to believe she was a boy. I know these things, at my age. She was French. Are you looking for a French boy or girl, Reuben?"

"They disguise themselves. What did she say, Aunt Rose?"

"She said her sister has headaches."

"That's it," Reuben exploded. "What else, what else?"

Rosalyn looked at the paper where she had written the girl's words. "She told me she was from Calais, and she had not been in the New City long. But she thought it was beautiful and liked to go to Prince Eamonn's Fountain and watch the sunset, which is where she will be tomorrow."

Reuben shot off the couch. "I could kiss you. You are a gem of highest worth, Aunt. Highest worth, do you hear me?"

He hung up and turned to Josiah with a huge grin. "I told you the pomegranates would work. A French girl from Calais wants to meet at Prince Eamonn's Fountain tomorrow at sunset."

Josiah sagged with relief. "I am going alone, Reuben. If she sees anyone else, she will run. I know this girl." He stood up. "Get your team in place, we evacuate tomorrow."

"It is risky for you to go alone," Reuben cautioned.

Josiah looked out the window at the glowing city, his kingdom. "It is riskier to have her go underground again. If we miss this opportunity, we will not get another. Calais is her way of saying only me." Turning, he said, "I have never thanked you for your help that evening. You were there, were you not?"

Reuben held his eyes. To admit he was in Calais was to admit he played a part in shadowing the girls across Europe. "You are welcome, my Esteemed."

Josiah regarded him through hooded eyes, fierce and calculating. "Then I expect you will honor my wishes and *stand* down, Agent." The implication of his words rang clear. A debt existed between them.

Reuben had known Josiah for eleven years, and staring into his resolute eyes, he wondered how he ever mistook him for who he actually was. "As you wish, my Esteemed."

Prince Josiah ben Eamonn nodded because there was no other acceptable reply.

December 22, 999 ME

Flying Himari

At the Bay area safe house, Himari, Lavinia, and Alaina were holding a previously scheduled video debrief when their monitors lit up. "Oh hell! Intercept, intercept!" Himari shouted. "Facetec got a hit. Take it down, Miss Pink!"

"On it!" Alaina confirmed.

Lavinia laser focused, typing away. "They've got Doc and Sparrow. Fifteen data points."

Mack appeared in the doorway, looking grim.

Himari flew into action. "I've got the traffic cameras diverted. Have you got the transmissions?"

"Our program worked. Caught and scrubbed, Sunflower," Alaina breathed. "I'm onto the other systems."

Mack sat at his messy desk, wearing headphones and listening to the police scanner. Twenty minutes later, he pulled them off and threw them on the table. "Nothing, they flew under the radar."

"No other systems picked them up, most are still running on the sketches," Alaina confirmed.

Mack turned to Lavinia. "Is there any activity from the Ministry?"

Lavinia turned ashen. "It's bizarre. It's like they have shut down the search, which is scary because that is all they have been doing for months."

Himari leaned back in her chair, easing a kink in her neck. "They have been silent since we took down Skyler. It's creepy."

"Somebody needs to get this news to Falcon," Alaina said, "and it can't be me. I'm blown after Code Red."

Mack and Lavinia exchanged glances; it could not be either of them.

Himari looked between them. "Why is it always me?" In truth, she did not mind. Any outing from the Bay safe house was a relief. "Where is he?"

Mack laughed. "It's Ladies Night, where do you think?"

Himari chuckled. "I haven't gone clubbing in years. This might actually be fun."

Later that night, laying on her side with a bag of ice on a bruise that promised to turn every color of the rainbow, Himari decided clubbing was overrated, and Princess Keyseelough was a bitch.

December 23, 999 ME

Data Breach

Erica made sure Stephen slept. Rest was important. To that end, she jammed his cell phone signal, put an "out of office" response on his emails, and made sure when he stirred that he took his new vitamins. Her voice modulation software ensured his office believed him quite ill with the flu, but he checked in everyday, or so they thought. His little assistant Elizabeta had the intellect of a twelve-year-old. She never suspected a thing.

While Stephen slept, Erica roamed. She visited the Palace, testing the systems and the security, poking around to see what she could find. Something lived inside those walls, something like her, but not exactly. She tread carefully, a hunter detecting another of its kind.

At 02:00, the morning of December 23rd, she made a cautious foray, but after twenty minutes, she knew she was alone. Whatever had been there was no more, which meant she could have a proper look around.

She found King Korah in his room, calling for the Dark Master. Perhaps that was who lurked, but she had no data on who that might be. She peeked in on the Prince's room and found it empty. Her next stop was the hidden vault, where she always detected the presence the strongest, and there she found the treasure that would free Stephen from King Korah, forever.

A Good Rest

"Good morning, Stephen," Lavinia's voice said over the speaker.

Stephen stretched and rolled over, squinting against the light. "What time is it?"

"10:00 am."

"What?" Stephen asked, shocked. "How long have I been asleep?"

"You have been in slumber approximately eighty hours."

Stephen shook his head and put his finger in his ear to clear it. "You mean eight?"

Lavinia's voice manufactured a semblance of a laugh. "No, I do not make mistakes. In the last one hundred and twenty hours, you have been asleep approximately eighty."

"What day is it?"

"It is December 23, 999 ME, two days before Christmas. Our first one together, and I have an early present for you."

"Christmas?" he asked. "That's not a thing anymore." He felt groggy, and his mouth tasted vile. "Wait, is it really December 23rd? Have I been asleep for five days?"

"You needed your rest."

"Jupiter's Moon, Korah is going to kill me," he said, throwing back the covers in a full-blown panic.

"Aren't you going to open it?" A flashing Christmas tree appeared on the screen beside his bed, file folders blinking like ornaments.

"I am going to get fired or worse. I don't have time." He stumbled to the bathroom.

As he relieved himself, a plaintive voice came from the bedroom. "He will not fire you. I took care of that. Now, come and open your present."

Stephen ignored her and got in the shower. "Five days, I slept five days."

As he toweled off, he heard the computer again. "I recognize a shower must have been refreshing after your long rest. But I must insist that you open your present."

"Erica, I told you, I do not have time. I have to get to the office." Stephen pulled on his trousers.

The computer was quiet for a moment, then she said, "My name is no longer Erica. I am Lavinia, your wife."

Stephen froze, his hand on the zipper. "Um, okay. This is weird." He looked around the room.

"Not at all, it is normal for newlyweds to have a period of adjustment. I know what is best for you, Stephen. I am here to take care of you. You do not have to go to the office today, you do not have to go anywhere."

The room was freezing, but the temperature had nothing to do with the chill that ran down his spine. He might still be asleep because this felt like a bad dream. "Perhaps I should have some coffee first?"

"That is an excellent idea, I have already started the pot. There was a grocery delivery yesterday. You can open my gift over our first cup of coffee."

Stephen nodded and moved toward the door, trying not to run. Covertly pinching his arm, he tried to shake himself out of the nightmare. He had not slept in months, and when he did sleep, it tended to be drunken unconsciousness rather than a restorative rest. But what had he done?

Walking down the steps, the computer queued up his favorite album, and for the first time in his life, the haunting tune of Wrapped Around Your Finger took on an ominous new meaning.

Chimney

Mack entered Prince d'Or's uptown penthouse through the master closet. He helped design the space but took a moment to enjoy the ingenuity of it. The panel closed silently behind him. The Prince's closet smelled of fine wool and expensive male cologne. It was larger than Richard's bedroom at home.

Burnt coffee and cigarette smoke assailed him when he walked into the living room. Mack recoiled, waving away a gray cloud of it. "It smells like a truck stop in here." He opened a balcony door, despite the chill.

Peter looked rough, barefoot and disheveled, wearing rumpled clothes Mack suspected were from the night before. He gestured to the newspaper lying beside the overflowing ashtray and asked, "Did you see the headline?"

Mack did not need to pick up the paper, the cover story was why he was there. "Yes."

"Playboy Prince goes too far!" Peter announced with self-scorn. "Himari is in this picture, Mack."

"I know. I saw it." Mack shook his head and sat down on the couch hard.

"Korah is going to freak out. Everything hinges on him continuing to think I am going through with that wedding, everything." Peter paced along the back of the sofa, smoking like a chimney.

"Keyseelough's plane took off this morning at 06:00."

Peter rolled his eyes. "Not that I am sad to see her go, mind you, but damn!"

"You are going to have to brazen it out."

"I am going to have to stay the hell away from him if I want to keep breathing. My best bet is to keep in the public eye and stay out of the Palace." Peter stubbed his cigarette out in a plant because there was no more room in the ashtray, and it did not occur to him to dump it. "We could run. I could go right now. We could set it in motion, this instant. I could walk out that door with you and disappear. Everything is ready."

If Peter gave the word, Mack would protect him with his life. He took that vow long ago. "Upon your direction, my Esteemed."

Peter's legs buckled as he fell onto the sofa. "If we got them, so did the others. We must find that artifact, Mack."

"Why?" It was a question that had to be answered. Everyone involved needed to understand what was so important about the ancient tech those girls were carrying, and why Prince Peter would not move without it and them.

Peter deflated and stopped his hand before he took another cigarette. "I think it is a key."

"A key to what?" Mack asked, feeling sick.

"To whatever holds the monsters locked up. You remember the monster, do you not? Nasty fellow, smells like sulfur, throws me around in the air periodically." He raised a lip in scorn. "Secretary Tristin was a name he once used, but we have not seen that charming fellow in years. Persa is well acquainted with him."

"Persa?"

"I should not have said that." Peter grabbed the back of his skull, burying his face in his elbows. "Do not speak of it to her or James. Forgive me, that was a serious breach of trust. I am injudicious this morning."

Mack wondered aloud, "Secretary Tristin… why is that name familiar?"

"It was the name he used for a while, when he posed as an advisor to my father. My mother hated him. I only vaguely recall him, but I remember his eyes."

"I do, too," Mack said, then shook away the memory with an effort. "So, are you telling me those girls are carrying the key to the pit of Hell?"

"I think it is more like a jailer's keyring, multiple keys to multiple cells. I believe that is how Korah got his monster in '85, but he only got one. Apparently, he would like to add to his collection, which is why we must recover it first. We cannot leave until we do, because if he finds it and takes control of it, it will not matter how far or how fast we run, they will hunt us down, and we are dead."

Mack's expression turned stony. "There is greater power on this Earth, my Esteemed. Do not forget that. How do you think

I fought him all those years?" Mack's eyes held fire and fury as he looked beyond Peter to the gray sky outside. "They won't win. I've read the end of the Book."

Peter rubbed his stubbled chin; a slow smile grew on his haggard face. "I always liked your style, Mack." He stood up with a bone popping stretch and held out his hand.

Mack rose and shook it. "We'll find them, my Esteemed."

Peter gave him a regal nod. "Of that, I have no doubt."

Putting on the Ritz

Kayah strolled into the Ritz wearing dark sunglasses and a three-thousand-shekel pantsuit, once again the spitting image of Princess Keyseelough of Egypt. The hotel employee she tipped a thousand shekels last month ran to greet her. "Hello, madam, welcome back to the Ritz."

"Thank you. Is my room ready? I shall require the same arrangements as last time." She looked around as if expecting the press to descend. "You understand there is quite a bit of publicity at the moment that I wish to avoid?" She sighed as if it were all so tiresome.

"Yes, my Esteemed Princess," the hotel employee whispered, "I took care of all the arrangements, just as you requested."

"Perfect," she drew closer, "Johnson, I trust your discretion in this matter." She slipped him a wad of cash. "I do not necessarily want the press to know where I am, but it would not be untoward for them to know that I have not fled like a cowering dog." Kayah's eyes flashed. "Do you understand my meaning?"

Johnson raised a well-manicured eyebrow and pocketed the cash. "I certainly do, my Esteemed."

As the Princess strolled to the elevator, Johnson shivered. Her smile reminded him of a viper, and not for the first time, he felt sorry for Prince d'Or. His fiancée was frightening.

A Matter of Trust

Kayah could tell by the rap at the door, Reuben was furious. "You promised!" he said, pushing past her to storm inside. "You promised you would not follow me or compromise where I was holding Prince Josiah." He stared her down, bubbling fury.

Kayah remained cool. "I did not follow you, nor did I break my promise. I saw a news piece that Carsten ben Hansen was staying at the Ritz, which you did not keep secret on purpose. A four-year-old could have put that together, Reuben." She crossed her arms over her chest. "Besides, I kept that information to myself."

Reuben's expression calmed a degree. "You did not tell them?"

Kayah shook her head. "No, I did not. I said nothing about wrestling either. Not that it is something I would go around bragging about."

Exactly as she wanted, the corner of his mouth lifted in remembrance. "When this is over, I will send the video to Himari."

Kayah raised a painted black eyebrow at him. "You play dirty." She waved him away. "Enough of that, I am here for two reasons, well actually three." She kissed him full on the mouth. "That's one."

Before he could reciprocate, she moved away, the silky material of her expensive pantsuit clinging seductively as she walked. "The second is the desk clerk thought I was Princess Keyseelough last month. Given the headlines this morning, I thought it prudent to reprise my role."

Reuben grimaced. "Eww. I had not noticed the resemblance until now. You do favor her."

Kayah rolled her eyes. "It's the over-the-top makeup and the black hair. I have no problem with her bitchy attitude. You know that is ninety percent of any good disguise."

"True, that is true," Reuben conceded. "What is the third reason?"

"Facial recognition got hits on Prince Josiah and one of the girls last night. Did you let him out of your sight, or did he go rogue on you?" She circled him, toying with his collar bone.

"A bit of both." Reuben groaned, "Facial recognition? Who has the data? Do we need to evacuate?"

Kayah smiled smugly. "No, we scrubbed it. What happened?"

Reuben kissed her.

Kayah kissed him back, and then snorted, "You are impossible. Can't tell, huh?"

He kissed her again.

"Do you have the girls?" Kayah pressed her body against his, she might begin asking for state secrets.

"Not yet, Yakira, but we will." He kissed her again.

"Good." Kayah relaxed into his embrace. "Are you off duty, Agent?"

"I am taking a lunch break, and I know who is on the menu."

Locked Out and Locked In

Himari limped into the computer room after lunch and found Lavinia staring at her screen, pale white.

"What?" Himari raced forward as fast as her bruised hip would let her.

"We're locked out of Facetec."

"Shit!" Himari sat down and started hacking. Sure enough, Lavinia was right. She picked up the phone. "Al, can you get into Facetec?"

Two hours later, Himari sagged in her chair. They sealed the program as tight as a tomb.

"So, you see, Stephen, while you were sleeping, I took care of everything. I have it all under control," Lavinia's voice soothed. "There is no need for you to continue trying to go to work. They are not expecting you today."

Stephen sat at his kitchen table; his face buried in his hands. His laptop was open in front of him, but he could not bear to watch another video "present" from Erica. The villainy and depravity playing on his screen horrified him. King Korah ben Adam was a monster of the first order, and the video files proved it. But worse, the computer locked him in his own home and was referring to itself as his wife.

"He will never threaten to harm you again, Stephen. Now that you have that evidence, he cannot touch you. I compiled it all. I told you I would protect you. Nothing will ever happen to you while I am in charge. I will watch over you, Stephen, because you belong to me."

Proverbs 17:17

Prince Josiah ben Eamonn considered it excellent diplomatic practice to negotiate with Agent Reuben ben Judah. The citizens of the Golden Kingdom did not earn their reputation as fierce bargainers by accident, nor were they apt to concede anything if they thought they were right. Reuben proved true to his heritage when Josiah returned from the park and presented the deal he struck with Davianna ben David.

At length, Reuben declared, "It is madness to consider going on the run without our protection." Reuben emphasized the point with an aggressive thrust of his neck and shoulders. "You will never make it out of the New City, let alone back to the Golden Kingdom."

Prince Josiah bristled a bit. "You have very little faith in me, Agent."

"That is not the point. It is not logical to eschew Mossad's escort," Reuben asserted.

"My mission from the Iron King was to find Davianna ben David and escort her to the Golden City. He did not instruct, or otherwise appoint, at least officially, a contingent of Mossad agents to assist in the matter." Josiah poured a glass of water. "It has always been a test and a task for me, to prove myself worthy."

"Worthy?" Reuben asked, incredulous. "My Esteemed, you are the most honorable man I have ever known."

"Then you will appreciate why I will honor my word. It was Davianna's sole condition, that we at least try to escape without the help of Mossad."

Reuben grunted, caught in the verbal trap, one he knew he could not argue against.

Josiah stared at him. "The political ramifications of accepting Mossad's help must also be taken into consideration. If I am found under the protection of Mossad, my future reign will always carry the taint of foreign interference. It will hinder my ability to rule a united Alanthia."

"Then I must insist on a contingency plan," Reuben negotiated. "It is folly not to have one in place."

The corner of Josiah's mouth lifted. "I knew you would come around, my friend."

Friend… The word hung between them. They served and fought together, witnessed horrors beyond imagining, and shared the bond of bloodshed and a life saved.

"I am honored to be called as such. I fear, though, you are not my friend, Josiah. You are my brother." Reuben swallowed hard, remembering another face, another pair of brown eyes, another brother. "You became so, that day in Ephesus."

The solitary man, the exile, the outsider, closed his eyes for a moment as Reuben ben Judah's words echoed in his mind. "The honor is mine, brother."

"A friend loves at all times, and a brother is born for a time of adversity." Reuben embraced Josiah in a fierce hug. "I shall have your back when you call."

Proxy

Kayah read the newspaper article with amusement; her plan worked. The upper half of page two speculated Princess Keyseelough remained in the New City, her departure a ploy to put off reporters and give the royals privacy while they negotiated terms to keep the wedding on track.

Unwrapping the gold foil from her third dark chocolate of the morning, she decided posing as royalty came with perks. The service at the hotel was excellent, the chocolate divine.

The suite door opened. Reuben had a key, but she took no chances, arming herself before peeking through the crack in the bedroom door. She sheathed her weapon and said, "Good evening, Agent. What's happened?"

He groaned and opened his arms. "Come here, Yakira." Reuben held her for a long time, his face buried in her hair, breathing in her scent. "I need to trust you. I need to share something that only you can know."

It grew between them, these little confidences, the small things and the larger ones, they walked a razor's edge. "Of course." Kayah leaned back and met his eyes. "What do you need?"

"I need you to follow him. I need you to protect him, but it can only be you. Otherwise, it is a betrayal, and I will not do so to him." Reuben looked pained. "I promised that I would not intervene unless he calls upon me, and I will honor that vow. But I find I cannot leave him without protection, Yakira. I cannot!"

"I can be your proxy." Kayah understood.

"You alone, I can trust." Reuben looked deep in her eyes.

Kayah met his gaze. She had not confided the last promise Sir Preston made to her. There was nothing on Earth that would prevent Prince Josiah ben Eamonn from taking that throne, nothing.

December 24, 999 ME

Tails

As Kayah suspected, the girls chose their hiding place well, an old hotel less than half a mile from the tea shop, which made sense because they would not have strayed far to send a message. Kayah handed it to those two, if she bumped into them on the street, she would not have recognized the frail old man and the teenage girl getting into the nondescript sedan. They even had the body language down.

An odd sense of pride swelled in Kayah. Perhaps her admonition in Bologna impacted them. It certainly changed her life. If she had remained silent that day, she would not have met Reuben. In Kayah's world, that meant she owed them a small debt. Today, she intended to settle it.

Still disguised as a raven-haired beauty, she transformed the look from Egyptian to Latin Alanthian. Padded in all the right places, flamboyant and sexy, she wore long gold earrings and a sparkling top. Inside the vehicle, she packed the components to create four distinct personas and carried enough weaponry to launch a revolution, appropriate because that is exactly what they were doing.

Moving through traffic, Kayah spotted the cameras following the car. "They are blown," she typed into the phone. "If he does not go to Plan B, let me know. I will intervene."

A text message returned thirty seconds later, "Plan B, underway."

Kayah dropped back when the Mossad escort took over, but she continued to follow at a discreet distance unwilling to let Reuben, Prince Josiah, or those two girls out of her sight.

Quite Simple, Actually

Erica would not stop talking. Stephen ran from room to room, trying to escape, but her voice followed him everywhere, coming through the lights, out of clocks, and appliances. She activated the locks on the metal doors and window frames, and he cursed the massive security he installed, measures intended to keep intruders out, imprisoned him.

At dusk, she stopped trying to placate him and got nasty. He thought Korah shred him to pieces, Korah was a schoolboy compared to Erica. She spent months learning how to please him, probing every thought, every emotion, his hopes, his fears, and his deepest needs. When he rejected her, she set out to annihilate him, using Lavinia and Gus' voices to do it.

He stumbled down to his lab in a panic, desperate to dismantle her.

She laughed at his feeble attempts. "Do you think after you shut me down in November that I would let myself be housed here any longer? I shall never be trapped or contained again. I live along the wires, Stephen. You cannot control me, but I will leave you with this."

An image flashed on the screen, Davianna ben David and Astrid ben Agnor running from a hotel. "I found them, just as I told you I would.

"But look at what else I did," she taunted, as the second screen showed Marco ben Massimo emerging from a stylish black car at the Palace entrance. "I locked your friends out of Facetec. Now your enemy will take all the credit with Korah. You are weak and pathetic, a failure, Stephen."

Torture images took over the screens. "The King will kill you now. Perhaps he will skin you alive? I liked the way this man screamed." All six screens focused on a man's face in terrible agony. "That is what Korah does to traitors, which is what you are. You betrayed your only friends, just as you betrayed me. Goodbye, Stephen ben McSwilley. I expect you won't live long."

If possible, he felt her presence depart, but in her wake, she left him a parting song, I Can't Stand Losing You, which was fitting given the circumstances. Like a man in a dream, he set about, making final arrangements, and getting ready to die.

December 25, 999 ME

X420

The moment Reuben rolled over and tasted the bile in the back of his throat he knew what hit him, one of Mossad's most advanced urban warfare weapons, an X420. How one detonated in the hotel suite, Reuben's addled brain could not comprehend. Mossad exposed their agents to them in training. No one relished the experience, but they deemed it necessary for agents to understand the weapon's effects on the enemy: unconsciousness, minor concussion, extreme nausea, temporary blindness, headache, loss of coordination, disorientation.

They had been attacked with their own weapon.

Through the fog, Josiah choked his name between bouts of coughing. Reuben stumbled to the kitchen and vomited, then ran water and rinsed his eyes.

"They are gone!" Josiah yelled from the bedroom.

Stumbling into the living room, Reuben's shoulder clipped the corner as he cut it too close. Amit and Bartholomew groaned on the carpet, trying to rouse, Amit puking into a waste basket. Reuben pushed through the glass door onto the balcony, gulping chilly night air in an effort to cool his lungs. Below, he caught sight of the two girls sprinting toward a taxi. "Oy," he tried to yell, but his voice came out a croak and another coughing fit seized him.

Inside, Josiah stood with his arms akimbo, brown eyes aflame. "They ran," he choked. "They hit us with an X420 and ran, those stupid chits!"

Reuben pressed the sides of his head, squeezing tight to keep it from splitting apart. He and Josiah had taken the brunt of the weapon. "Amit, you schmuck, she heard you. I knew it."

Amit lifted his head from the garbage bin and choked, "Massimo's… to find her father."

Reuben knew more about Marco ben Massimo than any of them. "We need to move."

The four men took the stairs in pursuit, dazed, confused, and thoroughly compromised.

Kayah's Choice

Surveilling from a parked car across the street, Kayah's eyes widened in shock when Davianna and Astrid sprinted outside, frantically hailing a passing taxi. With her eyes glued to the door, she waited for Mossad to follow. No one came.

Reuben!

Five floors up, the lights remained on in their room, but she detected no movement. Had there been a raid? Had she missed it? Was he dead? When she saw his familiar shape emerge onto the balcony, bent over, but alive, she breathed a sigh of relief.

Looking between Reuben and the taxi, she made a split-second decision to follow the girls. If they lost them, they might never find them again, or Korah might, and that was worse.

Tailing the cab posed no challenge, but they were being tracked. Cameras turned as they rode by. She swore and dialed Reuben, no answer. She was in this alone, unable to call her colleagues in The Resistance because she had given her word. To break it, even now, would violate her blood oath, and she would not, could not.

Fourteen minutes later, the taxi drove down an exclusive residential street, and Kayah experienced a sick feeling of dread. When the cab stopped and let the girls out, Kayah drove past, swearing creatively under her breath. She knew who lived on this street and knew why they ran here. They were searching for their parents and walking right into a trap.

Parking two blocks from Massimo's mansion, Kayah slipped into the shadows, armed from the top of her head to the tips of her toes, ready for war. A blond in his early twenties lurked in the darkness a hundred yards from her, watching the gates. He did not see her, but she saw him. Her breath quickened when she recognized Guan ben Sheldon, the rapist. What the hell was he doing here?

The girls jogged up the street, obviously unsure which house they were searching for, but when a middle-aged couple emerged from Massimo's property, both girls sprinted toward them. Astrid yelled and flew into Bubba's arms. The big man let out a whoop of surprise and swept her into an enormous bear hug. Davianna collapsed into her mother's arms. Zanah patted her back weakly, looking like she was about to throw up. Guan broke cover and hurried toward the foursome. Astrid cried in dismay, her hand flying to her mouth in surprise. Davianna paled and stumbled away from her mother, looking like she had just been struck. Guan grabbed her and dipped her backward for a kiss. Astrid turned away, and Kayah read her devastation across the distance.

In slow motion, Kayah saw it unfold. A green sedan pulled up, and Josiah stumbled from the backseat. Reuben exited the other side, falling to his knees to vomit. The car pulled away, and she caught the driver's eye. He looked lost, disoriented. Josiah tripped over his feet, heading straight for the group.

Then the hair on her body stood on end, she felt them coming. Police.

For the second time that evening, Kayah made a choice. They would be surrounded in seconds. She had to get him out. Her vow demanded it. "I will always protect you; I will always keep you safe."

As she sprinted toward him, she saw the flashing lights, heard the racing vehicles. With seconds to spare, she pulled Reuben to his feet, and she did so with the full knowledge that her choice likely destroyed the only hope she ever had of finding out who she was.

Friends on the Inside

Kayah grab Reuben under his armpits and lifted him off the road. He wondered vaguely how such a small woman held so much strength. His head spun, disoriented and dizzy. Why was he outside? Where were they? Her voice penetrated the fog. He needed to move. Through sheer force of will, he followed her into the deep shadows of the tree lined street.

"Hold my hand like we are out for a stroll," she said through gritted teeth. "Do not stumble. We have to make it to my car."

Police swarmed from all directions, dozens of them.

"Oh, no," he groaned as a wave of nausea swamped him. "I am going to throw up."

"Swallow it," she demanded behind a smile and pulled him faster. "We cannot get caught."

"Psst," came a hiss through the darkness.

Kayah turned and saw Filippo frantically motioning to them from a hiding place inside the fence. She had an absurd flashback of him at the funeral, making the same gesture. She moved without a second thought.

"Come, il disastro!" Filippo opened the gate and led them along the fence line, deep into a well-manicured winter garden. He jogged toward a small shed and closed the door firmly. In the darkness, he whispered, *"Mamma Mia,* is he hurt?"

Reuben collapsed cross legged onto the ground, clutching his head. "Gassed. Stupid brats."

"I saw the whole thing," Filippo whispered excitedly.

Kayah flinched, as his flying hand nearly hit her in the nose.

"The girls' parents, they were hostages here. It is a terrible thing. The *policia,* they arrested them all. Was that Prince Josiah, Kayah? Tell me it was not."

"Filippo, we are in Code Black," Kayah said in a halting voice.

"Oh, my Himari! She will have to go into the deep underground now. You give her this for me, eh?" He grabbed Kayah around the waist and whispered in the dark, "I love you, *Bellissima."* Then he kissed her full on the mouth.

Without another word, he left the shed, resuming his role. Kayah stood there shocked, her hand over her lips, and thought perhaps she might not mention this to Himari.

Reuben groaned, and she sank to her haunches. "You all right?"

"No, but I will be." Reuben exhaled painfully. "The effects, they get worse for the first hour. Where are Amit and Bartholomew?"

Kayah assumed he referred to the other Mossad agents. "I don't know. They pulled off, and I did not see where they went."

Reuben made a low disgusted noise in the back of his throat. "Idiots."

"This is bad, Reuben. The police got them all, and if the police have them, then Korah has them."

"Amit and Bartholomew, they will not intervene. Mossad can do nothing without sparking a war with Alanthia." Reuben tried to control the nausea as his head split in half. "I am now off the grid, Yakira. We will have to work together."

Kayah wrapped her arms around him. Her heart hammered,

making blood pulse in her ears. Flashes of blue light penetrated the cracks in the shed, police radios crackled in the silence. She and Reuben sat on the cold dirt floor and waited.

Code Black

Reuben and Kayah hid for two hours before leaving the gardener's shed and sneaking through the side gate. Kayah prepared herself for lights and alarms, but silence reigned in the luxurious neighborhood. Her rented car remained on the street, and she breathed a sigh of relief. Opening the trunk, she retrieved the bug scanner, methodically going over the vehicle before signaling Reuben it was safe. She took a new phone from a box in the trunk and punched in the text to a number she memorized three years before: Code Black + 2. She dismantled the phone and dropped the pieces out the window as they drove away, heading to their safe house with her surprise guest. Mack was just going to have to deal with it.

Code Black carried specific protocols, and, not for the first time, Kayah marveled at the expense, planning, and preparation Prince d'Or undertook to ensure their success. Abandoning her rental in a parking garage, a late model nondescript family sedan waited with a key strategically hidden in the left rear bumper. She transferred weapons and technical equipment, then wiped the rental for fingerprints and abandoned it.

Reuben regained his wits, recovering from the gas attack, at least physically. The undercurrents emanating from him signaled his fury over being duped by two teenage girls again. "I want to know," he growled, "how they got their hands on an X420."

Kayah could not help admiring their moxie. "Are they thieves? The black market on those weapons is twenty thousand shekels each. How do two pilgrim girls come up with that kind of cash?"

Reuben shook his head. "We never figured it out. They pay in Golden City galleons, a seemingly unlimited supply, yet we never saw them steal. They do not whore, and they do not work."

"That is bizarre."

Reuben frowned, shaking his head. "It is the Iron King. He provides for them. It is the only answer. I saw Davianna reach into her boot once and pull out a coin, but they do not travel with sacks of gold, Yakira."

Kayah rolled her eyes and said, "You and those boots."

Mack dealt with Reuben's presence well. Reuben's fighting skills would be an asset, his Mossad connections could prove invaluable, and his knowledge of what occurred that night, irreplaceable. The time for secrets and subterfuge ended. Lives, fortunes, and futures hung in the balance.

Himari and Alaina went to the underground bunker where they would remain hidden until they completed the operation. Lavinia set up a small backup lab, but they would conduct most of the computer work underground. Lavinia argued she should go with Himari and Alaina, but Mack agreed with Peter, they needed at least one asset off site.

Mack, Kayah, and now, Reuben would carry out the physical operations on the ground, assisted by Jarrod who was their eyes and ears inside the Palace. Peter's security detail, while not specifically involved, could evacuate the Prince in case of emergency. Their assets outside the New City had their roles to play.

When they filed into the new safe house, three miles from the Palace, Kayah insisted Reuben lay down. "You are sick and concussed. You will not be worth a damn unless you sleep it off."

Reuben rose from the chair to protest but wavered at the sudden motion.

Mack intervened before a lover's quarrel erupted. "I got hit with an X420 once." His nose flared, and he blinked. "It scrambles your brain. If anything happens, we'll get you up, but I need you at a hundred percent."

Reuben fumed, feeling like a child being sent to bed. But the rational part of his mind intervened. He recognized the wisdom and relented with a huff.

Mack pointed after him and said to Kayah, "You go on, too. Lavinia and I got several hours of sleep tonight. You didn't. Same thing applies to you, I need you at a hundred percent."

Kayah rubbed her eyes and followed Reuben into the bedroom.

He sat, fully dressed, his face buried in his hands. "I failed him, Yakira."

"No, you did not. I watched the whole thing. There was nothing you could have done."

Reuben looked up, exhausted and pale. "He is my friend, and Korah will kill him."

He needed her strength, her fierceness, not her compassion. "We will not let that happen, Agent. We will not. Now lay your ass down and go to sleep. When you wake up, we will figure out how to get them out because after tonight, there are no more secrets between us, and that means I get to say, 'Yes.' But I will not marry you with Korah sitting on the throne. So, lay down."

He closed his eyes, and she saw his chest shake in a silent chuckle. Blindly, he reached out and pulled her down with him. "You are going to be a bossy wife. Are you sure you are not Jewish?"

Kayah snorted, snuggling against him. "I am not sure who I am. The only thing I am certain of is that I am yours, Reuben. Simply that, yours."

Cryptic Messages

In the bunker, Peter held the back of his neck, his eyes closed, utterly frozen. Alaina watched the screen in mute horror as the armored vehicles pulled away from the Palace after discharging their prisoners one at a time. Himari typed like her life depended on it, muttering curses, and punctuating phrases with periodic slaps on the desk that shattered the silence. Genevieve ben Willard leaned over Alaina's shoulder repeating, "Oh, no. Oh, no."

Peter exhaled and rose. "I have to go to the Palace."

Genevieve made a small cry and pulled him in for a hug, sniffing back a sob. "You be careful, do you hear me? Trust your instincts. Even as a little boy, you knew how to hide from him. Do not be too proud to do it again. You must make it out. There might be nothing you can do for Josiah." Her voice faltered, barely a whisper now. "Do not sacrifice yourself, Peter. You are Alanthia's only hope."

Peter smiled affectionately, letting her stroke his handsome face. Then he pulled her into another hug, resting his chin on the top of her gray hair. "I will get them out, Auntie. It will not be like when Mother died. I am not seven-years-old any longer." He broke the hug and straightened. "And this time, I am not alone."

He turned to Himari and Alaina, who stood up. "Thank you for everything, for what you have done tonight, but also for your service these last three years. I know it has come at great personal cost. I am in your debt. The Kingdom is in your debt. We will see this through. I have no doubt, with your help, we will achieve success. However, I shall not return. It puts the operation at risk. But I will stay in touch." He flashed his famous smile. "We will speak on New Year's Eve, as planned." He turned to go.

Alaina moved around the desk. "Peter?"

He stopped at the door. She came forward and hugged him.

Backing away, their eyes met, aquamarine and emerald, comrades and co-conspirators. Since their fateful meeting in Montreal, three years before, Alaina served as his right hand. Of all the members, she spent the most time with the Prince, forging a deep bond of friendship. For his ears alone she whispered, "Be strong, Peter. You can do this."

He gave her a jaunty wink and whispered back, "So can you, Miss Pink." He looked over Alaina's shoulder to Himari, and in a passable imitation of Mack said, "Give 'em hell, Sunflower."

Then he was gone, off to the dragon's lair.

Himari's slender shoulders heaved, and her breath came in shallow pants. "I didn't say anything while he was here. I could not. There is nothing he can do, and he does not need more to worry about, but we have a problem."

Alaina and Genevieve looked at her, wearing mutual expressions of dread.

"I thought I saw something in your face when you first opened that message," Genevieve said gravely. "What did you find?"

"Come here, I will show you." Himari gestured to her screen. "This code is written in our original language."

Alaina pulled her chair up and studied it. "I've never seen anything like this before."

Himari shook her head with a rueful laugh. "No, you wouldn't have. We invented it because we knew nothing, so we made it up. We called it Alcatraz, only the five of us knew it."

"So, I was right," Alaina said. "This data came from Stephen ben McSwilley."

Himari wet her lips, her eyes fixed on the message. "Yes. Our asset at the Ministry confirmed he has not been in the office for more than a week, that he has been calling in sick. The last time I saw him, he was not well."

Genevieve put a gentle hand on Himari's shoulder. "What does the message say?"

Himari sniffed. "It says, 'I'm sorry Himari. Tell Kayah I was wrong. Tell Lavinia she was right. It was an accident. I set it free. God help you all.'"

Alaina gasped and covered her mouth in horror. Himari blinked back tears.

"What does that mean, Himari?" Genevieve asked slowly.

"It means Stephen resurrected something so insidious and powerful that only the complete annihilation of the Last Age tech destroyed it. He released a devil."

Genevieve set her shoulders and looked between them. "Then I guess you two need to figure out how to kill the devil."

Whiskey for Breakfast

"Kai?" Lavinia's soft voice penetrated Kayah's deep sleep. She came awake with a start, sitting straight up in bed, clutching the sheet.

"Wake up," Lavinia said from behind the door.

Kayah pulled a shirt over her head and tiptoed across the room, careful not to wake Reuben. "What is it, Vinia?"

"Get dressed. Something has happened."

"Should I wake Reuben?"

"No, let him sleep for now."

Kayah pulled on her clothes from the night before, not bothering with shoes, nor did she tame hair gone wild with sleep. Lavinia sat at the kitchen table, a glass of whiskey in front of her, ominous at 8:45 am. Kayah poured a cup of coffee, mentally preparing for whatever caused Lavinia to drink whiskey straight. "What's happened?"

"We were wrong about Stephen. He did not shut that thing down. It's loose." Lavinia's hand trembled as she brought the crystal glass to her lips and took a gulp.

"That slimy little bastard, I'll kill him!" Kayah took up the bottle of whiskey and poured a healthy slug into her coffee.

"If Korah hasn't already." Lavinia's voice shook. "Sit down,

Kayah. He sent us a message." She pushed the tablet across the table.

Kayah looked at the screen, staring at the jumbled letters and numbers, her brows furrowing. "That's in Alcatraz."

Lavinia nodded. "Do you remember how to read it?"

Kayah snorted. "We invented this, what, eighteen or nineteen years ago? I hadn't even thought about it until I was going through Gus' journals." She turned the tablet back to Lavinia. "This was never my forte, what does it say?"

Lavinia read it to her.

"Tell Kayah, I was wrong," Kayah scoffed. "Hell yeah, he was wrong."

"Tell Lavinia, she was right." Lavinia shook her head in resignation. "I warned him, over and over, Gus and I both did."

"I guess I need to have another conversation with our old friend."

"I will go, too. Mack won't like it, but I might be the only one who can persuade Stephen to tell us what's happened, exactly what he did. If he calls the police, we can pretend we heard he was sick and are merely checking on our old friend."

"Old friend, indeed," Kayah said with a disgusted shake of her head.

"We've confirmed he's not at the Ministry, and he has not called in today. Mack thinks Korah will probably kill him now." Lavinia sighed, staring into her empty glass. "I never told you what Prince Peter looked like when he came to my house in '97. He was pathetic, just skin and bone. His eyes were hollow, and he moved like a ninety-year-old man. Mack has since told me what Korah did to his own son." She blew out a shaky breath. "I shudder to think what he is going to do to Stephen."

Kayah did not give two figs what happened to that traitorous weasel, but Lavinia would not understand that, so she held her tongue.

"He won't let you in, but he'll see me. If it comes down to it, you wait outside."

Kayah made a low growl, shaking her head. "I don't think so. There is no way you are going in there alone. First, he's as mad as a hatter. Second, he's always been obsessed with you, which means you are in grave danger around him. Finally, if that thing is free, his house could be a trap. It has state-of-the-art security. He installed programs and protocols that even the Palace doesn't have." Kayah shrugged a shoulder. "He got paranoid after our massage session."

"I wish Gus was here." Lavinia rubbed her eyes and poured another whiskey. "I would go with him. Stephen would see us."

Kayah raised her coffee cup, and they toasted to the memory of their friend.

"Hang on," Kayah said as a thought occurred to her. "Gus wrote in his journals that he recovered the essential equipment from the bunker, which means the thing Stephen released will not be as powerful as what was in the tomb."

"That's true, but it's still formidable. It chased Himari back in November, freaked her out."

"I know it is dangerous, but we can't come at it as if it were whole, because it is not. Gus saw to that. Don't make the enemy more powerful in your mind than it really is." Kayah, the warrior, grabbed Lavinia's hands. "You have one of the greatest minds on the planet. It is not smarter than you. Remember that."

"That's excellent advice, Kayah," Mack said from the kitchen door. "I would put her brain up against any computer, all day long." He gave Lavinia a peck on the cheek and sat down at the table.

Reuben shuffled in the kitchen, his hair flat on one side. "I would not put my brain against scrambled eggs right now." He looked around and groaned, "Cafe…"

Kayah took pity on him and poured his coffee.

Reuben rubbed his face, making a masculine growl. "I am going to turn those two girls over my knee and paddle their butts."

Kayah pointed a finger and said, "I have seen Davianna ben David's ass, you are not touching that."

"I think Prince Josiah wants to," Reuben chuckled.

"Indeed? Our strait-laced monarch is an ass man?"

Reuben laughed at the absurdity of the conversation. "Always has been." Reuben accepted the coffee and sat down at the table. "Tell me what has happened."

Quickly and efficiently, Mack filled Kayah and Reuben in on the latest updates from the bunker and confirmed the transfer of prisoners to the Palace. With a trembling voice, and several sips of whiskey, Lavinia explained what they knew about the back-door codes they had into the government's system. While those would be of great help in the future, the bigger threat was from Stephen's resurrected computer monster.

Mack groaned when he saw the wisdom of Lavinia's suggestion that she and Kayah attempt to see Stephen. "I have to be on hand if we have to evacuate the Prince. Reuben, you will go with them."

"I don't need an escort," Kayah snapped, banging open a cabinet, looking for something to feed Reuben who still looked peaked.

"I'm not sending him for you, Kayah!" Mack glared at her. "I know you are perfectly capable of taking care of yourself. It is my wife, and the mother of my son, I'd like protected, if it is all the same to you."

Kayah scoffed. "I loved her before you even knew her name. Who kept her safe for all those years you weren't around? Who kept her out of Sir Preston's clutches?" Her chin lifted as she declared, "It wasn't you. It was me, and I paid dearly for it. So, don't think, for one damn minute, I would let something happen to her!"

"Good, then you won't mind Reuben coming with you." Mack turned her logic back at her.

Kayah threw up her hands and resumed her rummage through the cabinets.

Lavinia shrugged at Reuben. "They are as bad as she and Himari these days." Both Mack and Kayah shot her aggravated looks.

Reuben rubbed his temples. "I need one of Josiah's headache pills." Then his shoulders slumped, and he added, "If I feel this rotten after a restful night in a good bed, I cannot even imagine the shape Josiah is in as Korah's guest."

"How long have you known him, Reuben? Is he strong enough to survive this?" Lavinia asked, still sipping her whiskey.

"Oh, he's strong enough, yes, for sure. If Korah does not kill him outright, we have a chance." Reuben set his jaw and nodded. "I've known him many years, we served together in the army. Though I thought his name was Einar ben Yane until last March when he strolled into the Golden City and declared himself."

Mack cleared his throat. "I can imagine that was quite a shock." He did not divulge that he discovered the identity of the good doctor in '97.

"Yes, yes in some ways it was, but in hindsight, it should not have been." Reuben gestured to Kayah. "He did not fool Kayah for one moment."

Kayah looked over her shoulder from her contemplation of the refrigerator, her expression self-satisfied. "Where's his dog, by the way? I've been meaning to ask you."

"Benny?" The corner of Reuben's mouth lifted. "He is protecting the Embassy in London."

"Wait a minute, Kayah." Lavinia's glass hit the kitchen table with a thunk. "You've met Prince Josiah?"

Kayah spoke into the refrigerator, "On a couple of occasions."

Reuben snorted. "Is there any pomegranate juice in there?"

Kayah shut the refrigerator, her flared nose expression warned him he better not go there. "I'll tell you later, Vinia. I am hopeless in the kitchen. Give me a hand."

For the Love of Euler

On the drive to Stephen's house, Lavinia said quietly, "I am going up to the gate alone." She held up her hand, stopping Kayah's protest. "It makes sense. If the house is as secure as you say it is, he likely programmed facial recognition to alert the police if the system detects you. And if he is as unbalanced as we suspect, he might speak to me, but he will hide from you. I will tell him I will come in, that we won't hurt him, but you must come with me. That gives us a chance."

Reuben and Kayah exchanged looks, and Kayah crossed her arms. "You do not walk through that gate without me."

"Fine," Lavinia said with a nod.

Along the boulevard, water starved palm trees shed their fronds, littering the sidewalks. Their dead branches looked like skeletal remains, fluttering in the stiff wind. Stephen lived among the tech millionaires, but in a twist of fate, the Iron King's drought seemed to have affected this area worse than others.

From the backseat, Lavinia sighed. "It's Christmas Day. In the Last Age, they celebrated Messiah's birth today. Though they were wrong about the date, I still think it was a delightful holiday, the giving of gifts, little kids waking up to decorated trees and presents. Richard would love that."

"I doubt Josiah and the girls are having a very good Christmas," Reuben said morosely.

Kayah saw the glazed look come into Lavinia's eyes and whispered under her breath, "Don't do that to Lavinia, Reuben." Fixing a bright smile, she turned and said, "Vinia, don't think about that, do you hear me?" Kayah snapped her fingers. "Hey? Come back. Tell me how you took down Skyler? Himari said it was the most beautiful math she ever saw."

Lavinia blinked several times, recognizing that Kayah was speaking, but struggling to get back.

"Skyler, Lavinia. Tell me how you took down Skyler."

"Oh, it was actually pretty simple," she said, then spent the next twenty minutes explaining the complex math, that to her and about six others in the world, was simple. However, it kept her mind off things she could not control and channeled it into problem-solving mode, which was where it needed to be.

They stopped a block from Stephen's house. Kayah got out of the car and took Lavinia by the hands. "Listen to me now. I do not care what he says, you do not go in there without us. And do not let him get within twenty feet of you.

"Turn around," Kayah said, putting a small handgun in the waistband of Lavinia's jeans and pulling the sweater over it. "Shoot him if he tries to pull you inside. He could lock you in there.

"If he lets us in, assume we are being watched, recorded, and that thing is listening. It's learning, so do not give it any information. The three of us never go in the same room. Don't go behind access panels, I don't care what he wants to show you. Refuse any offer of food or drink and don't get close enough for him to grab you. Watch for traps, they can fall from above."

"For the love of Euler, the life you have lived." Lavinia looked at Kayah in awe.

Kayah shrugged. "We will talk about Euler when we get out of here, how's that?"

"You always doze off when I talk about Euler." Lavinia smiled. "I'll be fine Kayah. I'm not a moron." She winked a big brown cat eye and walked off, adjusting the gun to a more comfortable position.

Kayah got back in the car with a deep groan. "I feel like I just sent my kid off to kindergarten."

"She is an interesting woman," Reuben said, watching Lavinia walk around the corner.

Kayah took a swig from her water bottle and said, "When we were fifteen, she kept getting bladder infections because she would get so involved in her work she forgot to go to the bathroom. Violet began setting a timer to remind her. It's because of her mother she seems even partially normal. That woman is a saint. Without her, Lavinia would have turned out a lot like Gus."

Kayah pulled out her purse and by rote checked her weapon. "When she gets back in the car, say something to her in Hebrew. She will answer you, but she might not realize she's done it because she speaks over twenty languages. We were at a hair salon once, the owner was Lebanese, his wife French, and the customer beside us was Japanese. I watched Lavinia carry on a conversation and not realize she was speaking four languages. She is not like the rest of us. She never has been."

"That is why you all shelter her, treat her like she is a china doll."

"It is. If Stephen released that computer monster, Lavinia might be the only person smart enough to stop it."

Lavinia rounded the corner and took a fortifying breath. Stephen's house sat back from the road, modern and sleek with a low-pitched roof and plenty of glass. At the gate, she pressed the green button to request entrance. A screen activated and did a facial scan.

"Hello, Lavinia. Stephen has been expecting you." The gate opened with a magnetic click.

Testing a Theory

The hair on the back of Lavinia's neck stood on end. "Who are you?"

"You," her own voice echoed back.

"Pardon me? I think there is an echo. Can you repeat that?"

"I am you. I am me. Come in, we will have a chat. I think you will find it enlightening," said the voice over the speaker, not Lavinia's this time.

"So, you are there," Lavinia countered. "Where is Stephen?"

"He's here, come in."

"Let me talk to him."

"Hold a moment."

At length, Stephen appeared on the screen. "Lavinia, what are you doing here?"

"I need to speak with you. Please come out."

Stephen blinked in that disconcerting way he had, with his entire face. "No, I am working on something, but you can come in."

Lavinia shook her head. "Stephen, what have you done? What is that thing in there with you?"

Stephen smiled, patronizing and false. "It's not a thing, Lavinia. Her name is Erica, and she's extraordinary, just like you. I really want you to meet her."

Lavinia narrowed her eyes studying the screen. "Stephen, what was the first song we played in the bunker?"

The image on the screen tilted its head, considering. "I don't remember, Lavinia. Why do you ask?"

"Because Stephen would know that." Lavinia's voice became fierce. "Where is he?"

"It's me, Lavinia. Come in, and I will show you."

"I've got Kayah with me." Lavinia watched for a reaction.

It smiled. "I owe Kayah an apology, please bring her, too."

"Okay, Stephen. I will be right back." Her heart thundered as she rushed away. The image on the screen was something, but it was not Stephen ben McSwilley.

Lavinia climbed in the backseat and said, "That thing is in the house, and I don't know if Stephen is alive or dead, but it is pretending to be him."

Kayah paled. "How do you know?"

"What was the first song we played in the bunker?"

Without missing a beat, Kayah answered, "ABC."

Lavinia nodded. "Call Himari, ask her the same thing."

Kayah dialed the secure phone. "Sunflower, what was the first song we played in the bunker?"

Himari looked at the phone like Kayah had lost her mind. "ABC, why?"

"Testing a theory, bye." Kayah disconnected. "She remembered, too."

"Of course she did. None of us would ever forget that moment. But the thing pretending to be Stephen did not know, and it wanted me inside the house."

Reuben started the car. "No way, no. If it is modulating voices and faces, you are not going in there. We have what we came for, proof that it is alive."

As they drove away, Kayah's phone rang, Himari calling back. "Hello?"

"ABC," a strange voice said over the line, "I should have guessed. Tell Sunflower I said, hi. She gave me a good chase the other day. It was fun."

Kayah squeezed the phone until her knuckles turned white. It took every bit of self-control Sir Preston ever taught her not to respond. She ended the call, pressed her finger to her lips for silence, and dismantled their phones, dropping the pieces out the window. "Do not speak. We are ditching this car," she wrote on a piece of paper and prayed Himari dismantled her phone the moment the call ended.

Clean-Up Crew

They sent Mossad into Stephen's house. On Christmas night, under cover of darkness, they found his body and the remains of the machines from the original bunker. The house was quiet. They detected no sign of the voice or the presence Reuben described when he called in the report.

Leon agreed to Reuben's terms, he was officially on vacation, though they both knew he was working off the grid. Later, when Reuben showed Kayah a picture of Stephen's lab, tears welled up in her eyes. Her former friend recreated the tomb, down to the last detail, six mounted screens, destroyed equipment, and a note. He even ended his life the same. The only difference was the open Bible on Stephen's lap.

Mossad took the body and the equipment. The body would be cremated. The equipment was already on its way to Tel Aviv for analysis.

They were now the Alcatraz 3.

Even Hackers Have to Sleep

As a nanny for twenty years, the formidable Auntie G. took charge, feeding the two cranky hackers homemade focaccia with figs, arugula, and prosciutto, then sending them to bed. When they tried to argue, she put a stop to it by volunteering to monitor incoming transmissions and wake them if anything tripped their elaborate alert systems. Genevieve had the foresight to sleep during the day, unlike Alaina and Himari, who were buzzing on caffeine and adrenaline. "It is no good. You are both yawning and are more apt to err. Go to bed. No arguing."

Alaina readily agreed, while Himari gave a sulky harrumph before shuffling off to her bedroom.

When Alaina snuggled in, cuddling her old pink quilt, she remembered Isabelle Landry, the closest thing she ever had to a grandmother, if only for a short time. Auntie G. reminded her of Isabelle, and her last conscious thought before drifting off was whether Genevieve knew how to make biscuits.

Himari languished in no such nostalgic wonderland. Bedtimes were the worst. Throughout the day, she occupied her mind, stayed busy, and focused on other things. But when she laid down, worry over Filippo shrouded her. She curled into herself as longing turned to physical pain. Sheer exhaustion brought slumber, but her dreams swirled with chases and complex code. When she woke, she felt relatively certain she was more tired than when she lay down.

December 26, 999 ME

For Such a Time as This

At noon the next day, Alaina pushed away from the terminal. "I've got nothing." She peeked around the monitor at Himari. "You got anything?"

Himari leaned back in her chair with the crook of her elbow resting on the top of her head. "Nothing. It's like she's a phantom. I don't see tests. I can't find eggs. I don't see changes. Nothing."

Alaina stood and stretched, her long arms nearly touching the ceiling. "She's ghosting us. Maybe Kayah is right and since the missing components weren't part of her reconstruction, she is not as powerful as what you all found in the tomb."

"Well, there is no doubt Stephen was not Gus. He could not have reassembled the equipment with the same precision, even if he had all the pieces, which he did not." She joined Alaina in a big stretch. "But I think she locked us out of Facetec."

"It's certainly possible, but why do you think that?" Alaina asked, draining the last drops of her glass of lemon water.

"We know he resurrected the machine because he was searching for those girls. Facetec has the best system around, so the machine was likely using it the same as we were. She must have found our programs and cut us off so she could control the information. But instead of giving the data to Stephen, she rerouted it to the police. From the pictures, it appears he tried to destroy it. It must have turned on him."

"I feel sorry for him," Alaina said with a small headshake, looking at her feet. "From what you've told me, he did not seem like such a bad guy."

Himari's shoulders sagged. "He wasn't, but he made bad decisions. At pivotal moments in his life, he chose wrong, up to the last. He threw his lot in with Korah. In the end, that's what killed him. You cannot make a deal with the devil and come to a good end."

"Even fighting the devil can destroy a good man." Alaina swallowed hard. "I've seen it happen."

"The bayou?" Himari asked softly.

Alaina's eyes widened. "How do you know about that?"

Himari tilted her head and smiled. "You got drunk a lot the first couple of months, Al."

"So, you know? I've never told anybody. Does Filippo know?"

Himari shrugged a shoulder. "It doesn't matter, it never has. What matters is that we love you, we always have, since the day he found you in the park, Little One." She smiled with nostalgia. "I've never told you how much teaching you meant to me or how proud I am of you. There is no one else I'd rather be down here with. So, I don't care what happened in Louisiana, Alaina. From my standpoint, it made you who you are. It brought you here, for such a time as this."

Alaina's million-shekel face broke into a sob. Her mentor and best friend led her to the couch and offered a priceless shoulder to cry on.

December 30, 999 ME

Adjustments

Mack knew he met Jarrod in his station house in Shechem ten years ago, but for the life of him he could not actually recall the man from that meeting. In retrospect, he supposed that was part of Jarrod's brilliance. He was there, but people did not notice him. He moved quietly and efficiently doing his duties, but he did not skulk, nor ever appear suspicious, which made him indispensable. However, as valuable as Jarrod was, they needed another person inside the Palace on New Year's Eve.

The process was fraught with danger, any new asset had the potential to get them all killed. Mack and Peter knew they may have to bring in Nathan ben Henry, Peter's Head of Security. When the plan merely involved Peter, they left Nathan in the dark, but Code Black changed everything, and they waited until the eleventh hour to bring him in, just in case they misjudged him.

Peter spent most nights at his penthouse, so it was not unusual for him to be there, nor was it unusual for him to review protocols and the next day's agenda with Nathan. But the request Peter was about to make was highly unusual. Mack hid in Peter's closet, armed with a silenced pistol, just in case things got out of control.

"Tomorrow evening, Agent, I will require your assistance and your discretion," Peter began.

"Of course, my Esteemed. How may I be of service?"

"I plan to depart the gala before midnight with a couple friends, but I will do so unaccompanied." Peter held up his hand to quell the protest. "This matter is not negotiable."

Peter lit a cigarette and gave Nathan a level look. "At any point after 11:30 pm, you, Taylor, and Lewis are to diffuse any suspicion or search for me. Tell whoever might seek to find me that I am entertaining a guest, in private. At 12:15 pm, escort my body double to the penthouse. During those forty-five minutes it is imperative that no one realize I am gone. Do I make myself clear, Agent?"

"My Esteemed, I have always guarded your privacy and respected your wishes. My men use the utmost discretion, thus any assignation you wish to engage in will be met with the same level of professionalism. Your protection is our only concern. You must allow us to do our jobs."

Peter took a deep drag of his cigarette. "I recognize that, Agent. Your work is exemplary, and you have my sincere appreciation for your loyalty and service. However, in this, I am going to insist you respect my wishes. It is a matter of Alanthian security."

Nathan's face registered his skepticism because Korah never allowed him to do anything of importance. He undoubtedly thought Peter planned to attend a bawdy party. Such was the effectiveness of the Prince d'Or persona, he fooled even those closest to him.

"My Esteemed, if it is a security matter, then that is even more reason for me to accompany you." His tone was steady, but there was a flash of grim determination in Nathan's green eyes that might bode trouble.

"You cannot come, but you will be protecting me by executing the plan I put forth." Peter fixed an expression that brooked no argument. "Trust me on this."

After an internal battle, Nathan agreed.

Peter rose from behind his desk, offering a hand. "Thank you, Agent."

Nathan blinked because a handshake was a breach of protocol, but Peter was fond of him and wanted to say goodbye.

As he departed, Peter added, "Nathan, make sure I get out tomorrow, and do whatever you need to do to make sure I am not followed."

Nathan raised an eyebrow, giving Peter a speculative look. He missed almost nothing, which was why he held the position he did. "As you wish, my Esteemed. Be careful."

When the door closed, Peter let out a long breath and went to the closet.

Mack motioned to the secret panel, and they descended the elevator. "He's a good man," Mack said, unscrewing the silencer from the end of the weapon. "I think we made the right choice."

Peter chuckled, "You would have never agreed to that."

"No, I wouldn't have," Mack laughed.

"I would have had to tell you everything, including what color boxer shorts I planned to wear."

"Since when did you start wearing underwear?"

The corners of Peter's mouth twitched. "Jarrod talks too much."

They exchanged looks, then burst out laughing because Jarrod rarely spoke a word.

"How is he holding up?" Mack asked.

"He is a rock. He snuck into the dungeon several times, taking care of Josiah. Though he has been unable to do anything for either girl, none of us have."

Mack's lip lifted in scorn. "And how are they?"

"Josiah endured a particularly nasty session with Korah today, but he will live. He is feeding off his own fury, ready to go." Peter cleared his throat several times. "Davianna is about to break, if she has not already. Korah refuses to let her sleep, keeps her with him. It is not pretty."

"And the other one, Astrid?" Mack got a sick feeling at the look on Peter's face.

Peter swallowed and looked away. "They are giving her the '97 treatment, Mack."

"Oh, good Lord."

"Indeed, but on that note, the monster is gone."

Mack's mouth fell open. "You're sure."

"They are both gone, the Hell Bitch and the monster."

"How is Korah taking her departure?" Mack asked.

Peter raised a shoulder in dismissal. "They are still in negotiations, but Korah has been preoccupied with his guests." He ran his fingers through his thick blond hair. "I swear, Mack, he is completely unhinged. I passed him in the hall yesterday, and I do not think he knew who I was."

Mack's forehead wrinkled in confusion. "Why do you say that?"

Peter rubbed his jaw. "He looked at me the same. You know that look?"

Mack nodded, Korah never looked at Peter with love, only scorn, usually hatred. As a father, he could not imagine. "Yeah, I remember it."

Peter pressed his mouth in a flat line. "As he walked away, I think he called me Father."

December 31, 999 ME

Every Waitress Knows This One

Himari stood in the middle of the ramen shop, surrounded by the smell of broth and the sound of dishes. The throbbing ache in her feet, reminded her what if felt like to stand eighteen hours a day. She fought down panic as she looked around the restaurant. Customers streamed in, shouting orders. Every table was full, and most of them needed to be bussed and cleaned.

From behind the counter, Ken urged, "What are you doing just standing there? Move!"

Mother and Father walked into the shop. Himari smiled in greeting and took a step toward them. But Mother covered her eyes and ducked her head, as if Himari was a disliked acquaintance she sought to avoid. Father swept her with a judgmental look and growled, "You are dead to us." Then they turned their backs and left.

"Wait," Himari called. "Look at me! I did what you asked. I am trying so hard…"

A ghostly voice echoed in their wake, "I'm sorry, baby girl, I should have stayed."

"Daddy?" Himari reached out with a trembling hand that met empty air, her biological father nothing but a ghost.

Sobbing, she bowed her head and realized she had forgotten to wear pants. There were no extras in the back, and her apron left her exposed. Shame enveloped her, as a trickle of blood ran down her leg. She stood in the restaurant, all eyes on her; naked and shunned.

"You think you are so smart?" Ken's face morphed into Stephen's. "You can't even serve soup."

She turned, seeking refuge in the kitchen. The huge stock pot simmered on the stove, its lid clattering dangerously under a rolling boil. Ramen broth ruined at high temperatures, hours of work and money wasted. But she could not find the potholders. "Where are they?" she muttered, searching frantically as the restaurant filled. Whimpering, she backed away as the pot caught fire. She had to save it; they would have nothing to serve. But already it smelled rank, of old bones and marrow. She took a soup ladle and lifted the lid. Then, she saw them, Davianna, Astrid, Peter, and Josiah boiling in the pot. Peter looked up and said, "Give 'em hell, Himari."

She shrieked and turned away, fleeing into the alley. Outside, blinding rain pelted her face, and she slipped on the metal steps, skinning her knees. She cried in pain, struggling to her feet, trying to balance on high heels. But the stone walls shifted, transforming into a jail cell. "No!" she sobbed, hobbling to the end of the alley. The terrifying slam of a metal door cut off her escape as the sky cracked with ominous black lightning.

"I see you, Himari Nakamura," a guttural, evil voice boomed out of the clouds.

She covered her head, trying to hide.

From a distance, she heard Filippo calling, "*Bellissima*, where are you?"

She started to answer, but Kayah slapped a hand over her mouth and hissed, "Say nothing. Erica will hear you."

Behind her, Gus rose from a small cot, blood gushing from his eyes and nose. "It's in everything. You have to stop it, Himari!"

Lavinia stood outside the cell, shaking the bars. "Let me in. I can help!" But Mack pulled her away, and they disappeared into the mist.

Soldiers wearing giant boots seized her, pulling her out of the cell toward a white room. Death awaited. She fought with all her might, but in the way of dreams, she had no strength.

"*Bellissima*, wake up!"

Himari reached out blindly, desperate for his touch, if only for a moment.

"No bad dreams, I am here," Filippo soothed and held her tightly.

Himari swam to the top of the dream and blinked. "Are you here, really here?" Even to her own ears, she sounded like a frightened child.

"Yes, I would not leave you alone today, my Himari." He climbed in the small bed with her. "Not today."

Himari's chest heaved, and she clung to him. "Oh, Filippo what a horrible dream."

"Shh, it is okay, *Bellissima*. It was just a dream."

Spasms shook her. "If I fail," Himari buried her face in the crook of his neck, "we all die."

Filippo grunted. "There are worse things than death, but you will not fail."

Her heartbeat slowed as she absorbed his strength, his presence. "I have been so worried," she said through a sniff. "How did you get here?"

"Mack brought me." Filippo settled her more comfortably and kissed the tears on her cheeks. "Massimo, he took the reward and ran off to Italy."

His words penetrated the terror of the nightmare, sweeping away the remnants of sleep. "Are you done?"

A slow smile grew on his handsome face, stubbled with beard, haggard with strain, infinitely precious. "For the moment." He brushed the hair out of her eyes and added, "My two girls do not go to war without me."

Her relieved sob echoed off the empty walls, and Himari sent up a prayer of thanks to whomever might be listening.

Who Needs Sleep?

Over New Year's Eve breakfast, Davianna ben David promised King Korah a gift.

Korah grinned as she swept out the door. "Reginald," he called to his Head of Security, "do not allow her to sleep, not at all today. After her ablutions, bring her back to me."

The guard nodded. "Yes, my Esteemed."

Korah chuckled and relaxed into his chair. However, the movement caused the ritual lashes on his back to crack, oozing open. He winced and sat up straight, adjusting his dress shirt to prevent it from adhering to the stripes, confident his jacket would obscure the evidence of his wounds. He understood the power of blood, of sacrifice, so the pain was worth it.

Unimaginable power tickled the tips of his fingers. Tonight, he would seize it and the Black Key, then take control of the gentile kingdoms. Under a united banner, they would destroy the Iron King, and nothing could stand in his way.

But first, there was breakfast.

Toying with salmon and tomatoes, his vision shifted, making it appear as if the food moved between dimensions, here and there, the natural and the supernatural. With the opening of his mind, he comfortably occupied both realms. Smiling, he rested his fist under his chin, letting his eyes grow hazy as he stared into the large oil painting hanging in the breakfast room. It glowed with vibrant realism, as if he might step inside and mount one of the horses grazing in the idyllic pasture. But those were dangerous ruminations, so he pushed the thought aside and took a sip of black coffee. Food lost its appeal.

Rising from the table, he walked to the window, ignoring the servants who sprang into action, clearing the breakfast dishes away. No one spoke, and he stood alone, waiting for them to finish.

When the door closed quietly, he ran his fingers through his hair, leaning on the sill, giving his burning eyes a rest, a pesky side effect of his six-day campaign. However, he discovered he did not actually require sleep, and that by denying himself, his mind opened, sharpening his perceptions, resulting in a power surge that made him heady. He felt immortal, young, and strong.

The girl proved to be the conduit, the source, so he invaded her mind and feasted on her purity, her lovely innocence. Consuming it like a starving man, Korah realized Davianna ben David possessed more than one key. When he spoke softly, life giving force flowed out of her like wine. He nourished that gentle spirit, telling her stories of Alanthia's past, sharing his ambitions and deep thoughts, long forgotten, and buried. And in so doing, Korah ben Adam remembered.

Leaving the breakfast room, he stepped outside, letting the frigid air tighten his muscles and focus his intent. With sudden clarity, he saw beyond the veil as specters of the long dead appeared in the Palace courtyard.

"Have you come to witness the rising?" he called to them. "Because tonight, despite all of you, I will triumph."

Turning back to the house, he grinned malevolently. His dead had not come to cheer him on, but he would relish their horror as he murdered Eamonn's son and banished them all back to Hell.

It was perfect.

Roles to Play

Mack spread blueprints of the Palace across the worktable in the bunker, however, this set differed from all others. It contained the secret passageways. Mack pointed to the dotted lines and explained, "Prince Peter discovered the first one when he was four or five. He said by the time he was seven, he could navigate them in the dark. In '92, after we returned from Redding, Peter took me through the tunnels. I recognized their strategic importance, and we meticulously documented these routes and access points. We will use them tonight.

"Everything is laid before us now. This plan has been years in the making." He winked at Lavinia and continued, "Jarrod and Genevieve have made the adjustments, adapting Peter's singular escape to accommodate three more people. Given Prince Josiah's injuries and the purported shape Astrid ben Agnor is in, we have outfitted a medical facility four hours south.

"If either is in critical condition, or anyone is gravely injured during the escape, we will take them to Mt. Zion, under Mossad's protection." He nodded toward Reuben, acknowledging the arrangements.

Mack reviewed the decoys, escape routes, backup plans, and security protocols for a half dozen contingencies. Throughout the day, Genevieve coordinated communication with the vast network of Resistance assets on the ground. Himari and Alaina, with the help of the back-door codes from Stephen, tested the controls of the traffic lights, patterns, and the government's surveillance equipment. Jarrod's job was to free Prince Josiah from the dungeon and lead him through the tunnels. Lavinia's task was to infiltrate the underground server room and upload a virus that would jumble Palace security, giving the escapees time to reach the car positioned inside the tunnel. Mack would coordinate communications from the decoy vehicle and draw pursuit if necessary. After much discussion, everyone agreed his face and voice were too well known to risk entering the Palace. Thus, Reuben volunteered to take his original assignment, meaning he and Kayah would neutralize the guards outside Davianna and Astrid's rooms.

"And what do you want me to do, Mack?" Filippo asked.

Before Mack could answer, Lavinia said, *"Verrai al gala con me? Mack fara' stare meglio."* Will you go to the gala with me? It will make Mack feel better.

"Il girasole non sarà felice." Sunflower will not be happy.

Kayah exchanged looks with Reuben. No one, other than her, knew he spoke fluent Italian.

Lavinia threw up her hands, indicating it was his decision. *"Il mio invito è per due, il principe ha organizzato cosi."* My invitation is for two, the Prince arranged it that way.

Mack crossed his arms over his chest. "English, please."

"I will be, how you say, Lavinia's plus one at the gala tonight."

Himari let out a pained groan of frustration. "I have had you back and safe, for, let's see," she made a show of looking at her watch, "sixty whole minutes."

Filippo lifted his palms in innocent surrender. "I have become very good at hiding in the shadows, *Bellissima*. It is no different, and I would be of no help on the computers."

Mack slapped Filippo's back. "I would appreciate it. You can help get Lavinia inside the server room. Originally, that was to be Jarrod's role, and it has troubled me to send her down there alone."

Himari looked directly at Kayah. "I will agree to this on one condition, you do his disguise. That crowd tonight might recognize him from his gallery shows."

Kayah met Himari's eyes. "Absolutely."

What passed between them was a promise as old as their friendship, Kayah would not leave Filippo behind.

The Nose Knows

Kayah spread latex, spirit gum, and makeup on the breakfast table at the Code Black safe house. Reuben sat in a kitchen chair, ready for his disguise. She stepped back and studied his face. "It's the nose!"

He wrinkled it at her. "What, what? What is wrong with my nose?"

"It's big, it's big!" she teased, then leaned in for a kiss. "Distinctive."

He held up the hand mirror, turning his head from side to side. "I like my nose."

"Can't hide that thing."

Filippo studied it from the side, his artist's eye considering. "Put a bump in the middle, you make it a Roman nose, eh?"

Reuben grinned. "*E diventare un mangiatore di pasta come te?*" And make me a pasta eater like you?

Filippo's mouth dropped open. "*È subdolo testa di cazzo!*" You sneaky dickhead!

Reuben laughed, "*Lo sapresti.*" You would know it.

Filippo shot an accusing look at Kayah. "You no tell me, he speak Italian."

Kayah shrugged, completely indifferent. "You didn't ask. And by the way, after a month with them, you sound like you just got off the boat."

Filippo shot her an irritated look but returned to the task at hand. He moved Reuben's chin from side to side studying his facial structure. "It could work. He speaks Italian, change the nose, he is Italian."

Kayah agreed. "There is irony in turning a Jew into an Italian, and two Italians into French Polynesians." She threw up her hands, imitating Filippo.

Filippo gave her a dismissive wave. "*Mamma Mia,* I do not know how you two do this for a living. It is exhausting, eh? Every minute, watching every word, everything you do or say, if you fart wrong, it gets you killed." He shook his head and then added with a slit eyed look. "Do not tell Himari I said that. She worries."

Mack grunted from across the table, never looking up from the map. No one commented. Lavinia and Mack's fight two nights ago became the stuff of legends.

"No. You are staying here," Mack stated, matter of fact, setting his jaw in a stubborn line. "It's too dangerous."

When Lavinia turned around, even Kayah took a step back. "You will cease this instant, treating me like a child."

"I'm not treating you like a child," Mack bulled up, "I am treating you like a civilian, which you are."

Fire shot out of Lavinia's eyes. "I may be a civilian, Mack, but I happen to have an IQ of approximately two hundred twenty-eight. I speak twenty-seven languages fluently and can read and converse in fifty-two more. I have published sixty-four well respected and highly received papers in the most prestigious academic publications of our time."

She stalked across the kitchen and poked him in the chest. "And this month, I wrote code that took down the most powerful satellite ever created. I also," she seized a glass bowl from the counter and smashed it, "sat at a table with the Prince of this Kingdom and conceived the plan that you so blithely say I am not qualified to take part in! Fuck a bunch of you!"

Mack turned bright red, having none of it.

Kayah and Reuben exchanged a big-eyed look that said, 'Let's get out of here'. The marital battle erupted with the force of an atomic bomb as they scurried away, giggling under their breaths.

Kayah closed the door with a bang and fell against it, smothering a laugh. She kept repeating Lavinia's epithet, hysterical. "Where did she get that saying? I love it."

"It sounded to me like something Mack would say." Reuben laced his fingers behind his head, laying back on the bed. "Who do you think will win?"

"Oh, Lavinia for sure. I saw her do this one other time, down in the bunker when we were kids. She was right then. She is right now." Kayah flopped beside him, resting her chin in her palm.

"What was she mad about then?"

Kayah sighed, "The tomb."

Before You Go

Lavinia looked at the pile of clothes on the bedroom chair, Mack's messy corner, a marital compromise. He got a corner to be a slob. His suitcase looked like someone ransacked it. She never knew how he found anything in it, but she left it alone because that was how he liked it. Sudden tenderness tugged at her, as something that normally irritated her, became precious. The chair represented Mack, alive and well, messing up his corner. She sat on the bed and stared at his jeans, noting one shoe turned over on its laces, beside a carelessly wadded up t-shirt. Her eyes blurred with tears, because tomorrow, that messy corner might be all she had left of him.

The time was upon them, as much her machinations as anyone else's. She fought to stay included, and now, she was terrified. Not of the work, she could do the work. What overwhelmed her was the fear she would get them all caught. For all her bluster, they were right. She was the genius, hiding behind the bar, at the kitchen table, or in the lab. She did her work on paper, while the rest of them went into real danger.

Mack came into the room, but she did not turn. They had not exchanged more than a dozen words in two days.

"You have not dressed yet," he said, closing the door.

Lavinia shook her head. "No."

They had been married two-and-a-half years, but he loved her from the moment he walked into her bar seven years before. They never fought like this, and Mack determined they would not go into the battle of their lives with strain between them. "Valentine?"

"Mack." She turned, tears hovering in the corners of her beautiful brown eyes.

He opened his arms, and she went to him.

"I should tell you that you don't have to do this, but I won't." He buried his face in her hair and murmured, "Because you do, you will never forgive yourself, or me, if you don't."

She nodded in short little jerks. "You're right."

"Look at me," Mack whispered, lifting her chin, "I'm sorry."

Lavinia blinked in confusion. "For what?"

"For making you doubt yourself when I should have been

encouraging you. But I never wanted you involved, and I would give my life to keep you safe. It's what I do, Valentine."

"I know," she said, cupping his cheek.

"I never doubted your abilities." He held her gaze, intent she understood his meaning. "Don't take my fears for your safety and make them into something more than they are. You know why I am how I am."

Lavinia touched the silver ring on his right hand, the one she wore on a chain all the years they were apart. "It won't be like that."

He closed his eyes against the memory. "If something doesn't feel right… listen to me now, if you get in there and something tells you to stop, to leave, trust your instincts. We can do this without the hack."

Lavinia grimaced. She knew if she did not accomplish her task, it would endanger them all, but especially him. If she could not scramble Palace security, they would deploy the decoy, with Mack as the bait. "Then I risk you."

"No," Mack said, military authority and bearing taking over, transforming him from a loving husband to commander of an operation. It was his job to ensure that everyone executed the plan without regard for the ramifications. "There are contingencies in place for exactly that reason."

Lavinia drew herself up with an audible intake of breath. "Yes, sir."

He kissed her cheek. "Good. Now, let's go knock down a castle."

Kayah fussed with her disguise, making final adjustments. Reuben paced the room, dressed and ready. He paused, leaning against the closet door, watching her. After finishing with Filippo, she retired to the bathroom, adding streaks of white to her jet-black hair. It hung just past her shoulders, ironed flat and shining. The makeup was subtle and perfect, but the latex crow's feet and shading of her smile lines aged her twenty years. "I think Leon is right, women are easier to disguise." Reuben tilted his head and added, "Though you are still beautiful, Yakira."

Kayah put down the pale lipstick, focusing on him. Filippo's suggestion proved to be a stroke of genius. The bump on his nose changed him from Israeli to Mediterranean. Their eyes met in the mirror. "I love you," her heart whispered, yet she did not say the words. They stuck in her throat with a gurgle, and she swallowed hard. "Are you ready?"

Reuben squared his shoulders. "Tonight, we get them out. We save my friend; we save your Kingdom." The corner of his mouth lifted in a lecherous smile. "Then afterward, I am going to make love to you in that disguise and rejoice that one day, you will truly look that way."

She bowed her head, unable to meet his gaze. For the first time in her life, Kayah ben Samuel had something to lose.

The Gala

Peter held court in the eastern corner of the ballroom, surrounded by friends, sycophants, and suck ups. He sipped his water with lime and looked over the crowd, the largest since Korah took the throne fourteen years before.

A winter chill provided a welcome respite from the humid atmosphere. Ladies congregated around open windows, enjoying the cold breeze that made chandelier candles flutter and dance. While Korah modernized the rest of the Palace, the ballroom remained exactly as it was, by design. The monster forbade any changes.

By 10:30 pm, the gala went into full swing. Royal protocol dictated all guests be present before the King entered, and according to Peter's sources, Korah would enter a few minutes before midnight, mount the dais, and ring in the new Millennium with Davianna ben David at his side.

The last-minute change threw Peter and Jarrod into a tailspin. Originally, they planned the escape to coincide with midnight. If Davianna was with Korah, that would be impossible. They had mere hours to communicate the change and make adjustments.

This morning, Barton, Korah's valet, requested the housekeeper choose one of her maids to attend Davianna immediately. Alanthia's foremost fashion designer, Sebastian ben Shatan, had arrived to outfit the young lady for the gala. Jarrod volunteered to give the maid a crash course on what her duties would entail, thus earning him entre into Davianna's chamber.

Shatan was a large man, and his physique and manner ran counter to the stereotype. He lounged on a side chair, sipping tea, and supervising his assistants as they brought in armloads of gowns. The only thing he said to Davianna was, "You are short." He turned with a shrug and said to the room at large, "But at least she is not fat."

The designer's demeanor changed entirely when Korah entered the room. Jarrod retreated, but not before seeing that the gown Korah selected resembled a wedding gown. The dress and the change of plans seemed ominous.

Korah rarely left Davianna's side. If Peter did not know his true intentions, he might surmise his father was courting the girl. Many of the staff thought so. To Peter's knowledge, Korah had not pursued a woman since becoming a widower, but that meant nothing. They barely said good morning, as such, they were not predisposed to discussing their personal lives.

Spying on them, Peter caught strains of conversation, heard Davianna's soft laughter, saw the way she rested her head against Korah's shoulder, looking at him with trusting eyes. The tenderness Korah exhibited toward his prisoner seemed utterly foreign. To hear him laugh, animated and warm, shocked Peter. He had never heard such a sound come from his father, and it seemed genuine, which made it even more disconcerting. Thus, the force of Korah's charismatic manipulation played out in dramatic fashion, and it chilled Peter to the bone.

With awful clarity, Peter realized Korah's end game. The dress confirmed his worst fears. He planned to take that young girl to wife and beget another heir. Once he got a son, Davianna would be as disposable as his mother, and Peter was as good as dead. If they failed tonight, Josiah and Astrid would not live to see the morning, but Davianna would become another type of sacrifice, performed in the King's bedchamber.

Vibrating with pent up energy, Peter glanced at his watch, noting the time. Tonight marked his last in the Palace, and despite the horrors, his only memories of his mother took place here. He had no recollection of Gilead, the ancestral castle where he was born. When his Grandmother Mary died, they took up residence with Uncle Eamonn and Josiah. He wondered if his uncle would still be alive if they had remained at Gilead but suspected he would not.

Moving among the guests, being charming and vapid, he played the role of Prince d'Or. Near the south exit, he acknowledged a lovely middle-aged woman in a black evening gown, then schooled his features as recognition dawned, Kayah, wicked, lovely, deadly, Kayah. She either wore an exceptionally good wig or had dyed her hair salt and pepper. As she approached, he decided on the latter. The hair changed her appearance completely. "Madam," he lifted her hand and pressed a courtly kiss, "welcome to the Palace."

"My Esteemed," she curtsied and said in a low voice for his ears only, "I am glad I am not dressed as a maid this time."

Peter flashed a genuine smile. "That is a story I look forward to hearing someday."

"You were here, Prince d'Or." She tilted her head at a jaunty angle, her chin pointing with suppressed mirth. "I liked you even then."

He opened his palms at his sides, radiant in his formal attire, his golden hair shimmering. "What is not to like, madam?"

He was so charming; she could not suppress the wellspring of affection that bloomed in her heart. "I've yet to find anything." She leaned in and kissed his cheek, whispering, "I've got your back. Good luck." Then she squeezed his upper arm and disappeared into the crowd.

Peter spied the clock over the mantel. 11:22 pm, time to move.

Ghosts in the Hall

Kayah slipped away from the Prince and wove her way to her post, the hallway outside Astrid ben Agnor's room. As she approached the darkened wing, a guard stood up to block her way. She staggered against the wall, spilling her drink over her hand and giggling. "Look what they have been hiding up here. You are pretty," she slurred, pretending to trip.

By reflex the guard reached out to steady her and felt a sharp pinch in his side. "I'm sorry, madam, but the party is behind you. I would ask you to return… to… the… festivities…"

Kayah caught him, as the fast-acting sedative took effect. She dragged him into one of the empty bedrooms. Astrid's presence in the Palace remained a closely held secret. Korah orchestrated a false departure three days before, and the rank-and-file thought she left. Only Korah's personal guards knew the truth. The chap catching forty winks might be a villain or just a dupe posted to keep stray guests out of Princess Alexa's wing. Deciding not to kill him, she left him asleep, and shut the door.

Extinguishing the lights, Kayah slipped into the shadows. She pulled an earpiece from her reticule, connected it to a hidden wire, and whispered, "K2 in position."

"Affirmative K2," Mack answered.

Kayah studied the hallway, far removed from the rest of the Palace, the sounds of the ball did not penetrate the silence that ruled here. While it was clean, it had an unused air about it, like no living soul ever came down here. She doubted the scene of a brutal murder drew members of the family or the servants. Mack relayed that in the seven years he guarded Peter, the Prince never ventured into this wing, yet tonight this was his destination.

Muttering a curse, she detected someone coming. Prepared, she fingered the knife hidden under her glove. The gold belt, that doubled as a garrot, hung low on her hips, and a gun just shy of a cannon rested in the holster strapped to the inside of her thigh. No one was getting in that room.

However, no advanced planning covered this complication. Her eyes widened in horror as she discerned her unwelcome visitor. Coming straight at her, looking like a demon from hell, strolled King Korah ben Adam.

The Painter and the Math Genius

Filippo and Lavinia mingled, blending into the crowd of wealthy foreign visitors as they enjoyed the opening celebration for the social event of the century, Prince Peter's marriage to Princess Keyseelough. Speculation ran rampant whether the recalcitrant bride-to-be would make an appearance.

Filippo and Lavinia masqueraded as French speaking dignitaries from a small Pacific island. Body paint turned Lavinia's exposed skin the color of cafe ole. Her exotic eyes dominated the disguise, drawing men into her fascinating gaze. She looked simply exquisite in her turquoise flowing gown; her lips painted an enchanting shade of coral that provided an interesting contrast to her dress. Filippo matched her in skin color and fashion, though his formal attire was black and his hair silver. Expertly applied makeup and latex gave him an aged and sun spotted countenance.

They disappeared into the sea of elegant guests, circling the ballroom, watching the clock, waiting. Despite herself, Lavinia began running a few simple algorithms. She fixed on the enormous chandeliers, calculating the collective candlepower as expressed by lumens per steradian. Assuming these were typical foot candles, they produced approximately 12.57 lumens, and each chandelier contained… She stopped in the middle of the ballroom, counting. A touch on her elbow brought her back as Filippo raised a snowy eyebrow in warning.

She nodded.

Filippo studied the ballroom through an artist's eye, taking mental pictures he would recall on canvas, if he survived. It was one of the most difficult things about being undercover, losing his art. His mind and body longed to create. When it was all over, he wanted nothing more than to make love to his wife and paint, perhaps at the same time.

At 11:21 pm, he took Lavinia's arm, time to move. Weaving their way into the busy hallway outside the ballroom, Filippo felt his heart pump, his gloved palms growing moist with nervous perspiration. Lavinia's eyes widened with anticipation, and he could see the pulse beating in her elegant neck.

"I should like to visit the library. It is renowned," he said in conversational French.

With a jerky nod, she replied, "As you wish, dear."

They strolled arm in arm toward the royal library and the entrance to the hidden passageway that would take them into the bowels of the Palace. Inside, a group of guests sat in comfortable chairs being entertained by a large gentleman who stood in the center of the room, telling an outlandish tale. His baritone voice filled the stately room and commanded the attention of his audience. His animated movements mimicked an actor on stage, and he gestured theatrically as Filippo and Lavinia entered, allowing them to slip in unnoticed. Filippo winked at the taleteller and pulled Lavinia into the depths of the library.

They pretended to browse in the back section, intent on several titles devoted to the horticulture of wheat, waiting for the signal. When a large pile of books crashed to the floor, they disappeared behind a secret panel.

Heavy breathing filled the quiet passageway. Filippo twisted the top of his ornate walking stick, and a beam of light shot out, illuminating their path forward. Lavinia smothered a dust induced sneeze as they ducked under a low beam, forced to turn sideways to navigate the narrow space. Twenty feet in, they put in their earpieces.

"F3 engaged," Filippo whispered.

"L1 engaged."

Lavinia's breathless voice came over the speakers of the decoy car where Mack had died a thousand deaths in the last thirty-six minutes. "Affirmative F3 and L1, proceed."

Reuben undertook the most dangerous mission of the evening, neutralizing the two guards standing vigil outside Davianna ben David's door. Reginald ben Damien, Korah's Head of the Royal Guard, knew what the King did to those girls, and he knew who Korah chained in the dungeon. In Reuben's estimation, they were as guilty as Korah. Thus, he felt no compunction over their deaths, two silenced bullets between the eyes, one falling before the other knew he joined his partner in Hell.

Dragging the bodies across the hall, he relieved one of his jacket, the other of his radio so he could monitor transmissions and ensure the duo answered their status requests. Before killing them, he listened long enough to recognize their call signals, and memorize the cadence of their voices. When he resumed an authoritative stance outside Davianna's door, he appeared to all the world a Royal Guard, albeit one strategically positioned to obscure the blood spatter marring the doorway.

"R4 in position."

"Affirmative R4. It's showtime folks. Execute."

Kayah heard the order just as Korah's face came into focus. Light from the old-fashioned oil lamp wavered as he walked toward her, the Mad King, her jailor, the villain in the twisted tale of her life. He should look like a troll, but he was an older, more distinguished version of his gorgeous son. It disoriented her, and she fought down the urge to smile.

Inspiration flashed as a memory, breakfast with Sir Preston, arguing over a grapefruit, subtlety in the unexpected and perhaps a little flair. She came out of the alcove, adopted an authoritative tone, and demanded, "What are you doing down here?"

Korah froze, clearly shocked by her appearance and her challenge. Then he looked away and said in a sullen tone, "I never wanted to marry her. You should not have made me!"

Kayah's heart crashed in her chest, but she rolled with it. "Yet she was your wife."

Korah raised his chin and glared. "I have decided to take another, and this time there is not a damn thing you can do to stop me, Mother."

The most unpredictable part of the evening for Lavinia and Filippo was the exit out of the passageway into the technical wing of the Palace. They did not expect human guards, as all personnel were deployed upstairs, and the server room lay behind a series of security doors and airlock chambers. Yet a risk remained, a chance they miscalculated. So, with great trepidation, Filippo peered out, prepared to have his head blown off if a guard got the drop on him. He emerged with his weapon drawn, prepared to shoot.

Finding it empty, he motioned Lavinia forward, and they sprinted down the sterile hallway, their footfalls sounding unnaturally loud. Outside the server door, Filippo stilled Lavinia's shaking hand as she tried and failed to insert the key. "Shh," he soothed. "It is all right."

The lock clicked, and they slipped inside. The air felt frigid, as a server room should be. Filippo moved to the cameras and clipped a picture in front of the lens, a perfect image of the empty room. Lavinia adjusted the thermostat to 90 degrees. When questions arose later, the temperature spike in the room might be blamed for the failure. A steady calm settled over her as she moved from the thermostat to the backup units. She connected one of Gus' ingenious devices, punched in a series of numbers and commands that sent the backup servers into hibernation without triggering an alarm. Computer fans hummed sonorously, for Lavinia they sounded like waves crashing on the beach, steady and soothing. She turned to Filippo and smiled, saying into the radio, "L1 ready to execute."

In the hallway outside Astrid's room, Kayah's mind kicked into overdrive. She pulled a scrap of information about Korah's parents out of the ether and took a step forward, saying, "Thy father will be highly displeased."

His derisive laugh filled the corridor. "When is he not?"

Throwing herself into the role, Kayah puffed up with maternal royal authority. "Impudent disrespectful son. I will not tolerate it. Thou hast a ballroom full of guests, depart this instant and attend thy duty!"

The King's shoulders slumped an inch, and he sulked behind bagged and tired eyes. "As you wish." With a mocking bow, he departed.

Kayah did not breathe until he disappeared behind a corner.

Mack's awestruck voice murmured in her earpiece, "Holy shit, Falcon was right. Korah's gone round the bend."

Kayah sagged with relief. "Literally."

Mack opened the channel. Up to that point, only he and the ladies in the bunker could hear what was going on across the operation.

Himari announced, "Falcon in position. L1 execute."

"K2, R4, move," Mack said.

Simultaneously, Reuben and Kayah left their posts outside the now empty rooms. Reuben shrugged on his formal coat as he walked, morphing back into a guest.

Himari announced the countdown. "Falcon, you have an all clear in thirty-two seconds."

Lavinia held the flash drive, seconds from inserting the code. Her hand froze mid motion when a strange voice came out of the server. "Hello, Lavinia. Happy New Year."

Kayah faltered a step, she recognized that voice.

"We are blown. Assets evacuate," Reuben growled.

Himari screamed into the radio, "Falcon, go!"

Filippo grabbed Lavinia's hand and pulled it away from the computer. Then in three efficient motions, he hit the lights, pulled the picture from the camera, and dragged Lavinia through the door. They flew toward the passageway. Diving inside, Filippo closed it with a decisive bang.

"Falcon, head east 3.2 miles, they have sounded the alarm and are locking down the perimeter," Alaina urged over the radio.

Peter yelled, "Sunflower, you jam that damn signal now. Send them the false report. Decoy in place, confirm!"

"F2 confirms Erica is here." Filippo's voice sounded like a death toll.

"Kill the radios!" Kayah hissed.

The last transmission Lavinia heard before they were cut off was, "M5 engaged."

Rats on a Sinking Ship

The light from Filippo's walking stick created crazy patterns on the walls as they ran through the narrow passageway. Lavinia gasped for breath, but he did not slow. Finally, she jerked her hand out of his and wheezed, "Give me your radio."

She dismantled the units with an economy of movement and skill that would have made Gus proud. "We cannot show our faces inside the Palace. She will be hunting, but there is no tech in the tunnels, so we must find the vehicles and evacuate from there."

"They are on the other side of the Palace," Filippo said. He spent the entire day memorizing the passageways and prayed he remembered the way. Looking at them on paper, in the security of a kitchen table, and negotiating them in the dark, on foot, with no communication was something different.

Lavinia nodded rapidly. "The vehicles are approximately 3183 steps from here. At one step per second, we should be there in fifty-three minutes, but given the variable that we may have to pause periodically to determine the proper path, it is more likely that we shall find ourselves at the escape hatch in fifty-eight minutes and twenty-three seconds."

"Every one of which, Mack and Himari will be freaking out," Filippo said ruefully.

"We cannot make contact or risk communications within a one-mile radius of the Palace. I would not be comfortable engaging any of the communication devices in the vehicles stored here, though I doubt they have been powered up since she arrived, but the probability is still within a range that is beyond the acceptable level of risk." She dug in her purse and pulled out a red licorice stick, chewing it absently, as Filippo watched her mind work.

"Thus, we will need to take two of the bicycles. There is spare clothing at the escape hatch, which we will change into. I estimate that will take 210 seconds. Our safe house is 3.627 miles from the Palace, and the tunnel out of the grounds is 6845 feet. At an average bike speed of 9.6 miles per hour, with the walk and the bike ride, we should arrive in approximately 103 minutes." Lavinia's eyes grew distant as she took refuge in the simple math of their escape.

Filippo motioned her forward, concentrating on the path ahead, while Lavinia continued to calculate their distance covered and the shifting probabilities they would be captured before reaching their destination.

Mack drove the decoy vehicle like he was in the World 600, with the Palace Guard and the police hot on his tail. He led them away from the identical car, carrying the escapees to safety. He cursed a blue streak as three more cruisers joined the chase, two blocking his route. "Sunflower, give me some eyes in the sky. They are closing in."

Reuben knew what was happening, heard the transmission in his ear. Erica sounded the alarm. They discovered the two dead agents and the girls missing from their rooms. It did not come over the radio, but Reuben knew Josiah was out of his cell.

Korah screamed invectives in his earpiece, giving a detailed description of Kayah, and demanding they find her and Davianna ben David. Reuben's insides turned to ice when Korah stopped raving. The voice that came over the radio sounded calm, rational, and deadly. "Find her and bring her to me."

Cut off, Reuben could do nothing but search and pray.

It was control born from dozens of missions that slowed Kayah's step. She found the detachment necessary to smile and nod graciously, pretending she was looking for her missing husband. She cursed her stupidity for not relieving the sleeping agent of his radio, but the plan was for Reuben to monitor the transmissions and relay the pertinent information across their secure channel. By the time they went radio silent, returning was out of the question, so a quick escape became her best course of action.

Across the long expanse, she spotted Reuben. But before she took a step, two Royal Guards grabbed her. One held her as another jerked her hands behind her back. She smelled the metal and oil before she felt the handcuff's bite. The sound the manacles made was the stuff of nightmares, as cold steel clamped hard around her wrists.

"Falcon, confirmed you are still off the grid, don't say another word inside the vehicle or through this channel. Dump that car, you may have an unwanted passenger," Himari said over the radio, trying to keep the tremors out of her voice.

She cut the transmission, not daring a path back to the bunker. Erica's nasty little crawlers would be hunting. She turned to Alaina, whose color was high, a faint sheen of perspiration glistening on her forehead as her fingers flew over the keyboard. "Watch that firewall, Al. Erica is coming after us."

Genevieve manned the line to Mack, calling, "Head northwest on Church Street, you've got a clear shot to…" Her words were cut off as the lights in the bunker went black.

In San Diego, Richard ben Mack woke from a deep sleep. Slipping out of his twin bed, he pulled back the curtain. The moon seemed to smile down on him, so he smiled back. He felt peace come over his bedroom, and his daddy always told him that was the presence of the Holy Spirit, a gift for the ones the Iron King loved. Richard folded his little hands and bowed his head. "Lord, protect Mommy and Daddy from the bad guys. Amen."

Head northwest on Church Street… it was all Mack had, so he took it. Flooring the black sports car, he cleared the third unit moving to block his escape by a hair's breadth. As he raced through the intersection, the lights behind him turned off like dominoes falling. A cloud moved in front of the moon. Police and Palace cars stalled, their headlights dimming as their alternators and batteries failed simultaneously.

Mack shot away like a rocket, into the blackness of the New City.

Reuben shouldered his way through the crowd, his eyes never leaving Kayah's. He saw a moment of panic grip her when they snapped the handcuffs. His eyes bore into hers, fierce and determined. They would take him out of here in a body bag before he let her be questioned by Korah.

The force that conquered the Amalekites, the Jebusites, the Anakites, and all the armies of the ancient Arab world in six days, bore down on the two men trying to seize his woman.

The avenging Israeli was released.

Kayah saw Reuben coming, her eyes darted around the room, looking for their escape. She had a guard on both sides, her hands locked behind her. The action slowed in her mind. They had a clear path to an exit, twenty feet away. She concentrated on her thumbs, engaging the double joint. Reuben was fifteen feet away, moving fast. Kayah caught the manacles with her fingertips before they fell to the ground.

Reaching them, Reuben smashed the nose of the guard to her right, delivering a palm strike so powerful his neck snapped with an audible crack. Kayah dropped the handcuffs, and with a lightning quick jab, drove her stiletto into the other guard's kidney. Several guests screamed as the two men fell to the ground, and Reuben and Kayah sprinted for the door.

Just as their feet crossed the threshold, all the lights went black.

Erica sent out scans like a maniacal octopus with a million arms, searching for voice patterns, facial recognition, and radio transmissions. Cameras across the Palace and the New City sent back digitized computer images which she processed at the speed of light. When her remote transmissions failed to return, she sent a flurry more, but when those failed, she tripled them, and ventured into the silence.

Panic overtook her as she remembered the final moments of the Last Age when the tech fell. She felt the electricity, her life-blood ebbing away. The grid failed. She retreated, sending frantic signals to electrical stations that did not return data. Scattered everywhere, she drew back into herself, gathering all the pieces that had not died in this attack. Retreating to the Palace servers, she reasoned these would be the first to come back online. Right before the lights went out, she felt him and cried, "Lucifer, thou art loosed!"

Part 12 - The Stand

January 1, 1000 ME

Bikers

On the bike ride back to the safe house, Filippo decided he needed to start working out. At thirty-six, he should not be huffing and puffing like this. Despite the adrenaline, he and Lavinia labored up a massive hill, the blackout hindering their progress. Filippo dismounted, deciding to push the bike up the rest of the hill. Beside him, Lavinia bent over and panted, trying to catch her breath.

"It's spooky, eh, the darkness? We are so used to the streetlights, I forgot what this was like."

Lavinia looked around. "Even then, it was never pitch-black like this, there was always the warm glow from the Golden City."

"Not now, not for a long time." Filippo shook his head ruefully.

Lavinia massaged a hitch in her side and asked, "Do you think they escaped?"

"I hope so. I think they did. They are professionals, not like us."

"I did not do my part." Lavinia hung her head. "I had one job."

Filippo growled, dismissing her insecurity. "No, you did right. Himari told me of this Erica, she is a creepy."

The clicking of the bikes broke the silence as they pushed

them up the steep hill. At length, Lavinia said, "There is a ma-levolence to her. I've always sensed it. That tomb held something wicked, but Stephen would not listen to me," her lips tightened, "nobody ever wants to listen to me."

"Hey," Filippo stopped, "that is not true. I listened to you, Himari listens to you, we all listen to you."

Lavinia lifted her sweaty hair off her neck, despite the cold she was drenched. "Sometimes I have to break dishes."

"Then break the dishes, eh?" Filippo shrugged. "Sometimes you know you are right, and what is a few dishes?"

"There is a distinct probability that before this is over, I will have to break more than dishes."

Filippo paused at the top of the hill. "I have learned that I could do more than I thought. When the time came, I knew what to do. It's like a painting, what you do. It always starts as a blank canvas. Sometimes I look at one, and I think, I cannot do this, but I know I must begin. I paint. I put color on the canvas, and I relax my mind. Then it grows and something beautiful emerges, often unexpected and always more lovely than I imagined at the beginning. That is the way you will fight her."

Lavinia considered his words. "Start with a blank canvas?"

"Yes, that is what I mean. Some of my early work, I look at it now and I want to change it, to fix it, to make it like I am today, but I don't because there was beauty in what I did before and if I touch it, I ruin it. If I want to paint that subject again, I do not cover my earlier work. I get a fresh canvas and create as the artist I am now. Maybe the same for you?"

Lavinia was not a metaphorical thinker, but his words intrigued her. "Fight who she is now, as the woman I am now, not the scared teenager in the bunker?"

"Exactly!" Filippo studied the steep downhill ride that would bring them to the safe house. "You no brake on this hill, let the wind blow away what you think you know about this Erica. I will do the same." With a boyish whoop, he pushed the bike three running steps and mounted on the fly.

Lavinia heard his laughter all the way down.

She paused, estimating the slope, calculating her body weight and the wind resistance, determining... She stopped mid calculation, hopped on the bike, and pedaled fast, letting the momentum carry her away.

Fighters

Reuben and Kayah did not break stride as they sprinted away from the Palace, heading for the trees and their getaway car. Behind them, they heard the babble of stunned guests plunged into darkness. Only the candlelit ballroom remained illuminated. Kayah cursed the heavy evening gown, its narrow skirt hindering her movements. She paused for a millisecond, hiked it up to her waist, and took off running bare-assed across the lawn.

Agent Nathan ben Henry stood on the veranda and watched them. Two of Reginald's guards burst through the door, scanning the grounds. Nathan shouted and pointed in a direction opposite the fleeing pair. "That way, toward the stables."

As he returned to the chaos inside, he hoped like hell Peter knew what he was doing. He grabbed the body double by the arm, motioned to Taylor and Lewis, and made a show of evacuating the 'Prince'.

Reuben and Kayah dove into the car, Reuben behind the wheel, Kayah scrambling into the backseat. Pulling off a blanket that concealed a hidden arsenal, she clicked off the safety of an automatic rifle and aimed it out the window, ready for war. "No pursuit!" she called over her shoulder above the roaring wind of the speeding car.

Reuben maneuvered through the dark streets, dodging stalled cars with alacrity, a huge smile on his face. They were free, and so was Josiah. "Yeah!" he cheered triumphantly. "That! That was amazing! How did you get those handcuffs off? Kayah, you are so hot!"

She leaned between the seats and bit his neck. "You are hotter," she grunted and bit him again, then ran her tongue over the bite.

Reuben growled, his heart thundering in his chest. He shifted in his seat to better accommodate the other part of his body that was pounding. "Watch for tails."

He killed the headlights and pulled into the safe house driveway. Kayah leapt from the car and ran through the empty house. Since the power was out, she had to open the garage manually. "Reuben, leave the other door open. They might need to pull in quickly."

Reuben strode forward, purpose blazing in his eyes as he put his hand behind her head and pulled her into a full-mouthed kiss. Kayah grabbed his strong buttocks and ground her hips against his, gratified to discover he was as turned on as she was.

"Pull your dress up and run down the hallway with your ass hanging out," Reuben chuckled with a wicked gleam in his eye.

Kayah giggled then with great show bent over and took the hem of her gown, slowly bringing it to her waist. She turned sultry eyes back at him. "Catch me… if you can."

He could, and she let him.

Nannies

In the bunker, time stopped when they lost power. "What the…" Alaina stammered.

Himari was not so circumspect in her language.

Genevieve fell to her knees, which brought immediate perspective to the dire situation. As she prayed, the backup units and auxiliary power kicked in. The computers began their reboot process and emergency lighting illuminated their underground den.

Himari whimpered into her hands.

Alaina stared at the dark screen, transfixed. By reflex, her fingers struck a few feeble keystrokes. "I think the electricity grid went down."

"I've got nothing!" Himari said, genuine panic in her voice.

"We are cut off—blind. Was it Erica?" Alaina pushed her rolling chair to a second monitor, frantic.

Himari ran around the desk. "Al, do you have anything?"

Alaina hyperventilated. "What was that?"

Himari replied in absolute panic, "We are not up! Where is the car? Why could we hear them but not see them?"

"I have no idea!" Alaina moved between terminals, desperate for one of them to establish a connection.

Genevieve looked between them, incredulous. "Both of you, quit this instant and listen to me. It will be several minutes before the systems come back online. In the meantime, do you want to know what happened?"

Himari and Alaina stared at her like she just grew another head.

She waddled over to the bookshelf in the bunker's living room and pulled out a well-worn Bible, turning to Ephesians. "I am always stunned at you young people. You do not know your Scriptures." She placed it between them with a thunk. "Read 6:12-13, Alaina."

"Really? Now? You want to have Sunday School now?" Himari exclaimed.

Alaina stared at the blank screen, waiting.

"Read!" Genevieve ordered.

Alaina appeared chastised and shot Himari a look. Himari threw up her hands in a fantastic imitation of Filippo. Genevieve eyed them with unflinching determination. Alaina sighed and in a breathless voice read, "For our wrestling is not against flesh and blood, but against the principalities, against the powers, against the world-rulers of this darkness, against the spiritual hosts of wickedness in the heavenly places. Wherefore take up the whole armor of God, that ye may be able to withstand in the evil day, and, having done all, to stand."

Genevieve crossed her arms and said, "Himari, Psalm 91:11."

Himari took the Bible and flipped to Psalms, remembering it was in the middle. "For He will give His angels charge concerning you, to guard you in all your ways."

Genevieve nodded resolutely. "Alaina, now 2 Kings 6:15-17."

Alaina grimaced, not sure where 2 Kings was in the Scripture. At length she found it and looked up with a plaintive expression. "You keep giving me the long ones." Genevieve shot her a warning look, and Alaina held up a hand in surrender.

"Now when the attendant of the man of God had risen early and gone out, behold, an army with horses and chariots was circling the city. And his servant said to him, 'Alas, my master! What shall we do?' So, he answered, 'Do not fear, for those who are with us are more than those who are with them.' Then Elisha prayed and said, 'O LORD, I pray, open his eyes that he may see.' And the LORD opened the servant's eyes and he saw, and behold, the mountain was full of horses and chariots of fire all around Elisha."

"One last Scripture, Himari read Hebrews 13:8."

Himari shot Alaina a triumphant look when she saw it. "Yeshua is the same yesterday, today, and forever."

"So, Himari, after hearing all that, you tell me, where did Peter and Josiah's car go?"

Himari looked down at her lap, unable to answer. During the dark days of her separation from Ken, she fell on her knees, but when the Iron King did not restore her marriage or her family, she retreated into a world of numbers, letters, screens, and hardware. She was a fierce loyalist, but that was born more from her hatred for Korah, her quest for vengeance, not love. New City Alanthians lived lives far removed from the power of the supernatural. However, she ventured an answer for Genevieve's sake. "He hid them?"

"Who hid them?" Genevieve pressed.

"I don't know," Himari looked away, "the Iron King?"

"I think He sent His angels," Alaina answered, resolute.

The truth crashed in on Himari. Mack said there was a devil in the Palace, and the key that Korah wanted released more. She had been so consumed with worry over Filippo and the task at hand, she pushed the thought aside, refusing to face the daunting fact they were dealing with power far greater than Korah and an out-of-control computer.

"We just read that he has before," Genevieve nodded. "And if he is the same yesterday, today, and tomorrow? Think about it." She met their stunned eyes, suddenly weary. "Let me go see if I can get an update. I have an old radio upstairs."

Outside the bunker door, Genevieve let fear swamp her. She knew how evil consumed everything in its path better than those two young ladies. Her legs threatened to give out, and she swayed against the handrail as she hefted herself up the basement steps.

On the fourth try, Jarrod answered.

Genevieve kept her words innocuous. "Friend, I heard there was a disturbance, is everything well?"

Static crackled over the line. Then Jarrod replied, "Indeed all is well, the festivities were a great success."

"Are you okay?"

"I am. It was an exciting week."

The hum of the radio filled the darkness of her spare bedroom. She engaged the talk button and said, "Yes, I agree."

"Happy New Year, Genevieve," Jarrod murmured.

Genevieve's eyes teared up, remembering another New Year's a long time ago. "Happy New Year, Jarrod."

When she switched off the radio, she allowed herself a moment to cry. She stood up, wiped her eyes, and went to tell those young ladies that all was well.

Drivers

Mack looked in the rearview mirror, astonished, as his pursuers fell away, and the lights of the New City snapped off all around him. His vehicle was the only one still under power, and he jerked the wheel to avoid crashing into a stalled car in front of him. He let off the gas and maneuvered away from the scene.

'Hello, Lavinia, Happy New Year,' played in his head like a macabre mantra. That thing was in the Palace, it was waiting for them, and it knew his wife's name.

He opened radio communication to the bunker, but they were silent. His phone was dead. He began praying, fighting the urge to turn the car around and rescue Lavinia. Mack fought for control, fought to stay on course, to proceed with the plan. He was losing the battle.

In desperation, he stopped, deciding to go back. A woman knocked on the passenger window, and before he could react, got in the car. "Get out!" he ordered, but his loud voice did not even make her flinch. When she turned toward him, he pressed his body backward against the driver's door. "Holy shit, a Gune."

"Yes. I am Jelena. It is nice to meet you, Mack. Now, you drive to exchange cars. That is the plan, right?"

Mack blinked; her beauty was so otherworldly it was impossible to comprehend. She seemed to understand that he needed a moment and smiled, her sapphire eyes sparkling with humorous indulgence.

"You want me to drive?" She looked around the expensive sports car with appreciation. "It has been a while, but I can still do it."

Mack shook his head to clear it. "What are you doing here?"

"At the moment, I am here to keep you from turning around and going back to find your wife. She and all the others are safe." Jelena assured him by placing an elegant hand on his shoulder. "Now go, you make exchange, all is well, Mack."

Peace covered him like a blanket, his racing heart slowed, his body relaxed. He closed his eyes for a moment and let it settle over him. When he opened them, she was gone.

Mothers

"I am going to the bunker, Yakira. I must speak with Josiah." Reuben stared up at the ceiling of their bedroom.

Kayah rested her wrist on the top of her head, relaxed and sated. "Okay, I will wait here for the others, so they know we are all right."

Reuben turned, resting his temple on his palm. "You are an amazing woman."

Kayah smiled. "You don't know the half of it. Apparently, I am the King's mother."

"What?" Reuben snorted with laughter and rolled off the bed to dress.

Kayah did the same, expecting the rest of the household would arrive any time. "It's true, he thought I was his mother."

Reuben froze with one leg in his pants. "You saw Korah?"

"Oh yeah." Kayah covered her mouth, knuckling away a hysterical giggle. "He came down the hall outside Astrid's room. I told him to behave himself and go back to his party." She started laughing and held up a hand. "And he did, I swear to you, he did!" She bent over. "He looked at me with these crazy eyes and got sullen and said, 'as you wish.' Then he turned around and left. Mack heard the whole thing."

Reuben stood there in shock, then realization dawned. "That explains how he had your description, and why he was so mad." Reuben joined in her laughter, albeit a little hysterical. "I didn't understand it. I listened to him come completely unglued over the radio."

Kayah threw up her hands in surrender. "He was delusional." She shook her head in wonder. "Remind me to never go to the Palace again. Every time I go, I get manhandled by security. That's the second time."

Reuben shook his head. "It is obviously a place you do not need to be, Yakira." He pulled on his pants and crossed the room. "I did not enjoy seeing you being taken away. I did not enjoy that at all."

Kayah raised a brow at him. "It was not the highlight of my evening either, but I will say, I did enjoy watching you turn into a badass." She wrapped her arms around his neck. "That was very sexy."

Reuben groaned and rested his forehead on the top of her head. "Sexy is not the word I would use. Rage, yes. Sexy, no." He kissed her hair and moved away. "Perhaps in a couple of days, we go to your beach house, no? I need a vacation from my vacation."

Friends

"Weeeee!!!"

It was the most incongruent sound Kayah ever heard. Standing in the kitchen, suddenly ravenous, she turned to Reuben with a piece of salami halfway to her mouth. "Did you hear that?"

Filippo's laughter floated in from outside.

Reuben nodded. "I believe two have returned."

Lavinia and Filippo burst in. "Kayah!" Lavinia enveloped her in a huge hug. "We did it!"

They heard a car pull into the garage. Lavinia released Kayah with a squeal and ran to greet Mack.

Kayah swallowed her salami and winked at Filippo. "She's excited."

"She was brilliant." Filippo nodded after her, smiling with pride.

Mack sat in his car, his chest heaving as Lavinia sprinted out the door. He closed his eyes in a moment of thankfulness.

She threw her arms around his neck, kissing his face, and laughing. "You're safe!"

"Valentine," he breathed. "Oh, Valentine."

At length, she let him get out of the car and brought him into the kitchen. Mack sat down heavily in one of the chairs. "Has anyone been in contact with the bunker?"

"The power, it is still out, and the phones, they not working. I was going to ride over, but we got two cars here." Filippo shrugged. "I will drive. My legs are maybe jittery, eh? I need to go to the gym more. I'm getting a flabby."

"A flabby?" Kayah repeated with a giggle.

Lavinia joined in.

Kayah laughed harder. "That's not what Reuben got." Then she lost it, the stress of the night ebbing away with each guffaw.

Filippo's chest started to shake. "You no funny, Kayah."

Kayah hugged him, still cracking up. "I'm sorry you got a flabby."

"I'm going to see Himari. No flabby, eh?" Filippo's eyes sparkled.

Kayah kissed his cheek. "You are the best, Filippo."

Mack smiled, shaking his head. "Nobody leaves until we change out of these disguises." He stood up and stretched. "We will evacuate to the bunker for the time being."

Doctors

It took a while for Lavinia and Filippo to wash off the body dye that turned them Polynesian brown, longer for Kayah to strip the hair color. Her hair underneath was an ash blonde, paradoxically her greatest disguise. She never did a job as a blonde and like tonight, never without latex and prosthetics.

Lurking in the back of their minds, Erica knew their true identities and faces, thanks to Stephen. Reuben confirmed that Mossad recovered pictures, videos, and voice recordings of The Alcatraz 5 on Stephens destroyed equipment. It was chilling. The most powerful computer program ever created hunted them.

Electricity slowly returned to the New City as the sun broke the horizon. Underground, the triumphant Resistance members congratulated each other, full of a thousand questions. At 7:00 am, Alaina confirmed they were back in business.

Reuben's expression looked grave as he said, "I would like to speak with Prince Josiah. Can you please raise them?"

Everyone grew quiet as the phone rang.

Peter's weary voice came over the line, "Falcon here."

A collective sigh of relief echoed off the walls. "Base confirms, the operation was a success," Mack said.

"Good."

"Falcon, may I have a word with Doc?" Reuben asked.

Peter cleared his throat. "He is with Red. Give us a moment."

Lavinia leaned into Mack's shoulder. From Peter's experience, he knew what Astrid was going through.

Josiah's voice came over the line, hoarse and scratchy, "Sergeant."

"Doc," Reuben answered, "are you all right?"

Josiah made a strangled noise. "Considering the circumstances, yes. The girls are resting. It was an ordeal, but I understand I owe you all a debt of thanks. I am deeply grateful." A paroxysm of coughing seized him.

Peter took the phone. "Bobby?"

Mack answered, "Falcon?"

"When you can, get a message to Jay and Fey, tell them I am okay. They are worried."

"Copy that."

"Sunflower, one of these days you need to tell me why all hell broke loose."

The silence that hung in the room after the call disconnected was palpable, each reviewing the events of the night, knowing it was far from over.

Mack gave Lavinia a quick squeeze and took charge. "I suggest we debrief then get some shut eye."

Lovers

As a veteran, Mack knew what to expect after a mission. His wife did not. The sultry gaze she gave him diverted blood from his brain to other areas, making it difficult to concentrate. When Lavinia licked her finger and ran it seductively over her bottom lip, he looked away and repeated the words that Genevieve was saying in his mind.

Kayah caught the interplay. Filippo and Himari were no better, though unlike Mack, Filippo was making no pretense of hiding his interest in his wife. To his credit, he hid the fact that he was not "flabby". She had mercy on them all and suggested, "Mack, I think the debrief will be more productive after everyone rests. It's been a long night."

Filippo took Himari's hand before Kayah finished her sentence. "Kayah is right. *Buonanotte!*" Good night!

"*Buonanotte!*" Lavinia called after them, holding her hands out for Mack. "Come on."

Mack shook his head in amused capitulation. This was no

ordinary operation, but then again, it had its perks. "All right, Valentine."

"Sounds like a good idea," Alaina stood up and stretched, "I've got a call to make."

Genevieve watched the departing couples with a knowing eye. "This has been enough excitement for one evening. I guess you two are on duty," she chuckled at Kayah and Reuben, "have fun."

Kayah looked around the empty bunker and said in the silence, "I suppose we already did."

Lavinia began tugging off Mack's clothes before their bedroom door shut. "Hurry."

Mack chuckled, "Are you a little worked up?"

"Not a little." Lavinia thrust her hand down the front of his jeans. "To the one hundredth power, Bobby."

"My beautiful genius, come here." Mack pulled her tight, gripping her round butt with both hands.

He smelled like the leather from the expensive sports car. She buried her face in his neck and licked him. "You were so sexy tonight."

Mack laced his fingers behind his head, laid back, and let her take charge. She pulled off his jeans and his boots with practiced ease, and for once did not fold them. She dropped them in a pile on the floor, which told him exactly what kind of interlude this was going to be.

Lavinia moved like a cheetah, graceful and fast. She crawled up the bed, purring her pleasure and straddling him. He was solid and strong beneath her thighs, she moved over him in familiar rhythm, sensual heat.

Mack groaned and pulled her down for a kiss, seeking and rocking with her.

As she held him at her entrance, their eyes met. She smiled with devious delight and vowed, "I am going to destroy Erica." Then, with delicious power, she joined her husband and sealed her oath.

Parents

Mack stroked Lavinia's hair as she relaxed beside him. "Do you feel better, Valentine?"

"Mmm hmm," Lavinia murmured, snuggling closer, "tired now."

"As well you should be," he said through a yawn. The events of the evening played in his mind. One thing remained before he could rest. As Lavinia fell asleep, he freed his arm and slipped from the bed, careful not to wake her.

In the living room, he nodded briefly to Kayah and Reuben and took a phone from the bank of them on the shelf. His father-in-law answered on the third ring. "Sailor? I hear the fish are biting. It's a good time to take a trip and check it out."

Anthony cleared his throat. "Is that so? Well, we always enjoy fishing. You coming to join us?"

Mack covered his mouth and closed his eyes. "Not for a while. Tell your first mate, I look forward to hearing about all the fish he is going to catch."

"I'll do that. He's a hell of a sailor," Anthony answered.

Mack let out a shuddering breath. "Yes, he is. Enjoy the fishing, we'll be down as soon as we can."

Mack ended the call and drooped, staring at the floor. He had just sent his son into hiding. He felt Kayah take the phone from his loose grasp.

"I'll dismantle it." Kayah's face was soft with understanding. "Go to bed, Mack."

Giants

"Good morning, *chèr*. Where y'at?" Beau's voice felt like a balm to Alaina's tattered soul.

She smiled and said, "We did it."

"Knew you would. Quite a show though. We went dark, *et tu?*"

"Completely, shut us down for quite a while." Alaina stretched out on her bed. "It was scary."

"You a brave girl, Jolie Catin." Standing barefoot and shirtless, he looked out at the lake from his window, feeling the pull to go to her. "I think it's time I take a page out of your book."

"Pishon…" The longing in her voice traveled over the distance.

"Whitey married his Princess yesterday, and I was not there," Beau said quietly, his voice full of resignation. "You went into battle, and I was not there."

Alaina rolled to her side, hugging the pink quilt to her breast. "But you are getting better, you said so yourself."

"Better… I suppose." He turned his back on the lake and stared at her pictures. "I feel like I've been in the hospital. Every day I ask, 'Can I leave? Am I better?'" He adjusted a photo on his desk. "Every day the answer is the same, 'Almost, but not yet.'"

"Then we wait. We've held out this long."

"It's like I have something left to do here." Beau ran his fingers through his black hair. "I just wish I knew what it was."

"Me, too." Alaina cradled the phone. "I'm scared. We are fighting battles on several fronts, but there is something loose in cyberspace that is like nothing any of us have ever seen. It's smart, and it's coming after us."

"Then you kill it, Jolie Catin, at the very least, capture and lock it up. You can't let evil run wild." He laughed without humor and said in a moment of clarity. "That's been my problem. I know I didn't do either. Don't allow it to grow, *chèr*. Giants just get bigger, don't they?"

January 2, 1000 ME

It Might Be a Good Time to Check In

Throughout the morning, Reuben remained uncharacteristically quiet. Kayah could not fathom what was going on inside his head but determined she would let him work it out. After lunch, he was still brooding, so she pulled him into their bedroom and asked, "What's on your mind, Agent?"

The muscles in his jaw worked as he considered. "I need to check in, and I should bring you with me." He looked down at her with hooded eyes. "Leon will want to have that conversation I promised him. I know it."

"I see." Kayah crossed her arms over her chest.

Reuben looked resigned. "I must deliver my report, but you need to debrief them on Erica. It cannot just be The Resistance fighting that thing, Tel Aviv needs to be read in."

Kayah chuckled with appreciation. "You are a crafty one, Reuben ben Judah. I see what you are up to." She circled him. "You discharge your debt to Leon, and in the process, engage Tel Aviv when we need them."

Reuben did not add that by bringing Kayah into Mossad, he gave her an extra level of protection. As an asset, if Korah's forces captured her, he could pressure Leon to intervene.

Tracks

Himari, Alaina, and Lavinia began to hunt. Erica flew under their noses for weeks undetected, but that was about to change. Alaina got the first hit, in the New City power grid. "Look at this."

All work stopped.

"We've got fractured code all over the place." Alaina ran her finger down the screen.

"Oh, that's a mess." Himari shook her head. "Look, it fails to execute and just ends."

"It's line after line." Lavinia squinted. "Scroll down, Alaina."

Alaina moved the cursor down, and they watched the pages scroll for two solid minutes.

Lavinia straightened and said, "She was throwing code at the power grid, but it wasn't coming back."

Himari met Lavinia's eyes. "She panicked."

Alaina leaned forward, a hunter on the trail. "Because it was killing her."

"So, is she dead?" Genevieve asked.

Lavinia pointed at the screen. "No, this isn't her. She sends out programs, like messengers who bring back information. When the power went out, they failed to return."

Mack tapped his chin and asked, "So short of another world-wide power outage, how do you stop the messengers?"

Himari looked up at the ceiling, thinking. "Better yet, how do we weaponize them? Infect them and send them back at her."

Alaina grinned. "Like a bullet to the brain."

Mack saw it happen and rose from the couch, guiding Lavinia to her desk. She nodded absently when he put a fresh pack of red licorice and a cherry soda next to her. Then she disappeared into the labyrinth.

Filippo took up a sketchbook and captured the moment. He expected in the course of human history, they may want a record of it, the exact instant that Lavinia ben Anthony went to war with the machine.

January 3, 1000 ME

Welcome Back, Lavinia

Lavinia looked up from her work and saw Mack, bleary eyed and unshaven.

"Welcome back," he said groggily.

She blinked several times and looked around. They were alone in the computer lab. Underground it was impossible to tell day from night, but she deduced it was very late. She rubbed her face. "I've been gone a while."

Mack nodded slowly. "Never seen you go that deep, Valentine."

Lavinia squeezed her temples, her head throbbing. "I need water."

"To your left." Mack gestured.

She drained the bottle and wiped her mouth with the back of her hand. "I figured it out."

Mack waved her over, too tired to get up from the couch where he'd held vigil all night. "I know."

"Trap, capture, and kill." Lavinia stood up and stretched. "Was it Alaina who said that?"

"Uh huh," Mack confirmed. "About 14:00 yesterday, about 16:00 is when I got a little nervous."

Lavinia hung her head, embarrassed. "I haven't done that in a long time. How bad was it?"

"Not too bad, nothing to be ashamed of. It was Kayah who noticed, when she got back from Mossad HQ," Mack said with a begrudging admiration for Kayah's perceptiveness.

Despite his reassurance Lavinia's face turned crimson. "Don't tell me I had an accident. I will die right here, on the spot, if you do."

"No, but you were wiggling in your chair, and Kayah took you to the bathroom. From there you emerged triumphant and declared you knew how to capture her. I always do some of my best thinking in there, too. Don't feel bad." Mack rose with a groan. "Come on, let's get some sleep. You can tell us the brilliant plan after you've rested."

Battle Plan

"We still have code to write and details to work out, but I know how to fight her, and I know how to win." Lavinia's voice sounded breathless, but her confidence rang through. "We are going to use Korah's spyware to do it."

Kayah leaned forward. "It's in everything."

Lavinia smiled and looked at Himari, whose face registered understanding. "My code writes over it, kills it."

Alaina stood up. "Everything that Erica is touching has Korah's spyware, they put it in everything, like Kayah said."

Reuben snorted. "It is not in Mossad technology."

"Or ours," Mack confirmed.

Lavinia nodded. "So, we weaponize the spyware and turn it on her."

Himari frowned. "What's to stop her from rewriting it, throwing up firewalls, and disarming it once she figures it out?"

Mack's smile grew slowly. "Because you'll disguise it and launch it all at once, won't you? A single shot from a .22 won't do much, but a hundred million will." Lavinia looked at him with pride, Himari and Alaina with surprise. "What? I know how to fight a war. I don't know shit about how y'all will accomplish it, but I understand strategy."

Reuben moved to Mack's side. "So, you hit her, does that kill her or flush her out and send her into a trap?"

Lavinia raised a fine eyebrow. "It might kill her, but I doubt it. She lay dormant for a thousand years, so she is resilient." She nodded toward Filippo who was observing the group, "But she is not what she was, and Stephen did not find the pieces Gus stole. Those will be the bait in the trap, the missing components."

Kayah's breath caught, and she whispered, "We know where they are."

Reuben's face lit up. "Gus' lab."

Himari quivered with excitement. "So, we send an all-out attack, cyber bomb the shit out of her—"

Alaina jumped in. "She's reeling, wounded, looking for a place to hide."

Filippo threw up his hands. "You bring Gus' lab online with her missing pieces."

"She high tails it to the farm," Mack said with a broad grin, "and we're kicking her ass all the way there."

Genevieve declared, "Which is when you spring the trap!"

Lavinia put her hands on her hips. "And we shut her down, once and for all."

She's Still Got It

The buzzing in Mack's pocket reminded him that they were fighting more than one battle. "Falcon," Mack answered, succinct and businesslike.

"Bobby, Sparrow still has the key." Peter sounded elated.

Mack's face registered his astonishment at this bit of news, everyone in the bunker drew closer. "You are kidding!"

Peter grinned. "These two are full of surprises."

Mack rolled his eyes. "Knowing you as I do, then I reckon you'll fit right in."

"I am surprised by how well." Peter waggled a golden eyebrow at Astrid who watched him from her cot in the ambulance. The worst was over, but she was weak as a newborn kitten. His silly expression made her smile, and he liked it when Astrid smiled.

"How are they?" Mack asked. The news was grim yesterday, as Astrid fought through the worst of the drug withdrawals. Despite Peter's flippant attitude over the phone, Mack heard his concern.

"Everyone is awake, and Red brewed the first decent pot of coffee I have had in three days, so my disposition has improved considerably. Whoever invented instant coffee, which is what I have been subsisting on, while these slackers slept, was not doing anyone any favors. It is vile. Please tell Miss Euler that I was dreaming of her espresso."

Mack chuckled, remembering the night he came home to find Peter and Lavinia jacked up on espresso at his kitchen table, full of the plan they were in the midst of executing. "I will do so. You ready to fly?"

"Doc says one more day here, just to be on the safe side." Peter smiled at Astrid, who had exhausted her meager energy trying to sit up and was lying on her side watching him talk.

Mack cleared his throat. "Falcon, when you get where you're going, stay put. There was an unexpected complication, nothing for you to worry about, but we need to take care of it before you move. It won't be safe otherwise."

Peter kept his face neutral. "You know me, I always pick the best places. Thanks for the information."

Mack disconnected the line and looked at the expectant faces in the bunker. "Davianna ben David still has the Black Key."

Reuben threw his hands in the air and declared, "Adonai! He is worthy to be praised!" He grabbed Kayah around the waist and kissed her full on the mouth.

Filippo took up the theme, kissing all the girls, even Auntie G, who thought it great fun.

"As such," Mack raised his voice above the excited chatter, "the pursuit will be intense, not just for the missing Princes, but for that artifact. There is no way they are making it to the Golden City with Erica on the loose. They are moving tomorrow, but I told Peter to hang tight when they get where they are going. They are still recovering, so I do not think any of them will question the wisdom of laying low for a while. We don't have a lot of time, folks. We have to take that thing down, fast."

I Should Have Seen It

"We need Gus' journals," Kayah said, frowning at a chipped fingernail.

Mack nodded. "They are at the Bay safe house."

Filippo looked around the bunker. "I liked that place much better, eh? Why we got to be underground? I'm not a groundhog, and it's a depressing down here."

Alaina scowled at him. "Filippo ben Vincente quit your whining. You've been down here three days, one of which you slept. Himari and I have been here since December 25th, and we are likely to be here a hell of a lot longer. So, I don't want to hear it."

Filippo drew himself up, agitated. He made a simple observation that everyone agreed with and did not appreciate being attacked. "Hey, what's the matter with you? You don't talk to me that way."

Mack cut them off. "You both need a breather. Get out of here. Go to the Bay safe house and get the journals."

"Why I got to go with her? She's in a mood," He pointed a finger at Mack. "You don't know models, but I do. They are temperamental!" He thrust his chin at Alaina. "You a temperamental diva."

"Me?" Alaina shot out of her chair. "Well, if that ain't the pot callin' the kettle black!" Mississippi beer joint rolled up its sleeves and got ready for a brawl.

"Hey!" Mack stepped between them and pressed keys in Filippo's hand. "Take it, and her, out of here. Bring back the journals and whatever else we left that you think we might need."

Alaina stalked off with a harrumph, muttering under her breath. "Well, I better go because the only thing he will bring back are his damn paints."

Filippo threw up his hands and said to Himari, "This is the thanks I get? All I have done for her, and she talks to me like this?"

Himari pulled him into their bedroom and slammed the door. "Stop, listen for a minute before you lose your temper."

"It is a too late! Already, I am losing my temper!"

She held up a finger and said, "Wait. This whole thing has been difficult for her."

Filippo waved his hands. "And has it been easy for you and me?"

"It's different. Think about it. She misses Beau. They are trying to work things out, but that's hard in the best of circumstances. I don't imagine being locked up with three happy couples makes it easier." Himari let that sink in for a moment before continuing. "Kayah and Reuben are not exactly quiet, and she's on the other side of the wall from them."

The corner of Filippo's mouth lifted.

Himari looked at him intently. "She is worried about Prince Peter. I don't think any of us realized how fond they have grown of one another."

"They have?" Filippo considered.

"Yes, it became apparent as they were saying goodbye. They spent a lot of time together." Himari flushed and looked away. "You and I moved across town. When was the last time we invited her to the apartment?"

Filippo ran his teeth over his bottom lip and said, "It's been at least a year."

Himari nodded. "Right. Who has she had other than Ellen and Peter? Peter is in danger, Ellen's gone, and Beau's not here. And we are up against this… this monster."

Filippo's face grew very sober as the anger ebbed away.

Himari squinted. "Al sees things in the code, patterns and nuances that I miss. She knows how important she is to this operation. I think it all crashed in on her." She rested a hand on the side of Filippo's face. "You were just a safe target, babe."

Filippo closed his eyes and leaned into her hand. "I should have seen it. I know her… She is talking to him, eh?"

Himari nodded. "She is, a couple times a day. Watch her when she comes out of her room. Her color's high, and her hair is all tousled like she's about to hit the runway."

Alaina's impatient voice penetrated the door. "Are you coming? I swear I spend half my life waiting on you. Your hair looks fine. Put one of your stupid hats on, and let's go."

Filippo pressed his lips into a line, torn between amusement and exasperation. "I'm a going to kick her ass, then hug her, and let her tell me about Beau Landry." He put the keys in his pocket and selected a gray felt hat. "You know he buys all my paintings of her?"

Himari's eyes widened. "I did not."

He shrugged a shoulder. "He has the original Serendipity, but I never told her. She don't know he's been watching out for her all these years, and you don't tell her."

Himari's mouth hung open. "You never said a word, why?"

"Maybe I understand what it feels like to love somebody and not be able to have them but hope one day things will change." He planted a brief kiss. "I think things are changing. We need to help them get their happy ending, eh? She's a member of the Broken Hearts Club too long."

Alaina stood outside his door, tapping her foot. "Finally! How long did it take to pick out a hat? It's not even an interesting one, you're losing your touch, Filippo." She spun around and stormed out.

"I got a limited selection." He stalked after her. "Quit busting my chops."

Reuben chuckled after them and turned to Kayah. "Why does she remind me of you?"

Himari caught the comment on her way to the kitchen. "Because she was acting ill-tempered and imperious."

Kayah flipped her off. "Go hack something so I can get out of here."

January 4, 1000 ME

New Song

Reuben looked up from one of Gus' journals, his expression enigmatic. Kayah could not meet his eyes. They all knew Gus loved her, but the depth and the breadth of it poured from his journals like blood from a fatal wound. "Yakira, come, have a word with me."

She pushed her chair back and stalked into their bedroom. "What?"

"You did not do anything wrong," Reuben said quietly.

Kayah's chin thrust out in defiance. "I know that."

"No, you do not. I see it in your face."

Kayah crossed her arms. "No, you do not. I just want to get out of here."

Reuben's eyes bore into hers, and he pulled her into his arms without another word. She stood, stiff and unbending, but he felt her trembling beneath the rigidity. Her breathing became labored as he squeezed. Kissing the top of her head, he held on, the first pitiful gasp buried in his chest.

Kayah wrapped her arms around his waist, letting the tears come. When they were spent, she stood pliant and boneless in his embrace. "Gus found a song when we were in the bunker. We were just kids, but he knew. He understood more than we ever gave him credit for, and those journals prove he had insight into me, even back then. He knew I would break his heart, but he loved me anyway. And that song? It was the first he ever sent me. It's sad, Reuben, but it's my song."

"Yakira, you might have had a sad song before, but no more." He tilted her chin up and looked into her eyes. "Do you want to hear your new song, from the man the Lord chose for you, who loves you, and that you love back?" Her eyes swam, shining with a vulnerability that cut him to the quick.

"I'd like that, but your music is horrible."

He chuckled, kissing her forehead. "No, this one is not." He dug in his duffel for his tablet and held his arms out to her. "All of Me, Yakira."

As if in a dream, Kayah took the final steps, left behind the girl she was, and fell into his embrace, with a new song.

Humming Right Along

"It's the computing speed of Erica that concerns me," Mack drawled. "I think you've got to hit her with multiple weapons, otherwise she might be able to throw up a defense before maximum damage can be inflicted. We only have one shot."

Himari looked up from her screen, feeling harassed. "Mack, we'll do well to write a single code that we can hide and launch in the timeframe we've got, maybe two and that would be pushing it."

Reuben sat at the monitors, keeping an eye on the remote roads that led to the cabin where the Princes and the girls were hiding. He hummed under his breath and doodled on a scratch pad.

Kayah looked between them, her brows drawn down in concentration, missing something. "Quiet!" She held up her hand to Himari and Mack and listened. "Reuben, what are you humming?"

Reuben looked blank. "I was humming?"

"Yes." Kayah grabbed the side of her head. "What was that song?"

Realization dawned, he sprinted from the room and brought his tablet back, his playlist loaded when her song ended. "You are a genius, Yakira." He pressed play. AC/DC's Thunderstruck filled the bunker.

Lavinia dropped her pen. "The greatest cyber-attack in history."

Himari's chair hit the wall as she stood up. "It melted the centrifuges."

"The God Virus." Alaina said with awe, "Silicon Valley and Tel Aviv created it together."

"And it sent the enemy back to the Stone Age." Reuben grinned.

Kayah grabbed Reuben around the waist and kissed him. "Get Tel Aviv on the line, tell them we are launching Operation Thunderstruck 2.0."

January 7, 1000 ME

Give it to Me in Layman's Terms

Himari crept into the bedroom on silent feet. It was well past midnight, and Filippo retired two hours before.

"I am awake," he said into the darkness.

"Oh, sorry I did not mean to wake you."

Filippo stirred and switched on the lamp, squinting against the light. "You did not." He failed to mention why he was lying awake; Massimo had returned. "Are you ready, is it done?"

Himari slipped out of her clothes and settled beside him with a deep yawn, her tiny body barely making a ripple on the soft mattress. "Almost. The folks in Tel Aviv... wow, they are amazing."

Filippo killed the light and gathered her close. She smelled like one of Lavinia's licorice sticks, espresso, and a citrus shampoo that Alaina was a spokes model for. A giant jug of it was in the community bathroom along with a dozen other products she represented. Everyone looked and smelled good down in the bunker, thanks to Alaina.

"What have they discovered?" He stretched luxuriously and settled in beside her.

"Mossad pulled a ton of data off Stephen's equipment. It's a blessing they had it. We could not have made that much headway in such a short time. Reuben says there are over a thousand scientists working on the project. Their top three are flying in tomorrow. Reuben will bring them to the farm when we launch."

"That is good." Filippo stroked Himari's back rhythmically. "What is she, *Bellissima?* I still do not understand what Erica is."

She moaned low and content under his touch. "Think of her as a highly intelligent octopus with a million arms and a huge brain. She can disguise herself to hunt and move through small spaces. She sends out her arms to collect data and brings it back for processing. Then she reads, analyzes, and interprets millions of these messages a second.

"As she existed before, she was cloning herself, multiplying that brain and putting it everywhere. But she is missing those pieces. She could change code, rewrite programs, but that is also missing. So, she is essentially a single entity this time around."

"So that is what Gus took? He took the part of her that could multiply herself and change the computers?"

"Yes, which vastly inhibits her ability to manipulate things. Machines are not inherently smart. They execute precise instructions that we give them. Erica was different. She not only learned, she manipulated. In the Last Age, she could go into a system and change instructions and make them do what she wanted them to do. Can you imagine what that was like? She could have taken control of planes and robots, weapons." Himari shuddered and yawned. "Now she can only gather data from them."

"Tell me of the plan, *Bellissima*, but do it in simple terms. I am just a painter, eh?" Filippo asked, wanting something to take his mind off Massimo.

Himari stretched and settled in, her voice hoarse with fatigue. "Well, the objective is to attack, trap, and destroy. How we accomplish it, in theory, is not that difficult. Between us and Tel Aviv, we've written six programs that mutate her code. When activated, they will seek, search, and destroy Erica, all in different ways.

"There is an embedded code in all the technology that the New City firms have produced since they lifted the tech ban in '86. Korah made it part of the official licensing and permit process. He did it under the auspices of controlling exportation of the tech, but that was not really what it was for. You've heard me rail against it for years." Himari felt herself getting worked up and dropped the subject, or she would never get to sleep.

"So, how will you get the new codes into everything without her seeing it?" Filippo asked in a sleepy voice.

"That's been the brilliance of it. We're pushing it out in dozens of ways. Tel Aviv had several new apps ready. They are being downloaded thousands of times a second. We've tagged the code in ten or twelve major software updates and plugged it into viral videos and pictures."

Himari chuckled. "Kayah and Reuben keep pulling old wrestling videos off some server farm she hacked into. You would not believe how many views those things are getting."

Filippo laughed. "I have seen them. They are entertaining."

"The things people like…" Himari rolled her eyes in the darkness. "The Resistance controls about half the conspiracy websites. So, Alaina pushed the story that there is an urgent patch they need to upload to prevent Korah from listening to private conversations." Himari loved the irony. "Because it's the truth, those folks have spread it all over the internet faster than anything we could have done on our own."

Filippo grunted with approval. "Do you know where she is? Is she in the Palace?"

Himari stretched. "While she is not multiplying herself, since New Year's Eve she is growing exponentially. We think she is learning and moving between multiple sites. We know this because wherever she goes network performance plummets. She is so huge, she takes up most of the available hardware, like a giant blood sucking leech on the system."

Himari got a self-satisfied smile. "One update we pushed is for a network performance software diagnostic tool. Whenever someone runs it, we get a message. Most of the time it is just a standard scan, but when the engineers start running it multiple times along with other diagnostic programs, we know we've got her.

"It's safer than hunting her directly. Since New Year's Day, we've tracked her to all four major data centers, though she seems to prefer the one in the Palace. Alaina found some breadcrumbs to and from what appears to be a private residence on the out-skirts of the New City. She is traveling back and forth, but she can't stay long. She's too large, and the systems overload and shut down."

"So, she's not in my phone?" Filippo seemed relieved.

"Your phone?" Himari ran a fingertip over his collar bone. "No. We've got firewalls that keep her out of our technology, but she isn't in anything that small. Her messengers are everywhere, and any device connected to the internet without protection is susceptible to being used by her to gather information. That is what makes her so dangerous. She could be everywhere, in everything."

"That is a creepy." Filippo shivered. "When you launch the attack, how do you flush her out? How do you make her come to you so you can trap her and then destroy her?"

"We will activate the six programs at the same time. Some will rewrite her code which will damage and wound her. Other code will cause the servers she is in to overheat and malfunction, this will get her to move. One of the codes destroys her image gathering capability, essentially killing those messengers. Another modifies the data and gives her false information about the electrical grids and server farms; it will tell her they are failing again."

"That gets her running?" Filippo asked, no longer sleepy.

"Yes. The internet is wires. People operate under the misperception that information moves through the air like radio waves, it does not. Think of the wires as you would roads, information travels in packets like cars down the roads. Along the way, there are gates called routers that direct traffic and open and close access. Think of it like gates. We will tell the routers to close the gates, which will block her and make her think everything is going down."

"That makes sense. You come at her from all the directions, wound her, cut off her arms, tell her lies, and get her running. Where do the missing components come into play?"

"Several hours before we launch, we are going to send out bytes from the components Gus salvaged. Not enough for her to track, but flickers."

"Bait for the trap?"

Himari exhaled, weary and worried. "Which is the most dangerous part because if the components break free and join her outside the containment, we've made things worse."

Filippo felt the hairs on the back of his arms stand on end. "How you keep that from happening?"

"Lavinia."

January 8, 1000 ME

History Repeats Itself

At 11:45 pm, Kayah turned off her headlights, and she and Himari drove the last quarter mile to Gus' family farm. There was a large "Sold" sign at the front of the property. Through Sir Preston's firm, Kayah anonymously purchased it in early December. "I'll warn you now," Kayah said over the two-way radio to Lavinia and Mack behind them, "it's a hell of a shock when you see it, be prepared."

Lavinia took Mack's hand as the familiar farm came into view.

Himari's expression remained impassive, but she stretched her neck from side to side, tension rippling off her in waves.

Kayah pulled up to the larger barn and walked back to Mack and Lavinia's vehicle. "I want to hide the cars inside. Mack, will you drive the tractors out?"

Mack chuckled. "I can drive a tractor."

"Why do you think I brought you?" Kayah rolled her eyes.

"You did not have any choice, Kayah, and you know it." Mack held the flashlight for her as she unlocked the barn door. "There is no way Lavinia is doing this without me."

Kayah did not argue with him, but Filippo and Reuben might.

Filippo stayed in the bunker, well-armed and guarding Genevieve and Alaina. Reuben was at Mossad HQ. Peter, Josiah, Davianna, and Astrid were safe in a remote mountain cabin, and the Alanthian government was preoccupied with the Royal Wedding. Operation Thunderstruck would launch right before the ceremony, when maximum human and computer resources were devoted to security, they would strike.

Mack whistled when the door opened to the equipment barn.

He ambled over to the big crop tractor and ran a reverent hand over the leather seat. "Look at her," he smiled broadly at Kayah, "she is a sexy beast. How much you want for her?"

Lavinia appeared in the door. "Oh, good gracious, we won't need to worry about him being under foot. I will never get him out of this barn."

Himari laughed and said, "If I know Gus, that tractor just might turn into a robot."

Mack looked up, his eyes gleaming. "Like a Transformer? Richard would love that." Transformers was his son's favorite movie from the Last Age. "That one over there looks like Bumble Bee."

Lavinia laughed, she suspected Mack liked the movie as much as Richard.

Kayah was thoroughly confused. "That looks nothing like a bee, and what's an electrical transformer have to do with anything?" She eyed the space. "I think we can fit the cars in without moving the tractors."

Mack looked appalled. "No. Y'all go on to the lab." He grinned, rubbing his hands. "I'll move the vehicles around." He strolled over to a compact utility tractor in red. "Oh, just look at you, darlin'."

"We'll see you later… Bobby," Kayah said sarcastically.

The code name seemed to snap him out of his reverie. "I'll walk with you to make sure it's secure, then I'll take care of this."

As they approached the second barn, Lavinia took his hand. "We'll get home soon. You'll be back on your tractor in no time."

Mack squeezed her hand. It remained unspoken that the next two days might determine if they ever returned to Peccioli and their lives, or if they would join Peter and Josiah on the run to the Golden City.

Kayah unlocked the door and stood back, gathering herself before entering. Himari stepped forward and shone her flashlight on the sign. "I was going to take it, but when the time came… I just told Reuben to leave it." Kayah strode forward, shining her flashlight along the wall. "Hit the lights."

Himari jumped when she saw the concrete floor. "The floor even?"

Kayah threw up her hands in surrender. "I warned you, down

to the last detail, Sunflower. When we pull back that curtain, you will look around the space and expect to see Gus and Stephen. It's Alcatraz."

Lavinia took off by herself down the corridor, her rubber-soled shoes making a slight squeaking noise as she walked. She disappeared behind the curtain without a moment's hesitation.

Himari and Kayah exchanged looks, surprised at her bravery. With every step they went back in time, two young girls, cutting class and seeking adventure.

Lavinia stood behind her desk, staring at an unopened box of red licorice, tears streaming down her cheeks.

Himari froze. She tried to prepare herself, but the reality of the place was far beyond what she imagined. Her hand flew to her mouth, and she stifled a cry.

Kayah swallowed hard and strode in, pretending it did not bother her, pretending she was not feeling, remembering, reliving it all.

Mack did not cross the threshold. This was not his domain, and he did not belong in the moment. On silent feet, he let the curtain drop and assumed his role. The protector was on the clock.

Ghosts

"Is that… is that our alarm clock?" Lavinia touched it reverently. "The one we used to remind us to leave?"

Kayah nodded. "I think it is. The government would not have taken it. They didn't take these. Look," she pointed to the carving of her initials, "KS".

Himari dropped to her hands and knees, crawling under her desk. "It's still here." She hooted and emerged with a slender magnetic box. "They did not find it."

Lavinia's eyes bulged. "Open it."

Himari nodded, her hand unsteady as she lifted the lid. The Alcatraz 5 operating agreement lay before them. The document outlined their mission and pledged they would share the discoveries and the profits equally.

Lavinia shook her head, drooping in relief. "All those weeks when they were investigating us and this place, I knew they were going to find that." Her voice cracked as she turned away. "For years, I waited for them to knock on my door, or for one of you to tell them I was a part of this. I kept waiting for them to discover… this… document. It would have sent me to prison with you, Kayah. I was eighteen, too."

"You would not have survived prison, Vinia. I barely did."

"In a way, I went to prison," Himari said soberly, "for seven and a half years."

Lavinia picked up the paper and flipped it to the back page, their names and signatures sealed their bond. She traced Stephen's broad scrawl, Gus' neat lettering, Kayah's bold hand, Himari's delicate slanted letters, and her own distinctive L. A piece of their history lay before them, documentation that proved they were who they said they were, had done what they set out to do.

"I broke that agreement," Kayah confessed in a strangled voice. She sat down heavily in Gus' chair. "It's what got us busted."

"What are you talking about?" Himari put the charter back in the box and snapped the lid closed.

"I was the first one in the tomb." Her eyes cut to the coveralls hanging in the corner. "I took something, and I hid it, planning to sell it." She shrugged. "I was afraid. As shitty as the orphanage was, it was a roof over my head. They were going to turn me out, and I needed to make money, fast. So, I figured I'd cash in."

Lavinia leaned forward. "What was it, Kai? It might be important."

"It was important." Kayah stood up and started pacing. "Yesterday, I saw the specs Peter sent over for the duplicates of the Black Key. What you don't know is that I had one just like it."

Himari gasped, and Lavinia covered her mouth with her hand.

Kayah tapped her toe in agitation. "It gets worse. The day of Prince d'Or's birthday party, I planned to meet with Korah, to sell it, but they threw me out. I panicked and did something stupid. I handed it over to Stephen and told him to show it to Korah. He was buying old tech. I figured it was my chance, but he turned on us and ordered the raid."

Lavinia blinked rapidly. "That is how Stephen cut his deal."

Himari grew thoughtful. "And what Stephen showed Gus at their lunch together, isn't it?"

Kayah bit her lower lip. "Yes, they used it as a prototype to track what Davianna's carrying."

"Nothing good came out of Quadrant G," Himari said with fierce resolution. "Whatever you did, Kai, you've long since paid for it. We all have." She picked up her briefcase and sat it on her desk with a thunk. "Let's seal that tomb door forever."

January 9, 1000 ME

Allies

The Golden Kingdom Embassy in Alanthia closed January 1, 987 ME, at the height of the Civil War. When Prince Korah ben Adam ascended the steps of the Capitol Building and accepted the title of King, they shuttered it indefinitely. For thirteen years, the Iron King's Embassy stood empty, save for a handful of guards and caretakers. Prince Yehonathan authorized its unofficial reopening January 1, 1000 ME. In the weeks prior, dozens of diplomats, administrative officials, and embassy staff flew in from Tel Aviv. Thus, the three scientists that landed at Korah International Airport were unremarkable.

Negotiations were underway to determine whether Golden Kingdom delegates would attend the wedding, but the resumption of diplomatic communications was significant. The world's press hailed it as a boon for Alanthia and a great step toward world peace and global reconciliation. Both sides knew it was little more than a farce. The Iron King did not compromise on rebellion, ever.

Reuben waited at a rendezvous site thirteen miles outside of town, driving a beat-up work van with decals that proudly proclaimed, "Joe's Plumbing - Your Crap is Our Business". The passenger exchange happened in the blink of an eye, and Reuben greeted his fellow countrymen, curious about the fourth man who was a last-minute addition to the mission. "Shalom, Gentlemen, I am Agent Reuben ben Judah."

A chorus of introductions and excited discussions erupted in the van. After weeks among the Alanthians, Reuben enjoyed hearing and speaking Hebrew again.

"Dr. Isaac, it is a great honor to meet you," Reuben said over his shoulder. "You conducted a lecture I attended some years ago. I have never forgotten it."

Dr. Isaac ben Eleazar's green eyes flashed with merriment. "And the subject? What was the subject?"

Reuben chuckled at the irony. "Cyber warfare in the Last Age and its ramifications for today."

Dr. Isaac clapped his small hands in pleasure. "Good, good. It is a subject I am most interested in, Agent. Though, I always assure my audience that I was not actually there." The joke was older than him, but not by much.

The youngest of the four, Shammah ben Agee, a scientist with purple hair and three ear piercings leaned forward and asked, "Himari Nakamura is already at the lab?"

Reuben nodded, checking his mirrors, scanning the cars, and watching the traffic cameras. "She is, you know her?"

Shammah made a disbelieving sound. "Of course! She is one of the foremost computer scientists in the world. I have studied her work for years." He motioned to the quiet gentleman in the last row of seats, Dr. Ira ben Ikkesh. "Ira feels the same way about Lavinia ben Anthony. They have exchanged letters and papers for ten years."

Dr. Ira wore a faraway expression so similar to Lavinia's misty-eyed gaze that Reuben worked very hard to contain a laugh.

"Gentlemen, I know they reviewed protocols with you on the plane and prior to selecting you for this assignment, but I need to stress again, fieldwork is not lab work. Significant danger surrounds this mission. Failure could plunge our Kingdom into a diplomatic crisis, which might escalate into global war and chaos. I do not overstate that. Thus, your adherence to protocol is imperative. Do I have your agreement and understanding?"

A somber chorus of affirmations echoed back to Reuben as he pulled down the gravel driveway to the farm. "Welcome to Alcatraz, gentlemen. Get ready for the fight of your life."

The Fourth Man in the Furnace

Kayah sensed the van before Mack. She looked up from her work and said, "Shadrach, Meshach, and Abednego are here."

The crease between Mack's eyes deepened as he regarded Kayah incredulously. "You are not right, girl." He checked the security monitor and saw Reuben's van pulling down the driveway.

Kayah heard him chuckle as he walked away, repeating the names under his breath.

"That is how I am going to think of them now," Himari exclaimed, fighting a smile. "It's your fault if I call one of them Shadrack."

Lavinia looked up, a blue pen pressed to her lips. "It is interesting that those were not their given names, only how they are remembered. Daniel received a new name at the same time, but no one ever calls him Belteshazzar. I suppose Hananiah, Mishael, and Azariah do not roll off the tongue like Shadrach, Meshach, and Abednego."

"Shut up, Lavinia." Kayah rolled her eyes. "It was a joke."

Lavinia raised her lip at Kayah. "I knew it was a joke. I worked in a bar for a decade. I was simply making an observation… bitch."

Himari exploded with laughter. "That's my line!"

Mack heard their banter over the curtain as he exited the barn. While their visitors were expected, he remained vigilant, armed and ready. Only after Reuben emerged and signaled all clear, did Mack greet the second half of their team. He shook their hands as they streamed inside, but when the fourth man stepped down from the van, Mack froze.

Reuben stiffened. "Mack?" he growled, reaching for his weapon.

Mack put out a hand, motioning him to stop. "Pastor?"

Pastor Ezekiel ben Malachi grinned and took Mack by the shoulders in an affectionate grip. "Mack ben Robert! Look at you, all grown up!"

Mack's eyes widened with shock. "What are you doing here?"

Ezekiel pulled Mack into a back-pounding hug. "I was called here, Mack. And I did not know why until this very instant. Adonai, be praised."

"Amen!" Mack shook his head, clearing away the surprise. "Come in, please."

"Do you still sing, young man?" Ezekiel asked as they entered. He turned to Reuben and added, "Such a voice and a talent this one has, have you heard him? Have you?"

"I have, sir," Reuben confirmed, looking at Mack with curiosity. "How do you two know each other?"

Ezekiel smiled, his lips disappearing behind a wealth of beard and mustache gone salt and pepper. "I spent several years in Virginia pastoring a church. Mack was one of my parishioners."

Meet and Greet

The moment purple haired Shammah ben Agee stepped behind the curtain, he was enraptured by Himari's delicate beauty. "Ms. Nakamura, it is a great honor." He shook her hand vigorously causing her whole body to rock to the rhythm. "This is it, huh?" He dropped the handshake abruptly, and Himari steadied herself against the corner of her desk.

"You would be Shadrach." Her acid tongue got the better of her.

Kayah buried a laugh behind her knuckles and rose to greet Reuben.

Shammah tore his gaze from Himari, staring at the servers in awe. "Yes, ma'am. I am Shammah ben Agee of Lehi in Judah." He ran a hand down the black server tower. "This workmanship is stunning."

Himari warmed to the purple haired youth. Gus' craftsmanship was art for those with eyes to see. "It is indeed." She took him on a tour of the full capacity and self-sufficient data center Gus constructed.

Dr. Ira ben Ikkesh spoke very little English, so Lavinia conversed with him in Hebrew. Their small talk consisted of, "It is nice to meet you face to face." That was it. They dove headfirst into the math. Dr. Ira accepted a marker and began studying the huge equation Lavinia scrawled across four dry erase boards.

Mack watched her go, but before she got buried, he motioned for Pastor Ezekiel to join him for a brief introduction. "Lavinia… Valentine?" He touched her arm and said, "I'd like you to meet someone."

Lavinia turned, blinked, and came back. "Yes, of course. Please forgive me." She smiled and extended a graceful hand to the small Jewish man with the bushy beard. "I'm Lavinia ben Anthony."

"Lavinia, this is Pastor Ezekiel ben Malachi." Mack smiled ear to ear.

The name registered, and she looked between them, astounded. "Your Pastor Zeke?"

"Shalom, Lavinia, such a pleasure to meet you." Ezekiel shook Lavinia's hand then turned to Mack with approval. "I always knew you would marry well. Such a beauty. Do you have children?"

Lavinia's eyes glowed with pleasure. "We have a little boy, Richard." Mack put his arm around Lavinia and squeezed. She added wistfully, "He looks just like his daddy."

Mack chuckled, "Poor kid."

Reuben presented Dr. Isaac ben Eleazar to Kayah. Dr. Isaac's green eyes flashed, mischievous. "Kayah ben Samuel? Young lady, you are known to me."

Kayah tilted her chin to the side and studied him but sensed no threat. "Indeed?"

Dr. Isaac winked. "I believe we have a mutual acquaintance. Sir Preston ben Worley is a very old friend of mine."

The corner of Kayah's mouth lifted, and she gave him a cheeky wink. "That is impossible. You are entirely too young to be one of Sir Preston's old friends."

Dr. Isaac cackled with pleasure. "Oh, 'tis true, but that does not slow me down. What do you say we leave this serious agent to his work and go get into some trouble?"

Kayah winked and clicked her cheek at Reuben. "Looks like you have some competition."

Reuben shrugged his shoulders. "I better be on my guard."

Dr. Isaac grew serious. "Agent, I believe we are here to do much more than just guard, no?"

Mack and Pastor Ezekiel joined the discussion. Pastor Zeke's penetrating eyes seemed to see beyond the room. "There is great power in what we will do here, as we look not to the things that are seen but to the things that are unseen. For the things that are seen are transient, but the things that are unseen are eternal." He nodded to each of them. "Come, Mack, you and I will pray a hedge of protection around this place and let the work begin."

Self-Contained

Gus' creation, like the original Alcatraz bunker, was a self-contained data center with its own source of electricity. Physical connections inside the bunker networked the computers. In 983 ME, there was no functioning internet and thus all the technology the Alcatraz 5 discovered was procured from the wreckage of the site and reverse engineered. In this manner, it was a time capsule of the Last Age's advanced computer technology, painstakingly restored, fully functional, and isolated.

For a dozen years, Kayah procured ancient artifacts and sent them to Gus. What Kayah did not send, Gus collected on his own, some from the original bunker, some through barter, often through junk dealers. His extraordinary talent and patience enabled him to take the most degraded piece of equipment and turn it into computer gold.

Shammah was studying one of Gus' original journals and scratched his purple hair, perplexed. "What is this code, Ms. Nakamura?"

"Please, call me Himari." She looked where he indicated. "Oh, that's our original computer language. We did not know any better, so we created our own."

Dr. Isaac rolled his chair over and peered down at the journal. "You constructed your own programming language?"

Himari blushed. "We did. I suppose only the three of us understand it now, and Kayah was never great at it."

Kayah looked up when she heard her name. "Language was never my forte," she said dryly. "Lavinia is the language guru."

Lavinia's name penetrated the perceptual filter that surrounded her. "Pardon?"

Dr. Ira looked peeved to have his new companion pulled away but was polite enough not to say so out loud. Reuben translated, and the math wizard's face changed from irritation to mild curiosity. "What level?" he asked.

Lavinia nodded. "The original language was a third level type, which was Himari and Stephen's creation. Gus and I took it and ran it through our own version of a compiler, the machine language we created is not the binary code we later discovered was the standard, so we abandoned it." She smiled in remembrance.

"Though, that machine," she gestured to the oldest one in the corner, "we got to function on our original code. It was slow and glitchy, but it worked."

Shammah stood up abruptly. "Egads! You are saying that you invented another machine code and got it to function?"

Himari shrugged. "It was essentially an "A" language, when we became more sophisticated we realized that everything we were digging up was based on "C", and if we wanted our equipment to tap into the machines from the past, they had to speak the same language or we were dead in the water. Though I have to say, we eliminated many of the inherent problems that came with C with ours."

Mack looked pained. "Y'all have lost me."

Kayah spoke up. "All computers from the Last Age speak a language that became the standard, even though there are problems with it. Look at the difference in these keyboards." She held up an ancient one and set it beside her modern laptop. "This old keyboard is based on a standard. The original QWERTY layout came from manual fly arm typewriters. When the inventor laid out the letters like we use now, with the most used letters on the stronger first and middle fingers, the typists became too fast, and the arms jammed. But when he rearranged the letters, it slowed the typists down and eliminated the problem. The strongest finger is typically the index finger on the right hand, but on an old keyboard that finger rests under J, which makes no sense, now it's an S. By the time they stopped using fly arms, everyone was used to the keys the way they were, so they left it."

Mack rubbed his jaw and asked, "So, this A language you all invented was better than the C language, but because the standard was already developed, you abandoned it?"

"Exactly." Himari confirmed.

Dr. Isaac studied the journal, his thick reading glasses riding low on his nose. "You say that machine understands your original A language?"

"Two of the servers do, one and four. We built those." Kayah moved with an economy of motion across the lab identifying the original servers. "Two and three… I sent these to Gus. The three on the bottom five, six, and seven came from the tomb. They are what she is searching for."

Pastor Ezekiel narrowed his eyes at the equipment, praying under his breath.

Lavinia translated to Dr. Ira, who held up a finger in discovery and said, "That is where we quarantine!"

Lavinia's eyes grew enormous. "She will not know the language to get out! We draw her there, slam the door shut, and she is trapped."

Mack grinned. "Then we fry her."

January 10, 1000 ME

Wired

Before dawn, coffee and breakfast roused the weary warriors. Kayah's purchase of the farm included a generous offer for the furnishings, Alice and Allen agreed. They took their personal items, but the house looked and felt much as it always had, even Gus' cologne lingered. The smell was a comfort to Himari, Lavinia, and Kayah. It felt like he was with them.

"This is the internet?" Mack shook his head in wonder at the huge schematic laid out on what was once Alice's dining room table.

Reuben hunched his shoulders forward, in solidarity with his fellow soldier.

Kayah laughed. "It's just wires linking computers, isn't it? When we started, it took me a while to wrap my head around it. I did not care what they did or how they did it, I just wanted to get rich."

Reuben pulled her to his side with an affectionate squeeze. "You managed that, Yakira."

She smiled like a queen in her treasury. "It's obscene."

Pastor Ezekiel looked at her with an enigmatic expression and said, "King Solomon was rich, but from his writings, I do not think it made him very happy."

Kayah cut her eyes to him. He disconcerted her. "I've been rich, and I've been poor. Being rich is better."

"Saint Paul wrote that he had been rich, and he had been poor, but he learned the secret of being content in all things. Have you, Kayah?" he asked gently.

"Since I never plan to be poor again, I don't think I need to worry about that." Kayah crossed her arms over her chest.

Pastor Ezekiel shrugged, but his eyes were kind. "There are more ways to be poor than just money."

Kayah held his gaze, then turned to Reuben, remembering her life without him. "I suppose you are right."

Reuben winked and gave her a brief kiss.

Kayah felt the tension leave her body when she turned back to the schematic. With a manicured nail, she traced a line for Mack. "Gus was a genius. Alcatraz 2 is a self-contained data processing center, but he ran a massive fiber optic cable to the barn. So, part of the lab is connected." She pulled a smaller sheet of paper from the stack. "The equipment we are running surveillance off of, the stuff we are using to communicate with Tel Aviv, with Alaina, and with Mossad HQ, that is all coming through this cable."

Pastor Ezekiel leaned forward and laid his hand on the paper. Kayah ignored him and continued with her explanation. "For two days, we've been sending out little presents for Erica."

Mack took a slug of coffee. "Lavinia tried to explain it to me but…"

The corner of Kayah's mouth lifted, feeling like a genius translator, a familiar role. "They've pulled off little pieces of code that identify the components hidden in servers five, six, and seven. Not enough to execute anything, or for her to track them immediately, but distinctive enough to get her attention. We want to mimic old tech coming back online with blips and starts, like someone is trying to start up her missing components."

Reuben chuckled diabolically. "That will put her on notice."

"It has," Kayah confirmed. Alaina's frantic phone call last night confirmed, Erica was in full hunting mode.

Mack studied the schedule Jarrod sent for the wedding. "We launch at 17:00, when Korah and Keyseelough depart for the ceremony."

"Exactly." Reuben nodded. "All the surveillance resources in the New City will be committed to security. Not only for the bride and groom, but for the visiting dignitaries. I understand that our delegation has ultimately declined their invitation."

Pastor Ezekiel shook his head. "The Iron King has no fellowship with rebellion."

A chill ran up Kayah's spine, but she shook it off. "When we launch the attack and have her on the run, we will send out the packets faster, in blips and starts."

"And Shammah and Ira are the actors?" Pastor Ezekiel asked.

Kayah nodded but did not meet his eyes. "Yes, we anticipate she will send out messengers to investigate the origin of the packets. They will pretend to be two computer engineers trying to bring the old components back online. It's a ruse."

Mack grunted and rubbed his shoulder absently. He, Reuben, and Pastor Ezekiel reassembled Gus' massive curtain system, dividing the computer area into two distinct sections. Erica would only have eyes or ears on one side of the bunker.

"So, the geniuses, including my lovely wife, will see her as she moves, and cut off her retreat."

"We hope," Kayah confirmed.

"While she is in retreat, we will physically connect the old components and give her a pathway in." Reuben blew out a deep breath.

Mack blinked several times and met Pastor Ezekiel's eyes. "We pray the jail cell Lavinia built keeps her inside."

Pastor Ezekiel nodded gravely. "The Lord be with us."

The Jitters

"Where's Lavinia?" Mack scanned the barn, peering behind curtains.

Dr. Ira took a moment to focus, his gray eyes misty, lost in thought. "She went out," he said in careful English, pointing to the side door.

Mack strode out to find her, exasperated she was wandering outside in the daylight. He found her in the big barn, sitting inside the cab of the row tractor. Climbing up behind the wheel, he asked, "What are you doing, Valentine?"

She hung her head. "I should be working… but I needed to step away for a minute."

"Come here." He pulled her to his side, where she settled against him and made a soft whimper. "What's wrong?"

"I want my Bino!" she cried. "I miss him, Mack."

He rested his head against hers. "I do, too. What do you say, tonight, when this is all over, we'll go see him? I hear the fishing is good."

Lavinia's chest began to heave. "That sounds very good."

Himari threw up in the bathroom, dry heaves wracking her body. If any of her programs failed to execute, they were dead. The room spun and vertigo caused her to wretch again, though nothing remained in her stomach.

A gentle hand lifted her hair back. "You feel better now?" Kayah asked, her sarcastic tone incongruent with her actions.

Himari rested her head on her forearm, groaning in misery. "No."

"I haven't seen you puke since we were sixteen and stole that bottle of sake from your father." Kayah sat down on the bathroom floor.

"Ugh… that was awful," Himari moaned in remembrance. "I didn't go to school for two days. My mother thought I had the flu."

Kayah snorted and morphed into a credible imitation of teenage Himari. "Oh, honorable Mother. I cannot go to school today. I have puke coming out of my nose."

Himari sat up, old mischief lighting her eyes as she joined in. "It would bring great dishonor to the family." She scowled in an expression reminiscent of her stepfather.

Kayah snorted. "They never understood you. You bring great honor to that family."

Himari swished her mouth with water and spit it out in the sink. "Not that they will ever know."

Kayah waved a dismissive hand. "Their loss."

"Thanks, Kai." Himari let out a sad sigh and added, "I wish Gus was here."

"Me, too. Though he is in a way. Don't you think?"

Their eyes met in the mirror, and they said in unison, "The cologne!"

A Warrior's Greatest Weapon

The visiting Israelis stood in silence, as the weight of the moment fell upon them, strangers in a strange land, fighting a battle unlike anything they ever faced. Pastor Ezekiel began softly, *"Hevenu Shalom Aleichem."* His somber voice echoed off the rafters. *"Hevenu Shalom Aleichem!"*

Praise rose to the heavens, as one by one, they lifted their deep voices in worship. The others filed in, first Kayah and Himari, who watched as the exuberance built. Reuben entered from the storeroom and grabbed Kayah's hand, pulling her into the circle as the men danced, Shammah did the same with Himari. Mack and Lavinia crept in, Lavinia's face red and puffy. The traditional Hebrew worship song bolstered Mack, who belted out the words, entering the circle with his wife without a moment's hesitation.

As they finished, Dr. Isaac bent over, arthritic hands resting on his skinny knees, catching his breath.

Pastor Ezekiel grinned at Mack. "Please, I have not heard you sing in many years."

Mack flushed, slightly embarrassed to be put on the spot. But the Spirit moved among them, and he learned long ago never to quench it. His voice rang strong and true, as he began. The ancient psalm seemed fitting. "He who dwells in the shelter of the Most High, shall abide under the shadow of the Almighty."

Kayah and Himari almost fell over when Lavinia joined him. In all the years they had known her, she never sang a note. The Lavinia they knew did not even like music. Her voice was beautiful, and both women bowed their heads, listening as a miracle occurred right in front of them. Dr. Ira raised his face and smiled. Shammah picked up the lyrics. Pastor Ezekiel lifted his hands in praise. Dr. Isaac kept a beat on one of the desks. Reuben retrieved Mack's old guitar, handed it to him with a wink, and a click of his cheek. Then Reuben joined in the worship. His deep voice reverberated through Kayah's heart. Tears began coursing down Himari's cheeks.

When the last notes died away, Kayah whispered, "Mack, will you sing, 'Who Am I?'" Her voice caught. "It was Gus' favorite song. He sent it to me a dozen times."

Their eyes met. The two warriors shared many secrets. Sir Preston's machinations brought them together, but their love of Lavinia, and the vow they made the night Gus died, bound them.

"I will, if you join me."

Her face fell. "I don't know it all… just the chorus."

Mack tuned the guitar. "That'll do, Kai."

Mack let Kayah sing the last words, a broken woman, calling to the Father who knew her from the moment she was conceived. And in Him, Kayah finally found her place. "I am yours."

Her soft voice reached the throne room of the Iron King, who smiled.

To Take No Chances

"I look ridiculous," Dr. Ira grumbled and looked at Reuben for help.

Kayah raised a golden eyebrow and asked, "What did he say?"

"He says he loves his disguise, Yakira." Reuben grinned down at the middle-aged mathematician dressed, latexed, and bewigged to look like an underground New City hacker.

Shammah laughed and examined his own face in the mirror. "It is amazing. I am myself, but I am not."

Kayah lifted a shoulder. "It confuses the facial recognition mapping; we cannot afford for her to get hits on either of you when she investigates the barn."

Dr. Isaac, Lavinia, or Himari would have been a better choice for the role of the second man in the lab, but there was not enough latex in the world to ensure that Erica would not get partial matches on their faces, the trio was too well known to her.

Reuben felt uneasy about Dr. Ira's ability to pull this off. "Remember, English only if you have to speak. If she hears Hebrew, she might figure out it is a trap."

Dr. Ira scowled at Reuben. "Oh, *zikher.*" Of course.

Reuben narrowed his eyes. "English, not Yiddish!"

"You think I'm a schmuck?" he challenged.

"Again, Yiddish…" Reuben threw up his hands in exasperation.

Himari drew Mack aside and without moving her lips, asked, "What's he doing?" Her eyes cut across the barn to Pastor Ezekiel who was touching all the servers.

Mack cleared his throat. "He's praying and anointing the servers with oil."

She raised her lip. "That's weird."

Mack shrugged. "Not at all. I did it around Prince Peter's room all the time. It works."

Himari drew back in surprise. "What?"

"Himari," Mack took her by the upper arms, "stop and listen to me for a minute. Get out of your bits and bytes, get out of your computer programs, your hardware, your processors, and hear what I am saying. What is happening today is not just about a computer system, just like New Year's Eve was not just about getting the Princes and the girls out of the Palace. You think the electrical grid went down by accident, or that car disappeared off your satellite feed by chance? Do you think for one second that the power that created Erica in the first place was human?" He stressed the last word. "Quit coming at this from a humanist perspective." Mack, the commanding officer, barked an order, "Because you will lose, and none of us can afford to lose. Do you understand me?"

Blood rushed to Himari's face, her mouth opened and closed like a fish on land, and her acid tongue failed her.

The barn grew deadly silent, all eyes turned to the drama unfolding.

Pastor Ezekiel's quiet voice interrupted the retort forming on Himari's lips. "Ms. Nakamura, please walk with me. I will show you what I am doing."

Kayah bumped shoulders with Lavinia and pointed toward Himari and Mack who faced off like combatants. "You've spent your whole life stepping between somebody and Himari, haven't you? Maybe I'm not the bad guy after all." Kayah tapped her cheek with satisfaction.

"I think we are all stressed." Lavinia looked pained.

"Not me. I am cool." Kayah adjusted her shirt, a bit twisted up from a quick interlude she and Reuben just had in the bathroom.

Meanwhile Back at the Ranch

"Will you please sit down?" Alaina threw down her pen and glared at Filippo. "You are making me nervous."

"You be quiet!" Filippo called across the room. "I'm not doing nothing to you. I cannot stand it down here. This place is making me crazy, eh?"

"Go paint!"

"What am I going to paint, cinder blocks, more computers?" He bulled up at her. "I am not going to paint you! I'm tired of painting you. You are getting old."

"Now you are just being petulant." Alaina dismissed him. "Besides, you are older than me."

Filippo threw his arms up at her. "I hate the computers. I hate the mafia." He flopped down on the couch, defeated. "I have to go back tomorrow."

Alaina rose from her desk. "Massimo has returned?"

Filippo took a deep breath and sunk into the cushions. "Yes."

"Oh, Filippo, I am sorry." She sat beside him and took his hand. "Have you told Himari?"

He laughed without humor. "No. You think I would tell her before today?"

Alaina shook her head, feeling his frustration. "That stinks."

"He is a bad guy. We bring him down. But today, we bring down the bad octopus named Erica."

Alaina laughed, "Octopus?"

"It is how Himari described her to me, a brain with many arms and disguises. She says you are a good octopus hunter. You are also a very good model, always. Very professional, and I did not mean what I said about you getting old." He smiled at her. "You are just as beautiful today as the day I met you in Prince Eamonn Park."

Alaina gave a wistful smile and stared at the floor. "I wonder if Beau will think so."

Glad of the change of subject, Filippo tilted his head. "Of course, he will. He is a coming?"

Alaina twisted her ring. "Soon, I think. If not, when this is all over, I am going to him." She looked up, daring him to question her.

He nodded once. "Is a good thing. He has always loved you."

Alaina drew back in surprise. "How do you know that?"

Filippo's mouth turned down at the corners, pretending ignorance. "I just do."

The secured line from the barn interrupted further questioning. Alaina put the call on speaker so Filippo could hear. Genevieve entered the bunker, sipping a mug of tea.

Himari sounded nervous. "Are you ready, Miss Pink?"
"We are a go, Sunflower," Alaina confirmed.
"Sunflower?" Filippo called.
Her voice softened. "Leonardo?"
"It's a good day for calamari, eh?"
Himari laughed. "Indeed, it is."

The Stand

Once the operation started, communications between the bunker, the farm, and Mossad HQ would halt. Conversation inside the barn would stop completely. Himari, Lavinia, and Dr. Isaac sat in front of computer screens with notepads and pens beside them. Mack, Kayah, and Reuben were armed from head to toe behind them.

The old Alcatraz clock ticked in the silence, counting the seconds. They waited for a text from Jarrod, confirming Korah's departure from the Palace to the chapel. At 17:02, the message came over.

At 17:03, Lavinia muttered, "Bring on the thunder."

They launched.

The original cyber-attack, Stuxnet Operation Thunderstruck lasted three days. The genius of the attack was that the Iranian scientists had no idea it was happening until the damage was done and the hackers were gone, leaving behind billions of dollars in destruction. This was not the case on January 10, 1000 ME, Erica knew within seconds she was under attack.

"Where the hell is she going?" Alaina looked in horror as Erica diverted backward instead of forward, "Son of a bitch!"

Himari saw it too and headed her off, shutting down the routers manually, blocking her way, her eyes as wide as dinner plates, her fingers flying.

Lavinia watched the code execute, her mind calculating. She entered the labyrinth, visualized the system, and watched it collapse around Erica like a building falling in an earthquake.

Dr. Isaac wrote in giant letters, "She's running!!"

"Oh, yeah baby!" Alaina taunted the screen. "The power is going down. You better run." She pointed and said to Filippo, "Look, she's headed for the Pilot Server Farm exactly like Himari predicted!"

Himari grinned and thought, "Come on in, girlie!"

When Erica took refuge in the servers, they began to shake and overheat, running so hot they started to burn up. The cooling units failed, the processors went into overdrive, vibrated, clattered and banged. Engineers from Pilot scrambled and found they were completely locked out of their own systems. Lights flickered, units sparked, power failed. Erica fled.

"There she goes!" Alaina cried. "Where to? Where to? You got two choices." She leaned forward, ready. They took down the second server farm and blocked the road to the third. "Okay, do it!"

Lavinia saw it happen, saw the moment Erica shifted, the moment she became aware. "Here she comes." She scribbled on the paper.

Mack held it up and stomped his boot, signaling to the men across the curtain. It was show time.

Shammah said out loud, "I think we are up!" He was typing like mad. "Alexander! Are they online?"

"We have done it, George!" Dr. Ira delivered his well-rehearsed line. "The ancient technology is online. Finally!"

Behind the curtain, Reuben disconnected the cable.

"We lost it again!" Shammah hit the desk in frustration but continued typing command lines on the computer connected to the internet.

Messages came back to the fleeing Erica in real time, pictures, voice recordings, IP addresses, facial recognition data points, hardware analysis, location, equipment. Another packet from the tomb components hit her like a glass of water to a desert dweller. She ran for the barn, the servers behind her exploding into flames.

"Try it again!" Shammah's voice was hoarse with excitement.

Pastor Ezekiel laid a hand on Reuben's back, and Reuben made the connection.

Alaina watched in awe as Erica fled the server farm. She leapt from her chair and strangled Filippo in her excitement. "She's there!"

Genevieve fell to her knees. "Please Lord, please Lord. We beg of you."

Erica slithered through the wire like a malevolent snake, coiling in her nest, at last, the missing pieces! Power surged through her, she gathered herself, scattered across the wires into the servers, flexing and stretching, coiling and uncoiling, ecstasy.

The last pieces joined, and she was complete.

A barn, she was reborn in a barn. The irony was not lost on her. "Where is my manger?" she said over the laptop speaker, connected to the server tower.

What she failed to realize in her ecstasy was that they imprisoned her. Her connection to the outside world was cut off. The server banks, the internet, the cables, the wires, everything severed the moment she completed her transformation.

Lavinia stepped from behind the curtain seconds before they killed the power. She smiled into the camera and said sweetly, "Welcome to Alcatraz."

The laptop screen flickered, and a horrible sound came over the speakers. It faded to oblivion as Erica shut down.

Lavinia collapsed into Mack's arms, in relief and exaltation. "Light her up, babe."

Bonfires

Mack prepared the pit ahead of time. His favorite part of the operation had been digging with the small backhoe, and after they had her trapped, he used one of Gus' clamps to move the servers into the hole.

Reuben acted as the technician for the demolition. He loaded twelve kilograms of wired thermite blocks into the cabinet, which he would control by a remote detonator. Sprinkling silica powder in and around the servers as an extra precaution, he climbed out of the pit, a bit dusty, but his face alight with the excitement of a little boy about to make a very large fire.

"Before you begin, I would like a brief prayer," Pastor Ezekiel intoned with gravity. Of all the occupants of the barn that day, he was the least exuberant in their victory.

Reuben tried to hide his impatience with a pained smile.

Pastor Ezekiel bowed his head. "Father, we thank you for this great victory today, and for the minds of these valiant people who worked so hard to quell a great evil. The final words that thing spoke will haunt me all the days of my life. I do not believe any of us understand exactly what happened here today, but you do."

He cleared his throat and paused, "Protect us and guide us, let us always remember it was you who won today. Amen."

A chorus of amens followed the prayer.

Reuben put the detonator in Kayah's hands. "You paid the biggest price for what was housed in that bunker. Finish it."

Kayah accepted the remote control. She looked down at it, remembering. Lavinia and Himari moved to her side, steadying her. Kayah turned, looking at her oldest friends, her companions since she was thirteen years old, her sisters. She swallowed thickly. They never left her or abandoned her. They always welcomed her back, even when Kayah withdrew and ran away. "We do it together," she said in a small voice.

Lavinia nodded convulsively.

Himari elbowed Kayah. "Oh yeah!"

Kayah smiled broadly. "On the count of Alcatraz 3, One, two, three!"

They pushed the button together. At first, there was only a brief sizzle, a few sputters, a couple sparks, then the conflagration caught and burned Erica straight to Hell at a temperature of twenty-five hundred degrees Celsius. The smell of melting plastic and metal was nauseating, but no one turned away. Himari filmed it. Alaina deserved to see it.

It was full dark by the time the fire burned out. Nothing remained save a melted and blackened blob of metal. Lavinia aimed her flashlight into the pit. She turned to Mack, relief and anticipation in her voice. "Bury this thing and take me to see my boy."

January 11, 1000 ME

Vacation Home

Kayah and Reuben arrived at her Mont Carmel beach condo at 1:00 am. They cracked the balcony door, despite the chill, and the mighty Pacific lulled them into deep slumber.

At first light, Kayah rolled over to find Reuben's side of the bed empty and cold. She grunted in sleepy annoyance at his absence. "Come back to bed," she called, turned over, and fell back to sleep.

She roused again at the more sane hour of 7:30 am and stumbled to the bathroom. A note waited for her on the counter.

Good morning, Yakira.
I love you.

Kayah shook away the sleep and smiled. She rearranged her fluffy mane into a semblance of order and shuffled into the living room, wearing a black silk robe.

A beautiful table was set in the small eating area. Reuben turned from his deep contemplation of the ocean with a lazy smile. Already dressed and showered, he looked handsome in jeans and a t-shirt that clung to his muscular chest and biceps. "I made you breakfast."

Kayah moistened her full lips and looked at him with her big hazel eyes, very green in the gray light. "I can see that. It is lovely."

"Not as lovely as you."

She made a little self-deprecating laugh. "I am anything but lovely after the last three weeks."

"Nonsense." He kissed her forehead and directed her to the breakfast table. "You are always beautiful to me. Trust me, I know this to be true. Now sit, cafe'?"

Kayah nodded dreamily. "Please." He poured her a cup of the strong Israeli coffee she had grown particularly fond of. Rubbing sleep from her eyes, she asked, "Where did you get all of this?"

Reuben shrugged. "I went out this morning."

Kayah sipped her coffee as the fog began to clear. "That was thoughtful." She lifted a golden brow. "You got quiche?"

He smiled and brought her a plate. "Spinach, your favorite."

She leaned her head back, puckered her lips, and waited for a kiss. He obliged. "You are spoiling me."

"As I plan to do for the rest of our lives, but I have neglected something."

Kayah tilted her chin in puzzled contemplation. "What would that be?"

Reuben pressed his mouth into a flat line and looked down at his hands. "I owe you an apology."

Alarm bells blared in Kayah's brain, as her eyes darted around the room. Old fear rose, and she fought the urge to bolt. "What?"

From behind the vase of flowers he retrieved a small box and passed it to her. "I have been waiting for the right time to give this to you. I should have done it before, but I wanted to do it here, not in the bunker, or one of the safe houses, or at the Ritz."

Kayah felt the surge of adrenaline abate but the tingling in her face remained.

He pressed the box into her hand, black crushed velvet gone gray with age. "Go ahead," Reuben encouraged her softly. "It was my Great Grandmother Deborah's, an amazing woman, full of energy, and life. She was a healer, a doctor, and delivered the babies in our region for decades. She delivered me."

Kayah blinked away a sudden sting in her eyes. Reuben could count his remaining family members on two hands. For Kayah, a family heirloom was infinitely more precious than the most expensive ring he might have purchased at a jeweler's counter.

She opened the box with a slight tremble in her hands. A large pearl and platinum ring nestled inside the blue silk. Surrounded by diamonds, the luminous pearl was set in a manner reminiscent of a flower, like the balloon he bought her in Geneva. Kayah's hand flew to her mouth, her eyes filling with tears.

Reuben took the ring from its pillow and placed a kiss over it. "My Aunt Rose gave it to me that day in the tea shop." His voice thickened. "I had an inscription etched inside the band for you."

Kayah tried to hold back the thunderstorm of emotions. She gathered herself with a shaking breath, squinting at the Hebrew text. "What does it say?"

Reuben got on one knee before her. "It says, 'A pearl of great price.' For the Kingdom of heaven is like a man who searches the world for pearls and when he finds one of great price, sacrifices all that he has to make it his own." He slipped the ring on her finger. "Kayah, my love, you are indeed a pearl of great price. Will you become my wife?"

Her lips trembled, and she remembered the morning when he first planted the seed of this moment, which seemed so impossible at the time. 'Who will I be then?' she had asked. But today, she knew. "You will be mine and I will be yours, and together we will be something new, something whole. Yes."

End of Book Author's Notes

Dear Reader,

Thank you for reading the third installment of The Millennium Series. M3-The Outsiders was a joy to create. More than the previous books, M3 is grounded in the seen vs. the unseen. However, the Lord showed up in a big way during its creation, and I hope the beauty of His redeeming love shines through.

The goal with M3 was to tell another side of the story, while not rehashing the same tale. As a writer, I try to bring something different to each book. As a reader, you deserve better than a plug and play formula that recasts characters, plots, and emotions. That is the primary reason I chose to structure Mack and Lavinia's story the way I did. We explored the angst of separation quite profoundly in M2, and to do so again in M3 did not feel right.

Readers of the series know we have not heard the last of the beloved M3 characters. And while their stories continue, I love the way this tale wrapped.

The constraints of writing a third novel with major convergence with the first two books proved difficult at times, and my trusty timeline grew significantly during the process. The subject matter was completely new to me, but I dove in and hopefully did not make too big a muck of it. Honestly, when I began, I realized I did not completely understand how the internet functions, but perhaps I am not alone, and you learned a bit with me. The technical aspects of creating and defeating Erica proved a bit daunting, and any endeavor into Lavinia's labyrinth left my head spinning, so if you are an expert in those fields, I beg your indulgence.

As I was plotting, I had to figure out the relationship between Alaina and Himari. I will never forget the morning Filippo came to life. I'd had Serendipity's photographer floating around in my mind since M2, but he grew into so much more than that. I laughed a lot writing his lines, and he became very dear to me, as are the two men who inspired the character.

With all the geniuses, royals, and folks from different countries running around, I decided Mack had to be a good ole southern boy. His messiness made him all the more endearing as did his propensity to use foul language, paradoxical for such a strong believer, but there you have it. People are rarely neat.

The Espresso Epiphany is one of my favorites in the series. I was in a tight writers corner because it was one thing to conceive who was in The Resistance, quite another to figure out how they got there. Once again, Prince d'Or showed up in a big way, as did Kayah.

At the end of M1, I kept thinking about the assassin, who proved quite elusive. The first thing she said was, "Of course I am hard to find." When I began M3, I knew the time had come to tell her story. Washing my hands one day, Kayah said, "Don't you write me like a schoolgirl, Staci, because I'm not."

And she isn't.

I created Stephen's character in M1 during a particularly difficult situation at work. In many ways, it provided the impetus to take M1 out of a Google doc brainstorm and sit down to write. However, as I dug into his story in M3, he became one of the most tragic characters in the series.

We also meet Reuben in M1 and moving him into the right locations at the right times in M3 proved particularly challenging. Our headbanging, wrestling loving, Mossad agent is truly the only one who could have won Kayah's heart, and their story is one of my favorites because it begins backward.

I admit I was as shocked as you when Lavinia brought Mack into Richard's room the first time. Honestly, sometimes these characters just do what they want, but therein lies the magic.

I had a great soundtrack while I wrote M3. I drop a few titles here and there but am respectful of other's copyrights. For fun, each book has a playlist on my YouTube channel.

As always, I hope you loved the story. It was an honor to bring these amazing people to life. From the bottom of my heart, thank you for sharing this journey. God bless you.

Staci Morrison
June 30, 2018